Barry,

An early happy ( )

to you! Hope you "enjoy")

it, and looking forward to

a little partying this year.

MW01482601

EXECUTION ISLAND

by

Thomas Alton Gardner

www.ThomGardner.com

Execution Island is entirely a work of fiction.

Any resemblance to persons living or dead is purely coincidental. Where the names of actual people, places, and historical events do appear, it is understood their purpose is for verisimilitude, and any situation in which they are placed is entirely fictional.

Previous works by Thomas Alton Gardner, including but not limited to "Confessions of a Corporate Spy", "Home on the Strange", and "Holy Tequila!" are available for purchase at most online booksellers.

Execution Island is dedicated to Maya and Kaitlin, who taught me what "family" really means. One wonderful evening on a Nicaraguan beach, near the spot where a famous reality TV show had been filmed the prior year, I sipped a cocktail and watched them play in the ocean. As they frolicked, silhouetted against a setting sun in the Pacific Ocean, the seeds of this tale began to sprout in my mind. That memory, that scene, will live forever in my heart, as will the two of them.

THE CASTAWAYS

Taylor- Creator and host of the hit television show, Execution Island

Old Joe- Season 18 winner, 57 year old country boy from West Virginia

Kinnary- Season 12 and MVP Season winner, beauty, brawn, and brains

Susan- Season 19 winner, cutthroat businesswoman, multi-millionaire

Matthew- Season 20 winner, one of the best physical competitors ever

Amy- Season 21 winner, swimsuit model, tremendous social game

Randy- Season 15 winner, gambler, one of the game's smartest players

Leticia- Season 16 winner, highly disliked, brutal player, no social game

Franklin- Season 7 winner, former NFL player, physical threat

Darius- Season 9 winner, father of three, physical, social, nearly broke

Danielle- Season 14 winner, mother figure, great social, no physical game

Jason Oliver- Season 11 winner, notorious bad boy, wicked smart

Tonya- Season 5 winner, very high IQ, no physical game

Malik- Cameraman

Carl- Cameraman

Ricardo- Sound man

Sato- Lead medical doctor

Jeremy- Assistant medical doctor

1

Day 3 ~ Game On

Remote, idyllic Cocos Island, source of legendary adventure and mystery for centuries. Frothy, white capped waves crash against boulders of limestone and lava. Giant fruit bats float with muscular grace on floral scented South Pacific breezes, while emerald green palms sway like exotic dancers over platinum sands that glitter and flash in the bright sunlight.

High above those glittering sands, twelve pairs of hands struggle painfully to cling to twelve identical poles, ten feet high, brightly colored, and arranged in a circle. Feet aren't spared in this strange torture scene either, standing on two shorter poles arrayed out from each main pole, turning the the bodies to which they belonged into a human "Y", their torsos dangling precipitously in between all three in a perpetual plank position.

Taylor Woods paces like a rabid hyena as two cameras follow him through the scene. Looking like the product of an unholy union between a camping store mannequin and a tacky seventies game show host in his trademark safari adventure garb, his own feet twitched in sympathy with those of his players as he waited for the cue from his sound man, Ricardo. When the red indicator lights suddenly flashed on, the cameras went live, and Ricardo's upraised arm dropped to bring this circus to life.

The final season of the hit reality TV show, Execution Island, was on.

"Castaways! Are you ready!" squealed the maniacal carnival barker.

All but one contestant hooted right back at him, ready to get this biggest of all games on. But, high on pole six, Susan was distracted. For just a moment she thought she'd seen something moving in the jungle, just beyond the circle that had been cleared for today's challenge.

"Susan, are YOU ready?" Taylor demanded, noticeably irritated by her unwillingness to contribute to his charade.

No stranger to intensity, she quickly shook her head to re-focus. "Hell yes!" shrieked the winner of Execution Island nineteen, a millionaire even before she won that season. Jaded and tough as an alligator briefcase, the successful businesswoman was not about to let nerves keep her from this first victory. The others made no secret that they despised her, and rubbing this win in their faces would feel even better than it had the first time.

"Then GAME ON! The winner of this game will last longer on the poles than anyone else. At stake in this very first competition of the most dangerous game ever played is something you are all going to want very badly . . ."

Taylor paused for dramatic effect, before strutting to a small crate and removing the first reward item.

"A tarp and enough line to make a rain shelter! It gets mighty cold and awfully itchy when it rains here, and as lush as this island is, you can probably guess how often that happens. The winner will skip tonight's execution, and be spared the boat ride of shame back to the mainland!"

He paused once again to increase the tension, the master of twenty-three hit seasons at work.

"At least . . . for one more week."

As if on cue, large drops of rain began to appear on the hands and feet of the contestants, quickly making their foot holds not only painful to grip, but very slippery as well.

Taylor ate it all up with a self-loving grin, raising his arms in the air as he walked towards the camera.

"People, I am NOT God, but sometimes I DO feel like it!"

Malik, behind camera two, caught Leticia rolling her eyes over on pole four, and quickly marked the video for an edit.

The rain grew in intensity while Taylor pranced back and forth across the circle like a mouse across the face of a clock. He taunted the contestants, the consummate salesman playing the audience at home.

"Darius, looks like your left foot is cramping up! Hang on, man," he said, turning his back and strolling away, *"you've got ten million reasons to stay in this."*

Darius' lip quivered from the pain in his feet. When the rain began his left foot began to twist in on itself, his size thirteen double E's straining to hold his large body across the gap to the single pole where his hands scraped for any kind of grip. He shifted to his right, which for the time being was holding, and hung his left in the air for relief. He tried to stretch it with muscle strength alone, but to no avail. Gritting his teeth, he simply tried to focus past it.

Taylor's mockery continued.

"Jason Oliver! Winner of Execution Island eleven! One of our all time greatest villains! Doesn't look like you're holding up so well!"

Jason was lucky in that he weighed next to nothing, and though he had little strength, it was almost enough to hold that light load. All brains and zero brawn, his skinny arms struggled to hold their grip on the slippery pole, while his feet turned sideways in an effort to maintain theirs on the smaller ones below.

But it was no use. A moment later, he plummeted to the ground.

"And we have a LOSER!" Taylor shrieked in delight, as he walked over and extended a hand to the first of the fallen.

Jason swatted it away and popped to his feet.

"That's okay, Taylor! Don't need this one." Extending both of his middle fingers to salute the remaining players, he sneered at the camera and strolled calmly to the bench to wait for the next victim.

"Our fans will remember that this particular contest is often won by a woman, and so far, this one looks to be no exception. The women look strong, and except for one or two, the men look rough! Ten million dollars at stake, people!"

Kinnary, who'd won this very competition on her way to winning season nine, gripped her high pole like a woman possessed. Glancing around she saw Amy, America's sweetheart, looking strong, as did all but one of the other women. Danielle, the mother

9

figure from season fourteen, was slipping. Age before beauty, thought Kinnary, a wiry grin spreading across her face.

As for the men, she saw only two who might last as long as the women. Randy, the professional gambler and winner of season fifteen was notoriously good at competitions, incredibly smart, and might be her toughest opponent in these games. And Old Joe, the Redneck and fan favorite from Kentucky, was also a competition freak, but lacked the mental abilities that she, Randy, and perhaps two or three others possessed.

Yes, she thought, she and Randy were the ones to beat. Brains, brawn, and at least in her case, beauty all rolled into one. When the shit really began to hit the fan, she might have to work some alliance magic with him. But, not yet.

BOOM, two heavy bodies hit the dirt almost simultaneously, as both Darius, beaten by his twisted left foot, and Franklin, former NFL player and winner of season seven, thundered to the ground.

"It looks like size DOES matter! Our two big men have come back to Earth! The bigger they are, the harder they fall!"

The impulse was just too strong to fight, and Malik rolled his own eyes behind the camera. How much did they pay this jerk to spew this crap?

The two fallen giants took their places on the bench and watched. Moments later, Danielle gave in and fell to the ground, yelping as her tailbone hit the dirt.

"And then there were eight!"

Tonya, winner of season five, scanned the remaining contestants. No way she would last as long as them. Heavily built and her arms shaking from it, it was her high IQ that brought her victory in her season, not her body. Realizing she'd at least not finished last and that this was definitely not her competition, she exhaled, loosened her grip, and prepared to jump.

But before she could, a loud "CRACK!" exploded underneath her, and pole seven split in two below her shaking hands.

The top half of the pole broke away and her hands, now freed from it, scraped furiously at empty air. But with nothing left for them to grab, her heavy body collapsed forward, impaling itself on the sharp, jagged point of the pole's lower half.

Amy was the first to scream, and as she let go her grip to cover her eyes, she tumbled to the ground.

"Jesus Christ!" Taylor yelped in shock, before gathering his wits and yelling "CUT!"

He sprinted to the shattered pole, all but two contestants following closely behind. Tonya's twitching body dangled four feet above the ground, her eyes had rolled back in their sockets, and her tongue swung lifelessly from her mouth. The five inch thick pole had torn clear through her abdomen. Dark blood covered it, blackening its surface.

"MEDICAL!" Taylor coughed into the wind.

Old Joe and a few others helped to lift her body from the stake. He and Matthew yanked the pole onto its side, while the two big men pushed up against Tonya's bulk with their shoulders, finally freeing her limp body, which slid onto the glittering sand with a sickening sound.

Sato and Jeremy, the two person medical team, arrived on the scene within seconds. But it was too late. No one could survive a five inch wooden dagger through the gut, and Tonya was no exception.

"My God, she's dead," Sato gasped grimly, before pulling the reward tarp over Tonya's still body.

Kinnary spun around at what she thought sounded like laughter, coming from the jungle. Her eyes scanned the dense foliage, but seeing nothing, she shook it off. Frayed nerves, she reminded herself, were both expected and acceptable in a horrifying situation like the one before her.

Some players stood alone, sobbing, while others huddled together for comfort, the merciless rain beating down upon them.

Taylor stood, and wiped his brow. Dazed, but always on the job, he sauntered over the wet sand to the two cameramen and asked, very quietly so none of the contestants could hear, "Did you get that?"

Above the chaos, one lone figure still gripped tightly to her poles. Much like Taylor, Leticia, winner of season sixteen, was all business.

"Hey!" she screamed at the medical team, "Don't you dare cover her with that tarp! It's mine! I won it, fair and square!"

2

Taylor ~ Seven Months Earlier

"It's a corpse, Taylor. Dead. Do not resuscitate."

The host paced the room as Davis spoke, feeling like he'd been stabbed in the heart with a very sharp fountain pen. And in essence, he had.

"How can you say that?" he asked. "This is the most profitable show in television history! It invented the genre! How can you reject the show that brought this network back from the dead? That built *my* career? *YOUR* career!"

Davis leaned back in his padded leather chair, and spun around to face a massive picture window that overlooked the city of Burbank. He took a deep breath before continuing, partly for appearances, and partly, because he needed it.

"Taylor, you're right," he declared. "It *was* original. It *was* profitable. It *was* a game changer. But the operative word in those sentences is, *was*! Ratings have been slipping for years. I mean, we're talking about a steady ten year slide! It's time for something new. Millennials don't give a shit about this kind of show. Competition just isn't their thing. We need new blood, especially in the Thursday night slot."

Taylor continued pacing, nervously running his fingers through his hair as if it were the only thing left to grip. There had to be a way. His livelihood— a house in Malibu, another in San Miguel, the boat, the kids' college tuitions, hell, Sandy's spending habits—

everything in his highly leveraged Hollywood life might vaporize if the show, *his* show, went to the morgue.

"Look, Davis," he pleaded, "all we need is a reboot. A shock injection to get people to pay attention again. Something big. Something even more revolutionary than the show was when it debuted."

Davis shook his head. "Unless you're going to hang people on live TV, I don't see what the hell you can do to get anyone to watch! The audience no longer believes in the premise. They think it's scripted. Oh sure, we know it's really not, but you do edit the hell out of it to create storylines, to make it more exciting than boring old real life, yes?"

Davis, the executioner, spun around to face his victim. "And you make it look like they're in the middle of nowhere, when a mile away people are sipping piña coladas and spraying sunscreen while their kids play in the surf! No one is fooled anymore!"

Davis felt awful saying these things. Taylor was a good soldier. Instrumental in building the very empire he now sat upon. But entertainment is a business like any other, and when assets underperform . . . they get cut. Unfortunately, it was his job to put a toe tag on this cadaver, or wear one himself.

"It's not real, Taylor," he softened, "It's a show. It's a show with a longer run than even the best of them. Seinfeld. Friends. All in the Family. Happy Days. You name it, your show has run longer. But it has also run its course, just as they did. So unless you've got a plan in your pocket to mindfuck America back into believing it's *really* real, and boy, it would have to be a doozy, we're done here."

Taylor's brain raced. Real. That was the original idea, but it was corporate assholes like Davis who gutted his creation right from the start. They wanted predictable. They wanted storylines. Show-mances for the female viewers. Villains to hate. Blood too, but not so much that they might get sued. And so each season smelled a lot like the last one and the one before that, no matter what "twist" was added. It worked for a while, a *long* while, but he knew in his heart it hadn't *really* worked, for years.

Real. What the hell does that mean in the plasticized, digitized, and homogenized twenty-first century, he wondered?

Really real.

"What *is* real," he thought out loud as he continued pacing around the office. "Dirt. Blood. One on one battle. Real battle, not bullshit puzzles and games. Hand to hand. Mano a Womano. Guts. Glory. Pain . . . "

Death, he thought, *inside* his head this time. Nothing more real than death. But that was a bridge too far. There was no way he could incorporate death into a TV show. Could he?

Could he?

"What if we make it really, truly real?" he blurted, stopping in mid-step on the carpet, a pile of loose nylon wadding up in front of his Gucci clad toe like a wave. "I don't mean bullshit real. I mean *real*."

Davis looked incredulous.

"You can't let people *die*, Taylor. Are you off your fucking rocker? How desperate are you, man?" Davis stood, walked around the mahogany desk, and put a hand on his former star producer's shoulder.

"Something else will come along. This show isn't everything. You'll get another idea. Now," he reached across the elephant-leather covered desk and grabbed a huge, cow-leather bound checkbook, "I'm gonna write you a large severance check, right here, right now. And since you've made us all so much money, I'm adding 10% more than your contract calls for."

But before the pen touched paper, Taylor yanked the checkbook out of Davis' hand, and flung it across the room.

"Hell no, you're not! And you know why? Because I'm gonna save this goddamn network, and *your* fat ass . . . AGAIN!"

The clever ad ran for a week in primetime, starting with the Sunday NFL playoffs, all the way through a popular Thursday night cop drama and two barely-breathing sitcoms. It ran on YouTube, it ran on Facebook, Instagram, and Snap news feeds across the country, and it was blasted hourly on Twitter. It was clear, it was provocative, and it had the desired effect. No video, no sound, just glaring words on a screen, scrolling in *Star Wars* fashion, punctuated only by thirty seconds of absolute quiet.

In the era of overstimulation, nothing screams louder than silence . . .

PREVIOUS WINNERS OF EXECUTION ISLAND

Are you *REALLY* a winner?
Can you win for *REAL*, or just on a fake TV show?
Did *YOU* win, or was your victory handed to you in a script?

There are 23 of you. Which of you are real, and which are fakes?

It's time to show us. It's time to show the World.
But only twelve of you will get a chance to prove you aren't a fake.

The real question is, do twelve of you even have the guts? Do you?
Let's find out who the *REAL* winner is.

Coming in September.
No rules. No teams. No food. No help. No outside contact.
No B.S.
An unprecedented $10 million prize for the *REAL* winner.

The final season of EXECUTION ISLAND.

Reality TV Just Got . . . REAL!

Taylor admitted it was way over the top. Alienating and humiliating the very people he had exalted and held up for praise was certainly sleazy. Admitting the show was a bit less than real hurt his pride, but experts assured him it was the only way to really start fresh. First admit blame, then ask for another chance. It was the American way.

Besides, he realized, this is network TV. Nothing is sleazier than that.

During the week the ad ran, Google's search ranking for "EXECUTION ISLAND" rose from 2,724th place to the top ten. Every time the ad ran, people called, texted, re-tweeted, shared, and discussed how the network could possibly pull it off. Few believed it. The show's reputation had fallen so far, had become so synonymous with plastic and fake, that it seemed like yet another parlor trick.

Still, even detractors admitted it was one hell of a parlor trick. One hell of a pitch.

Previous winners were pissed off. Some filed defamation suits.

Network lawyers screamed. Did anyone realize how difficult, how downright impossible it would be to indemnify the company, let alone the producers, from liability on this thing?

The insurance company went through the roof, until they were assured that there would indeed be a few unmentioned precautions- a small medical team on the island, and a boat that would come once a week to remove that week's losers. And ironclad, ninety three page indemnification clauses in the contestant's contracts.

The media called it a farce. A lie. A gimmick.

The affiliates groaned. Would they really be forced to run another season of this roadkill that was costing them valuable ad space?

And yet, something funny happened on the way to production.

Fans clamored. They raved. They wanted one more season, a season to end all seasons. Viewers who hadn't watched since the first three seasons emailed to ask when the premiere would be. Chatrooms and boards lit up with rumors and lists of who might be the final twelve. Fans promoted their favorites, and Netflix reported that the previous seasons of the show on their network had become the top twenty three watched television shows they ran, of any kind. Even people who had never seen the show wanted to get a look at those who might actually have the guts to put their reputations on the line, maybe even their lives if all was to be believed, in order to gain those same reputations back.

Boarding a ship bound for the remote Cocos Island, a place unaltered by man and uninhabited by Costa Rican law, Taylor Woods felt the wind at his back for the first time in years. Studios were calling. His family was elated to see him out of his funk. Even the media was once again using the long-neutered term "genius" to describe him.

But Taylor was soon to learn that wind, the most fickle of nature's forces, has a way of changing directions, just when you think it's finally got your back.

3

Day 1 ~ Island of Mystery

Randy peered across the Pacific, holding Amy, his fiancée, tightly to his chest. A thick fog that had long obscured the lovers' view was just beginning to clear. Behind the slowly dissolving veil of the misty curtain, he could just barely make out the outline of an island.

"Holy shit!" he yelled across the deck to Matthew. "Looks like something out of King Kong, doesn't it?"

Matthew nodded, awestruck. "Central casting, my friend. Unbelievable."

Like most on board, Matthew's eyes were transfixed on the dark green blur coming into focus across the deep. It loomed, leaping out of the water to impossible heights, a mass of cliffs rising hundreds of feet into the clouds. The bases of two tall mountains rose above the rest, their lofty peaks still mired in a thick shroud of white.

Taylor glowed, standing at the front of the ship with his foot on the bow like a conquering pirate.

"See what I mean?" he gloated with a self satisfied smirk. "Cocos is the best backdrop we've ever had. This is going to be a historic season, and you're all part of it!"

A whoop rose from the gathered, twelve contestants, four production staff, two medical staff, and six Costa Rican laborers who would set up the challenge area and execution grounds, before returning home with the ship.

The story Taylor had been telling for months appeared to be true. Cocos truly was the treasure island that loomed in the mind's eye of public consciousness, an island of legend, complete with pirates, shipwrecks, myth and mystery. Three hundred and fifty miles off the Costa Rican coast, alone in the Pacific Ocean and only five miles long by two miles wide, it was the very portrait of a deserted island.

Human settlements had never survived here for long, though that hadn't stopped them from trying. The soil simply would not support crops. Giant rats were known to bite off chunks of settler's exposed extremities while they slept. Steep mountain ridges, rising one after another, thwarted human attempts at agriculture and cross island travel. Heavy monsoonal rains were frequent and could last for days. Raging streams, plunging waterfalls and mystical caves added together to make it the stuff of tall tales, an emerald jewel filled with adventure and intrigue.

Normally, luxury yachts filled with wealthy divers trolled the azure waters for glimpses of hammerhead sharks and sea turtles. But no permits had been granted for weeks, and theirs was the only boat to be found for dozens of nautical miles in all directions.

Taylor was right. It was the perfect place for Execution Island to make a last stand, to fight for its *own* survival, or die trying.

Tonya and Old Joe stood together next to the railing, sheltering each other from a steady wind that seemed to blow straight from the island itself. Now about a mile out from the green hulk, they saw an impossibly high waterfall plummeting onto a white, sandy beach, with a small bay nearby. Caves opened up on sheer cliff sides as though the island were a block of Swiss cheese. It was an intimidating scene, to say the least.

Tonya shivered. Not from the wind, but from the realization that something epic was about to unfold.

"Dang," Old Joe whispered to her, "looks like a lotta hikin'. Not a flat spot on the whole gol' durn thing."

She nodded, but said nothing. Tonya was not exactly athletic, winning her season by putting her massive intellect to work. This season would require a new strategy. She made a mental note to align immediately with someone strong and lean, like Matthew, in order to last long enough in the game to find a way to win.

Leticia smiled, seeing the very same scene through a different lens. She had an edge. Born in a barrio in Buenos Aires, but having lived in Brazil for the past ten years by skimming off the tourist trade in Fortaleza, she was used to the intense heat and humidity they were about to face. She could climb coconut trees and had been fishing since she was a small child. She gazed in delight at the weaklings around her and couldn't help but laugh out loud.

Darius' muscly arms flexed nervously as he noticed the "Bitch from Buenos", laughing alone into thin air. Everything in his life now hinged on this mysterious island. He desperately needed a cash infusion or he would lose his family home, and his children's future. A father of three, he'd invested the winnings from his season in a failed business. Now he *had* to win again. And as he stared at those impossibly high cliffs and thought of his children, he knew he would, no matter what awful things he might have to do to make it so.

Amy broke from Randy's loving embrace and exchanged a high five with her old friend, Kinnary. A good climber and all around athlete, Kinnary would be sure to make coconuts, and their electrolyte rich fluids, a staple of each day. She'd use the climbs to scout out where others were camped, and perhaps sabotage them, or steal from their supplies.

She smiled back at Amy, the bikini model. Randy, a professional gambler originally from Chicago, was her friend's ride or die. Their show-mance from the MVP season was beloved by viewers, and by using their friendship she might gain access to him as well. Like Kinnary, he had a superior mind. But, turning her gaze back to the imposing island in the distance, she realized that this time brawn would be every bit as important as brains. She and Matthew had been dancing around a relationship for a long time, and now she would kick it up a notch to be sure he and his lean, muscular frame were fully under her control.

Franklin, a former NFL player, stood with one of the all time classic villains of the game, Jason Oliver, who won his season partly by pretending he had just beaten cancer, using that sympathy from his team to save him from an important vote. That vote led to a merging of the teams, which then led to his victory.

Franklin won the old fashioned way, with muscle. Everyone had aligned to vote him off the island once it came out late in the game that he was a pro ball player, but when he won all of the last five execution challenges, the jury had no choice but to make him the victor. Jason knew that win had come in a place much like the one he was now staring at, a place that was mountainous and physically demanding— the volcanoes of Guatemala. A human stick figure, Jason had quickly sidled up to the big man and proposed a union of brain and brawn. Franklin, despite the obvious stereotypes, was no dummy, and immediately realized they could form a powerful whole from two opposite halves.

Danielle and Susan stood together too, but for no other reason than neither one had a natural partner in this game. Susan, a multi-millionaire from Hong Kong, was despised by most of the other players. She'd been ruthless in achieving her victory, and was famous for perhaps the worst social game in Exccution Island history, minus Leticia's. Yet she was incredibly cunning. That cunning had allowed her to slip under the radar as someone her competitors believed couldn't possibly win even a single jury vote, and that herd belief led her to make it all the way to the final two, as the one person every player was certain they could beat.

They were wrong. Her final speech in defense of her carefully crafted gameplay was considered the best in the show's history.

Danielle also began her season with an awkward social game, but quickly turned it around, becoming a monster in the last few challenges. She not only made it through the weekly executions, but earned enough credit in doing so to win by a single vote. But this time she had a new plan. Her eyes slipped softly across the bow of the ship, noting the numerous young players, far from home and family. She would become the camp Mom. She'd aged into that role since her season, and planned to use it as an advantage here.

Nobody wants to kick Mom off the island. Nobody.

Taylor, still doing his best Leonardo DiCaprio impression, felt once again like a god. This was to be his greatest victory, the season that would rebuild his legendary status in the entertainment business. And much more. For he was not only here to provide the network with the greatest ratings numbers in history. Oh no.

Taylor Woods, like every other person on this deck, had a plan. A plan far more ambitious than reviving a hit tv show. A plan that would ensure not only that he kept his place among the middle echelon of the Hollywood elite, but would also secure his own well funded, independent production company, ripping him permanently from the teat of the corrupt and creatively bankrupt studio system.

A plan, in fact, that had nothing to do with his tv show, whatsoever.

He knew they were coming. During his time on the island, he'd hidden outside the ranger stations at night, listening as drunken conversations seeped through their thin walls before vaporizing into the misty night air. He'd heard the rangers talk of the vast sum of money paid to the Costa Rican government by a television company, to gain access to *his* island for a period of three months. This revelation filled him with dread, for he had not yet reached his goal.

Life on the island was difficult, even for him. Rats were the true owners of Cocos, large and aggressive, they tormented him daily. The constant rain gave him fungal infections he could not seem to shake. Food was hard to come by, and he had taken to carefully raiding the ranger's trash pits, as well as stealing from the occasional diving party that illegally set foot on the island.

Now, for three months, these invaders would take over his island. He didn't have three months. He would be ready to leave in only a few weeks. And he couldn't wait. He wouldn't wait. But he also couldn't continue his work with these ridiculous tourists in his way.

And so, he too came up with a plan.

Now, sitting atop a coconut palm, camouflaged by thousands of other similar trees that from the blue waters of the bay appeared as one solid green mass, he watched these pampered travelers from America topple onto the beach like children. He saw men, and he saw women.

Women. On his island.

He watched their boat beach, watched them jump off as if they were real adventurers (they were not), watched them wade ashore pulling crates, boxes, and small barges with equipment. Loads and loads of it. He saw chainsaws, shovels and ropes. He saw colorful flags and signs. He saw camera equipment, communications equipment, and boxes and boxes of food (they would be very lucky if the rats didn't get it all within days). He saw water purification equipment, tarps and tents.

And then he saw something else.   Something not totally unexpected, and yet, something that sent a chill through his hungry body. At that moment he knew these fat, sloppy, rich invaders from the north had not just come to Cocos for some silly game show.

No, he realized as he slid from the tree to make his way back to his cave. They had come for what was rightly his, and he would not let them take it.

4

Day 3 ~ Game On, Continued

"It's ok. We're insured for this," Taylor mumbled reassuringly to himself, unaware it was loud enough for the anxious contestants gathered before him to hear.

These were not the wise words of assurance the distraught group was looking for.

"*That's* what you're worried about? Tonya just *died* on your fucking show!" Danielle screamed, an angry rumble rising from the players around her.

Taylor quickly made an attempt to pull his head out of his ass and calm the mob, before they calmed him permanently. He suddenly found himself so grateful they had left their machetes outside the door.

"People!" he shouted above the din, "That's not what I meant! I'm upset too! Tonya was a friend." He paused to gather his rapidly diminishing wits. "But this is no bullshit out here. You all knew that when you signed on!"

The intensity in the room dropped, just a little, but the faces around him betrayed a mix of fear, sadness, and simmering rage.

"Look," he corrected, "All I meant is that the show *will* go on. It *must* go on, and we all know Tonya would want it that way." Emboldened now by a few nodding heads, he continued, "This was a freak accident, period. It will not be repeated. We'll double and triple check *every* single event from now on, until the very last day when the winner is crowned and we all get the hell out of here."

Ricardo shook his head in disagreement, and looked to his fellow crew members, Carl and Malik, for backup.

"Look, man, we *did* triple check that shit! Last night, right after we got the whole thing set up. All three of us went over the rigging, the pegs, the pole mounts, the whole thing. And there wasn't a damn thing wrong with pole seven!"

"Hundred percent. I stood on the damn thing to test it," nodded Malik.

Carl nodded too, but felt less certain about it. They must have missed something. The three of them, four including Taylor, were the final safety net in the game. Now Tonya was dead. Not exactly one for the resume when the show faded into history, probably in the very near future.

"Well I guess you fucked that up!" argued Jason Oliver. He shook his head wildly and continued, "Hundred percent? As if! C'mon, man! That ain't good enough. I'm not putting *my* ass out there without a real guarantee."

Taylor laughed derisively, having had just about enough of his children's whining. "Guarantee! How about I guarantee you don't win ten million if you don't get your ass out there and compete? How 'bout that? How about the headline that Jason Oliver, bad boy and everyone's favorite villain, chickened out when shit got real? How about that? What will your fans say? How's that podcast of yours gonna do when they know that's what *you* do! How about I *guarantee* your reputation is at stake here!"

Calmly, and with his trademark sneer, Jason Oliver replied, "And what about yours, asshole?"

Taylor nodded, fully in agreement. "Mine too. No bullshit, I know we've got to get this right. No, I know *I* have to get this right, or the next time you see me I'll be serving fucking fries at McDonald's!"

He kicked his chair across the room, briefly silencing the horde. Running his fingers through his hair, he felt bewildered that things could have fallen so far so fast. And not one single solitary episode in the can. He'd have to call the network, but boy, he was not looking forward to it.

"Carl," Taylor broke the silence, "get the booze."

Carl didn't move. "But that breaks all the rules. Players aren't allowed to partake in . . ."

"Get the fucking booze!"

Jason Oliver threw up his hands with a smile. "Finally, somebody is making sense!"

Carl left the cabin, returning a few moments later with a bottle of blended scotch, and handed it to his boss. Taylor cracked the seal, faced the ground and poured a few drops, before looking up at the mob.

"For Tonya, may she rest in peace."

"For Tonya!" the players repeated like good little soldiers. Their host had cleverly managed to regain control, at least for the moment.

He took a swig before passing it to Jason Oliver, who chugged, coughed, and then passed it on in turn.

The bottle drifted silently around the room, meeting lips and warming throats, greeting heads bowed in respect for their dead comrade.

When it reached Amy, she asked sheepishly, "Can I get a glass? The germs. . ."

"Really, Amy? Are you kidding me?" Taylor humiliated her, "Do you even remember where you are? What you're here to do?"

Snickering derisively, Leticia snatched the bottle from the beauty queen's grasp, and chugged. Finishing with a sneer aimed right at Amy, she added, "Prissy bitch."

The awkward moment passed, and the bottle was slowly and ceremoniously drained. Taylor paced anxiously, realizing he needed to think quickly to keep his minions in hand. He'd managed to quiet them, but once the bottle was gone, anything could happen. If he failed, they might revolt and be gone on the next boat, taking his renewed career prospects with them.

"Here's what I can do," he began, crafting the plan while he spoke. "Before each and every event, you'll each get to inspect your own course. Not anyone else's, mind you, just your own. We can't completely exclude the possibility that someone in this room might actually be a saboteur, so we've got to be strict about that."

The crowd murmured, it suddenly dawning on them that Tonya's death could have been caused by one of their own.

"Now, look," Taylor waved them down, "there's no evidence of that, but we should still be cautious, considering what happened.

That's all I'm saying. So, self-inspection of one's own competitions. Agreed?"

Voices chimed in harmonious assent.

"Excellent!" Taylor's spirits lifted, "Let's finish that bottle, and then get out there tomorrow morning and win ten million bucks!"

They clapped, the bottle was emptied, and the revelry continued, though still a bit subdued, as Tonya's ghost never left their minds. No longer the focus of their attention, Taylor slipped quietly out the door with his satellite phone.

"Davis," he began when his boss came on the line several minutes later, "I've got horrible news."

"Already?" he was incredulous, "Shit, Taylor, this better not be a deal breaker. I've got millions in this thing, and advertisers are chomping at the bit!"

"We . . . We've had a death." There. It was out. He closed his eyes and waited for a response.

For a few seconds there was none.

"I'm sorry? Did you just say there was a death? Is that what you said?"

Oh boy, Taylor thought, here we go. "Yes, there's been a death."

Now the response was quicker. "That's what I thought you said. Well, we're insured for this, of course," Taylor rolled his eyes as Davis continued, "and it was always a possibility. We knew that, and everyone involved did too. Don't beat yourself up, they all knew the risks." A pause, and then, "Wait, are we talking one of the crew or a player?"

"Player. Tonya, the girl with the high IQ. A freak accident, right in the middle of the first event."

The line was silent for several seconds, and then the conversation took a sudden turn. "Did you get it on camera? Please tell me you got it on camera, Taylor."

"Yeah, yeah, we did, but . . ."

Noise and static took over the line, and then, "Taylor, you fucking genius! Do you know what this will do to the ratings? Holy shit man! Through the roof! THROUGH THE ROOF!"

5

Day 3 ~ Nests

While Taylor, his crew, and the medical team slept comfortably in the ranger cabins at Wafer Bay, the eleven remaining players were scattered in much less pleasant camps of various types. Some stayed close to the beach, while others scouted further out, realizing that once things really got going, there would be camp robbers, confrontations, and other chicanery afoot.

Old Joe was one of those.

He grew up in rural West Virginia, and was accustomed to steep hills, thick vegetation, trees, and critters. He happily reckoned that there was more wildlife on this tiny island than in his entire home state. It was dense, and no one had ever lived here long enough to over-hunt it. Joe was an outdoorsman from way back, and could survive better than anyone else in the game if tossed to the winds. Yet, remarkably, he'd won his season with his social game, rarely winning competitions. Somehow staying right in the middle of every alliance at once, he proclaimed ignorance when asked if he knew of anyone else's plans, very skillfully remaining off the "threat radar" of other players, until it was far too late to do anything about it.

Joe made his camp near a stunning waterfall about a mile into the island's interior, right near the center of the northern half of Cocos. He had plenty of fresh water there, and could hunt animals that came in to drink. He'd already seen a dozen or so very large rats that might end up on his plate in the near future. A few goats too, but they were wily, stayed high above in the hills, and would prove difficult to catch. He spotted some large bird nests near the cliffs overlooking the ocean. Those eggs were big, and if he could avoid getting slaughtered by the boobies, they would get him pretty far.

As comfortable as he was in the bush, he felt terribly unsettled by Tonya's death. The two of them had watched others pairing up on the boat ride to the island, and quickly made plans to do the same. Her brains and his woods-smarts would have gotten them far in the game. Now he'd have to make it alone on his wits, hoping that as the numbers dwindled and players left the island, another single might pop up for him to work with.

Sitting in a high tree near the top of his thundering waterfall, he busied himself knitting large palm leaves into a sturdy platform on a mighty limb, where he would scc trouble before it saw him. And hear it. Even over the thundering of the falls below, he could hear an occasional laugh or hoot rise up over the island. What in God's name could they be laughing about, he wondered? A woman, a very nice, innocent woman, died today in a horrifying way! He had only played this game with a few of them, but knew them all by both reputation, and the occasional Execution Island cast gathering.

There were some real dirtbags in this cast— Jason Oliver, that kid was an evil whack job as far as Old Joe could figure. Randy, way too smart and even more cocky. Susan, the sleazy millionaire that everybody wanted to take out. The bitch Leticia, and of course Kinnary, probably the best of the best, who won the MVP competition a few years back. That girl scared the hell out of him. At least with the others he could tell when they were lying or getting ready to stab him in the back, but not Kinnary. She was good, *real* good. He didn't trust his instincts around her, and that meant he had to stay away from her as much as possible. Off her radar.

That left Darius, Matthew, Danielle, Amy, and Franklin as players he might be able to trust. He'd seen Matthew hanging out with Randy, Danielle with Susan, and Kinnary with Amy, so that meant that Darius might be a single. Leticia too— but nobody would actually choose to join up with her unless they were forced to— so Darius, a family man, might be the guy.

He made a mental note to test that option as the game went on.

But tonight he would build his treetop shelter. While not as comfy as one on the ground, it would be far more tactically valuable when the game kicked into high gear. And tomorrow, he'd begin building makeshift weapons for the hunt.

Tonight he was alone, but not lonely, listening to rats scurry, bats flutter, the waterfall growl, and occasionally, one dipshit American voice rising up to spoil it all.

He wrapped another vine around the massive tree limb and saw a light come on down river, about halfway to the beach. Then, sure enough, another god damn whoop went up to accompany it.

"Cooking with gas! Nicely done!" Franklin hooted in excitement as Jason Oliver made the little tufts of wood shavings start to glow. The glow became a flame, and in a few minutes, the flame became a campfire.

"I do have a couple skills, Frank," the bad boy smirked, slamming his machete into a coconut to get at the life saving waters inside.

"High five!" said Franklin, extending his hand, more than a little surprised that this scrawny kid might help punch his ticket to the end. One thing was for sure, he thought as a toddler's hand slapped his giant paw, Dr. Evil, as Jason had been named by the fans, would have very few votes from a jury if he ended up sitting beside him at the final vote.

The celebration over, they went in search of rocks to make a ring around the fire. Once that was done, they rolled in larger rocks to sit on, and then sat together enjoying the fruits of their labor. Each competitor was given a three pound bag of quinoa and a cooking tin at the game's start. Quinoa was much more nutritious than the rice they usually were give, and this game would be far more strenuous. They would be given no more, however, so eventually they would have to wean themselves off the grain, and onto whatever sort of island fare they could scrape up.

The two men prepared their dinner in a silence that was inevitably broken.

"Thoughts on the accident?" Jason pondered softly across the smoke.

Franklin huffed. "Accident? You get a look at that pole?"

"Yeah, but not that close. Why?"

"Well, I worked construction with my Dad during college. And while I can't be sure, I think there may have been tool marks on that thing."

"What?" Jason scoffed, truly shocked. "No way! You're saying she was murdered?"

Franklin swatted the thought away with a wave of his hand. "I'm not saying that! But it just didn't look right, y'know? It looked like there might be tooth marks, like from a saw, right around where the pole split. Wouldn't have taken much, just had to be in the right spot. And she was a pretty heavy woman."

Jason stared into the fire, contemplating what his temporary teammate had just said. "Shit, man, *if* that were true, it would change the whole game. I mean, change everything."

"No shit," Franklin nodded. "Which is why I'm glad we get to inspect our own courses from now on. I'm going over each and every one with a fine tooth comb."

Jason's waking interest led immediately, as it often did, to perverse excitement. "Okay, okay. *So*, if there is a killer among us, who is it? I got odds on Randy. That guy's smart enough to hide his work *and* make it look accidental."

"Maybe. But me," Franklin grinned, "I got odds on you!"

Jason feigned offense, though in truth he was very flattered. "Get the fuck outta here! Me? Why?"

"I'm half joking, but half not. I don't doubt you could kill somebody, I mean, there is your rep. You're a devious little bastard. Which, of course, is why I'm at your side right now instead of on your hit list."

"Smart man. Of course I could still whack you with my machete while you sleep."

"Yeah, there is that. But you need me right now. For the time being anyway. Truthfully though? I've only got two suspects." He considered for a moment, and then added, "Nah, make that three."

Jason's excitement grew with each passing word, silently hoping he was still on the short list. Being an asshole really got him off.

"Come on man, spill!"

"Well, there's Kinnary. We all know about her brains. But I don't think she'd be motivated enough to kill. I mean, the girl won twice!"

"Yeah, true," Jason agreed, "but then again, she's arrogant as hell, and you know she wants to stay the goddess of the game Who knows what she might do to make that happen?"

"And that's why she's still on my list. But the guy most likely to be able to pull off the sabotage without being obvious? Old Joe."

This time Jason shook his head. "Nah, no way man. That guy is a good egg, much as I dislike the type. Hero complex. Too nice a guy. Which brings us to?"

"Which brings us to the guy I think is most likely. Taylor."

This time Jason absorbed the name silently, leaning back on his rock, deep in thought.

"Taylor," he finally spoke, breaking the silence, "Now that I believe. The guy is really laying it on thick. His show is in trouble, and he's cooked up this little soiree where the stakes are really high. But what might make them even higher, *and* make the ratings go up?"

"My thoughts exactly. Murder. Death. Mystery. Call it what you like, it's gonna make people watch like crazy when they catch wind of it. And who stands to benefit the most from that?"

Jason rose and stirred his little pot of quinoa. "I got to admit man, you got me thinking. And watching, that's for sure. I'm gonna be watching him like a hawk."

"You and me both, amigo. And there's something else."

"About Taylor?"

"Probably. I dunno. Could be one of the crew, or some of them, or all of them for that matter. Did you get a look at the gear they hauled off the boat?"

Jason thought back, but drew a blank. "Didn't give it much thought."

"Yeah, neither did I, but now with the Taylor thing, I'm thinking about it again. I'm pretty sure I saw a GPR unit."

Jason drew a blank. "And that is?"

"Ground penetrating radar. The kind they use on archaeological digs. I've seen it used on big construction sites, and I'm pretty damn sure that's what it was."

"How sure?"

"Hey man," he laughed, "I was focusing on the island just like you. But I'd say eighty percent."

"So what, you think there's like artifacts here?"

Franklin shrugged. "Could be anything really. Hell, could just be that that the government makes them to use it to set up competitions, so they don't disturb grave sites or something."

"But no one is supposed to have ever lived here, at least not for long, right?"

"Look man, I just play football. I'm no expert. But again, let's keep our eyes open."

"Yeah," Jason replied with a glint in his eye, "I dig."

Down on the beach, Leticia was within eye shot of the cabins. She'd made her brand new tarp into a nice shelter, and sat in the soft sand feeling hungry. She hadn't yet figured out how to make fire, and that would be a problem if she didn't do so soon. She'd need to hook into another single, maybe the old guy, to be sure she could eat. But since they all disliked her, she realized she'd have to sweeten her attitude if she was going to get any help.

And it would probably have to be one of the men— they were stupid and she could easily play the sexy kitten if she needed to. The women would see right through her no matter how she played it. Except for maybe Danielle. She might be worth a try.

Her stomach growled. It looked like a long night ahead, but at least she was still alive. Unlike Tonya.

Rising, she strolled to the water's edge, where the Pacific Ocean sleepily slapped the shore. It was hard to believe the weather here could be as brutally violent as they'd been told. Tonight was warm and the air was calm and smelled sweet. She felt at home. Cocos wasn't that much different than Fortaleza. But damn was she hungry.

Then, just as she turned back to her little camp, she noticed the glow of a fire just up the river. Smiling, she grabbed her quinoa and cooking tin and headed towards it, gleefully kicking huge rats out of the way as she went.

With any luck, it would be a couple of boys. Reaching down, she ripped the side of her shorts to show a little more thigh, just in case.

6

Leticia ~ Seven Years Earlier

Stairs. Lots of stairs. The barrios of Buenos Aires were built on steep land no one wanted, vertical slopes dangling on the precipices of lofty hills, so to get from any point A to any point B, one was forced to hike an endless serpentine network of stairs. Leticia's sturdy legs made quick work of them as she climbed through myriad concrete steps, sandwiched between buildings placed far too closely together. It was a netherworld of concrete and steel, in a forest of shoddily built structures made of the same.

And yet, people did what they could to make those shabby structures into real homes. Rusty, patchworked tin roofs floating on a drab sea of graystone blocks and makeshift wooden remnants, these hovels nonetheless blazed with the wild colors of Argentina. Brightly toned football jerseys flapped from homemade flagpoles and clotheslines, colorful sheets served as draperies to block out the pounding tropical sun, and beer signs served as talismans of a good life that might someday come this way and splash the residents with its golden fluids.

Leticia paused, looking back on the shimmering city below, its beaches and urban streets teeming with life. The white masts of sailboats floating on the Rio de Plata looked like bedouin tents floating upon a turquoise mirror. Gilded skyscrapers and glittering hotels reflected the brilliant sun back at her, forcing her to shield her eyes with her arm.

But the glittering paradise below was not her world. Her world was here, in the cramped alleys of the favelas. She'd lived here on her own since she was 9, when her parents decided that taking care of a willful young girl was more than they could handle. So they simply left. To where, she didn't know, and now at 16, she didn't care. If they came back someday, she might just hand them a knife in the belly for their troubles. Or she might not. This was the conflict that raged inside her every day. Light to dark. Good to bad.

She was innocent, once. Or at least what passed for innocent on these streets. And the truth was, she was still soft as down inside, filled with light. But she knew well that if she dared show that sweet side, it would quickly be stolen from her and sold to the highest bidder.

So she kept it hidden deep underneath, far from the view of prying eyes, buried beneath layers of venom and brutality that formed in the years following her parents' abandonment. A callous over the soft tissue below.

No, she thought as she pressed on, steeling herself against what she must do next, that world of shimmering glass and sailboats would never be hers.

Arriving at her destination a few minutes later, her thick, muscly legs still yearned for more of the climb. Stepping into a doorway that had only a swinging blanket as a barrier to the outside world, she slipped instantly into her steely skin.

"Melinda!" she yelled with authority, but heard no response.

"Melinda, it's Leticia! I am here to collect Raimundo's rent! You cannot hide from him, Melinda! You know what I must do if you don't pay!"

She knew too, but she wouldn't unless she was forced. If she could coax anything, even a few coins out of the woman, she would let it rest until tomorrow. Raimundo gave her a small bit of latitude in her role as rent enforcer to the female residents of his blocks, but not much. Still, he was one who knew there was a soft side to her. And though he was a slumlord who wanted arms and hands and sometimes legs broken if rent went unpaid, he had compassion for the tough job his enforcers had to do.

But Melinda better get her ass out here now or…

A figure emerged from the bedroom just beyond the kitchen, pushing a cardboard door out of the way as he moved towards her.

35

He was bare from the waist down, a sweaty tank top barely clinging to his bony torso.

"Well, well. And who are you, young beauty?"

Leticia's heart beat quickened. After all these years of fending for herself, she'd developed a sense for when things were about to go sideways. And the look in the eyes of this man twice her size said "run". But she also had learned that if you do run, they'll beat you twice as hard when they catch you.

She stood her ground.

"None of your fucking business,," she spat at him, "I'm on business for Raimundo—this is his flat. So get the hell out of my way, and point me to Melinda."

The greasy beast paced around the kitchen. She could smell his sweat, and something else. Sex. The scent of intercourse flowed from his pores and filled the room with a sickly sweet stench.

When he paused in the middle of the kitchen, she noticed something in his hand. A knife. A very large knife.

"Yes, yes," he grinned, "of course! I can take you to her. She is right through that door, in fact. Go on, go ahead, see for yourself!" He waved his knife wielding hand at the makeshift door.

Leticia's breathing became heavier, her lungs rising and falling, processing the heavy, wet tropical air saturated with this pig's stench. She wanted to vomit. She wanted to run. But she refused to give him the satisfaction of either.

"Melinda!" she yelled without taking a step, "Come on out! If you don't in the next minute I'll go get Raimundo!"

She heard a sound, but it wasn't a voice. It was thumping. Intermittent scuffling and thumping sounds.

"I'm afraid," he said, scraping the knife's edge on the counter, "she can't come out right now. But why don't we join her? You go first."

Leticia's body tightened. She scanned him for signs of weakness, and quickly found them. Telltale signs under his nose. He had been huffing, paint, or fuel, or something. That and his pinhole eyes told her that this piece of shit was very high, and a man who was that high wasn't seeing things as they were. He would make mistakes.

It was all she had.

"Sure, I'll go in," she feigned a smile, loosening her tense stance as much as she could. "But you go first. I'm right behind you."

The predator laughed, raising the arm that held the blade into the air.

"No, no!" he chuckled uncontrollably, "I insist! My friend here," he waved the blade in front of his eyes, "he insists!"

She put her hands up in surrender. "No problem. I'll go."

She slowly sidestepped towards the door, keeping the creature in her sights while slipping ever closer to the room. Reaching the cardboard sheet, she pulled it aside, then quickly spun through the opening and slid to the right, so that her back was against the inside wall of the room, protected from the animal's knife for just a moment.

Melinda was face down on a dirty mattress, her arms bound behind her back. She was drenched in sweat and her underwear were pulled down to her ankles, a filthy bandana shoved in her mouth. As she craned her neck to see Leticia, her eyes spoke volumes.

They were huge, bloodshot, and shifted rapidly towards and away from the door as if to say "he's coming!"

Leticia tried to slow her breathing, but it was no use. Reaching behind her she tried to grab her own blade from where it was tucked into the small of her back, but before she could unsheath it, a grimy hand clamped down on her shoulder and shoved her to the floor.

She focused on Melinda's eyes, knowing they would tell her all she needed to know about what this creep was doing behind her. But just as quickly as he shoved her to the ground, he spun her to face him with his hand, her knees scraping along the concrete floor and starting to bleed.

Looking down on her with his knife in his free hand, his chemical-stinking sweat dripped off of his chin, and onto her legs.

"Stand up now, slowly," he began, a maniacal smile spreading across his face. She did as she was told, feeling her own blade waiting, still pressed against her spine.

"Now take off your clothes, slowly. I want to see you unfold before my eyes, like a flower."

Leticia stepped backwards until she could feel the edge of the mattress against her heels, and began to comply.

Carefully she slid her t-shirt, emblazoned with the image of Rio's Sugar Loaf mountain, over her breasts, then slid her arms through the sleeves and pulled it over her head.

"Oh," he leered, "I am going to like this. And you are going to like it too!"

Reaching back to undo her bra strap, she felt the handle of her weapon touch her fingertips. It was an Indonesian Kris, with a wavy blade designed to shred a victim's guts when thrust into the abdomen.

"Yes," she smiled back at the creature, "I will like this very much. But you? I don't think you will like it as much as I will."

She flicked open the catch on her bra, allowing her heavy breasts to spill out of their cups and capture his gaze for far more time than she would need. Gripping the handle of her Kris with her right hand, she thrust out her left hand, grabbed his shoulder, brought her blade up quickly and planted its hilt against her stomach, the point facing his belly. Pulling him to her, she used her heels as a fulcrum against the filthy mattress, and he toppled forward onto her as they fell together towards Melinda.

Instantly gored by the undulating steel, his pleasure seeking eyes briefly met hers, then turned to stone. His warm entrails spilled out across her chest and stomach, his knife dropped harmlessly to the bed, and all fell silent.

Leticia closed her eyes. She thought of the boats floating serenely on the waters below, their passengers completely ignorant to the life and death struggle that had just taken place far above them in the shanties on the hill.

And it was certainly not the only one.

She opened her eyes, suddenly aware of Melinda thrashing underneath her. Shoving the bloody mess off of her, she rolled first to her side, and then back onto her knees. Steadying herself, she reached for her bra, but finding it a bloody mess, discarded it. She found her shirt near the door, and slipped it over her bare torso.

Leticia walked back to the thrashing Melinda, cut the cloth ties that bound her arms and legs, and yanked the gag out of the woman's mouth.

She was instantly sorry she had.

"God damn you, Leticia!" the woman shrieked as though her life had not just been saved. "Look at this mess! How am I gonna clean this up? He was fucking done, for God's sake!"

"Yeah, he was done," Leticia sneered at the ungrateful woman, "with you!"

"He was a paying customer," Melinda raged at her savior. "He paid for this! Now you've taken money out of my pocket! That's one less client for me! What you gonna do about that!"

Flaming mad, Leticia strode to the corner where the man's pants had been tossed, and ran her hands through his pockets. Yanking out several bills and stuffing them in her pocket, she turned back to Melinda.

"Did he pay you?" she screamed, "Where's the money!"

"You can't have it! It's mine!"

"Look, Melinda," she dropped to her knees, shoving the blade under the woman's nose, "give me that money or join this asshole in hell. Now!"

Melinda backed off, quickly rolled to the far side of the bed, and ran her hand under the mattress while Leticia, her reptile brain fully in charge, prepared to fight.

But instead, the hand came back with a fistful of money, and threw it in her direction.

"There! You happy! Now I have a mess, *and* no money!"

Leticia scraped up the bills and quickly counted them.

"Well you better get back to work, because you're still short. I'll be back tomorrow, and if it's not all here, I'll take a finger."

Leticia, bloody, yet victorious, strode confidently towards the door that led back outside to relative sanity.

"A finger, huh? How about this one!" Melinda squealed, her middle finger extended to the sky.

Leticia didn't even turn her head, knowing good and well which finger was pointed in her direction. "Makes no difference to me, bitch. At 3 o'clock, if you don't have the money, we'll start with that one."

7

Day 5 ~ Game On . . . Again

A tense mood gripped the Castaways as they gathered on the beach for the second competition. Each player walked their course's extent very slowly, scanning for anything out of the ordinary. Today's game was a standard on each season of Execution Island. Players would begin by being tangled by the crew in mesh commando netting, which they would have to untangle as they moved in and out of it, release themselves from it, and then commando crawl on their bellies under an more netting in the sand. Escaping that, they climbed over a high wall, dropped, and then ran to complete a puzzle at the end. If they were the first to solve it, they'd light a fuse with a waiting torch and fireworks would signal their victory, guaranteeing they would remain on the island when the boat of shame arrived to take the loser back to the mainland.

Each of them had completed this course in a prior season, some twice, so they knew right where any possible injury spots might be, and looked them over carefully.

Taylor waited on the sidelines chugging water from a coconut, just wishing they would hurry the hell up. Noticing that Jason and Franklin were stroking every piece of wood on the whole damn course, for just a moment he wondered if they might know something he didn't. But then, chuckling at his own paranoia, he realized no one out here knew more about what was *really* going on than he did.

No one.

Fifteen minutes later, all but one contestant were ready at the starting line.

"Jesus, Franklin!" Taylor was losing his patience, "What's the holdup?"

Franklin shot him a nasty look, but then jogged in to join the others moments later.

Jason Oliver quickly made eye contact with his new buddy and mouthed the words "See anything?"

Franklin just shook his head to say no, and nervously took his position. The crew worked quickly to wrap him the specified number of times in the mesh netting, like a fly in a spider's web, and then jogged to their own positions.

"Better late than never! Are we rolling?" Taylor asked.

Carl waved an arm to say yes, and then, shocking everyone in attendance, Taylor suddenly turned on something few believed he could— thoughtfulness. Quietly, and with at least outward sincerity, he began.

"Before we get started, I want to address the tragedy that has happened to our family. Tonya, one of the smartest players we've ever had, passed away two days ago in a tragic accident. Through no fault of her own, a freak occurrence led her pole to snap, and she was killed instantly, and by all accounts, painlessly. I'd like to send my condolences to her family, and our little family will then begin today's challenge in honor of our fallen sister, with a moment of silence."

The players bowed their heads. Some cried, while others just waited impatiently for the game to start, too focused on the challenge to come to let sentimentality fog their vision.

Taylor's rarely used thoughtfulness meter shortly reached its limit, and he slipped quickly back into himself. "With that, I dedicate this challenge to our sister and friend, Tonya." A quick beat, and then "*Players ready!*"

Hands rose to signal readiness, while hearts raced with a butterfly-inducing mix of anticipation and fear.

"*All right then! GO!*"

41

Feet scraped furiously, straining for purchase in the soft sand. This first half of the challenge was not about brawn, but about being lithe, agile, and quick. The larger men, Darius and Franklin, got stuck behind in the netting with the usual stragglers, Old Joe, Susan and Leticia, while Jason, Amy, Danielle, and Kinnary shot out front. Matthew and Randy were right in the middle of the pack, the athletic pair sure to move up once they cleared the nets.

Franklin tore at the heavy mesh with huge fingers and kept his head on a swivel, eyes scanning the course for anything that might spell M-U-R-D-E-R. He'd made a calculated decision to stay near the back of the middle of the pack to be sure he survived to fight another day. He watched Taylor prancing as usual along the edges of the course, but nothing in the host's attitude looked out of the range of normal, at least *his* normal. The ringleader seemed truly absorbed by the competition, screaming his usual shtick into the boom mic that followed him, as he followed the action.

"This course has nothing to do with brawn, and as you can see, the big men are far behind the smaller men and women! This is truly a competition to be won by someone agile, although once out of the spider's web, it favors the competitor with the fastest legs! Even Jason Oliver, who almost never wins a competition, is in this one!"

Jason enjoyed the overdue recognition as he slipped out of the mesh and sped across the beach to the commando crawl. Hitting the sand, he snapped his head to his left and saw Kinnary ahead of him two lanes over, while Amy dropped into the sand at the very same moment he did, right beside him. Matthew grunted right behind on his right, apparently having cleared the nets as well.

Randy, like Franklin, didn't plan to win this one. He was holding back, moving quickly enough to avoid suspicion, but not quickly enough to become a bigger target in the game. Sure, this game was different than the others, but there would be twists, twists that might give one of the players the power to send a big target home, and he was determined not to be that guy. Always thinking two, sometimes three challenges ahead, Randy knew that in doing so, the odds of him winning the whole thing increased.

Danielle was tiring rapidly at the far side of the crawl. She'd flown through the nets with furiously fast fingers, but now age began to show itself in the thick sand. Slowing noticeably as flying sand from her thrashing competitors flew into her open mouth, she knew she must keep going to stay competitive in the game, and that she would do. Let the Bitch from Buenos get eliminated. That would make everybody smile.

No one noticed that Franklin had stopped dead in his tracks, staring into the jungle.

Amy's golden legs kicked the sand as she slid on her tight, toned belly. The swimsuit model used her narrow form to easily clear the wires hanging just inches above her back. Quickly passing Jason, she saw Matthew's long arms shoot out in front of her as he rapidly made up ground. He would be nearly impossible to beat, but she reminded herself that in this new version of the game, all she needed to do was not finish last. It seemed a foregone conclusion at this point that her strategy was the correct one, right up until the moment her stomach suddenly split open, its contents gushing out of her belly and onto the reddening sand.

Matthew thrust his muscular arms forward once more, clawing the sand and throwing it behind him as quickly as he could. He blew by Amy, who stalled quite suddenly as though she were stuck. All he could hear now was his heart pounding as he focused on the only pair of feet in front of him.

Kinnary cleared the crawl and got to her feet, sprinting for the wall as fast as she could. She felt Matthew on her heels, his feet kicking so hard at the sand that it flew forward as well as back, right past her. One them would surely be the winner of the first completed Execution Challenge.

Old Joe had just cleared the webs that still held Leticia, Darius, and Franklin, when he heard Jason Oliver scream.

"Amy!"

Taylor's heart threatened to leap from his chest as his worst fear suddenly came to life. "EVERYBODY STOP!" he screamed as loud as his panic stricken vocal chords could muster. He began to run to Amy's aid, but remembering what his boss had said, first turned around and saw Carl and Malik dropping their cameras to the ground, joining the effort to help the fallen beauty queen.

"NOT you two!" he yelled, moving quickly to Amy's side, "Keep rolling!"

The cameramen glanced at each other, shocked. Carl shook his head in disgust, while Malik said just loud enough for his companion to hear, "You think we're *still* insured for this?"

Taylor and the medical team dove on top of the commando rigging and wiggled to Amy's side, the other players keeping their distance. Each of them had fully awakened to the shocking but inarguable fact that something was seriously wrong with this game, and there was no way to be sure the afternoon's carnage was over. Jason lay stiff, frozen in the lane next to the eviscerated woman in scared silence, eyes tightly closed.

Sato saw the pool of blood under Amy's body, and a piece of intestine poking from her side. She motioned to Jeremy, her assistant, to move to the girl's other side.

"She's been gashed open! We need to *very carefully* roll her over! Somebody cut this god damn netting loose so we can move her!"

Ricardo dropped his boom mic and took off with Darius for the starting line, where machetes had been left by the players after the trek to the competition site. He handed one to the big man, and took off running with one himself. Lunging into the commando netting, they chopped and hacked at it until it went limp. Gathering it in their arms, they rolled it carefully over the medics and the motionless girl, until all were freed from it and could stand.

Sato took charge as Taylor dove into the sand next to Jeremy, waiting for instructions.

"Taylor and Jeremy, very slowly, very carefully, roll her over towards me. That's it, easy . . . slower, I don't want to risk injuring her any further. That's it, easy now . . ."

"Oh my god!" Jason Oliver shrieked, before his mind succumbed, and he passed out on the crimson sand.

"Get this fucking child out of here!" Sato screamed, and Randy, tears streaming as he gazed down at his fiancée, jumped into action, grabbing Jason's legs and very forcefully dragging him to the side of the course.

Amy's entrails slipped from her belly, instantly covered in sparkling sand. Her abdomen was ripped from belly button to sternum, a large hunk of pointed bamboo hanging from her torso.

"Aww fuck," moaned Taylor, as Sato checked her pulse, and then hung her head as it shook from side to side.

The second Castaway from the final season of Execution Island, was dead.

All of their efforts for naught, the two medics fell back in the sand, breathing heavily.

"She's gone," Sato said matter of factly as she regained her objectivity, wiping the blood from her eyes.

"What? How can that be!" yelled Kinnary, more angry than afraid. Far down the beach and nearly finished with the puzzle, she had just realized the competition was over.

Matthew and Old Joe stepped in to help move the dead girl's body. Jeremy and Matthew grabbed her feet and began to pull her from the course, but Old Joe paused, his wise old eyes catching the terrible truth of the moment.

"Hold up guys! Stop!"

The two men paused, while Joe reached in and grabbed the chunk of bamboo. He struggled to remove it from her body, as it had caught between her ribs when they flipped her over. But once it was out, he wiped it on his shirt, instantly realizing what they were up against.

"This wadn't no accident, y'all! This here was *murder*!"

Silence. The entire Execution Island cast and crew held their breath, in their shock choosing to disbelieve the old redneck's muttering, until he offered something more in the way of proof. It didn't take long.

"See here, Taylor, look ... these marks was made by a man."

Taylor wiped the sticky sand from his eyes, struggling to snap out of his stupor, before leaning in to see what Old Joe was talking about. When he did, he saw in a glance that there were indeed marks, serrations which made it very obvious that the hunk of sharp bamboo hadn't gotten that way naturally.

"But that ain't all. Look at this here."

Joe wiped more blood from the device and pointed to the unsharpened end of the bamboo dagger, where a thicker, flatter piece of bamboo had been tied to it horizontally with vines, rising a few inches above the stabbing end.

"Adding that piece to the back of it made it a lever. Looks to me like somebody buried this thing in her lane so nobody could see it, but she come along and her hand, or her chest, hit this here bar, pushed it down into the ground, which at the same time . . ."

"Pushed the sharp end up and into her gut," Taylor finished the sentence, horrified, yet marveling at how such a simple device could so easily kill someone. "Jesus Christ."

A deep, calm voice rose from behind them.

"I saw him."

Taylor spun to see Franklin, standing stone-still in the middle of the spider course, his eyes focused on a spot in the jungle. Darius stood nearby, gripping his machete like a tether to life itself.

"What are you talking about?" Darius asked, his voice betraying panic, "You saw . . . what?"

"Somebody! I don't know," he shook his head, confused. "Something," Franklin raised his thickly muscled arm to point, "in there. Bushes moving. A figure."

"One of us?" Taylor probed, realizing the plot had thickened, both suddenly and profoundly, in his little game of pretend death.

"No!" Franklin suddenly snapped awake, tearing violently at the mesh that held him. "A man! I saw a fucking man! Get me out of here, I'm going after him!"

Fear replaced by action, Darius leaned in, hacking at the netting with his machete until Franklin was free.

"Now hold on!" Taylor yelled, running towards the two men "There's no one here but us! The authorities assured me!"

Franklin just shook his head and grabbed a machete from the pile. "Well I saw something, and it sure as hell looked like a man, right when Jason screamed! Who's with me?"

Matthew and Darius flew instantly to his side.

Old Joe raised his arm. "Now before you boys go a runnin' off, ya gonna need somebody who kin track. And only one here fits the bill." He calmly stepped to the machete pile, grabbing his own. "I'm comin' with."

"*Everybody fucking stop!*" Taylor yelled, trying to regain control of his meal ticket. "No one is going anywhere until we have a plan!"

"*Who the fuck do you think you are, Taylor?*"

The host spun around to see that Jason Oliver had somehow come out of his funk and stood next to him, wiping blood and sand off his body as quickly as he could.

"The way, I see it," Jason Oliver continued, his blood apparently having gone to his head instead of out on the ground, "you aren't in charge of shit! We've had two people die on your watch. TWO! So, it seems to me that your *leadership* is limited to the minutes between clicks of the camera shutter. So, shut the fuck up, and get out of our way."

Scrawny, unlikely badass Jason Oliver shoved his way past Taylor, joining the others already moving into the jungle behind Old Joe.

"I'm coming!" Kinnary added, running to join the men.

Taylor hyperventilated. He looked down at Sato for support, but the normally stoic physician just shrugged her shoulders. His cameramen came running, having finally left their cameras on the sand.

"Look boss," Carl said, "we better a*ll* go. No telling what this guy, *if* he exists, has cooked up for anybody staying behind. If we all go, we can track him down *and* overpower him. Either way, in this case it's best we stay together."

Taylor begrudgingly nodded, realizing the truth in the older man's words.

"Okay, grab machetes and some water, and follow Old Joe. Ladies?" he waved his arm to the last remaining players, Danielle, Leticia, and Susan, who jogged over to join him.

Randy, though, just sat in the sand, cradling Amy's head, softly rocking back and forth, sobbing like no one had ever imagined he could.

"Hey, Randy, you all right?" motherly Danielle asked as she kneeled next to him.

No reply, he just kept running his fingers through the dead girl's hair, rocking back and forth with his eyes tightly closed.

"Hey man," Taylor entreated, "you want to stay with her while we go find this guy? No one's gonna blame you, not a bit."

Suddenly Randy's eyes snapped open, he took one long look at Amy's rapidly whitening face, and set her head softly in the sand before leaping to his feet.

"No way," he said, grabbing his machete, "I'm gonna kill this fuckin' guy."

8

Randy ~ Fourteen Years Earlier

"Tell me you're a dick sucker!"

Pinned on the ground, Randy struggled against his attacker, twisting and thrashing with every drop of strength at his disposal. Boys laughed and pointed all around him, just waiting for him to say those magic words that would send them all frothing into the stratosphere with glee, and tar him for months with their derision.

I suck dick.

A few girls stood in the circle too, but the truth was that they'd rather be almost anywhere else.

All except Gina. She was there to support her younger brother, but was not about to save him. At least not yet. A small boy, Randy had never figured out how to defend himself. Instead he allowed the many bullies in their small, blue collar town, boys whose fathers no doubt bullied them as well, to pick on him and push him around, call him "fag", and generally make his elementary, middle, and now high school years a painful stroll through all seven levels of hell.

Eventually, of course, Gina would step in.

No way would she let her little brother get beaten to a pulp, she just wanted him roughed up enough so he didn't forget what it felt like. She'd been waiting years for him to stand up for himself, to fight back just once, knowing full well that's all it would take for this bullshit to stop for good.

The only thing a bully understands, she knew from her own experience, was another bully.

But, as Eric stuffed dirt clods in Randy's mouth, punching first one side of his face and then the other, the familiar feeling crept in yet again that today was not to be the glorious day when he would show those boys he was done being fucked with. No, she realized sadly, that was still her job.

"What will he do when I go to college next year?" she wondered.

Hesitating, she watched Randy roll and twist, trying to avoid both the blows, and choking on the clods of dirt being shoved into his mouth. That dirt was beginning to clog his airways, and in mute agony he quite suddenly realized that he could no longer breath at all.

"HMMMMPH!!" he tried to scream, but that's all that came out. Eric just kept sitting on his chest, the crowd kept laughing, and his sister kept staring down at him with a combination of disgust and pity.

He didn't know which was worse.

His body convulsed as he tried to buck the bigger boy off, and his legs kicked hard, grasping for purchase on the slippery gravel road behind the school.

"What's that?" Eric put a hand to his ear, "Did I hear you say you suck dick?"

Tears were pouring down Randy's cheeks, turning the soft, brown dirt on his face into mud. He swung his arms with all his might, but each time Eric managed to catch them before they could land. He was as helpless as a baby turtle in an eagle's claws.

"MMMMMPPHHH!!" he tried again. This time he was actually trying to say the dreaded phrase, the one he would hear replayed for years to come if those gathered around the fray could actually make it out.

Luckily for him, they couldn't. And then suddenly, it was over.

Gina slammed into Eric, sending him skidding across the gravel, clods of dirt transforming into clouds of dust as he scrambled to halt his tumble.

"That's enough, Fuckwad! We're done here."

"Eric got his ass kicked by a girl!" somebody yelled from the throng.

"Fuck that!" Eric stood up, shouting down the heckler, "That bitch is no girl! Unlike her brother, she *doesn't* suck dick! Fucking Lesbo!"

He spit towards her, but as he did, she bull rushed him and knocked him right back on his ass.

"Say that again Fiedler, and I'll kick your fucking teeth out," she panted above the bully. "C'mon, asshole. Say it again!"

Eric Fiedler stood and began to back away with his hands up, showing he was no threat. "It's cool, it's cool. I'm not gonna hit a girl, even a Lesbo. But watch out, bitch. I got you in my sights."

And with that the bully walked off, joking with his buddies about the whooping he had just doled out, along with a few tired tidbits about lesbians in particular.

Randy rolled over to cough out the dirt, and then began the slow work of picking the clods from his nose.

"Thanks, Sis," he said sheepishly.

Gina stood over him, her legs straddling him as Eric's had just moments before the beating.

"Damnit, Randy! When are you going to learn? These assholes won't stop beating the shit out of you until you make them! The only thing that's keeping Fiedler from killing you is me, and I'm only here a few more months! What you gonna do then?"

Randy had no answer. He slid to a seated position and wiped the blood off his face with his shirt. Then he combed his fingers through his curly hair and shook out dirt and small rocks that had become one with his scalp during the scuffle.

Gina reached down to help him to his feet. Despite her disappointment, she loved her brother, and wiped the wet mud from his eyes as he looked back at her like a puppy dog.

"Oh, Randy," she sighed. "You're gonna have to get smart and beat them with your brains. I know you can. You just have to figure out how. And," she shook her head sadly, "you're running out of time."

He nodded with his head hung low, and watched as she turned to walk home across the desert. She was right. This was his third beating since tenth grade began. Two of them by Eric, who was a year older, and would still be there when Gina was long gone next year.

He watched her walk away, disgusted with himself. He felt like less than nothing. Like a void.

This, he told himself, was bottom. And as he slowly shuffled his tired feet through the sand, he felt an ache inside that told him there was no way to go but up. In that moment of clarity, a plan began to form in his incredibly sharp brain, a brain that would one day help him win a tv game show and bring him millions of dollars from both that win, and wins at the poker table against the best of the best.

Before going home he made a detour, and took some quick measurements by placing his feet end to end, pacing in a straight line.

Then he swung by Jerry's place and stole some fishing line from his dad's tackle box, which he always left in the bed of his truck, parked far away from the house to avoid waking Jerry's mom in the morning when he left early for work.

That night he sat on his bed, twisting successive long strands of fishing line, rolling them tightly together so that they made a thick rope. An almost translucent, clear rope. When he was finished, he stuffed his creation under his bed, and went to sleep with a smile.

The next day he put on a hat and slipped out before his mom could see him. His Dad was long gone for work before Randy even got up. His teachers asked about the black eyes. He told them he fell, again, and they gazed silently back at him with the same pitying stare as his sister. In the hallways people pointed and giggled. Pulling his hat down low, he just got on with it as he had so many times before.

For the last time.

When the day was over, his heart pounded in anticipation. His time was at hand. Revenge, served still lukewarm, would be his.

He knew Eric had basketball practice until six, which, now that it was winter in the Mojave desert, was just after dark. Mom wouldn't expect him for dinner until seven, and he'd told his sister he'd be at the movies alone, just trying to forget what happened yesterday.

He bought a ticket for that movie, then slipped quietly out the rear exit right after the opening credits.

Heading to his chosen spot, he slipped on a pair of leather work gloves his dad had given him for chopping wood, and pulled the translucent rope out of his bag. Carefully he looped it around the wooden light post at the far side of Benson road, a quiet side street about halfway between school and Eric Fiedler's house. Measuring with a length of cord in his gloved hands, he tied it tightly at just the right spot. Stretching it across the street, he laid it on the ground so that any passing cars would simply drive over it, and then dove into the bushes to wait, the rope coiled around his thick gloves several times so there was no way it would slip from his grasp.

A car passed. Then another. He prayed his rope hadn't been damaged by their tires, but he was not about to turn back now. And then, he heard it.

Revving high at every turn, it was Eric Fiedler's old Honda Trail 90, the one he used to get to and from school and practice every day. A moment later, a single headlight flashed in Randy's eyes as Eric turned the corner.

Predictably, Eric cranked on the gas on this long, straight street, which was exactly why Randy had chosen it. The tiny 90 cc engine strained under Eric's weight, but managed to accelerate to nearly 35 miles an hour just before it reached the two light poles.

Sweat pouring from his brow and his heart pounding in his chest, Randy pulled on the nylon rope with all his might, bracing his legs against a large boulder to avoid being yanked into the street by the force of the impact.

When the rope met flesh, Eric's head snapped instantly backwards and Randy was jerked forward, only to fall back hard on his back when the rope snapped in two. The driver-less motorcycle kept rolling, twitching left and right, its headlight beam splashing here and there, until finally it smashed down against the pavement, skidding to a stop twenty feet later.

Eric Fiedler lay on the ground, his neck bearing a huge red welt and leaning strangely to the side. Blood trickled from the back of his head where it slammed into the pavement. The translucent cable lay in two pieces, the spring-tension of the impact having sent it recoiling to either side of the street. Rushing to gather up the remains of his weapon, Randy dared not even stop to check his victim, but instead ran home as fast as he could.

Outside his back door, he struggled to calm down. He shook his head vigorously, and took deep breaths in and out to consciously slowing his breathing. When clarity finally returned, he walked over to the woodpile, grabbed an armful of wood, and calmly stepped through the door.

"Mom, I'm home!" he yelled as he strode to the wood stove and dropped his armful. A warm heat was already rising from it, but it didn't matter to him if it was about to go out or was blazing like an inferno. Opening the stove's door, he yanked open his backpack, looked around to be sure no one could see, and then pulled out the revenge rope and quickly shoved both it and his gloves into the blaze. He watched as the nylon melted slowly over the logs inside, black smoke billowing from it in huge clouds. Throwing another log on for good measure, he shut the stove's door, and went to say hi to his mom.

"How was the movie?" she asked as she began to set the table for dinner.

"So good! Seriously the ending was spectacular."

The next day Randy was questioned by the police at school, his mother and the principal next to him. He showed them his torn movie ticket and described the end of the movie (Danny Turner told him all about it a week ago). The police, however, wore grim expressions, still fairly certain he was the one who had broken Eric Fiedler's neck, paralyzing him from that point down.

But there was, and remained, no real evidence, and though the investigation went on for months, it went unsolved.

When he'd answered all of their questions and they finally let him go back to class, things had quite suddenly changed. The other kids paused as he passed, gazing at him with a mixture of admiration, fear, and awe. Randy smiled back at the gawkers, enjoying the warm glow it gave him inside, and then simply went about his day as he normally would, this time with his head held high.

No one ever called Randy a fag again.

9

Day 5 ~ Chase

Old Joe worked quickly while the others beat back the jungle. His eyes scanned the ground, and his nose sniffed the air. All of his tracking senses combined together in the hunt for clues as to where the mysterious interloper had fled. While he was used to tracking much smaller game in the Hill Country, raccoons and the like, this quarry, which appeared to be a full grown man, was much easier to follow.

Up and down they went, hiking up one jungle covered hill, then down the other side, wading through a river, then doing it all over again on the next set of hills and valleys. Old Joe led the entire band of Execution Island contestants and crew behind him, all of whom were dead tired by hour two of the search.

Joe stopped before a glorious ocean vista on Gissler point to catch his breath, allowing the whining hordes behind him to catch theirs as well.

"There's a faint trail here," he said, gulping water from one of a string of coconuts tied around his waist. "Ain't much, but it must belong to this fella we're chasin'."

Taylor peered through the thick foliage ahead, seeing only an endless sea of green shrubs, green bushes, greener trees, and big, brown rats running between them all.

"I don't see it."

Joe smiled. "Don't figger ya would. Like I said, it ain't much, but I bet this ol' boy walks it a coupla times a week. Ever since we left the beach, this here trail— which disappears now n' then 'cause the dang bushes grow so quick 'round these parts— this here trail has been right where he's aimin'. Here, look back where we come from..." He pointed down the hill towards the last creek they crossed.

"Now, if ya' follow the line of our path, you'll see it takes a perty straight route. It's 'bout the easiest track a body could make 'cross these hills. Only come about a mile so far."

"Easiest?" Matthew mused while munching a handful of coconut flesh, "Man, that's about the toughest mile hike I've *ever* seen."

Joe chuckled knowingly. "Ya mighta noticed, son, but there ain't no such thing as an easy hike on Cocos. This thing is one goddamn green stepladder after another. But that there trail? That was made by a body who knows the island, and knows how ta break this hilly sumbitch down into the softest bits possible. Which," he grinned, "are 'bout as soft as frickin' barbed wire."

Kinnary joined in, her mouth overflowing with coconut pulp. "But they told us no one but the rangers lives here. You're saying somebody *else* does? Like, permanently?" She was one of only a few, Matthew and Old Joe included, who weren't lying flat on the ground, panting from exhaustion.

"That's 'zactly what I'm sayin'. Maybe these rangers ain't go no idea this ol' boy is here. That'd be my guess."

Taylor's eyes darted around nervously as Old Joe finished, and Jason Oliver, despite being half dead and huffing on the ground, took notice.

"Something wrong, Taylor?" he asked, a wry smirk somehow spreading on his hyperventilating face.

Taylor shot him an angry look. "What the hell is that supposed to mean? Yeah, something's wrong! Two deaths this week, and now there might be a killer on our island! Yeah, Jason, something is actually wrong!"

Susan, just as tired but her mind still sharp, replied, "Seems like it's his island. Not ours."

"Damn sure is, damn sure," Old Joe nodded before taking his own seat on the ground, and tearing into the flesh of the coconut he'd just drained.

55

But Jason Oliver wasn't through. "Oh, I don't know," he teased. "Seems like Taylor might be a little extra freaked out that somebody might be on *his* island."

"Got something to say, Oliver?" Taylor snapped, his eyes betraying a mean streak that was now just below the surface.

"Who, me?" Jason's smirk grew with every smarmy word that left his lips. "Nah, but I thought you might? Maybe about all of that GPR equipment you brought? Just how exactly did you come to pick *this* particular island, anyway? Huh, Taylsie?"

Having quietly stayed in earshot, Randy stepped even closer to see if he could pick up on what the hell was *really* going on. Right away he saw by the look on Taylor's face that he wasn't just shocked, but was also alarmed by whatever Jason was implying. Something was most definitely amiss.

"And just what is this GPR equipment?" Randy asked, more in an attempt to continue the conversation than because he didn't know.

"Ground Penetrating Radar," Franklin happily obliged. "I saw it when we offloaded the boat."

Randy observed Carl, Malik, and Ricardo moving in as well, eyeing the proceedings with what struck him as perhaps too much interest.

"What's the scoop, boys?" he probed in their direction, "The three of you know something the rest of us don't?"

Malik spoke first. "I don't know nothing 'bout nothing. First I've heard."

Carl nodded. "Me too."

"Well one of you better speak the hell up," Susan warned, "or the posse here might toss you off this cliff!"

Sitting down nonchalantly, Taylor bit off another hunk of coconut meat, and took a moment to think.

"Nice little conspiracy theory you got going here, Jason," he began his quickly crafted defense. "But if you must know, the GPR was *required* by the Costa Rican government. There may be artifacts here, and we aren't allowed to disturb any if there are. So, Ricardo and I go over the courses each time, to be sure we aren't destroying any archaeology. *That's* your big fucking conspiracy."

Jason Oliver caught Franklin's eye, and then Randy's. Neither of them were buying it. He put two fingers up to his eyes and then pointed them back at Taylor. The other two nodded, feeling exactly the same as he did.

Randy looked again at Carl and Malik. Both looked surprised, and didn't seem to be buying the "artifact" explanation either.

Old Joe, who really couldn't care less, ignored the scrum and stood near the cliff's edge to take one last look at the beauty spread out below his feet. He took in the endless green of Cocos, framing both Wafer Bay to their right, and his very own waterfall behind that. Golden cliffs lined the deep blue Pacific, dropping hundreds of feet below his shoe tips. His ears caught the roar of the waves pounding the pebbly beach far below. If he'd just take one step forward, he thought, he'd become part of that idyllic scene forever.

But instead, he turned back to the far less pleasant scene behind him. "Best get moving, 'fyall are done with yer little dance," he chided. "Not sure why the hell all that crap matters right now, anyway. We got a killer ta catch."

Intent upon cutting off any response, he quickly stepped through the group and moved back into the jungle. His team of bushwhackers, machetes at the ready, hopped up to join him, and the rest, tired or not, soon followed.

They kept on for another hour, the tropical sun pounding down on them while birds screamed above, warning their nested companions that two legged monsters were approaching. Lizards scurried out of their way, but the rats just stood their ground, forcing the invaders to either step over them, or kick them aside and maybe lose a toe in the process. The jungle became more dense as they hiked on, and a darker, more foreboding shade of green.

Finally, the trail stopped winding up and down through endless river valleys, and instead made a beeline up a ridge, towards the highest point on Cocos, Mount Iglesias, rising another 1500 feet above them. Old Joe led them through a gap in that ridge, and they found themselves perched above yet another gash in the island's side, deeper, and cut by the largest river they had yet seen.

Old Joe paused and held up a flat palm, bidding the others to stop. They did so gladly, dropping to the ground to munch on quinoa and coconut, swilling whatever little bit of water each had left.

The old hunter turned and looked at Taylor. "I ain't sure what ta say. It just stops."

Confused, his brow sweaty and his mind suffering from heat exhaustion and lack of water, neither did Taylor. "What? What stops?"

"The gol-durn trail, that's what. Just stops, right here. If ya look down below, you can see there just ain't no more of it."

Taylor looked, but saw only a pair of raggedy goats, far below on a rocky ledge. "I'll take your word for it."

"You're saying he's given us the slip?" Danielle asked. Older than all but Joe and Carl, she was dragging badly and would gladly borrow any excuse to call it a day.

Thinking it a silly question, Old Joe didn't bother to answer. Instead, he put his senses back to work and continued the search, while the others sat and rested.

His mind spun as he watched massive fruit bats twist through the air like pterodactyls of old. He'd tracked much tougher game than this. Bears, bobcats, mink. There was no way this guy was going to out maneuver him. Still, it was truly strange. Scanning the thick green of the scrub around him, he saw no signs of anything pointing to a man's footprints being through here in the last week. Sure, he thought, the jungle grows fast, but not *that* fast. It reminded him of a time he tracked a mountain lion, and after several miles, all evidence of the creature's existence just completely vanished. He remembered thinking then that it seemed as though the ground had just swallowed the beast up. And then . . .

Instantly alert, Old Joe turned and barked orders at the ragtag band of wannabe bounty hunters.

"Ever'body up! I want y'all to look down, right under yer feet! Poke around, kick the dirt, turn over rocks, uproot bushes. There's a hole here, and I think this ol' boy done went in it!"

"A cave?" Randy asked, already tearing through the bushes as he spoke. All around him the others began to do the same, kicking dirt, moving rocks, and scanning the hillside.

"More like a hole," Joe corrected him. "When ya say the word cave, most folks think 'bout a big ol' gapin' doorway on the side of somethin'. But this here island is just one big volcano. And volcanoes, they got lava tubes, and lava tubes, most often they don't have a big, open mouth like that, they got a hole. Now, that hole can be big as a house, or tiny as a mouse. I'm guessin' this one here is small, just the right size fer a man ta squeeze into." Pausing to roll aside a large boulder, he added, "If, that is, I'm right at'all."

The searchers continued to dig, scrape, and kick. Minutes later, Old Joe was indeed proven right.

"I got it!" Darius shouted, sending a large palm tree trunk rolling across the ridge. Then he stood, staring down at the spot where it had been.

Joe ran to his side, and there it was. A small crack, about a foot by two feet with jagged sides. Just large enough for a modestly thin person to fit through.

"Who are we sending in?" asked Leticia, hoping it wasn't her. As she saw it, this guy had kindly removed two of her competitors and was no enemy of hers . . . yet. Besides, he might have a weapon.

"We all go," Taylor answered, "the larger our numbers, the better."

Franklin shook his head. "That's too tight a squeeze for me. Besides, somebody, or two or three, needs to stay here in case he comes out."

"Good idea," Taylor nodded. "Who's going in? I sure as hell am."

"You know I am," Randy said, cradling his machete with bloodlust.

"Man, I wouldn't miss this for the world!" Jason smiled.

"Show of hands?" Taylor asked, and all went up except for Leticia's, Franklin's, and Carl's. He was also a bit thick around the middle, but for different reasons than Franklin.

"I'll stay," Sato added, "just in case we need medical up top. Jeremy and I shouldn't be together, the way things are going. Too risky."

Jeremy agreed. "No problem, I'm in."

"Aren't you all forgetting something?" Leticia smirked. "It's a cave, right? And caves are . . . dark!"

Behind her, Carl tossed his pack on the ground and rummaged through it. "Me and Malik each have a pair of lights, Ricardo too. They're nothing special, just little LED jobbies, but they should work."

Malik nodded and took off his pack, and Ricardo followed.

"That means we got eleven folks goin' in, and six lights. Teams of two? Means we need one more," said Old Joe.

And there was only one more to be had.   "Leticia?" Taylor prodded the angry beast, "One for the team?   The other two won't fit."

"Fuck!" she shouted unapologetically, kicking the dirt to show her dissatisfaction. "Team, my ass!"   Folding her arms across her chest, she pouted. "Whatever.   Fine."

Satisfied, Taylor grabbed a light. "Let's pair up."

"Now hold on, y'all," old Joe paused their descent, "I think two oughta go in first, just ta scout a bit.   Who knows what we're walking' into here.   Might not even be room for more than one or two.   These caves is unpredictable."

Taylor agreed. "Volunteers?"

"Me," Randy was determined, and no one could stop him.

"I'll go with him," Darius   added.   "Did a bit of caving back home."

"Done.   Now y'all check 'er out, and if she looks good, come right back up and let us know," instructed Old Joe.

Randy was first through the hole, hell bent on slaughtering Amy's killer. He was thicker than some from living the good life of a mid-level, professional gambler, complete with dinners out in Vegas nearly every night. Grimacing when the sharp lava caught his belly, and tore a small cut in his side, he was relieved a moment later when his feet touched down on a narrow ledge below.

Pointing the little flashlight around, he could see very little. All around him was black lava. Tiny sparkling specks like stars captured the light and shone brilliantly back at him. Looking down he could see that the ledge on which he stood veered downwards, plunging deeper into the hole at a walkable angle, then disappearing around a huge pile of rocks that had fallen from the ceiling above.

Feeling a tap on his shoulder, he quickly spun around, ready to dispense sharp justice with his machete. But it was only the tap of Darius' feet as he dropped in behind, so he moved down the ledge to get out of the bigger man's way.

With Randy in the lead, they crept down the ledge. A thirst for revenge raging inside him, he picked up a knife-like wedge of lava to use as a weapon, only to drop it later when he found a better one. These tight quarters, he realized, might render his machete useless.

60

But when they rounded the corner behind the fallen rock pile, the room suddenly got much larger, opening into a huge chamber that could easily fit a five story building.

Randy stopped. "Hey," he said when Darius caught up, "go back and let them know we're good."

Darius nodded, and with the quick moves of an experienced caver, ambled back up the ramp to the hole. Once there, he did a pull up on the hole's edge, popped his head through, and ordered, "It's on."

One by one the team ambled downwards over a mountain of hard debris, sharp lava left behind by the raging hot river that once flowed where they stood.

"Watch your heads," Darius commanded as he bent low to clear a ceiling of sharp, thick lava drips, "those things bite harder than you'd think when you hit one."

Despite his warning, every so often a shriek rose up behind him. Some of them, apparently, hadn't listened.

It was tough work climbing down over, under, and through a five story pile of sharp rocks, but their efforts were soon rewarded with a breathtaking sight.

The twelve of them stood at the bottom of the huge chamber, ankle deep in water. A series of just-barely-human-sized tunnels extended in several directions. Ocean water, or perhaps an underground river, flowed languidly through the cave. Their lights illuminated hundreds of bats hanging in bucolic brown bliss, just above their heads.

Kinnary reached down with her hand, scooped up a handful of water, and put it to her lips. "Slightly salty," she declared.

But Jason Oliver had other concerns. "Anybody know if those bats are dangerous?" The only thing he hated more than regular rats, was flying rats.

"Cave bats," said Old Joe. "Harmless. They don't go in much for human flesh. And they won't wake up 'less you touch 'em. But if you do, it's gonna get loud in here real quick."

"Note to self," Jason replied in a shaky voice.

"Good thing we split into teams, because we've got a whole hell of a lot of ground to cover," Taylor announced, anxious to get on with the search.

His nerves were at their end, yet he couldn't help feeling he was closer to his goal. He doubted anyone had ever found that little hole in the ground before, other than the guy they were tracking. And that guy just might hold all of the information he needed, but didn't yet have. It was key that he and Ricardo were partnered in this little chase. And although he realized anything could happen with this many different tunnels, he'd better be ready to explain if his plan was somehow exposed.

"Ricardo and I will take that tube to the left there," he declared. "Let's all plan on meeting back here in a half hour or so."

"That's funny," Danielle laughed nervously, "since not a single one of us has a watch!"

"Guesswork is good enough."

"And what the hell do we do if one of us finds him?" she asked. "A signal or something?

"How 'bout a whistle?" Carl asked.

"I can't whistle," she responded.

"Well then," Old Joe jumped in to put an end to the fruitless discussion, "clap your hands real loud, n' if we don't hear it, we'll sure as hell hear them bats when you wake 'em up!"

10

Day 5 ~ Caves

Taylor and Ricardo

Once they were out of sight, Ricardo grabbed Taylor by the shoulder and spun his boss around to face him.

"They know!"

Obviously irritated, Taylor shoved him away, and looked around cautiously before answering.

"They do *not* fucking know! Relax!" He took a moment to gather himself, and continued a bit more calmly. "They don't. It's still just you and me. So let's keep it that way."

Ricardo's grimace displayed his inner paranoia. Ignoring him, Taylor turned and hiked on.

"I think that rat bastard Oliver knows," Ricardo continued, "maybe Randy too."

"Really?" Taylor teased, before crouching to avoid a sharp overhead chunk of lava in their path, "and just what is it you think they know?"

"How the hell should I know!" Ricardo spat nervously, "I think they're wise to us, that's all."

Taylor focused on the beam of his flashlight, as ripples from his feet made the water sparkle and flash in the otherwise placid glow.

"Something could be *anything* as far as they know, and they don't know shit. And even if they did, who cares? We've studied the island, tracked down the truth in the legends, followed the paper trail, all of it. All they know is that Cocos is spooky, filled with waterfalls, has huge caverns under it, and there's a psycho roaming the jungle? Seriously, is that what you're afraid they might know?"

Ricardo shook his head, nearly whacking a sleeping bat with his long, black hair in the process. "All I mean is, now it's gonna be a lot tougher for us to get out of here without anyone the wiser. Just look at the GPR convo."

Taylor nodded. "I see your point. But we'll deal with that if and when we come to it. For now, stay calm, and stay on plan."

Their crouched creeping continued, but the ceiling of their section of the tunnel kept getting lower and lower. A hundred yards later, they were forced to crawl, their bellies soaked in the salty brine.

"Shit!" Ricardo groaned, his knee striking a sharp spike of lava under the water, "I don't like this, Taylor. Not one fucking bit."

But Taylor had tuned out. He was thinking like a treasure hunter, not a whiny little sidekick. Moments later though, he came to a dead stop. On his belly with water up to his neck, his head pressed against a ceiling of compacted sand, he met an impenetrable rock wall, just inches from his face.

"Damnit!" He hung his head until his nose hit the warm water, "looks like the end. Let's go back and pick another tunnel before somebody finds something they shouldn't. Back out, slowly, so I can get out."

But there was no response from his sound man, no rustle in the water, no "ok, boss", no nothing. Taylor craned his neck over his shoulder, flashlight in his teeth, to look for Ricardo.

But he was gone. Taylor was alone, neck deep in water, and at a dead end.

Kinnary and Matthew

Kinnary led her sometimes-boyfriend, as she so often did. Although Matthew didn't take a back seat to anyone else in the game, he was well aware that if they were ever going to stop dancing

64

around being a couple, he'd sure as hell have to get used to it. And there, as they say, lay the rub.

"Thoughts, milady?" he asked, watching her shapely brown legs part the waters before him.

"Well that's an awfully big question, Wonder Boy!" she replied with a grin, his gaze burning into her from behind, "About what? The murders, Taylor, the game?"

"Well," he smiled back, "let's take the game first. This island is seriously vertical. Climbing trees, hiking hills, getting food, it's a physical season. Which, I'm thinking, favors us."

Kinnary shook her head. Her man was good to look at, as proven by the fact that he received the most fan mail during his two seasons, mostly from teenage girls, divorced women, and gay men. Marriage proposals. Dirty panties. Sex toys. The whole gamut. But the one thing he lacked was the one thing that set her apart. Brains. Brawn he had, but the balance between the two was not as even as was hers. So though in a romantic sense she wanted to be with him, in a strategic sense, she doubted she needed him.

"Are you even sure there's a game left?" she asked, trying not to sound condescending. "Two players dead? A killer who could be right in front of us? And you're talking strategy?"

He chuckled. "Oh, you bet your sweet ass there's a game. Hell yes, there's a game! I've been listening. People think the murders mean a ratings boost to the powers that be, sick as that may be. But what that means is, game on."

Kinnary had to laugh at her own arrogance. Once again Matthew exposed the one thing he *did* have over her, the thing she discounted at her own peril. A social game. People loved him, while they feared her. He could get right up close to anybody and make them feel comfortable enough to spill the beans, but when she did, they just clammed up.

"Well, you might be right. But only if Amy's death is the last one. Then you've still got the possibility of the Costa Rican government investigating, maybe forcing us to go home."

She stopped, eyes still focused dead ahead. "But, for the sake of argument, let's say there *is* still a game. There's just one person here I see as my competition, and I'm happy to say it's not you, my lovely man."

She quickly turned around to soothe yet another wound her big mouth had caused, grabbed him by the head, and planted a very long kiss on his already pouting mouth. Her practical mind, which was almost always in charge, saw him as another player, but her far less capable heart wanted a relationship with him, even if she had to be the one to make it happen.

"No offense, Loverboy," she put on her best smile. "And if you'd grow a pair and commit instead of all this stop and go dating stuff, I might even share my prize money with you! "

Matthew rolled his eyes. "Gee, no offense taken," he sneered, her kiss only partially effective, "What am I, Batwoman? You see me as your freaking Robin?"

"Hey," she continued, glancing at his shirtless torso just long enough for her eyes to melt from the sight of his impossibly-sectioned abs, "I'm just teasing. I just mean this is more than a physical or mental game. It's an *outdoorsman's* game. And there's only one of those here."

"Old Joe. Now you're talking my game."

"Bingo. Old Joe. So the question is, how long does he last? I mean, the guy is in his late sixties, right? How long does his body hold up out here?"

"I don't know," Matthew replied, "but he sure as hell whipped that hike. We were huffing and puffing more than he was."

"True," she nodded, realizing that his social mind had once again picked up on something she'd missed, "but it's early. Like I said, *endurance*."

Matthew fell quiet, letting the sound of his feet shuffling through ankle deep water soothe the jitters he'd felt at the hole, when the reality that they were actually chasing a murderer into an abyss took hold.

Moments later, he broke the silence. Though she definitely liked to be the boss, he knew the reason he'd not yet gone as far with her as she wanted was that she *expected* to be. Until she began to see his input as valuable, instead of just directing it how she wanted, he just couldn't take that next step. And in that small act of rebellion, *he* got to be the boss in the relationship, for once.

"Look, job one is getting Old Joe into our circle. Nobody wins without him. Nobody."

"See," she smiled, happy to hear something assertive leave his lips, "you're not just a pretty face after all! Now how do . . ."

"Shhh!" he quickly put his hand over her mouth. "Hear that?"

Kinnary went stiff, craning her ears. It took a second, but then she did hear . . . something. She waited . . . there it was again. A rock, maybe, hitting another rock, or a piece of metal.

But it wasn't behind them, where the others were.

It was in front of them.

Danielle and Darius

Darius led the way, and Danielle was glad he did. He was a big man, not quite as big as Franklin, but a hell of a lot bigger than she was. If some wing nut with a murder fetish came around a dark corner, she wouldn't have to greet him. And she wouldn't wait around while he slaughtered her friend, either. She'd run like the wind, in the opposite direction.

She'd already decided on a new plan. This was not the game she signed up for. She was forty seven years old, her daughter was grown and on her own, and she still had half the money from her win in season fourteen. She had only come back on the show to prove to herself she could still play, but had quickly discovered the truth.

She couldn't.

"This some crazy shit or what?" chatted Darius. His stride was nearly twice as long as hers, and she had to quick-step to keep up.

"Beyond all recognition," she replied. "But, really, do you see any point in this? I mean, what are we even *doing* here?"

"You mean trying to catch this guy, when we have no idea what we're up against and should probably be back at camp, packing our bags?"

Danielle sighed, relieved. "Thank *God* somebody is thinking the same thing! Yes, that's exactly what I mean! Seriously, what are we going to do if we catch this guy? Me, I'm running. And I'm not gonna stop running. When that boat gets here in three days, I'm on it."

Darius stopped in his tracks, and turned to face her, a shocked look on his face. "You mean, you're *quitting*?"

She tried not to look as hurt as she felt from his obvious derision, but her entire body burned from the heat of his shaming gaze.

"You're really surprised?" she replied indignantly, her backbone beginning to rise again. "You really want to stay here? Maybe get killed?"

Darius shook his head, resolute. "We catch this guy, nobody's getting killed. And this ain't no joke, I got ten million reasons to stay. Ten." He glared, an inner pain blazing through his intense eyes. "Yeah, I'll admit, I didn't do do well with my money the first time, and I got three kids counting on me. Ain't no way I'll quit. Couldn't *drag* me offa this damn rock!"

Danielle was stunned. She was so hoping everyone else felt like she did. Practical. Smart. But Darius sounded totally reckless. Sure, she wasn't a risk taker, she was a home maker. But to think that people like Darius, a nice guy, and a *Dad*, would choose to stay here and risk death?

"Ok then, tough guy," she continued, tension on display both in her voice and on her face, "I ask you again then, what do we do with this guy if we catch him? How can we be sure he won't escape and kill again?"

Darius looked at her in disbelief. "Escape? You seriously think we're gonna let him live? Really? This is kill or be killed, Danielle. Which one *you* votin' for?"

She quite suddenly found herself in the unenviable position of being even more scared than she had been just a moment before. Prior to that moment, Darius, the sweet, hard working father of three was the last person she would ever expect to scare her. Money really does change people, she thought. To their core.

"My guess," he elaborated, "is we throw his ass off that cliff back there. Easily explainable, too. Then we get on with what we came here for. Ten million bucks."

Danielle shook her head. "Can you hear yourself? You want to be a *murderer*? For *money*?"

"Oh get off it, Danielle. That's not murder. That's self defense! The guy lives, we die. Simple as that. You said you're going home in three days, right? You think you'll be safe for even three more days if he's alive? Do you?"

That ugly little scenario hadn't exactly occurred to her. But now it did, and as her companion turned his gaze back to the tunnel ahead, she couldn't even be sure that *she* wasn't on board with murder, as long as she didn't have to be the one to give him that final shove into blue oblivion.

Susan and Jason Oliver

Susan, the consummate professional with ice water in her veins, wasted no time.

"What the fuck is going on here, Oliver!" she demanded.

Jason, following her through the tube, cackled wildly. His hand held tightly, knuckles white, to the knife-rock it carried.

"Who, little old me? Whatever might make you think *I* know anything?"

"Knock it off, Jackass! There's a little shitstain trying to kill me, and I am *not* in the mood for your shtick. You're nearly as ruthless as me, and almost half as clever." She paused, turning to face him. "I caught your little act back there. You weren't showing all your cards, and I want to see them. Now."

He laughed again, just slightly less maniacally this time. "Look, all I know is me and Frank spent a night theorizing about just what is *really* going on here. We all know this is Taylor's last stand, right?"

She nodded, her tight, pointed features casting twisted shadows on the cave wall. She was so Type A, so inherently nervous all day long, that she rarely stopped twitching long enough to eat and thereby fill out her bone structure, remaining perpetually gaunt as a Peruvian mummy.

"A goddamn child could see that, Jason. Get on with it before this asshole puts a knife in your back."

"So," he ignored her standard aggression and went on, "there's this GPR equipment, right? But have you seen these guys on the beach, checking for *artifacts,* even once? I haven't. No one has. Because they aren't! So then, what the hell *are* they doing?"

She thought for a moment. Taylor was definitely even twitchier than normal. And that was *before* the murders of two of her competitors.

"Ok, I'll bite. What did you two Agatha Christie society dickwads conclude?"

"We didn't. We ended up talking about Tonya's death, and how it might be murder. And who we suspected might have done it."

Susan was now not only intrigued, but impressed. Jason Oliver had unknowingly just jumped up a peg on her who-do-I-take-out-first list. "You thought it might be murder before we knew it was? Nobody was thinking that!"

He shook his head. "Wish I could take the credit, but it was Franklin. He noticed some marks on her pole, and realized somebody made them. Somebody crafty."

"And you think Taylor is crafty? *Our* Taylor? That's a stretch!"

"Ok," he chuckled, "that one was my idea. I just thought, for reasons already covered, that he was suspect number one. The show is failing, right? What would get ratings up, fast?"

A grin spread across her face. "A death. That would do it. People would suddenly believe it was real again!"

Their two wicked smiles matched in intensity, evil twins grinning like comic book villains. "Bingo, sister. Give mama the big prize."

"Ok, so now that there's been *another* murder, how does that advance your theory?"

His evil grin slid halfway down his face, resting on his chin as a self-satisfied smirk. "Show me yours, and I'll show you mine."

Her gaze lost itself in the glimmering mica sparkling in the walls, while she constructed a mosaic of facts in her mind's eye.

"Well," she replied, "Taylor needs a hit, and he needs it fast. Maybe he hires this creep we're chasing to kill a couple contestants to get the ratings up? And, maybe there's something buried here that he and this creep plan on digging up, maybe using the GPR to find it? Something valuable that gets his debt ridden ass off the hook, even if the ratings *don't* blow up."

Jason nodded wildly, adding an extra creepy, "yes, yes, yes," in between each point. "That's good. That's *real* good! That's as good as I've got, almost to the last detail."

"Which means," she continued, ignoring his worthless praise, "this thing we're on is a total fucking goose chase. Taylor knows we won't find this guy!"

Jason quickly mulled her words over, quickly realizing there was something she had missed.

"Right, except for one thing. Old Joe led us here. Taylor had no way to know that was going to happen. Old Joe seems damn sure the guy is down here."

"Yeah, you're right," she agreed. "Which means we have to keep an eye on Taylor, no matter what happens down here today. Day and night, if for no other reason than to keep the sleazy bastard from taking *us* out. And," she added, "so we can heist whatever the hell it is he's looking for, if he finds it."

"Damn!" he yelled in glee, "That's some first rate, super-villain shit! I'll let Franklin know you're in on it. Randy is too. That gives us four sets of eyes on him."

"Something else though," she revealed, "something I've been thinking hard about, and if you're throwing in with me . . ."

"You mean you're throwing in with *me* . . . right?"

"In your dreams, Bucko. You ride with the she-wolf, you take the ass end. What I've been thinking is that Tom Sawyer's Island here is firmly in the wheelhouse of one and only one Castaway. Got a guess?"

Jason huffed. "Ain't gotta guess, 'cause I know. And I'm with you. We need to work on him, get him in the fold."

He looked at her, she looked at him, and in unison they said, "Old Joe."

But as the popularly spoken name left their lips, there came a scream, and they began to run.

Randy and Leticia

Two awkwardly matched teammates pushed on through the dark tunnel, dodging sleeping bats, steel-like frozen lava drips, and climbing over large piles of black boulders that had once belonged to the ceiling above them. The water was cool on their feet, a welcome relief from the stagnant, hot air of the caves.

Leticia hung behind while Randy moved quickly through the tube. She was the last kid chosen on the playground, and he'd begrudgingly accepted her only once there were no other possible partners left. This season was supposed to have marked a turnaround in her image. After the fallout from the last one, when she was dubbed the "Bitch from Buenos" by fans and players alike, she'd

71

resolved to be nicer, calmer and sweeter this time. React less. Interact more. She would renew her image, and then turn that revival into something financially lucrative back home.

But soon after her arrival on Cocos, the darkness set in again. She was isolated from the others, even when standing right next to them. No one had forgotten how she'd behaved before, and with each passing moment that they ignored her she grew even more bitter, until the sunny new attitude she'd tried so hard to cultivate simply leaked right out of her and slipped away into the silvery sands of Cocos Island.

And now with a heaviness, she realized the Bitch from Buenos was back.

But it wasn't her fault. Abandoned by her parents when she was small, she was left to run the barrios of Buenos Aires as a street kid, making her own way by taking what she needed to live. She'd been robbed, raped, and sold like property. Daily cuts, beatings, and bruises were her way of life.

But then she did something remarkable. She got on this show. And she won.

So fuck them, she thought. Fuck the whole damn bunch of pampered first world babies. She'd show them they were wrong about her by doing just one thing. One more incredible thing.

She would win. Again.

Watching with detachment as Randy's flashlight disappeared around the next bend, she stayed behind to let her eyes adjust to the blackness. She wasn't the least bit afraid down here. If anything, she told herself, the killer should be scared of her!

Far ahead, Randy moved quickly. Enraged and devastated at the shocking loss of his fiancée, he wanted desperately to be the one to find the guy and cut him in two with his machete. He wasn't worried either. This guy hadn't killed his victims by facing them down in cold blood. No, he simply set traps under cover of night, and let them kill themselves. And Amy? Why did it have to be Amy? Why someone with a beautiful heart, who wouldn't hurt a flea? Why not the nasty girl behind him? Why not evil Susan? Why not fucking Taylor himself?

Randy wouldn't be tricked that way. The gambler's all seeing eye kept him safe wherever he went, and as he kicked through the water, forgetting completely about Leticia, he was determined to make this kill as soon as he had the chance. Later, he'd cry. But now, he'd kill.

Behind him in the black, Leticia's eyes adjusted to the darkness. Mica specks sparkled around her like stars in the Amazonian night. It was impossibly beautiful, and her shriveled little heart skipped a beat at the itty bitty bits of light the tiny stars captured and cast over the water from Randy's rapidly fading beam. The dark, she knew as one who had slept outside much of her life, was even more beautiful than the day, looked at the right way.

But as her other senses grew stronger in the blackness, she noticed something. Something peculiar. The water was flowing very slowly, almost imperceptibly, down the tube they were exploring. Yet she could hear it rushing somewhere, not enough to change the flow of the stream, but enough to make a sound.   That was something else she had learned about the dark. If you remove all light and turn down the volume of the day, you can hear forever. And right now, she could hear something that almost none of the others would have, except possibly Joe. Certainly not the emotional buffoon in front of her.

She crept slowly towards the sound, which seemed to be coming from the wall itself. Her body hugged its lightly shimmering surface and her fingers probed along it, feeling, sensing, struggling for something that might give way. Kneeling in the shallow stream, she worked her fingers under the water, until at last, she found it.

A rock, or rather, a large, flat plate of black lava, that at first moved just slightly when she got her fingers under it, and then moved all the way to the side as she gave it a heave. As it toppled into the slow stream, a sudden rush of water took its place, flowing through a gap in the wall where the stone had been. Feeling around again with her hands, she discovered that the gap was just big enough for a small person to squirm through. Her skin tingled, and an excitement in the real adventure beyond the wall overtook her. There was no time to waste. Looking back down the tube and seeing no sign of Randy's flashlight, she very quickly dropped into the water, and wriggled her body into the hole.

When Leticia popped out the other side after a short swim, she found herself in a huge lava chamber that was somehow filled with light. Her eyes took a few moments to adjust to the brightness, and then she saw something remarkable! A brilliant smile spread across her face, like a sunrise spreading over the bay on a beautiful morning in Buenos Aires.

The other Castaways might not want to be her partner, but Fortune? Fortune did.

Several hundred feet down the tunnel, Randy stopped dead before a solid wall of lava. So solid, that the water stopped too, deepening into a sand filled pool. He scanned its surface below him, but soon found that there was no outlet for the stream. It just stopped cold, doubling back on itself.

In a rage, he pounded the black wall in front of him with his fists and cursed it aloud. This was not the way the killer had gone, and he was wasting precious time. He'd never forgive himself if someone else made the kill before he did.

Randy turned quickly on his heels and began to run through the knee deep water, only then realizing that Leticia was no longer there. He ran, leaping rocks and crawling over boulders, hurrying to get back to the central chamber so he could pick another route, the right route, that would lead him to the piece of shit that killed Amy. He had to be the one. Had to be the one to kill him.

Had to.

Rounding a bend he found Leticia sitting in the water, her hands underneath it as though she was digging for something.

"What the hell are you doing?" he screamed at her. "Don't you care about finding this guy?"

Leticia looked up at him, satisfied that her tracks were covered. "I slipped and went down," she began, "not that you even noticed, running off with the light! Thanks for the help, asshole! Such a gentleman!"

Randy gazed at her in disbelief. "Go fuck yourself!" he roared, "Try being part of the team for once!"

He moved past her and began to run.

"That's ok, I'll be fine!" she yelled after him. "And no, by the way! No, I don't care if we find this guy! Seems like he's the only one on my side!"

74

Joe and Jeremy walked along without speaking. There wasn't much to say, as they had never really met. The medical team was always kept isolated from the players, until the shit hit the fan and they were desperately needed.

For his part, Jeremy felt relieved that Old Joe was his partner. The guy didn't look like he'd be much in a fight, yet his very presence instilled calm and a confidence that, no matter what happened, he'd be able to find a way out of it. But Jeremy, like Danielle, would vote to end this little game if there was a vote, if non-players actually got one. His pay for this gig was only about forty thousand bucks, certainly not enough for him to stay on this rock and risk his life.

The wrinkle in that plan, however, was a stiff penalty built into his contract for abandoning the show. And not only a financial penalty, but a possible blacklisting from any further work in Hollywood. He loved being a Hollywood medic— the pay was good, the travel perks were great, and though the hours often sucked, there was usually very little actual work to do. That suited him fine. Being paid for doing nothing had always been his life's goal, and he had managed to achieve just that.

He understood that things were different for the others, of course. The players, and the host, had large stakes in this game. Maybe if ten million were coming his way, he'd think differently. And Sato, his boss on this gig and an experienced M.D. mandated by the insurance company, was a stodgy, duty-driven Japanese woman. There was no way she would break her contract, even if it *actually* killed her.

The other guys? The camera guys and the sound guy? Maybe they'd join him in a little rebellion. And if they did, who could refuse them? There would certainly be no show without them, and there was far less safety to be had with just one medic. Certainly the insurance company would flip out if he left, if there was any way to let them know. But how *would* they find out? Taylor controlled the only communication with the mainland, and the boat wasn't due for three more days. Perhaps, he thought, he could sneak into the producer's cabin, and use the radio transmitter.

No matter what, he'd have a powwow with the other subordinates after this little chase was over. He had no dog in this fight, and was ready to run if trouble reared its ugly head his way.

Joe, on the other hand, was exhilarated. He hadn't felt this alive in years! Chasing badgers, raccoons, and deer was one thing, but a man killer? That was the kind of thing he'd always wanted to do, and now he was doing it! Not only that, but he was good at it. He was sure this creep was down here somewhere. Certain of it.

But, what to do when he caught him? That was another matter entirely, and it depended on many factors. How big was the guy? What kind of weapons did he have? And how many of his fellow competitors would be around when he met him face to face?

Joe wasn't a fighter by nature, but he was crafty, and skilled in anything involving Mother Nature and her environs. Just now, creeping through the water, he barely made a sound. Looking behind him with mute satisfaction, he saw that Jeremy was copying the way he strode and stepped, so as to make the same sort of silent steps through the stream.

At this point, he wasn't certain the game would actually continue. But if it did? One thing was for sure. After his little Daniel Boone performance tracking the killer today, the others would be coming for him. And that was both good, and bad.

The bad part was that they'd be coming for him as the guy with the big target on his back, and they'd do whatever they could to get him out, since at this point he was clearly top dog.

But the good part, he knew from his last trip through this game, was that some of them would also hope to form an alliance with him. This bunch of ragamuffins had about as many outdoor skills as a five year old kid from the inner city. These young urbanites needed him, just as in past games they had needed guys like Matthew, who could sprint through a challenge course while others were still getting their feet set. Or like Austin the merman, who could practically catch fish in his fingers and toes and clean them with his bare teeth, or like Kinnary, who dominated any challenge that required brain juice to squeeze out a victory.

This time? This time it was him. Old Joe. This was his game to lose, and as long as it continued, he was going to be a threat. And he was going to be desired, until the moment they didn't need him anymore, and then he'd be a goner. At least, he suspected, that was what *they* were thinking.

But his thoughts on the subject were stopped cold by a blood curdling scream, and turned to find that Jeremy's medical instincts had quickly taken over, and he was already rushing to find its source.

Taylor ~ solo

Taylor hesitated. He'd been diving on other Execution Island excursions, of course, but never in a cave and without equipment. He could feel the water rushing over the sand on which he rested his knees, rushing directly under the wall in front of him. Ricardo was no longer there, but Taylor still had the light firmly in his teeth. He had to look, he just had to. There was clearly more ahead, and one thing he'd promised himself when he arranged this little trip to Cocos, was that he would leave no stone, no tree, no beach unturned in his hunt.

Steeling himself for the swim through the narrow shaft, he sucked in a deep breath, and dove.

He swam as hard as he could with so little room to move his arms. His feet kicked and shoved along the bottom, and more than once he bumped his head on the hard lava above. The air pocket he had hoped would be there just wasn't. Ten seconds into the swim he began to panic, and then . . .

He bobbed to the surface, gasping for air. The stream spread out into a large pool before him, in a chamber the size of a hotel room. He struggled to his feet in the soft sand at the bottom of the pool, stood, and then nearly shit his pants.

In a bizarre turn of events, purely by accident, driven by Providence, pushed forward by Fortune herself, he had quite suddenly and inexplicably arrived at his goal. A goal sought by hundreds of men over equally as many years, with only scant reward shared between them. Men had given their lives for this. Men had literally gone crazy trying to find it. And yet here he was, with all of his technological advantages, careful scheming and planning, and in the end, he just plain fell right into it.

No, he realized as his greedy eyes took in his new found wealth, he just plain *dove* right into it.

Taylor Woods placed his hands on his hips and expelled an enormous belly laugh that echoed loudly off the black walls of the chamber. In the strangest of places and in the wildest of circumstances, chasing a serial killer for god's sake, he had found at least one of the buried treasures of Cocos Island. Which one he did not know, as there were so many stories, maps, and legends about Cocos that he couldn't be sure which had chosen to bless his life, but at this point, knowing which would have been mere icing on the cake made of gold, staring right at him.

That he should find one of the most sought after treasure hordes in the world after only mere days, without even trying? It boggled his mind. How could one so regularly unlucky suddenly have so much luck that it couldn't be quantified?

Struggling out of the water, he fell into the golden cache that lay on a small beach at the end of the room. Hundreds, perhaps thousands of gold coins made up the stash. They had clearly been piled here fairly recently, as there was neither dirt nor sediment on top of most of them, save those at the bottom that were half buried in sand. He raked his hands happily through the coins, letting them fall through his fingers like golden rain.

He simply could not believe it was true.

But the daze finally wore off, and he held his light to the treasure. The coins were Spanish, as expected. He looked at the dates on them. 1795. 1797. 1794.

These were the same range as the dates on the few coins August Gissler himself had found. The German spent seventeen years living on the island in the late 1800's and early 1900's, searching for this very treasure, but found only thirty three coins.

His mind reeled. Gissler spent seventeen years of his life looking for it, his last words on his death bed affirming his belief that the treasure was still on Cocos. The British navy brought dynamite and blew up portions of the beach and river looking for it. Other men, their names lost to history, had searched for this very pile in front of him, among others, and all they had discovered was a few Spanish doubloons and a cryptic carving on a coconut tree that said simply, "The Bird Has Flown."

But here it was, proof that it hadn't flown at all, and that someone craftier and quicker than he not only found it, but secreted it here bit by bit in a place that would be incredibly difficult to find, only to have it discovered by an American television host soon after he deposited it.

Taylor then realized else something wonderful. Now he didn't have to share it with Ricardo! He, Taylor, and Taylor alone had found it! No one knew, and no one would. Ricardo had his chance, but he chickened out, or was killed—either one suited him fine at this point.

No, the treasure was his. Fuck the show. Fuck Ricardo. Fuck the Castaways.

One final thought hit him like a bolt of lightning, sending him instantly back under the little wall that would now hide *his* fortune from the world.

The killer, whomever he was, knew his secret. He must die, and die soon. And when he did, Taylor Woods' secret would die with him.

11

Day 5 ~ The Chase, Part Two

Old Joe entered the central chamber to find a wide-eyed, chattering group already gathered there. Kinnary was at the center of it, so he moved closer.

"A foot," he heard her say, "That's all I saw!"

"Which cave?" demanded Randy, ready to fly as soon as he was pointed where to go.

"There!" she pointed, and off he bolted into the darkness, Matthew hot on his heels.

"Tell me ever'thing ya saw" Joe pleaded.

"A foot . . . we heard a banging noise, and when we went to investigate, I saw this foot, in a boot, going out through a hole in the wall. I screamed, but he was gone. I saw daylight— maybe it's another entrance, or an exit. But he had it covered with a flat stone, like a giant plate, and what we'd heard was him removing it. Then, we ran back here to get help."

Ricardo quietly materialized out of the shadows and into the glow of the gathering, alone, and without a light.

Jason Oliver took notice. "Where the hell is Taylor?" he asked.

Ricardo shrugged. "Who knows? Who cares? Not me. Guy was crawling in the muck last time I saw him, making zero sense. So, I split."

Jason began to ask more, but the moment was quickly hijacked by the chaos all around him, and he soon forgot about it.

"Ok," Joe continued, "I'm goin' in too. Who else wants in on this?"

On the surface above them, Franklin sat and waited. And waited. And waited.

He threw rocks into the ravine below to burn some time. He hiked up the ridge towards the peak of Mt. Iglesias to burn even more time and see what he could find. The answer was more of the same, lush green, and endless blue beyond that. Three goats eyed him warily from the rocky hillside above, far out of range of any hungry Castaways.

Down the slop a bit, Sato had spread herself out over the grassy ground, soaking up the warm evening sunshine.

"I thought doctors were afraid of skin cancer," Malik noted, searching for something halfway intelligent to say to the golden-skinned beauty before him.

She peeked out from under her hat. "True. But Japanese people have a pretty low skin cancer rate, so I figure I'm ok. Besides," she smirked, "what else am I gonna do while we wait?"

Malik thought of a few things, but she quickly tucked her dark eyes back under her hat to deflect the innuendo oozing from his gaze. Rebuffed without even firing a shot, he strolled over to where his old friend Carl, lying just as prone on the ground but in a sleeping rather than a tanning pose, was curled up with his eyes closed.

"What do you make of all this, old man?" he asked.

Carl's eyes popped open. He gazed back at Malik with the irritation of one who is just about asleep, but suddenly finds himself shocked awake by an unwelcome intruder.

"What?"

"I said what do you make of all this? The killer? The shit that went down between Taylor and the cast? Ricardo?"

Carl rolled his eyes and quickly closed them again.

"Shit if I know, and shit if I care."

Now it was Malik's turn to be irritated.

"Carl, you lazy piece of crap! How long have we known each other, man? I don't believe you for a second. I know you care, and I know you think something's up."

Carl sighed, but kept his eyes closed while trying to look as passively pissed off as possible. "Okay, so I think something's up. Big freaking whoop. We both know Taylor is a piece of shit, right? So tell me, why then are you surprised something's going on that we aren't in on?"

Malik sat on his haunches next to his longtime friend, gazing at the horizon.

"We've done what, eleven seasons with him? How many has Ricardo done?"

Carl moved his eyebrows as if his face were shrugging. "Seven, eight?"

"Yeah, something like that. So if we've known him longer, and we've at least *pretended* to be friends ..."

"*You* have, anyway ..." Carl smirked.

"Yeah, yeah, whatever. Still, if there's something valuable here, why the hell ain't we in on it? Seriously man, I've given a chunk of my life to this game, a lot of time away from family, a lot of opportunities missed while I sat on some god damn rock! Where's *our* payday?"

Carl groaned and rolled onto his side, away from Malik.

"Jesus, Malik, you think too much. We're not in on it because Ricardo is the only one as sleazy as Taylor. Mystery solved. And what even makes you think there's a payday?"

Malik shook his head at the stubbornness of his colleague.

"Ground penetrating radar? Man, are you serious? That shit is for treasure, or artifacts. Something *worth* something, man. You can ignore the whole thing if you want, but I'm telling him I want in on it, period."

"Or what?"

"Or I'm gonna turn Sinatra and start spreadin' the news, *that's* what! I could start a revolt with the Castaways, or I could catch the next boat and spread the word back home. Either way, I'm gettin' me some. This is our last parlay on this little gameshow, and we are not on the ten million dollar guest list. I'm gettin' mine!"

"Well then," Carl leaned up and smiled with a total lack of sincerity, "since I can out *your* sorry ass just as easily, let me know when you're done with all that and I'll be there. Besides, you think corporate is going to let the game go on once they hear about death number two? Not likely. We'll be out of here on the next boat."

Carl paused to roll towards Malik, and added, "Now, scoot over a little and block the sun for me, will you?"

Malik hopped to his feet and walked off as he shouted "Ingrate!". Carl returned the gesture with a silent middle finger held high, before closing his eyes and daydreaming of the luxury of real sleep.

Back up the ridge, Franklin sat down. An hour had passed, yet no one had popped out of the hole to tell them they either caught the guy, or lost him. Glancing at the horizon he could see the sun sinking. There was maybe an hour of light left, and they still had to get back to camp.

Just then a dark figure appeared between him and the sun, perhaps a quarter mile away— a small figure, seemingly emerging right out of the ground. But the hole the search team had gone down was the other way! Without a moment's thought, he sprang to his feet and gave chase.

Malik heard the big man's footfalls, and spun around to see the him heading into the Sun.

"Now where the hell is *he* going'?" he asked the air. But as his eyes adjusted, he too saw a dark speck slipping off the high ridge and into the jungle. "Aww, Shit!" he muttered, and took off running as well.

Randy and Matthew quickly arrived at the hole in the wall where Kinnary saw the killer disappear. There was indeed a large and very thin slab of rock laying on the ground beside a man-sized doorway in the lava.

Randy exploded into the hole with Matthew close behind, but both soon found it tough going. The small gap was made for someone no taller than five foot six, and neither of them were less than six feet tall. Still, they squished their bodies up and pressed on, their skin constantly poked and scraped by sharp edges and points on the surface of the narrow tube.

Kinnary was next into the gap, with Old Joe and Darius right behind. But Darius took one look at the hole and knew he wouldn't fit.

"You guys go on," he huffed and puffed, "I'll go back and tell them to hit the exit in case he pops out somewhere else."

Joe nodded, and slipped quickly through the doorway.

"Ain't much light left," Joe noted before squeezing in behind her, "if ya don't hear from us before the sun starts to drop, y'all git on back to camp. Don't want to be responsible for this guy takin' y'all out in the dark."

With a nod, Darius turned and sprinted back down the tunnel.

Kinnary quickly caught up with the two larger men, still painfully twisting and turning their way through the dark tunnel. The tube began to angle upwards, and soon was softly lit with a faint shaft of light from above. Slowly the trio climbed up and over the rough lava, until finally, Randy's sweat drenched body popped through a small crack and flopped onto the dirt. Covered in bodily juices and grime, he felt like human toothpaste.

Matthew and Kinnary were right behind. Their lungs, finally able to expand to full size after the compression of the cave, struggled to replenish their oxygen, while their eyes struggled to adjust to the brilliant tropical sunlight.

A blazing figure appeared before them, lit up by the sun at their backs.

"Hey!" Malik yelled just as Old Joe's head popped out of the hole, "Franklin took off after him! He ran into the bush!"

Exhausted and soaking wet, Randy nevertheless hopped immediately to his feet.

"Where?" he gasped.

Malik pointed towards the north end of the island, where none of the Castaways had yet tread.

"In there, 'bout a minute ago. Didn't say a word, he just took off after him."

Wiping the sweat from his brow, Randy gazed around at the others, anguished strain clearly visible on his face. "I'm going in! Who's coming?"

"Now hold on jus' a minute, son," Old Joe began, before pausing to exhale a blast of stale air, "That there sun's 'bout ready to call it a day. We don't want this whole group ta be sittin' ducks in the dark for a guy who knows this here island like the back of his hand. Ain't no sense in you runnin' off after him. That jungle's thick. More than likely you're gonna get lost, it's gonna get dark, and then you're on yer own 'cause I'm gettin' the rest of these folks the heck back ta camp. Already got one guy ta track down, sure as hell don't need one more."

Panting like a wild animal, Randy's angry eyes bored holes through Joe's skull.

Old Joe did his best to soothe the savage beast, waving his hand passively in the air as he continued, bent over, to try to regain his breath. "You'll git another chance, son! I promise, and I'll be right by yer side."

Kinnary, her race trained lungs faring a little better, nodded in agreement. "Joe's right, Randy," She put her hand on his shoulder, instantly feeling the seething hot rage pulsing just under his skin. "He's gone, unless Franklin can catch him, and I doubt he can. The guy was small, and small moves a lot quicker through jungle than somebody Franklin's size. Or yours."

Randy balled up his fists, leaned his head back, and screamed. Kinnary jerked her hand from his shoulder and backed off, just in case the cork in his mind was about to pop.

Further up the ridge, mole-like figures with tightly closed eyes begin to emerge from the ground, one by one, struggling to adjust to the sunlight, heads turning to and fro to try to get a grip on the situation.

Just then the jungle beside them began to move and shake, and moments later, Franklin, scraped and bleeding, joined the group on the ridge top.

"Lost him," was all he could say, as he dropped to the ground, gasping.

Old Joe nodded. "Not your fault. Guy's a native. Wadn't a chance to begin with."

The mole people straggled slowly down the hill from the original hole. In the confusion, no one seemed to notice Taylor's late arrival. Slipping quietly through the original entrance far behind the others, he cautiously made his way across the open hillside, and joined the team.

Now that the whole group was assembled, Franklin and Joe quickly passed on the little they knew of the killer, before Joe stressed the need to get back to camp, and pronto.

"Well," Taylor tried to sound involved, "at least we know there's just one guy. We'll get him."

With that, they began their march into the jungle, heading in the opposite direction of the killer.

But privately, Old Joe had doubts they'd actually catch him another day. The guy had holes, tunnels, escape routes. Probably many more than they had found. He could seemingly come and go at leisure, without being seen, already proving he could outrun them if they gave chase.

He was, Old Joe grinned, just the kind of prey an old hunter lived for.

Back at camp, they gathered around the fire pit at the Execution Grounds to chat about the day's developments, and their chances. More than one brought up a desire to leave on the next boat, which would bring a sudden, fatal end to the final season of Execution Island.

Worried that his treasure hunt was also about to end, Taylor slipped away from the group, beelining back to the cabin he shared with his crew. Making sure he wasn't followed, he pulled out his satellite phone and made a call.

The voice that answered spoke Spanish, but Taylor quickly forced its speaker into broken English.

"Yes, that's right," he said for the second time, as the voice on the other end struggled to understand, "No boat this week. Una semana mas, sí. We'll be fine until next week. No, I mean it. No boat. Sí, sí, no barco. It's very important that it not come this week. Es muy importante. It's for the game. Yes, si´. Gracias."

Taylor hung up, satisfied that this would not be the week that spoiled his plan. He would provide no easy outs for *his* Castaways. He had given them both his life and his career, the latter of which seemed to now be at an end. Typecast as the "Execution Island guy", there would be no easy gigs for Taylor Woods in the near future. The very least these wealthy degenerates could give back to him, after he'd made them all rich, was a little retirement plan.

Outside the window, a pair of bare feet made soundless tracks in the mud, as their owner left the scene with an earful.

12

Day 6 ~ The Turn

Taylor barely slept. How could he? He'd expected a long search. He'd been prepared for a slow, painful dig. He'd planned for night after night of frustration. But instead, the universe had handed him a silver platter full of golden treasure before he'd even begun to look for it. Shocked by such a rare piece of luck, his calculating brain had no choice but to move on to a surprising next step to secure his sudden fortune.

Murder.

No, murder was too strong a word for it, he told himself, since you can hardly murder a murderer. He preferred to think of it as island justice.

And so he awoke at 4 am before anyone on the beach stirred, and drew out his plan. It would begin, as many days in Execution Island history had, with the construction of a competition course.

He'd keep it simple. Coffee in hand, he strolled behind the cabins to the large, temporary quonset hut, erected by Costa Rican laborers the first day on the island. Opening the door, he gazed at his legacy. Yards and yards of colored lumber, bamboo poles, floats, ropes, puzzles, flags, and construction equipment spread out before him. The simple tools of the game. Simple tools that Taylor Woods would now use to ensure he would leave the show as a very, very rich man.

His hands moved lovingly over the items in the hut, realizing with each tactile moment that soon he would never see, nor touch these things again. They were so much a part of his life, more, he realized, than the actual people who'd won or lost millions competing amongst these lifeless items.

A tear slid down his cheek. This really was the end of the greatest chapter of his life.

"Knock it off, Taylor," he chided himself. "Go out with a bang. You single-handedly changed television history. Show 'em how it's done."

Hours later he was on the beach, instructing his masses to come in closer.

"I don't want him to hear," he warned them. "Kneel down on the beach with me. The waves should muffle our voices."

Eyes filled with confusion, they complied.

"Now look. I know you're all scared." His eyes met Randy's, still blazing a day after Amy's death. "Most of you, anyway. But, here's the thing. This piece of shit killed two of our own. In cold blood. Murdered them like animals. I think it's time to return the favor."

Predictably, Danielle stood up to leave.

"Seriously? Listen to yourself!" Her voice quivered. "Let's do the right thing here. Let's get the hell off this island, and let the authorities tear it apart looking for this guy. I'm getting on the boat! The game is over, Taylor."

But the host just shook his head, and replied with a total lack of emotion, "There's no boat."

Suddenly Danielle wasn't the only one on her feet, confusion swirling around the shocked players like a fog.

Malik shot an "I told you so!" glance at Carl. In return, Carl raised his eyebrows as if to say, "yeah, I guess you did."

"What in God's name do you mean there's no boat?" Jason Oliver prodded, his nervous smirk taking on Joker-like proportions.

"I mean it's not coming this week. They called this morning. The weather is a mess on the coast. High seas. No way they can make it, and the boat we use has other charters during the week. They'll come nine days from now, back on schedule."

Danielle collapsed to the ground in tears. Kinnary knelt to comfort her, while the others took turns hurling expletives at Taylor, one after another. Randy sat silently grinning, just thrilled that he wouldn't be forced to leave. Leticia bathed in the glorious chaos and fear all around her, while Old Joe just sat quietly, observing.

Taylor took the abuse in stride, before continuing his pitch. "Do you all feel better now? I mean, it's not my fault. Someone has to be the messenger here, and that's me. So fine, shoot me, I don't care anymore. But what I do care about is that we make it through the next nine days alive, and that means we have to kill this piece of shit."

"Amen!" Randy agreed.

"Did you even *tell* them there had been two murders!" Danielle screamed through her tears. "Did you?"

"Of course I did!" Taylor maintained his lie. "But the boat can't make it. This isn't America. We're on our own, and we're not even Costa Rican citizens, so they aren't going to risk any of their own to come and save our asses! When I told them it looked like just one guy, they suggested we take care of it. And so, we will."

Old Joe finally rose and stepped into the fray. "And how's that, son?"

Taylor peered around, twisting his neck from side to side, gleeful to move the conversation on to his murder plot. He gestured for them to come still closer.

"A competition. We know he uses them to kill us. So, we set one up. We make it look like business as usual. And of course, he'll try to sabotage it. But this time we wait, and watch. Sentries. Traps. We catch his ass. And we survive, but this time, for real."

"And *after* we catch him?" Susan asked, "What's your big disposal plan, Osama?"

"He doesn't need one. I'll do it," Randy spoke up.

Taylor held his hand up. "Now, hold on there. They said to be sure to make it *look* like an accident, or at least self defense. We don't want anyone spending time in a Costa Rican jail while they sort this thing out. So, yes, to answer your question, Susan, I do have a disposal plan. And it's right there."

Taylor pointed toward the high cliffs looming beyond Gissler Point. Each set of eyes followed his arm as it slowly unfolded towards the spot, like the bony finger of the Grim Reaper. And instantly, they understood.

89

Minutes later they split up, each knowing his or her place. It was quickly decided that the contestants shouldn't help build the course, as that was certainly not the pattern the killer had seen before. Everything they did must lead him to the conclusion that a legitimate competition was about to take place.

Taylor chose a swimming competition for a very specific reason. Those courses were in deep water, which would make the killer's escape, once he was discovered, much more difficult and slow. And it would also give them time to get to him in the water, while he struggled to get out of it. Matthew was the best swimmer, and shouldered the challenge of getting to the killer first and wrapping him up.

Though not tasked with constructing the challenge, the Castaways had a much more gruesome task to perform. With the boat still nine days away, the two bodies, one of them days old, had to be attended to. Temporary graves were hastily built on the hillside to the west of Wafer Bay. The two women were wrapped in tarps from the quonset hut, so they could easily be extracted from the ground once the boat finally arrived to take them all away.

That task completed, they returned to their "game lives"— swimming, strolling the beach together, and heading back to their camps to cook quinoa while they waited uneasily, nervous eyes scanning the bush for any sort of movement.

And they waited. And waited.

Old Joe's time was spent in his tree, listening, thinking, sharpening the arrows he'd made, adding sharp stones to his spearpoints, creating a strong recurve bow from a sturdy branch cut from the very tree in which he sat. He'd originally intended to use these items to hunt birds and rats, and he did manage to nail three of the fat little rodents to share with the others at dinner. But as he sat in his tree lacing together vines for his bowstring, he knew chances were good that these arrows might be buried in human flesh by night's end.

Which didn't bother him one bit. Prey was prey. And sometimes, Joe knew, prey was people.

13

Joe . . . A Long, Long Time Ago

The grand prize was a '62 Ford pickup. Not a new one, of course, but a set of wheels nonetheless. And young Joe Stabler needed a set of wheels.

Growing up on the eastern border of West Virginia, Young Joe had no game, or at least not with the young ladies he so craved. Sure, he was about the best hunter there was, at least the way he saw it, but when it came to impressing beautiful high school girls? Well, taxidermy and gamey meats just didn't get the job done.

His Pa had made it very clear there was no money for wheels. Hell, there wasn't money for anything. The mines had already begun their slow, inexorable slide towards certain death, forcing Joe's father to endure an endless cycle of job on, job off, a cycle that would eventually send him to an alcohol soaked grave, only six years later.

No matter what, if Joe wanted a car and the young women he could carry around in one, he'd have to go get one himself.

But until this week, that had seemed an impossible task. There were few jobs for people his age, and what passed for work in Mercer County paid minimum wage at best, and more likely, far less than that under the table.

But an unlikely salvation had suddenly arrived at Joe's doorstep in the form of a contest. A contest geared specifically to Joe's personal special-ity.

Hunting. And not just any kind of hunting. Coyote hunting.

Now, the coyote was just about the darnedest creature on god's green earth, thought Joe. Hard to hunt, smarter than most people he knew, and best of all, plentiful. Mother nature was in no danger of running out of coyotes, which meant Joe could hunt them anytime he wanted, and almost anywhere too, since they were considered a nuisance to farmers, ranchers, and cat owners alike.

Truth be told, though, Joe liked coyotes. They reminded him of himself. Lean, wiry, at home in the deep woods, excellent at catching game and hard to outsmart, he felt a kinship with them. More often than not, though he'd certainly never admit this to another living soul, when he came across one he'd gaze down his gun barrel at it, but never pull the trigger.

Instead, he'd sight in on their heads, set his finger to the side of the trigger, wait for eye contact, and then yell "bang!", just to see what they would do. And no matter what they *did* do in that moment, it was always entertaining.

But now, for a truck? Joe would indeed pull the trigger, and as many darn times as he possibly could. He'd be 18 in three months, and had gone far too long without a car, and even worse, far too long without touching the soft skin of the girls who liked to ride in them.

He signed up immediately at the local grange hall. There were thirty-odd boys on the list, most of them known to him in one way or another, and not one of them did he consider a formidable opponent. The contest would last a week, and at seven pm on the following Saturday night, the boy who piled up the most coyote carcasses would drive home that old Ford pickup. And even though the contest was to start at seven the next morning, Joe ran straight home, grabbed his rifle, and set off into the woods.

He got his first just before dark that night, but was smart enough to wait until ten the next morning to bring it to the grange hall in his red wagon. With a confident grin, he savored the slap on the shoulder from the councilman in charge of the count. His was the first, and there would be many more to come.

But the rest of that first day passed without Joe getting a single one. As he slunk home after dark, he check the leader board at the grange. Two other boys had managed to tie him that day. Still, he slipped into bed without a worry, knowing he would stretch out his lead in the coming days.

But the next day went the same way. Not a single coyote. And that night, Steve Wilcox actually managed to pull in front of him, with a total count of two. Meanwhile, four other boys had moved up to one coyote a piece.

Wednesday saw Joe up before the crack of dawn. He pedaled his bicycle down the county road for six miles before diving into the woods and stashing it behind a bush. He rode further out this time, figuring that the problem was range. He needed a bigger one, because the other boys were clearing out all the coyotes close to town.

Luckily, it worked, and he managed to get one just after noon that day. But, it turned out, so had Steve. And two other boys had tied him with two a piece.

As Thursday morning dawned, Joe was already ten miles down the county road on his old bicycle with the wagon dragging behind, his flashlight taped to the bars, bobbing to and fro as he pedaled. Ditching his childhood wheels, he launched into his work, sniffing and scanning around for game trails where he knew coyotes would eventually be found. Once he found a good spot, or God willing an actual dead prey animal like a rabbit or a squirrel, he would cover himself in leaves fifty paces out, and wait in silence until one of the wily beasts finally came along. This time, a dead possum played the bait, while Joe lay in wait.

And it turned out that God was indeed willing, because three hours later, a female coyote happened along. Joe dropped her before she even knew he was there.

Once again, Steve Wilcox, the dirty son of a bitch, managed to keep pace.

Friday. Joe was nervous and sick to his stomach as he strapped his wagon to the back of his bike. Two days to go, sunup to sundown. Wilcox was up by one and Davey Peterson sat in third, one behind Joe. It was a tight race, to be sure, but Joe couldn't shake the feeling that he was being had. Wilcox wasn't half the hunter he was. Not nearly so. And one coyote per day? Like clockwork? Come on.

So he changed his tactics, and headed for Steve Wilcox's trailer home before dawn. He stashed his bike behind the dumpster at the trailer park, and waited, his eye solidly on Steve's door.

And he waited.

Wilcox didn't even step outside for three hours! How the hell was he beating Joe, a dedicated, rise-before-dawn, real deal hunter, by rolling out of bed at nearly ten am?

Joe's sixth sense was cranking now. The contest leader was definitely pulling something.

Wilcox went to his own bike and began to roll while Joe stayed far behind. Luckily, Steve's bike was even shittier than his was, making a squeaky caterwauling that would not only mask any sound Joe made, but surely send any nearby coyotes running for the hills.

Once again, Joe shook his head. None of this made *any* sense!

But then suddenly, it did.

Steve pedaled his beaten old bike leisurely while Joe struggled to stay far enough behind to not be noticed. And then Steve turned quickly off that county road leading into the forest, and made a beeline down a dirt road that led only one place.

The city dump.

Joe fumed. The dump. Gathering place of coyotes, vultures, bobcats, bears and anything else that liked to eat garbage. Of course! Why hadn't he thought of it! Joe was hunting for his prize the only way he knew- the hard way, the honest way, the traditional way, while Wilcox had gamed the entire system, probably spending just two or three hours a day rubbing his body against other peoples' garbage, while Joe came in sore and scraped up every night after nine or ten hours in the woods!

Joe seethed. He now hated Steve Wilcox with a passion. Worse, he hated himself for being so damn straight and narrow to not have made that Ford an absolutely sure thing, like Steve Wilcox! But now that he knew how it was done, he made a plan.

Just as he figured, Steve didn't want to make it look like a runaway victory, and only took one coyote, just two hours after entering the dump. Joe could see more of the beasts further out at the very back of the dump as those hours rolled by, but Wilcox, sitting with his transistor radio, humming a tune and eating a twinkie, finally shot one that got close enough to pop without even having to hold his breath as he squeezed the trigger. After all, he only needed that one to stay ahead of Joe, so why not make it look legit.

"Fuckin' cheater!" Joe mumbled as he lay between bags of trash, just a hundred yards from Wilcox. His scope was trained on the bastard, and all he'd have to do was squeeze the trigger …

Steve rolled out of the dump with the coyote in his wagon, and Joe went to work.

Moving rapidly through piles of rubbish, rotten food, dogshit, and moldy mattresses, he took a bead on the first coyote. "POP!" it went down with a whimper, and he moved to the next one. "POP!", and it too was down.

Now Joe might not have been as crafty as Wilcox (them trailer park kids is always schemin' 'bout somethin'), but he was no dummy. He waited until nearly dark, loaded the two animals in his wagon, and rolled in to tally the count.

All tied up!

With only one day left, the competition was now squarely between Joe and Steve, as Davey hadn't gotten one that day and was two behind.

The next morning, he played it the same way. Following Steve out to the dump, he waited. This time he was pretty sure Wilcox would take two, because nobody could logically get three (except Joe, of course), and that should ensure a tie, at worst.

And even if for some crazy reason Wilcox took three, it would be a tie, and a tie would mean a runoff with one more day to bring home the bodies. If that happened, Joe would be sure the councilmen found out about Steve's loophole. It would surely be banged shut, and then his victory would be assured.

No goddamn way Steve Wilcox could beat him in the *real* woods. No goddamn way!

Just like the day before, Steve popped one pretty quickly. But after that, he just climbed to the top of a forty foot mountain of trash, surveyed the scene, sat down with a comic book on top of an old freezer, and began to read.

After that, he sipped a coke, set up some bottles and broken car windshields, and began to plink away at them with his rifle.

After that, it was tin cans.

And after that, he just played the radio and danced on of his hilltop freezer-fortress.

It was getting late, and Joe hadn't gotten a single coyote yet. He'd expected Steve would get two and then roll right on home. Meanwhile, he would get three, be proclaimed the best coyote killer in the history of Mercer county, win the contest, and hopefully get laid within a month!

But Wilcox wasn't making it easy, and almost seemed to be toying with him. Dark was rapidly approaching, and at seven pm the contest would be over. It would be dark by six thirty, so if Wilcox didn't roll soon, Joe would scarcely have time to get his animals shot and loaded before he ran out of time.

His heart pounded mercilessly. Sweat rolled down his brow, clouding his vision. The plan was falling apart right before his eyes, while Wilcox danced the night away on top of that damn freezer!

Joe's blood boiled. Visions of Wilcox behind the wheel of *his* Ford pickup tortured his nervous mind. More than once he aimed at the boy, wanting desperately to shoot the kid's feet out so he fell and couldn't make it home, but knew there would be no way to escape being caught if the kid took a bullet.

All of a sudden Steve finished a dance move with a flourish, leapt from the freezer to the ground, and disappeared down the other side of the trash hill, apparently heading for his pair of winning coyotes.

Joe didn't stop to think. Rage drove him straight to his feet and right up the side of the trash hill. Arriving on top, he saw Wilcox picking his way down the far side of the mound, about a third of the way down. Without a moment's hesitation, Joe strained against the heavy freezer, managing to tip it up to a standing position. Lining it up as best he could, he gave it a mighty shove towards the unwitting Steve Wilcox.

Joe dropped to the ground and watched as the two hundred pound chest freezer bounced and hopped down the steep side of the pile. Wilcox's tiny brain was still focused on the little transistor radio swinging in his left hand as he picked his way through the garbage, and didn't hear the crashing of the freezer until it was too late. When he finally did, he turned his head up the hill to see it, and quickly tried to jump out of the way. But his right foot punched through the side of a rusty muffler, and he was trapped.

The freezer slammed into the eighteen year old boy, flattening him to the ground as though he were a dry autumn sunflower, before the heavy metal box left his broken body and continued to thunder down the hill.

Joe froze in terror, realizing what he'd done. He prayed he hadn't killed Wilcox. He wasn't a bad kid, just a cheater. And while cheaters might deserve a broken arm or an ass whooping, they didn't deserve to die.

He slipped slowly down the hill, fearing both being discovered, and finding Wilcox dead. Moving cautiously, he kept an eye out for some kind of escape, just in case Wilcox stood up.

But he didn't.

Joe finally made it to where the broken kid lay in a bundle of rusty auto parts, and looked him over carefully.

Eureka, he was still breathing!

Without so much as a second look, Joe raced back to his gun and moved to a spot closer to the far off coyotes at the back of the dump. He dropped to a prone position, sighted in, held his breath, and before they even had a chance to jump, popped off one, two, and three shots from his semi automatic rifle. Three of the beasts dropped to the ground, and Joe quickly began the laborious work of hauling them back to his wagon, carrying them one by one over his shoulders while the rest of the pack milled around and sniffed, waiting for him to leave so they could dive right back into their evening meal.

Wilcox still hadn't gotten up when Joe rolled into the Grange hall to claim his victory. The councilman patted him on the back, a small crowd of parents and executives from the mine cheered and hooted at his amazing success, and when the clock ticked seven, a set of car keys was dropped into his hand.

Steve Wilcox wasn't found for two days, and didn't go back to school until nearly a week later. By then nearly everyone knew he had been out shooting coyotes at the dump when a huge freezer had somehow toppled onto him, breaking his left leg and foot in several places, and leaving him unable to crawl out until a search party found him. The discovery made Joe's achievement seem even more amazing. Since Wilcox was now a proven cheater, Joe had beaten the nearest competitor by a whopping four coyotes, a margin larger than any other boy had even managed to kill all week.

Truly amazing, it was proclaimed. Joe's fame as the best hunter in Mercer county grew from that day forward, until he was considered a legend.

And better than that, thought Joe, he had wheels. Wheels that, combined with a new top-dog status, got him laid not within a month, but within a week.

The day after Louise Bannon gave up the goods on the bench seat of the old pickup, Joe strode cockily into school to see Wilcox standing, with the help of a pair of crutches, at his locker.

The week, and the previous night's sexual conquest had only served to grow Joe's cocky hatred of Steve Wilcox, and as he slipped confidently behind the broken boy on his way down the hall, he whispered venomously into the loser's ear, "Fuckin' cheater!"

14

Day 7 ~ Trapped

Night fell on Wafer Bay, silent and moonlit. Around the beach the Castaways slept, or at least pretended to. There were regular watch changes so each of them could get a few hours sleep before their turn, with at least three players scheduled for each three hour watch.

But as the soft morning light slithered its way through the jungle behind them, one thing was painfully clear. The killer had not shown himself.

Whether the water challenge proved too difficult to sabotage, or he'd somehow caught on to their little plan, nonetheless, he failed to fall for their carefully laid trap.

Taylor's shrill whistle brought them out of their beds and back to beach center, where the "competition" was to have begun. Long faces and bleary eyes ruled the morning. Feet kicked sand to and fro, releasing nervous, *very* nervous, energy from the night's tortuous dreamscapes.

"He's on to us," Jason broke the silence, his bushy hair matted into a leaning wad by his hard, sandy pillow, "in fact, I bet he's watching us right now."

"Are we still doing this thing?" Susan asked. Her own nervous energy, as always, was translated by her mind into a command to "do something!"

"Why would we!" shrieked Danielle, her stained face betraying that tears had dripped down them at some point during the night. "So he can take potshots at us from the trees? No goddamn way! Count me OUT!".

"Yeah," Kinnary nodded dejectedly, "she's right." Normally she was up for a bit of danger, but instinct told her that this time, chasing that buzz would be foolish.

"Time for a new plan, Bossman," Jason grinned from ear to ear, enjoying Taylor's failure nearly as much as he would his own success.

Old Joe stood alone behind them, quietly facing the jungle. His weathered eyes scanned the trees for any signs of movement, or perhaps a lens flash from a pair of binoculars. But there was nothing. Nothing but a miasmic, swirling flight of birds and the glare of the new day's Sun, rising above the trees.

Taylor's head hung low. He'd bought himself some time by canceling the boat, but now everyone, himself included, would spend that extra week fearing the killer in the jungle, who, it seemed, remained one step ahead of them.

"Fine. I give up. He beat me." He paused to sigh and catch his breath. "One of you can come up with something. Everybody here?"

Scanning the group, they soon discovered they were a pair short.

"Med team's not here," Carl said.

"Go get 'em, would you, Carl?"

The cameraman took off up the hill to the edge of the beach, where the ranger cabins sat like twin remnants of a lost civilization, slowly being swallowed up by the voracious wild behind.

"Randy?" Taylor turned to the tall man behind him. "You're a gambler. Your brain is used to these kinds of puzzles. You got a hole card for this kind of unwinnable situation?

"Not really," Randy shook his head. "The key obviously is what you tried last night. Figure out what he really wants, and use it to draw him out. We clearly aren't going to go to him, so we have to find a way to bring him to us."

"Which didn't work," Franklin reminded him.

"Right. It didn't," Randy nodded. "Which means the bait wasn't strong enough. So then, what does this guy *really* want?"

"I'll tell you what he wants!" Danielle screamed. She couldn't believe they were even having this conversation. "He wants us the hell out of here!"

Matthew put his arm around her as she began to sob. Others, however, didn't feel quite so charitable towards their group's weak link.

"Look Danielle, you're not the only one in this," Susan wagged her finger at the sobbing mess before her. "*All* of us are out here, there's no boat coming, and turning into a god damned jellyfish and spreading your sad baggage all over the beach isn't going to make any goddamn difference! In fact, it might hurt. None of us can think clearly with your little pity party going on, so *can* it!"

"Jesus, Susan!" Kinnary defended Danielle, "Who made you Queen? You don't get to speak for all of us."

"Who said I was?" she gathered herself, "I'm speaking for me. We need to think. And we need clarity. And crying ain't it!"

A muted groan rose suddenly from behind the gathering, and the Castaways spun en masse to see Carl stumbling from the ranger station, his normally calm face pulsing with dread.

"They're dead! Sato… Jeremy… they're dead!"

Danielle fell to the sand in a puddle as Matthew dropped her like a hot rock. Taylor's mouth hung open, shocked, while Franklin and Darius immediately sprinted towards the cabin.

"*Both* of them?" Taylor said very slowly, in disbelief. "This guy is tiny from all accounts, how could he kill Sato *and* Jeremy? At the same time? You've got to be kidding!"

Old Joe peered cautiously into the jungle before following the two big men up the beach, Randy at his side.

When Darius hit the doorway, what he saw inside did not compute. Sato and Jeremy appeared to be sleeping. There was no Manson-esque blood splatter on the walls, no sign of struggle, just the two of them lying in their beds, blankets pulled up around their necks like sleeping children, each facing the wall.

Darius stood stunned in the door as Franklin blew past, headed for Sato first, and ripped back the blanket.

Her neck was sliced down to the trachea, one side to the other. Blood pooling underneath her had begun to thicken. Moving to Jeremy, he saw the same dark tale repeated.

Old Joe slipped through the door as Darius stepped out to clear his mind. The hunter stopped in the doorway too, but for an altogether different reason. He wanted to survey the scene as it was, and by doing so, maybe figure out just exactly what had gone down as they all slept nearby.

"Franklin, mind backin' off fer just a minute? I wanna get the whole scene. May be important."

Franklin slowly lifted his eyes from the horror before him and turned. "Gladly."

He stepped out just as Randy moved in behind Old Joe, beginning his own scan of the room.

"Blood drops, on the floor," he pointed.

Old Joe nodded. "More like little puddles. Footprints smeared in 'em. Our boy's got 'bout a size 9 shoe."

Bending down closer, Joe observed the directional patterns in the droplets. "They come from Jeremy, like he's tryin' to reach her."

He moved closer to Jeremy's side, while Randy inspected Sato.

"Hey, Joe, there's something in her mouth." He very softly turned the dead woman's head to get a better look. "It's cloth. Canvas maybe."

Old Joe checked Jeremy's mouth, but found no such cloth.

"Nothin' here. Let's peel back the blankets, real slow like."

Each man carefully pulled back the blanket on his chosen corpse. Sticky with coagulating blood, they made creepy, slurping noises as they came off.

Behind the unlikely coroners, a crowd had gathered. Matthew gagged and quickly left, while Susan, Jason, and Malik stood transfixed by the investigation.

"Bruises. She's covered in them," Randy announced. "Guy beat the hell out of her."

Joe scanned the corpse in front of him. Jeremy was black, and a man, so bruises would be much harder to detect on his body.

"Not ol' Jeremy. Nothin' like 'at here. Looks peaceful as a lamb."

Randy straightened again and stepped back towards the door. His eyes fed data to his brain as quickly as they could, scanning from one side to the other and then back again, picturing the scene just as the killer might have.

"I see it," he said with authority, and all eyes, even Joe's, turned to him with anticipation.

"He opens the door," Randy began, "Jeremy is sleeping, and being a fairly big guy, clearly the more dangerous of the two. So, he goes quickly to her and shoves a gag in her mouth. Before she can make a sound, he lunges at Jeremy and slices his throat. Jeremy wakes up, and before passing out tries to get to his killer, just as he's slicing Sato's throat. She must have woken up when he gagged her, but it took her a moment to realize what was happening, and by that time…"

"By that time," Joe nodded, "Jeremy's damn near dead n' she's only moments from the same. I think you got 'er, son. Which means our boy's quick, he's got a knife, and he ain't afraid 'a big strong men. All of which," he turned to the group at the door, "ain't good."

A voice rose from far behind the throng. "The radio!" Ricardo shrieked, "It's smashed! And everything else! Cameras, the booms, sound equipment, all beat to shit!"

Like a crowd watching a three ring circus, the audience pivoted to the second cabin. Inside was a Manson-esque scene of destruction they had avoided at the medical cabin, only this time the victims were electronic. The cameras were bashed to pieces on the floor, and boom mikes were bent and broken like long necked birds God had twisted into pretzels. But the worst part was that the rangers' radio, their primary link to the mainland, was not only completely destroyed, but doused in water for good measure.

"Nobody panic!" Taylor's voice came from the rear of the crowd, "I still have the satellite phone! We're not cut off."

"Don't panic! Did you just say don't panic, Taylor?" Darius lunged at the host, grabbed him by the throat, and pinned him against the wall outside the cabin.

Not a single member of the Castaways or the crew moved even one single inch to help Taylor Woods.

Darius was rabid. Tonya's death was, at first, thought to be an accident. Amy's death was immediately followed by a search through the jungle and the underbelly of the island. That search had taken some of the edge off of those first two, bizarre deaths.

But for Darius, there was no taking the edge off of two brutal, cold blooded murders within a hundred yards of where he slept.

"Taylor," he tightened his grip on the smaller man's throat, "I've got three kids man. They depend on me to *live*! And some guy here is killing us, one by one! You're going to tell us right fucking now *why* it is that he wants us dead!"

Taylor's body twisted and contorted left and right, his face beet red as he began to run out of air.

Old Joe moved in next to Darius, machete at the ready.

"Back the fuck up, Joe!" Darius yelled, eyes ablaze, "I won't let you save his sorry ass!"

Old Joe grinned like a wise old owl. "Hell son, who said I was gonna save the sumbitch! I'm on yer side! But you gotta let go his pipe or we ain't gonna git nothin' from this here jackass."

Darius peered sideways at the old codger, unsure whether to trust him or not.

"Darius," Franklin added, "Taylor's not going anywhere. We're all with you."

Old Joe put his hand on the big man's arm as Taylor's eyes rolled back in his head. "It's all right son. We got yer back."

Darius released his grip and Taylor collapsed to the sand. Gasping, he winced anew when Kinnary pounded her foot into his groin.

"Talk, you piece of shit!" she screamed.

Taylor rolled on the ground, while Ricardo took a few steps back to avoid joining his boss on the pain train. But a hand landed on his shoulder, and Matthew glared into his eyes. "Where are *you* going?"

Ricardo surrendered, throwing his hands in the air. "Hey, nowhere, man! I'm cool."

Darius scanned the crowd. "Carl! Malik! Get the fuck up here!"

Malik leapt to the front of the crowd, his highly advanced instinct for self preservation taking over.

"Y'all," Malik faced the crowd with his back against the wall, "I'm here to tell you, there *is* definitely something going on here, only me and Carl don't know what the hell it is! But *that* piece of shit…" he pointed at Ricardo, "*is* definitely in on it. Me and Carl been trying to find out what we've been cut out of for days."

Ricardo felt a hand bite down on his other shoulder as Darius reached across three people, and dug his fingers in, hard.

104

Carl chuckled indignantly. "Don't include me in this, Malik! You just told me something might be up yesterday, and if you remember correctly, I told you I didn't give two shits, either way."

Carl turned away and walked towards the beach, his middle finger indicating yet again that he actually and truly did not give even one single solitary shit.

"So then," Darius cranked down on Ricardo's shoulder, dropping him to his knees, "who wants less pain? Seems like it's gonna be the first to talk."

"And that would be me . . ." Ricardo gasped through his pain, his eyes tearing up.

"Ricardo! No..." Taylor begged, only to fall silent once more when Kinnary again slammed her foot into his testicles, and he fell face first into the sand.

"Fuck you, Taylor," Ricardo continued, "I bet you weren't even gonna split it with me anyway!" He paused, sucked in a lungful, and then sure as hell let one out. "Treasure. Lots of treasure! This place is supposed to be rolling in it."

"Fuckin' A, I knew it!" Jason Oliver nodded about as hard as his chicken neck would allow without his head leaving it, "I fuckin' knew it! Treasure, man! And we're sittin' on it!"

"Well, now, ain't that a fine kettle a' fish," Old Joe found himself smiling for the first time since the game began.

Susan's eyes blazed with gold, which just happened to be the same color as her favorite mascara. "Sure seems like you boys got some 'splainin' to do. So c'mon now, Ricky Ricardo, spill it!"

"Gissler," he continued, "like Gissler point? He landed here in the late 1800's. Lived here for years. He knew of at least two treasures buried here. One from a pirate called "Bloody Sword Bonito". Well, Gissler got hold of his diary. And then another pirate named Old Mac. That one had a map. And there's more of them than that. This place was a legendary pirate stop, because it was off the beaten path, uninhabited at the time, and lawless."

Randy had questions. "So this Gissler guy," he began, "you say he lived here for many years? But he didn't find the treasure?"

"Yes, and no," Ricardo shook his head, sensing he was winning the war against pain. "He found thirty three gold coins from the late 1790's, but that's it. He found a tree marked with the words "the bird has flown", and some people think maybe one of the treasures got dug up. The English navy came here in the early 1900's and used dynamite, but we don't know if they found anything or not. Gissler himself left in 1908, after his colony abandoned him. Couldn't grow crops in the dirt here."

"Wrong crops, I bet," giggled Old Joe, who, for once, couldn't seem to stop smiling. "Dumbshits."

"And, let me guess," Franklin sneered, "here comes the GPR."

Ricardo nodded. "That's what it was for. But we haven't gotten a chance to try it yet. We were gonna wait until the game got down to fewer players, so we could do it without being found out."

"Taylor, Taylor, Taylor," Susan teased as she stood over the host, "I don't know whether to kick you in the balls, or kiss your stupid face! Wait. Yeah I do."

Bam! Her size 6 shoe slammed into Taylor's already inflamed groin.

Taylor doubled over again, but, growing used to the pain by now, quickly tried to rise to his knees, only to have another hand grab his shoulder.

"You better add something valuable, quick," Darius warned, "or you're gonna be my new punching bag."

Taylor put up his hand to ward the big man off. It was now, he figured, surrender or die time. And he had no intention of dying.

"What none of you realize," he squealed in a pitch far too high for TV, "is you are sitting on Robinson Crusoe's Island. Or at least many people think so. The maps, the landmarks, they all match. And not only that, it's the model for Treasure Island, the book. This is not a joke, people. There's treasure here. Enough to change all of our lives."

He calculated for a moment before speaking another line. The truth, as he saw it in those few seconds, was there was simply no way he'd ever have to share his gold with all these people. The killer would see to that. He'd just have to wait them out. So then, would he dip a toe into the truth, or launch into a full cannonball?

He chose to make a splash big enough to soak all of them.

"And I've found it." He paused for effect, the master showman raising the blood pressure of all in attendance, and raising his own, as always by the power he had to do so.

"*What!*" Ricardo screamed, launching across the sand to slam his fist in Taylor's face, knocking the cocky host right back to the ground. "You fucking asshole! When *exactly* were you gonna tell me? We were partners!"

"It's in the caves. There's a wall you'll have to swim under. My guess is he dug it up somewhere else, and stashed it there. And, I think he may still be stashing it."

He paused again, sensing the moment the crowd was about to explode, while Leticia's eyes nearly doubled in size under a furrowed, angry brow. She took a step back from the group, just as he finished with a flurry.

"You want to know the reason why he wants to kill us, Darius? Well, how about tens of millions of them."

Jason Oliver squealed giddily, and Old Joe leaned his head back and hooted at the sky.

"Taylor, you are the hostest with the mostest!" Jason extended him a hand, "Damn man! That is the best freaking thing I've ever heard!"

"Sure is," Susan grinned greedily, "and now we're *all* partners!"

The host wobbled his way onto two legs. "That's fine," he lied, "I don't mind sharing. The situation has changed, and we've got a killer on the loose. I hadn't bargained for that."

"Shit," Randy popped back to reality, "the killer. Christ, we've still got a murderer to take out. But there's something I don't understand here. The radio cabin. Your cabin, Taylor. He smashed all that shit up without the four of you knowing?"

"The last watch," Ricardo rushed to explain before the mob set on him again, "we had the last watch! No one was in there for the last four hours."

"Which means he murdered them and smashed the cabin up in the last four hours," Randy calculated.

"And another thing," Leticia added, lurking at the back of the group, "why didn't we hear him kill them? Does that make sense to anybody?"

"I got that one," Old Joe nodded. "Y'all walk over here with me, just a few steps."

The crowd followed him towards the beach, until he turned to face them. Even Carl returned from self exile at the water's edge to hear the old guy speak.

"All right. Ever'body quiet. Now Matthew, if you'll do me the favor 'a headin' up ta the radio cabin, then just bang around n' make some noise— much as ya can."

Matthew did as he was asked, and disappeared inside.

"Hear that?" Old Joe asked after a few seconds.

"Just waves crashing," Leticia answered.

"That's right. Look y'all, this guy ain't no dummy. He knows this place inside and out. The fact he was here jus' before dawn tells me he's probably still close right now. Real close. I bet he's got a place nearby he kin run to, and c'mon back soon after."

Skin crawled, goosebumps rose, and accidental gasps flew out of the open mouths of those gathered.

Ricardo, sensing another chance to get out of the doghouse, stuck his pointer finger into the air.

"Shit," he began, "Joe, I think I might know where he is."

With those words, Taylor, still hoping for a few more of his "partners" to die by the killer's hand, died a little inside instead.

15

Day 7 ~ Game Changer

Ricardo led them up the hill north of Wafer Bay, along a steep ridge that towered hundreds of feet above the sea on each side. All were silent, anxiously expecting blow darts, boulders, or arrows to rain down on them at any moment.

Danielle camouflaged herself right in the middle of the group, preferring to live to see her newfound fortune rather than pretending to be tough, as some of the others seemed to be doing. But the news of the treasure had served to brighten her mood, at least a little bit.

"Up here," Ricardo whispered as they moved closer to their goal. "Gissler's cave. It matches the location of Robinson Crusoe's cave, almost exactly."

A few yards later, Old Joe stepped quietly to the front of the line and raised an open hand.

Everyone froze as Joe knelt to the ground. When he was sure, he pointed to his shoe.

Footprints. They understood immediately, having followed the outdoorsman halfway across the island just two days before. Old Joe's junior rangers knelt down and waited while he, Darius, Franklin, and Randy crept forward along the ridge. Thirty steps later, the mouth of Gissler's cave came into view, gaping hauntingly at them from the brush, only fifteen yards ahead.

Joe pointed to his ear. Necks craned and attention focused, but there was no sound whatsoever but the far-off drone of crashing waves. He held his hand up again, telling his advance team to stay put while he crept back to the larger group. When he reached them, he motioned for them to close in around him, and whispered as loud as he dared.

"I want y'all to form a line, like a net, 'round the cave. If he comes a runnin' out, I don't want him ta have nowhere ta go."

Danielle's fear leapt to the front of the conversation, yet again. "No goddamn way! I will *not* be part of this! What if he comes out with a weapon!"

Joe waved frantically for her to please shut the hell up, and now. Others were not as kind.

"Listen, bitch!" Leticia whisper-yelled at the woman she'd quite gladly choke to death right in front of everyone if someone would just give the okay, "You help, or you get no treasure. Got it!"

"Well now *you* listen, bitch!" Danielle shot back, her lip quivering uncontrollably from the confrontation, "*You* don't make the rules!".

"You're right, Danielle, she doesn't," Susan whispered angrily back, "but for once, she's right! You leave, you're out! Am I right?" she asked the crowd.

Without the slightest bit of hesitation, the entire group nodded to approve Leticia's new rule.

"Then fuck *all* of you!" Danielle yelled at full volume, before charging down the hill to the relative safety of the beach.

"Maybe I'll cut *your* throat tonight!" Leticia shrieked in return, before Joe, appalled at her choice of words, silenced her by putting his hand over her mouth.

"Jesus H. Christ," he whispered into her ear, "let's be smart about this'un, ok?"

Her mouth still gagged by his hand, Leticia nodded in reply.

Randy stuck his hand into the gap in the circle of players, and added, "Remember, he's mine."

One by one they crept into line, forming a half moon shape around the cave's mouth. Randy stood directly before the opening, with Darius and Franklin each on one side of the cave, and the rest arrayed in a semi circle.

"All right you piece of shit!" Randy braced himself for anything that might come flying from the darkness, "we know you're in there. Come out now, or we're coming in!"

Silence, except the sound of waves crashing, far below them.

"Maybe there's a back way out, like the other cave?" Kinnary asked.

Taylor shook his head. "No way, I've seen photos the rangers took from inside. Ends in solid rock."

Old Joe left his place in the circle momentarily, returning with a pile of dried palm leaves. He tore a few into tiny strips, wadded others into a ball, broke a branch in two, and then began to rapidly twist the smaller piece against the larger one, just behind his little pile of furry tinder.

Noticing that the group was watching him, he quickly chided, "Y'all, please keep your eyes on the cave, y'hear? I'm a sittin' duck."

Chastened, they returned their gazes to the entrance. Minutes later, a ball of flame grew from the pile Joe had made, and he ran to grab more fuel. When he returned, he waved Randy aside and with his feet shoved the burning pile right into the cave's entrance, creating eerie shadows on the granite walls inside.

"Ol' Injun trick," he smiled. "Smoke him out."

The fire grew rapidly until it began to produce clouds of thick, black smoke. Running off again, Joe came back with much larger, living palm leaves, and began to wave them against the fire like bellows, pushing the smoke deeper into the cave.

Minutes went by. Eyes filled with tears as smoke blew in and out of Joe's Indian fire.

More minutes went by.

"Whoever's coughing, quit it!" Leticia yelled suddenly.

They peered around the circle at each other through the thickening smoke. The sound of coughing was unmistakable, but no one's lips appeared to be moving..

Bracing himself for the fight, Randy yelled, "Aww shit! Here we go!"

But no one anticipated what came. Seconds later, the thick smoke blocked the killer's appearance in the mouth of the cave. With fast feet he kicked the flaming pile into the group around him, causing his would be captors to wince and pull back as burning embers pelted their skin. He sprinted from the cave, aiming for a tiny gap left by the retreating Castaways.

Old Joe dove to his knees to block his way, but the killer leapt right over him like a college halfback.

Randy caught one of his legs as he flew over Joe, and held on with all his might. His brief flight over, the killer thudded to the ground, twisting and contorting as others came to Randy's aid. Leticia and Franklin pounced on the little man simultaneously. A bandana covered his mouth showed how he'd held out as long as he had against the choking smoke.

Small but agile and lean, the killer broke free of Franklin's huge hands with the quick slash of a knife's blade, and the big man jerked away in pain, blood flowing freely from the new gash in his arm. Somehow Leticia managed to keep her grip on the killer, rage rising within her as it always did when someone dared act against her, a state in which she was not to be trifled with. Nearly as short as the killer but more thickly muscled, she kicked hard at his groin and bit his arm as he slashed at her with his knife. Darius reached in to help, but got his hand ripped open for his trouble. A large man himself, he just wasn't fast enough. This was a fight for the small, the agile, and the quick.

In a moment of wonder, Randy thought to himself that it was like watching two trained fighting dogs in the arena.

Each person there wanted to stop the killer, but not a single one of them was willing to risk death to save Leticia, the least liked member of the group by a long shot. Instead they selfishly watched as she and the killer rolled and twisted on the ground as one, until a lucky slash of his blade cut her left shoulder to the bone. She screamed, more in anger than in pain, and immediately jumped off of him.

The killer leapt to his feet and stood frozen on the edge of the cliff, briefly observing these strange people who he'd been trying to evict from Cocos all week. So very close to leaving the island himself, he had decided to stop moving the rest of the treasure to his stash hole, and instead to begin the laborious process of loading it into his boat for a nighttime escape. He could always come back for the rest later.

He could, or so he had thought until now, when there was no doubt that his secret was exposed.

Regaining his senses, he waved his blade in the air menacingly and peeked over his shoulder at the drop off behind him. For a brief moment he considered jumping down the cliff, hoping to grab on to something and then make his getaway by side-stepping down to the water. No one would dare follow him if he could, not even the crazy girl. Glancing at it once more, he looked in vain for a tree or a vine to latch onto, just as his right leg exploded in pain.

Instinctively he slashed down with his knife as he screamed. Leticia's teeth were buried squarely in his right calf, and she wasn't letting go.

Less than a second later, Randy slammed into his chest, and the killer was airborne. His legs twisted around Leticia's body just as Franklin blasted into him as well, misty red droplets from his bloody arm spraying into the ocean breeze.

The force of the two large men was too much, and both the killer and Leticia were blown out over the sea into thin air. Horrified to see her caught by his own lunge, Randy's helpless eyes locked briefly with Leticia's as she realized her fate. But even now, on the way to certain death, she continued to bite and tear at her foe. They looked like two alley cats, each still intent on clawing the other to death after falling from a skyscraper.

Twisting as one they fell, each still fighting for the knife despite mutually assured destinies. Then, finally, the thud of their bodies slamming into the rocks below hammered the air, the sound rising above even the thunderous roar of the waves.

Rushing to the cliff's edge to see if Leticia had somehow been spared a fatal impact and landed in the water . . . Kinnary immediately saw she had not. Two small bodies lay motionless, just feet from the rising tide.

"Fuck!" Franklin screamed in guilt. "I didn't mean to hit her!"

"It's not your fault, man" Randy sighed, staring into the abyss beside Franklin. "I hit him first," he said softly, emotionless, "it couldn't be helped. She just got hung up."

"Jesus," Susan wondered out loud as she took her turn to peer over the side, "she was *actually* trying to help! I didn't think she had it in her!"

Far from the edge, Taylor stood alone. He didn't need to look. But his mind quickly did the math. One less portion to share.

"No," he spoke matter of factly, a poor man's Rod Serling standing just off camera, summing up an episode that had played only in his head, "she was just trying to win. That's all she knew how to do. Fight, and win."

When the shock finally wore off, the fire was put out, and the tattered Castaways began to make their way back down to the beach, the pounding surf quickly claiming the bodies of the fallen fighters in its foam. By the time they made it to where Danielle had sat alone, watching the battle on the cliff's edge, the two bloody corpses were gone, buried at sea in the mighty Pacific.

"Good riddance, Bitch," Danielle whispered bitterly into the rushing ocean air. "I hope you float all the way back to Buenos Aires."

16

Day 8 ~ Game, Changed

The day ran to its inevitable end. A bonfire was built and set alight. Crew rations were opened up to all for the first time. Songs were sung, mostly poorly. Wine was swallowed and friendships made. And Leticia was toasted and honored, something none of them had ever thought they would witness, let alone be part of.

For the first time in many days, the Castaways felt safe. The killer was gone, and they could finally sleep through a night with both eyes closed. Leticia's malignant camp presence, no matter how quickly forgotten it might be, was gone. Malik was happy he'd finally get a piece of the action. Even Taylor dropped his guard, no longer in possession of a secret to protect at all costs. The game was a long forgotten trifle, as now each contestant would go home with what would probably end up being millions of dollars. They were so happy, in fact, that a vote was taken, and Danielle was cut back into the deal ... for a half portion.

It seemed for the moment that all the thorny issues, all the competition, all the irritation and strife had left Cocos island. Now all they needed to do was wait seven days for the boat to come and take them all away. Seven days to move the treasure to a new spot of their very own, a spot they would return to before long to claim what was now theirs by right. Rights handed down through the ages to them from pirates like Bloody Sword Bonito and Old Mac, through

August Gissler and his German colonists, by the British Navy and a nameless troll-like killer, to the remaining crew and competitors of the final season of Execution Island, paid for with buckets of blood.

"Taylor," Randy yelled across the fire's glow, "I need to see that treasure in the morning."

"Hah!" Jason Oliver agreed, "you're not the only one!"

Taylor lay back with a belly full of wine and food, and smiled for the first time since he'd left his treasure room. "I'll take everyone there in the morning. There's nothing to worry about now, might as well relax and take it easy."

The host stood, wobbly on wine soaked legs, and greeted his masses, semi-officially, for the last time.

"I hereby crown you *all* the winners of the final season of Execution Island!"

"Here, here!" Malik cheered, finding himself included in the winner's circle for the first time. His whooping cry was quickly seconded by the very players he'd been so jealous of for so long.

All went to bed drunk and happy, awaking the next day to yet another brilliantly beautiful island morning.

Several hours of daylight passed before the hangover ridden gang was ready, but with Old Joe taking the lead, soon they were off, trodding the well worn trail back to the high ridge of Mt Iglesias. Spirits were high despite pounding headaches and sick stomachs, a few of which relieved themselves along the way.

"*Buried treasure*, Jason," Susan cooed the words almost pornographically, pausing briefly to kick aside a pair of mating rats as she strolled happily through the emerald green of Cocos, "Just think of it."

"I know. Never thought I'd hear those words with my name attached. How very kind of that son of a bitch to find it for us."

"Right. Hard to hold a grudge, no? I feel bad for the dead, but I'm sure glad we lived to see it."

"Don't jinx it! We haven't yet!" he replied.

They laughed, but only halfheartedly, as just a hint of gloom still hung in the air between them. Both knew well by now that virtually anything could happen on Cocos Island.

And had. For centuries.

By the time they reached the original entrance to the lava tubes, Cocos obliged that hint of gloom, and her sky opened up with a drenching rain. Relief came only when when they quickly slipped into the caverns and escaped the deluge. Even Franklin, lubricated by the pounding rain, found he was now able to squeeze into the small opening leading to the caverns below.

Once inside the smiles returned. Hands were slapped giddily as they traversed the spiral flumes of lava leading to the cavern bottom. Randy wisely suggested they mark Taylor's tunnel so they could easily find it later, and Old Joe brought a homemade torch to mount in the rocks near it. It was ceremoniously lit with whoops and hollers, and the accidental treasure hunters continued towards their bright destiny.

But a few minutes later, Matthew groaned. He was forced to stoop lower and lower with each step, as the lava tube's ceiling became ever closer to the floor. "Jesus, Taylor, you didn't mention how tight this thing got." His six and a half foot frame, though lean, was challenged constantly by the rough, sharp ceiling of black stone. More than once he bashed his head, until finally it began to bleed. Franklin was treated to the same fate.

After about the seventeenth exhortation of "Shit!", Taylor bade all to stop. At this point the cave was about five feet high, and only wide enough for single file.

"Look, this thing gets a lot worse," he explained, "not only does it drop to about a foot high with a belly crawl for about 60 feet, but you're gonna have to duck under a wall and then swim for another twenty. That's downright cramped. Franklin and Darius, and my chubby old buddy Carl, are going to have a hell of a time with it. I doubt they'll make it, frankly."

Darius, sensing a future for his three kids just over the next bend, was neither pleased, nor inclined to trust Taylor.

"You trying to cut some of us out, Taylor? I mean, this *is* Execution Island. Some folks get to go on reward trips, others stay behind, right? One winning team gets together over a meal, the other over their bitterness at *not* getting a meal, and voila, they plot against each others. You sure that's not what's going on here?"

"Jesus Christ, Darius!" Taylor barked. "You *can* turn the game off now."

"Can I? Really?"

"Look," Franklin nodded, "I feel the same way. How 'bout you Carl?"

Carl sneered in Taylor's general direction. "You took the words right outta my mouth, Darius. Where's *our* insurance, host boy?"

"Well thanks for the goddamn gratitude! And by the way, you're welcome!" Taylor yelled, sick and tired of being the brunt of everyone's disdain. Taking a moment to breathe it out, he calmed, and hit on a decent solution.

"Pick someone. Each of you. Somebody you trust. That way you'll each have a proxy inside. Three people you can trust to tell you the truth of what happens inside that chamber."

"Danielle," said Darius.

She smiled, but shook her head. "I'm flattered, D, but I'm not even sure I want to attempt the swim."

Darius looked at her, his eyes like daggers. "I need you to. Frankly, you need you to. These folks might just try to cut you out again. I don't want to see that. Do you?"

Danielle considered his warning, realizing the truth in it. "God, when you put it that way…"

"I got Matthew," Franklin pointed to his fellow athlete.

Matthew grinned confidently. He knew *somebody* would pick him. "I got your back, Frank. No sweat. At least," he noted, rubbing the blood off of his forehead, "if I don't knock myself out on the way in."

"C'mon Carl," Taylor grumbled, "we don't have all day."

"Old Joe. Hands down."

Malik felt insulted. "Screw you, man! I thought we were partners!"

"No offense," Carl shook his head, "but you're a wee bit shadier than Old Joe. You know it. You wouldn't pick you either."

Malik cracked a knowing grin. "Well played, my man."

Old Joe's leathered hand reached across the others and shook Carl's. "I gotcha. Done deal, buddy."

Satisfied, Taylor turned back to the task. "Onward."

And onward they went, dropping to their knees in another hundred feet, then to their bellies in a slow caver's crawl after that. Matthew kept on bashing his head, but he wasn't the only one.

Arriving at the swim, Taylor didn't even turn around to explain what was coming. He just dove in, and disappeared.

"Holy sheepshit!" Joe gasped, watching Taylor's feet vanish. "That there looks a might bit wilder than I figgered."

Susan, right behind and pinned uncomfortably between Joe and Kinnary, wasted no time with his bullshit weakness. "Joe, we can't turn around, and there's no way to get around you. *Dive, god damnit!*"

The old hunter closed his eyes, held his breath, and dove just like the mean lady said.

Cold! The water was cold, and though he'd been in much colder, he realized right away that some of the crew behind him were going to panic when they hit the icy fluid. But soon he could see a light. A small one, but he was grateful it wasn't pitch dark in the water. That *really* would have scared him.

Moments later, his head popped out of the water and into a scene from a blockbuster movie.

"Son of a muffin top!" he yelled in excitement. "This sumbitch is the real deal!"

Taylor, proud as a peacock and twice as puffed up, sat like a king on his pile of gold coins, under a tiny shaft of white light, shining down from above.

17

The killer ~ Seven Months Earlier

Every head in the room craned forward, and every backside on every seat slid towards the front of its chair.

In the very back of the small, dimly lit bar, sat a small, dimly lit man, alone. He'd squeezed his diminutive frame into the corner, leaving the larger spaces for the fishermen, longshoremen, and assorted rabble-rousers one tends to find in small, dimly lit bars near the shore.

It was his third week in Panama City. He'd come to wrap up the affairs of his recently deceased mother, the wife of an American canal worker who had refused to leave when the famous shipping lane was handed back to the Panamanians. They were a stubborn lot, he and his mother, the latter of which earned a small amount of local fame for throwing rocks at the American forces as they departed the canal garrison, leaving her soon to be dead husband out of work.

The hairy, little man was set to ship out for the States in three days time. But somehow, by the fickle finger of fate, he'd stumbled into this place, and into the spinning of a yarn that would determine the path of the rest of his short life.

On a barstool a scant twelve feet from him sat a large, bearded man, telling a tale of pirates, of settlers lost, of bounty undiscovered, and of a mysterious island that loomed over the room like a phantom.

The man was nearing the end of his circuitous and mysterious tale. A tale of pirates through the ages with names like Don Pedro "Bloody Sword" Bonito, and Old Mac. Of a man named Bartels in the South Pacific who obtained a map from Old Mac himself that supposedly "marked the spot". Of a British navy captain who tried to dynamite areas of the island based on some sort of map he may, or may not, have possessed. Of a burly German named August Gissler who obtained Bartels' map, talked the Costa Ricans into making him Governor of the island, and tried to settle it in search of the treasure supposedly buried there. And of his followers who had lost their minds, and their lives, trying to help him live out his obsessive dream.

The storyteller was nearly done, and about to set the hook.

"And when he died in Germany," he led into the finale, "though he'd found but a few gold coins, Ol' Gissler's last words were these. 'The treasure is on the island, but it will take money and a good deal of effort to unearth it. I have gone through many hardships and dangers, and perhaps shall do so again, but this will not keep me away.'"

The old codger let the room go silent, and then let that silence grow to obesity. Asses shifted in chairs. Glasses scooted from side to side on small, sticky tables. For the better part of a minute, no one spoke. And then, finally, he hit them with the closer.

"Gentlemen, I'm here ta tell you all that I, Freiderich Schaible, am at this very moment in possession of August Gissler's map."

Gasps filled the room, and the little man in back stood up on his chair so he could see over the crowd. But the showman still wasn't quite done.

"Now, I'm old. And worse, I'm near broke. Boys, I hate to say it. I've no choice but to let the map go. For a fair price, that is."

And quite suddenly, the room erupted with laughter. Large men slapped each other on the back and guffawed, sloshing their steins in the old man's general direction. When they'd had their fill of their initial fun, they let him have it.

"You mean the one that *didn't* lead him to the gold?" the first joker blasted him.

"What's to keep us from beatin' it outta ya!" one particularly hairy man near the front yelled.

The old storyteller now took his own turn to laugh. "You fellas don't think I'm stupid enough to carry something that valuable on me person? Not likely!"

More laughter rose as the men continued to write off the prospect of his story even being partially true.

"Do you know how many men scraped offa the boot of the World have pitched this story hereabouts? Huh, do ya!" yelled one, before hurling his glass at the old man's head.

Ducking more rapidly than one might have thought possible, the tale spinner was unwavering.

"And what's the difference between them and me? I knew Gissler's grandson, that's what! I've got photos with him to prove it! And I've got the map, guaranteed! You show me the money, I'll show you the map!"

"Ahhh ya probably drew it this mornin' ya geezer! Git on outta here!"

That last call reverberated and was repeated around the room. More beer was thrown at the old man, until his shirt was soaked in its stinky fluid. Worse yet, once that beer was gone, the now empty glasses came next.

Having had enough, he stepped down from his stool, dodged one last beer stein, dropped a green bill on the bar, and made a quick exit.

Turning the next corner he found he was being followed, and not just by the curs at his feet who smelled his brewy essence wafting on the warm Pacific breeze.

"I told ya!" he yelled at this final tormenter, "I don't have it on me! Now leave me alone!"

The small, dark stalker quickened his step and passed the old man, before stopping cold, right in front of him.

"I'm interested in your proposition, sir," he said.

The old man looked him up and down, which didn't take long.

"You, uh. . . you got money?" He very much doubted so, by virtue of the little man's unkempt, ragged appearance.

The little man nodded. "Inheritance. Just got it. I'll need to see what you're selling, of course. And also any sort of provenance you might have to prove it's real."

"Provenance!" the old man laughed. "Oh, you'll see provenance, sonny. Provenance ta beat the band! But before I take you to where I've got it holed up, how much are we talking here?"

The little man shifted his feet uneasily. "I . . . I don't know. How much do you want for it? Provided, of course, it's all you say it is."

The old man stepped back to kick one of the dogs at his feet, rubbed his hand over his beard, and studied the dirty little fellow.

"What sorta money you got? American?"

The little man nodded.

"Fifty thousand is the price," he blurted out quickly, having been ready for this moment for a long time. "She's worth a damn site more than that. But, it's a hardship sale."

The little man looked down at the ground. Something wiggled in his beard, and he plucked it out and tossed it to the dog the old man had just kicked.

"I don't have that much. Not even close."

The old man picked at his own beard for a moment, suddenly and disturbingly certain that he too felt something moving in the thick tufts of hair on his chin. Satisfied there was nothing alive in there, and disappointed that his figure had so quickly been rebuffed, he nevertheless intended to land a sale, tonight.

"Well then, what *are* ya offerin'!" he commanded. "Don't waste my time, boy. This thing's hotter than a pistol!"

"I've got ten. Ten thousand," came the sheepish reply.

The old man considered for a moment. He looked around. No one else seemed to have taken his story seriously, and this was the third bar he'd tried this week. Beggars, he decided, had to eat too.

"Well then, since you're a fellow American, I'll cut you a break, son. I just want you to find it! Someone has to, I know it's there! But," he paused, "I want you to swear on your mother's grave that you'll give me the other forty thousand once you do."

The little man's face brightened as much as it could through the crust and dirt, and he smiled up at the grizzled old man. "I swear it!"

The old man shook his head.

"No, sonny. I really mean *on* your mother's grave. Where is she buried?"

Five minutes later they hailed a cab, and rode off to see the little man's dearly departed mother about a contract.

Two hours later, the little man saw the map and its provenance, which consisted mainly of the map being very old, bearing August Gissler's signature and a stamp from the Stuttgart Archives, a set of

123

Wikipedia listings on the pirates in question, the aforementioned photo of Schaible with a man who, according to Google images, was indeed Rudolph Gissler, and, the very best piece of proof, a shiny, Spanish gold coin marked with the date 1794.

He was hooked. The next day he handed the very happy old man a stack of bills adding up to $10,000, American.

And three days later, under cover of night, the hairy little man stole a boat from the Panama City harbor, and floated quietly out to sea.

Six months later

It took several months, but he'd finally found it! It hadn't been easy, and he'd had to to constantly outwit both the park rangers who roamed the island, as well as the ever-present scuba divers pointing binoculars inland from their party barges. The latter weren't allowed to set foot on Cocos, but if they saw him they might alert the authorities, and it would be game over.

He lived in the caves directly below where he now stood for all those months. Even the rangers didn't know they existed, nor, did he believe, had the numberless pirates and treasure seekers who visited this emerald isle of the Pacific over the centuries. He stumbled on the caves by accident when his boat, which he had feverishly tried to hide from all of the above, became entrenched in a thick mass of vines and bushy growth on the wilder side of the island, near Cape Discovery.

A storm had thrown his skiff into a cliff wall that was covered with a massive crop of thick vines like none other on the island, and when the tide dropped to its lowest point, those vines tangled around his boat and suspended it eight feet in the air. He was frantic, imagining his precious transport being dashed upon the rocks and destroyed should that foliage suddenly give way. It was not just his only means of escape, but also his only means of transporting the treasure, should he somehow find it. Peering over the side he moaned out loud when he saw that the rocks below, uncovered by the angry tide, were very sharp indeed.

Grabbing the vines in his tiny fists, he climbed up into their massive, dangling roots, trying to find a way through them to solid land to sit the storm out. But as he did, his foot punched through the back side of a mat of green leaves and hit empty air. He kicked again, yet still could find no purchase. Holding tightly to a giant root with one hand, he reached for the trusty blade that was always at his side, and swung it against the leaves with all his might. But their solidity proved an illusion, and they gave way so quickly that the knife flew right out of his hand. Yet instead of being upset at its loss, he was overjoyed to hear it clatter to a stop a moment later, on what sounded like solid rock.

He plied the thick leaves out of the way with his hands until he too dropped onto terra firma. Quite unexpectedly he'd found himself in a huge cavern, large enough to fit his boat three times over. Over the next two days he cleared the brush just enough so that, on high tide of the third day, he floated his boat right into the cave, quickly covering the hole behind him before anyone was the wiser.

Now, he stood far above that cave on the western ridge of Mt Iglesias, crouching with his eyes to the ground, walking ever so carefully. He scanned the earth for a sight of the tip of a long stick he'd shoved up through a tiny crack in the ceiling of a lava chamber, a chamber he believed would make the perfect hiding place for the treasure, which now really was *his treasure.* Research back on the mainland, a leap of faith with ten thousand dollars, brutal digging, chopping, and route finding here on Cocos had finally paid off. The last piece was the brilliant idea he'd had when he came across this little room with a beach at one end, hidden in a nearly impossible to find portion of the massive cave system under Cocos.

Elated with the sheer mysteriousness of the room itself, he discovered when his light suddenly, and quite alarmingly, flashed off for a brief moment (only a battery connection, thank God!), that there was a shaft of light from above piercing the darkness of the cave.

And now above it, seeing his stick standing out against the black, barren, lava strewn ridge top, he was about to put his plan into action. Instead of trying to pull it up, he shoved the stick back down through the hole. Moving with greedy speed, he peeked around to be sure he wasn't being watched, and then yanked off his backpack and opened it wide.

Shiny, beautiful gold coins glowed up at him in the tropical Sun. He grabbed one, kissed it, and then dropped it through the hole where his stick had just been. Listening carefully, he happily heard it thud on the ground some twenty feet below.

Smiling like no one who'd ever met him would have thought he could, he did the same with the rest of the little golden pieces of freedom, pirate booty from an age long gone by, kissing each one before it fell. He would perform the same ritual with each and every one of his coins, all nine thousand of them, over the next several weeks.

The last one of this first batch safely pounded home below, landing with a "clink" this time, instead of a "thud".

His smile shone brightly against the dark lava landscape. Taking a moment, he crossed his chest to God, blew a last kiss to the sky, grabbed his backpack, and went back for more.

"Fort fuckin' Knox!" he yelled as loud as he dared.

18

Day 8- Return to The Game

When Danielle, the last one to make the swim, finally emerged from the water, the little cavern was about as full of people as it could possibly be without someone getting hurt. Nearly levitating out of the pond with newfound energy, she, like the rest, immediately grabbed a handful of gold coins and ran them through her fingers.

"My God. It's true…"

It was as if they were five years old and had just entered Disneyland for the very first time. Cavorting in childlike wonder throughout the small chamber, they played in the water and threw coins at each other, giggling and enjoying a sober moment together for the first time in a long time. Even Old Joe forgot the past few days for a moment, greedily pacing off the pile to map out just how much gold was actually there. Laughing like a little boy, he eventually gave up, deciding there was a hell of a lot and who really gave a rip after that.

Taylor, satisfied in the moment but still scheming, stepped back and eyed the group. He watched the lusty way they caressed the gold, tasted it, held it to their cheeks. He observed them playing, tinkering, and rolling in the coins. He wanted them to fill their souls with the lust for gold. To get drunk on the greed he'd lived with for so long. Greed that intensified in a major way once he'd seen the same pile. Greed that led him to mislead everyone without hesitation, and occasionally even root for their permanent removal from the island.

His island. He wondered if the killer felt the same way, shortly before his death. It seemed to Taylor that the next person in line for this throne of gold was the true owner of Cocos— anyone else was just renting.

"Man, how do we even value this thing?" Jason peered out of the water like a hippopotamus, blowing bubbles as he spoke.

"There's a shitload of coins here, that's for sure," Randy said, "thousands. Does it really matter? It's so much!"

"We've got to get it out of here first," the ever-practical Susan spoke up. "I guess that means handful by handful, swimming out the way we came."

"Yeah, been thinking about that," Taylor rose from his stupor and stepped forward. "We'll start a chain, one person swimming out with a bagful, handing it on to the next, then the next, and so on."

"Man, that's gonna take a long freaking time," Randy said doubtfully.

"Right," Taylor nodded, "and we've only got seven days."

Alone, high on the corner of the pile, Ricardo let out a softly maniacal cackle as the others debated what he saw as an instantly defunct plan. "C'mon man!" he yelled at Taylor with a grin, "You know we got a better way! One we brought with us."

Taylor shook his head nervously, giving Ricardo the side eye. "That wall is a good six feet thick. No way that works. Way too thick, and not only that, no way we want to take a chance on accidentally sealing it off for good."

Ricardo cackled again, visibly drunk on the golden vapors in the room.

"I'm not talking about the wall, man! Just look up."

He pointed to a small hole in the ceiling directly above the pile, his arms jostled by the players still goofing off around him.

Taylor gazed at the tiny shaft of light above the pile of gold. Only about the size of a silver dollar, he suddenly realized its potential to change everything

"Holy shit, you're right! We can dynamite that hole out, and raise the treasure out by bucketfuls instead of hauling it the long way! Genius!"

Susan stared at the two excited men like they were circus monkeys. "What? You guys brought dynamite? Here?"

128

"You gotta be kiddin' me!" Malik yelled. Visibly angry at the gall of the two conspirators, truth be told, he was even more pissed off he'd been left out of the plan to begin with. "I can't believe you risked everyone's safety for a god damned treasure hunt!"

Had he actually been in on the plan, though, the truth was that he would have gladly carted dynamite through a day care center to get to this spot.

"Well, now aren't you glad we did! Again, how about a little gratitude?" Taylor chided. It was bad enough he'd have to share, but to share with an ungrateful jerk? Or twelve of them, as the case was?

"*Gratitude?*" Kinnary took her turn. "We're supposed to be grateful you could have killed us? Could have sunk the ship we came in on? Could have blown up our camp? What if the killer found it and used it on us?"

"You really are an unprecedented bastard, Taylor. Really." Danielle shook her head in derision. Of course, she wasn't the least bit surprised, and couldn't even muster enough emotion to raise her voice.

"Ok, ok, I get it! Shit on Taylor time is here again! Hallelujah! All right everybody, dump all you want, but save some of your shit throwing for Ricardo, too. And when you're done, we can get moving on this thing. The boat gets here in seven days, and you can all pussyfoot around and piss and moan, but that won't get this gold where we need it to go."

"What if the whole roof collapses?" Susan asked the obvious question.

"Lady, that there is solid lava," Old Joe answered, "we'll be lucky if we can even crack 'er. Ain't no chance of it fallin' in." Coming from Joe, that settled the question as far as all were concerned.

Randy, ignoring the emotional bullshit and instead focusing on the task at hand, interjected.

"Which brings up another problem. How the hell do we get the gold out of here, and onto the boat? I mean, this is a lot of weight. A good ton or so. Did you evil twins have a plan for that?"

Ricardo spoke as his eyes scanned the hole above for clues as to how much wiggle room it had, and how strong it really was.

"Not really. Ideas... yes. Plans...no. We thought we might ditch some of the construction gear for the challenges, fill those boxes and tubes with the coins. Or, like Taylor said last night, we just figured we'd stash it and come back later."

"No goddamn way we're doing that now," Jason Oliver stepped out of the water, "No offense," he gazed around at the others, "But I don't trust a single solitary one of you at this point. Just takes one asshole to charter a boat back before the rest, and poof!"

"He's right. I don't trust anybody either" Matthew added, a bit out of character.

"Et tu, Matthew?" Susan replied, shaking her head. "My, how the holy have fallen."

"This is gold, Susan. Not chocolate Hanukkah coins. You gonna tell me *you* trust the rest of these guys?"

Susan smirked, "Hell no. Just surprised the Angel of Execution Island has joined us all down here on Earth, that's all." She reached over and patted his still bleeding head, adding "Welcome to my World, Wonder Boy!"

"There's still one more little problem here nobody has mentioned," Randy continued to plan a step ahead, "Let's say we blow the hole and the get the coins out. Then we figure out how to get them on the boat and back to the mainland without having to share it with a bunch of sailors or laborers on the docks, should one of the boxes crack open. We still have to get it back home after that, and there's no way Customs is going to miss this much gold. No freaking way."

"Ricardo?" Taylor smiled.

The sandman stepped down from his perch on top of the pile where he'd been assessing the ceiling. His eyes glowed with wild hopefulness, tinted with a bit of reckless malice.

"Doesn't anybody wonder why our super selfish friend Taylor actually included *me* in this little caper and *no one* else? Anybody?"

"I sure as shit do," Malik chortled.

"Well," he grinned like the Cheshire Cat, "as it turns out, I happen to be a Panamanian citizen. And Panama is the next little backwater below Costa Rica, no? Why don't you take it from here, Boss."

"Panamanian banks." Taylor folded his arms confidently across his chest and exhaled. "Ricardo can get us across the border, we grease some palms, and then we deposit the money in a loose

Panamanian bank. That way we can access it from anywhere, without raising suspicion."

"Everybody there is on the graft," Ricardo continued the tale. "The money train. The banks operate outside international norms, and money laundering is common. Trust me, it's taken care of."

"Nice and neat," Susan agreed. "Hard to believe you two came up with it."

"Beautiful, just beautiful," Jason added, "Now, if we're done with logistics, I vote we get out of this little hole and get to work. Get back to camp and start collecting gear. Wheelbarrows, shovels, and this fancy-assed, secret dynamite stash."

"Yup, let's move," Joe waded into the water, preparing himself for another unpleasant swim. At least this time he knew where he was going.

But Taylor wasn't quite ready to go. No, he thought, it was time for a test of this new partnership.

"We'll do that, but first, let's have a little chat. That's a lot of gold, isn't it?"

The stench of an obvious Taylor caper suddenly filled the room, and while everyone could smell it, no one spoke. Instead they waited with dread tinted glares pointed nervously in his general direction.

"And I want to be fair about this, but when you come to think of it, it's not *that* much, is it? I mean, split thirteen ways?"

"Get on with it, Taylor," Susan tapped her foot impatiently on the sand.

"Well," he began his pitch with his best facial imitation of a weasel as he pointed at the wall they were about to swim under. "There are three guys out there right now who have no idea how much is here. If we work quickly, we could hide a whole shit load of it where they can't find it. Bury it under the sand in the water or something. Then at night, we come back, and we add it to our own portions. In our personal belongings or something. Nobody knows, and nobody is hurt."

Jason and Susan quickly exchanged unspoken glances, before sharing them with Malik. Those were the easy sales. That made 5 probable conspirators, with Ricardo and Taylor. But there were four goodie goodie types left and that meant…

131

"Shut the hell up, Taylor. We're not screwing anybody," Matthew said firmly.

"Well, well," Susan teased, "looks like the Angel hasn't fallen *that* far, now has he?"

"Shut up, Susan," Kinnary shot her a look as she patted Matthew on the back, "I'm with you."

"Me too, Ol' Boy," Joe nodded. "Me too. Ain't no cheatin' gonna happen on my watch."

"Well now," Malik smiled a knowing, crazy grin, "that's all nice and good, ain't it Country Boy? But there's a whole lotta them thar days left until that boat a come' a slidin' in, now ain't thar?"

The four dark siders tried to hold back twisted grins, succeeding only to varying degrees. But the other four were quickly enraged.

"Is that a threat, you piece of shit?" Danielle spit at Malik.

"Boy," Joe stuck his arm in front of her and took a step forward, "ya come after me, ya better pack a lunch, 'cause you're gonna be there *all god damn day.*"

Taylor wisely realized the test was over, and jumped back into the role of statesman.

"Now, now! Come on! Nobody is threatening anybody here— totally out of line, Malik! Forget I said anything about it. You're right, Matthew, the whole thing should be fair and square. I just got a little gold fever, that's all," he paused to glare at Malik, "and apparently I'm not the only one. Besides, no way it would ever work. Somebody would get wind of it, and then all hell would break loose."

"All hell," repeated Malik, glittering gold flashing in his eyes.

Thirty minutes later they were topside, heading back to camp, with none of the three outsiders wise to the fact that they had nearly become junior shareholders in the plot to raid Cocos Island.

19

Malik ~ The Nineties

"Have you seen the sheets yet?" she asked.

"No," Malik suddenly felt a lump in his throat, "are they up?" He hadn't eaten anything today and had barely spoken to anyone, not even to Lindsay, his roommate. Too much hung in the balance.

"Yep, just heard from Delia. They're posted. She got a PA job."

Malik froze. "She say anything about me?"

Lindsay shook her head. "Nah, but I didn't get jack shit, thanks for asking!"

Malik didn't waste one single second on soothing her, but instead turned on his heels, bolted out the door, ran from the apartment, and hit the street.

He jogged to the bus stop and took his place in the queue. Anticipation tore through his brain. He wasn't surprised Lindsay hadn't gotten anything. He loved his friend, but she was nothing special. In a town where you had to shine to be noticed, her bulb was barely lit. She was average at best, and that wouldn't get you a job on a production in these parts, no way.

But Malik was different. He was at the top of his graduating cinematography class. In fact, he *was* the top. He was born to be a director of photography, if ever anyone was. The final project he worked on before graduation elicited a standing ovation, and special mention was made of his work with the camera by the department's judges.

Malik was meant to be behind the lens, and today, he fully expected, would be the start of that life.

The bus finally came and he floated onto it. Twenty minutes later, after chewing his nails to the core, he arrived at the USC campus. As part of the graduating class, he was eligible to be chosen to work on a real, low budget, three million dollar film being made with a crew of mostly graduates from his class. It was a big reason USC was such a great place to get a film education, other than the obvious possibilities brought about by its location. Placement in the industry was a little bit easier with a degree from the home of the Trojans. Even getting a job as an assistant DP would be tough in the initial stages, but with this one he'd go straight to the big chair, being able to put his own stamp on a real film. No matter it was only a three million dollar budget.

And the head of the department told Malik he would be getting his recommendation for the job, virtually guaranteeing it was his.

He sprinted to the School of Cinematic Arts, and through its open corridors to the Production Division bulletin board. Several other students he recognized were milling about, chatting about their good, or bad, luck. He saw Professor Devlin and beamed a huge smile at him. His day had come.

But Professor Devlin's own smile slipped away as soon as he made eye contact, and Malik's heart sank.

It couldn't be.

The professor stepped through a crowd of students and over to him, putting a hand on his shoulder.

"Malik. I... I'm sorry. They went another way. I don't know what to say."

Malik knew exactly what to say. Nothing. His throat closed, his tongue swole up to fill his mouth, and no words would come.

"Look, I gave them my strongest possible recommendation. I really did. I don't know why they chose Walter, but I promise I'll get on the phone tomorrow and make some calls. We'll get you something. This production isn't worthy of your skills, anyway."

Walter? Fucking Walter Thurman? Over him? It couldn't be. They were two totally different classes of camera jockeys. Thurman had no inventive quality whatsoever to his work. What were they shooting, a documentary?

"Walter? Really?" he croaked.

Professor Devlin shook his head. "I know. Makes no sense to me, either. But son, you have a seriously bright future in this business. This *craft*. Walter's going to be shooting tv commercials in ten years when you pick up your first Academy Award. Just hang in there. This is an anomaly, I assure you."

But Malik was distraught. His brain had shut out any and all sound. He no longer heard Professor D. He no longer heard either the jubilant nor whining students gathered around him.

Malik was enraged. He turned and immediately left the building. He needed closure on this, and he needed it now. He'd told his parents, his friends, his erstwhile colleagues in the program that he was a lock for his first job as a DP. And now somehow, he wasn't.

He walked back to the bus stop, fuming. He boarded the 913 this time, not headed for home, but for Burbank, the home of Sizzlepic films.

On the short ride to Burbank he tried to calm himself. He wanted to know why the choice had been made, but he dared not make a scene. Hollywood, and by association, Burbank, was a small town, and if he blew his top and flipped out on a producer before he even had his first job? Well, he could be sure he wouldn't be getting even an assistant DP job anytime soon. And then, like so many before him, he'd end up shooting porn in the Valley.

The bus arrived in downtown Burbank and Malik double checked the address on the submission form. He got off at Magnolia and walked three blocks to the building where the office of Sizzlepic sat amongst other fly by nights, in shabby suite 314.

"May I help you?" asked the receptionist, an elderly hispanic woman. Her eyes were glued to a small, portable tv on the desk in front of her.

"I'm here to see Jonathan Lindner. He's expecting me."

She looked up at him with doubtful eyes.

"And you are?"

Malik thought quickly, realizing there was no way some shmuck, Burbank, low budget producer was going to meet with the guy he just screwed out of a job, unless he had a death wish. People had killed for far less in this town.

135

"Walter Thurman, USC."

The receptionist dropped her eyes and hit a button on her intercom. A moment later, Malik was ushered into the inner sanctum.

Lindner had his back to the door, but spun in his chair when he heard it close.

"Hey, Walter! Glad you're here, are you ready to… Hey! What the fuck, kid! What are *you* doing here?"

Malik was choked up again, but managed to squeak out a few words. "Mr. Lindner, I'm sorry for the subterfuge, but I knew you probably wouldn't see me."

Lindner was livid. "Subterfuge! What are you, a fucking librarian? Why don't you call it what it is, kid. It's a lie. You told a fucking lie."

Unbeknownst to Malik, Lindner's right hand was resting on the drawer where he kept his pistol, just for little pissants like this one.

"No, no, I'm sorry. I just didn't see any other way. I apologize, really."

"Good, then get the hell outta here, ok? I got shit to do."

Malik nodded his head, shuffling his feet. "I will, I will. I just need to know, sir. Sir, why exactly *did* you pick Walter Thurman over me? I mean, Professor Devlin said he gave you his highest recommendation."

Lindner's hand relaxed and fell back into his lap.

"And he did. You can rest assured that he did do just that. But in the end, you weren't right for the film. That's all, kid. Look, you're talented. You won't have any trouble getting something. Just persevere. That's free advice to you, since you came all the way down here. Talent is fine, but in this town, it's all perseverance. And frankly, you showed some today. I'll make a note of it."

Malik wasn't buying it.

"Thanks. But can you tell me *why* I wasn't right for your film?"

Lindner shifted in his chair. This is where things could get sticky, he knew well from previous experience.

"You're a little too good. Thurman, he's more, oh, I don't know. Workman-like. No big flourishes, just a blue collar type of straight ahead, right at you, no false moves kind of DP. And that's what we're looking for on this particular film."

Malik smiled. "I can do that, you know. I've shot a lot of simple, straightforward stories. Professor D can vouch…"

"Look, kid, not this time, ok? You just don't have the sort of makeup we're going for. This thing's going to play heavily in Scandinavia. We need that sort of hand at the wheel. Thurman fit the bill."

Malik's blood began to churn. It was just as he'd thought.

He stepped closer and looked down at Lindner, heat pouring from his eyes. Lindner's hand shot back to his gun drawer, opening it just a crack.

"It's because I'm black. Just say it."

"No, I did *not* say that. I did not fucking say that. I said we need a different sort of hand at the wheel. Don't put words in my mouth! And don't be so god damned sensitive."

"But that *is* what you meant, right?"

Malik was starting to look a bit too menacing for the producer's tastes. Now he slipped his hand *inside* the drawer, wrapping it around the hilt of his .45.

"Kid, you've got ten seconds to get out of here. One."

"You know," Malik began to rant, the rage of the ages creeping into his forehead, "we were told this sort of shit doesn't happen in this town anymore!"

"Two."

"That creeps like you don't exist anymore. The whole, 'Jews keeping the blacks down' shit."

"Three. Back up, kid. Now."

"But it does! You're sitting right here. A guy in a leisure suit, pushing a black kid back to the back of the line!"

"Four."

"Well, I've got news for you! I'm gonna file a grievance with the PGA."

"On what grounds? You've got nothing. I didn't say what you think I said. And you know what, I'm skipping five. Six!"

"Being black is *not* a handicap!"

"Seven, and who the hell said it was? Jesus, it got you into USC, right? I'd say that's the opposite of a handicap!"

"What? You think I got into USC because I'm black?"

"Eight, and no, I think a lot of white kids, who may have been better than you on paper, *didn't* get into USC because you're black!

137

Now I am warning you, at nine this gun comes out of my drawer, and you better be the fuck outta here before I get to 10!"

Malik stared. 1995, and this shit was still going on. In an industry that could be counted as one of the most progressive in the country. He was out of words. And now, he was out of time.

"Nine you little prick! Now get out!"

Lindner drew the gun from the drawer and pointed it across the desk. Instinct finally engaged, and Malik ran out of the office, out the front door, down the stairs and onto Magnolia avenue. And he kept running.

Four blocks later he collapsed on a bus bench and began to cry. He cried because he was helpless, cried because he was angry, cried because he would look like a fool when he told everyone he knew that he'd been wrong about the job, and that he'd have to get back in line like any other graduate. In fact, if other producers out there were like this asshole, he'd have to get in the *back* of the line.

Malik had done bad things before, and the only thing that kept him from jumping across the desk at that racist jerk was the gun. Guns he respected. He'd grown up just blocks from USC in Inglewood, and had known too many friends that hadn't respected them. But he also wasn't about to roll over. There was a principle, and Malik Jones was a man of principle.

He got to his feet and found a pay phone. On the other end, a familiar voice answered.

"Who dis?"

"Malik."

"Malik? Who da fuck Malik?"

"Man, fuck you, man. You know who da fuck Malik. Asshole."

The voice broke into laughter. "Awwww, *dat* Malik! Man, where you been! Ain't seen you in a year or mo'. And why da fuck you callin' me now, Boy?"

"I need something. Something you can do for me. I can't touch this myself."

There was a pause.

"Ok, Mister Malik done lost my number 'til his fool ass done *need* somethin'. Why you think I'm gon' help?"

"'Cause I got money."

The pause was shorter this time. "Well then, shiiiit. What you need, my brotha?"

Jonathan Lindner left the office, gun lodged in his waistband, heading for his leased Jaguar XK. It had been a screwy day, what with that kid almost taking one in the chest, right in his office. But he'd met with the crew of the new picture that afternoon, and everything was on track. These kids, they kissed his ass like he was the goddamn Lion King, like this was a cherry job. But what they didn't know was that he was the one that should be thanking them. Hiring college kids would save him a shit pot of money on this one. Which was good, because it was headed straight to the international markets, do not pass go. And it would turn a profit, much of it thanks to them.

Screw that artsy little prick!

He hit the clicker and heard his car beep. Strolling over to it, he stuck his key in the door, and was instantly knocked to the ground from behind.

"Well now! Looky here, boy! Man's done brought us a car!"

His eyes fogged over, and he felt a set of very strong hands holding him down, while another set went through his pockets.

"Mother fucker!" the voice yelled as he felt his gun being ripped from his pants. "Nice gun, hombre! I'll be takin' that."

Then went his wallet. Then an envelope stuffed with five hundred new bills that he was on his way to deliver to the local Teamsters boss, incentive to ignore the illegal laborers he'd hired on another low budget production he was working.

The big hands rolled him over, and he saw his two attackers. To his extreme chagrin, neither of them was that god damn kid from today. He was so hoping to blackball that bastard.

Then came the blows.

The two men kicked, punched, and rolled Lindner across the pavement for several minutes, before taking off in his Jaguar for some late night fun. When they'd had their fill, they ditched it off a cliff up on Mulholland.

Malik watched all of this from across the street, tucked in behind a row of cars in a parking lot. He smiled as Lindner was beaten, bloodied, and then left to swim in his own fluids as his two old friends did exactly as he had asked.

And as he left, walking a couple dozen blocks to Cahuenga before catching a bus home, he felt better.

But not nearly as good as he would have felt, had his own fists been handing out the beating. And it was not the last time Malik Jones would feel such powerlessness in the face of the Hollywood establishment.

Lucky for him, though, he had friends in low places.

20

Day 9 ~ Fall Down, Go Boom

The next morning, Taylor loomed over the hole with a single stick of dynamite, his eyes blazing in the tropical sunlight. He took that stick, bent down to the ground, and wedged it into the hole. Pulling a lighter from a pocket in his trademark expedition vest, he lit the fuse and sprinted back down the hill to where a small group huddled, waiting for the bang.

A moment later it came, and when the dynamite exploded a hard, black rain showered them with tiny bits of very sharp rock. Dust filled the air and darkened the sun, but when it cleared, several sets of feet scampered furiously across the ridge to see what had become of the killer's piggy bank.

It was wider, but not by much. The formerly dollar sized hole was now about the size of an average donut. They would be able to get coins through it, but only at the rate of a few at a time. Still, it was an improvement.

"More dynamite?" Darius more spoke than asked.

"More dynamite," Taylor smiled, waving to Ricardo to bring it.

"Two sticks!" he yelled across the hillside, "we've got a bigger hole now!"

Ricardo brought the sticks, and quickly scampered back down the ridge. Taylor wedged the next two into the donut, lit one, and again ran back down the hill.

This explosion was louder, the dust was thicker, and the black rain was heavier.

"Shit!" Kinnary squealed, a hot piece of lava slamming into her leg and tearing a tiny hole that immediately began to bleed. The rest covered themselves as best they could, but this time the radius was twice as wide, and the sharp chunks that flew through the moist island air were twice as big.

"Buenos noches!" marveled Ricardo, standing tall amidst the falling rock, the whole adventure juicing him up to another level of crazy.

"Jesus Christ!" Taylor yelped as he dove under a tarp, which was quickly burned full of holes by the artificially reheated black lava. When the hard rain finally ended, the Castaways lifted themselves slowly and cautiously off the ground, like drowned rats emerging from a flood. Taylor ran to the hole and saw, not surprisingly, that it was now a mere two donuts wide.

Franklin strolled to the edge to have a look.

"Apple fritter," he commented before heading back to help the mildly wounded.

"That's it, I'm out!" Danielle announced with the back of her hand, her feet already winding down the well worn path back to camp. Being filled with black buckshot was just not part of the deal she had agreed to.

Matthew and Old Joe wrapped Kinnary's leg, and helped her hobble down the path as well.

"So, a couple things are apparent," Franklin, the only one with any kind of experience with dynamite, explained. "First, we need some kind of cover. Hard, firm cover. Second, this is gonna take a while."

"How big does it need to be in order to get the gold out?" Taylor wondered, wiping black dust from his eyes.

"Dunno," Franklin replied, "probably big enough to get a five gallon bucket through. So, maybe 8, 10 times bigger."

"Well, damn me all to hell," Malik sighed to the sky. "That is gonna take a while."

"I agree," Carl jeered, "Damn you all to hell, Malik."

"Enough, Beavis and Butthead," Taylor laughed. "Let's head back to camp. We'll get more dynamite . . . A lot more, I guess. And we'll grab some wood to make a shelter with."

Falling in line behind the others on the trail, they returned hours later with sheets of plywood. Under Franklin's supervision they quickly constructed a military style, pill box enclosure. For the rest of the day, Taylor, Franklin, Darius, Matthew, Ricardo, or Malik would pack the hole, first with dried palm leaves so the dynamite would stay in place in the growing void, and then slip in the TNT, now up to three sticks at a time, light it, and run like the dickens back to the box. Towards the end of the day, Matthew proved to be the only one fast enough to keep making the run to the little box, about a hundred feet away.

Just before dusk, one last explosion ripped away a final, piercing point of rock, and the six men gathered around the hole.

"That looks like a bucket to me!" Franklin proclaimed.

"Yup," Old Joe returned. He'd spent most of the day watching, lacking the speed to run back to the pill box.

Taylor gazed around the hole at his new team, for the first time feeling grateful they were there.

"Gentlemen," he spread his arms in a grand gesture, "that was some fine work! Couldn't have done it without you!"

"Yeah," Darius laughed, "but you'd have tried!" For a moment, they laughed together, each man actually finding himself not hating Taylor.

They laughed, but Old Joe thought it strangely out of character that Taylor was laughing too, at his own expense. Was he softening them up for something new he was cooking, or was it legit? He couldn't tell.

Taylor was tricky that way.

"All righty then!" the host continued, arms held to the sky like he was the Emperor of Cocos Island, "Tomorrow we feast!"

That night, Danielle and Susan, both insomniacs on or off the island, experienced something similar, though separately.

Danielle, sleeping at the jungle's edge with a group that included Kinnary, Matthew, Franklin, and Darius, heard the sound of foot falls at about three in the morning. She rose and looked around, but couldn't see a single thing in the dark, moonless sky. Sleepy though sleepless, she thought no more of it and tried yet again to fall asleep.

Susan also heard something that she assumed was the door of the quonset hut opening and then, minutes later, closing. But she couldn't be sure, as she and her group Jason Oliver, Randy, and the newest member of the dark siders, Malik, were even closer to the crashing ocean waves.

The camera jockey had that night stepped away from the crew, choosing sides in the growing battle for which group might successfully screw the others out of their loot. Still angry that he'd been left out of the original plan, he turned sour. Then, once his eyes had met the treasure, greed crept into his mind and took root.

Gold fever had come to Execution Island, its pernicious fumes drifting amongst the competitors like an airborne virus.

Malik and Carl had never been close to begin with. Besides Old Joe, Carl was the odd man out on the island simply due to his age. And much like Joe, he preferred to remain self reliant and neutral. Both men suffered from old codger syndrome.

Noting that Malik wasn't in his sleeping bag, Susan thought no more of it, and put her head back down.

Old Joe slept peacefully in his tree, far from the others as might be expected of an old codger. He had no trouble sleeping, thanks to the soft roar of the waterfall below him. Like a running fan, or wind in the trees, it was the kind of sound that rocked a man's mind to sleep no matter what thoughts happened to run through it at that moment. His bow and arrows lay by his side, just in case some wayward goldbug tried to take one more stakeholder out of the picture.

Not that he'd be their first choice, he figured.

Carl, Taylor, and Ricardo were tired. They'd done much of the work during the day, and none of them had Matthew's youthful endurance. Men of a certain age, they snored like hibernating bears.

Those snores were so loud, in fact, that not one of them heard the sound of approaching feet, the light of a match, or the creak of the cabin door as it opened.

But one of them, Carl, did manage to barely crack his eyes open as that swinging door began to close. His sleep blurred eyes were instantly drawn to the floor between their bunks, where something hissed and glowed mysteriously.

He wiped his eyes as the door banged closed hard before bouncing back open briefly as such doors tend to do, and was surprised to catch the briefest glimpse of someone he recognized.

"Hey, what the…"

Old Joe bolted instantly upright at the shocking roar of the explosion. Flames leapt into the sky from the direction of the beach, fiery debris raining down as far as he could see. A golden orange glow lit up the treetops like the brightest sunset, and through their branches he saw people scurrying to avoid falling chunks of flaming cabin.

Grabbing his weapons, Joe flew down the rope he called his hillbilly elevator. Stumbling on river rocks at the bottom, he realized he forgot his shoes, but teetered on into the night nonetheless, heading towards that ball of flame on the beach.

Danielle was the first beach goer to leap from the ground and run towards the water. She didn't know exactly where the sound had come from, but her mind screamed "flight!", and she knew she had to run. Seeing her in the glow, the others in her group quickly followed, soon reaching the water's edge and relative safety.

Chunks of burning debris fell upon them as they ran. Hair singed and stunk like burning rubber while tiny bonfires littered the sand, adding an eerie, 'vacation in hell' look to the beach.

Old Joe burst from the jungle and instantly ducked to avoid being hit by a fiery wad. Turning towards the inferno, his eyes instinctively closed to protect themselves from the heat and the glare. But before they did, he realized that the radio cabin was gone. Anyone or anything inside had been turned to powder, right along with the cabin itself.

The quonset hut, which was metal, had survived, but burning debris had set the second cabin alight, and there was no saving it out here where the nearest hydrant was a thousand miles away.

Old Joe gathered himself, jogged slowly down the beach as the debris fall ceased, and walked right into a screaming match.

"You lying motherfucker!" Susan faced Malik with her finger in his face, "you *weren't* there! I wasn't asleep, I heard a sound, and you, you weren't there! I saw your empty sleeping bag!"

Malik was attempting rather poorly to defend himself, and already wore not only the sizable hands of Darius and Franklin on opposite shoulders, but also the angry glares of the strangely unified group gathered around him.

"I took a piss, ok! Shit, I didn't do nothin'! Just took a leak!"

"You piece of shit!" Matthew jabbed him with a stick, spittle flying from his gaping mouth, "*Nobody* believes you, man. Nobody!

You want us to believe you *just happened* to get back thirty seconds after the hut blew sky high? And you *just happened* to be away from camp, right before that!"

Malik saw the writing on the wall, and was growing frantic. "Look, you guys, I know how it looks. C'mon now, Danielle... Kinnary... Joe! You know I wouldn't do this!"

Old Joe shook his head, a thin, knowing grin spreading over his face. "No? You, the *same* sumbitch threatened me yesterday? Somethin' 'bout there bein' a lotta time left?"

"Joe! That was a joke! I was just messin' with you, man!"

Danielle stood with her arms folded across her chest, a severe look on her already severe face. "That was not a joke, asshole! Nobody took it that way, and you know god damn well you meant it."

Malik's mind roiled. "Gold fever, man. It wasn't me! Sure, it was a jab, but…"

Joe turned, lit his headlamp, and walked into the jungle. Crouching low, he scanned the ground.

"No way we can sleep with this piece of shit still alive." Darius spoke dark words that others merely thought.

Gold fever had, for the moment at least, been replaced by paranoia.

"And what the hell does that mean?" Malik wailed, jerking free of Darius' grip for a moment before being shoved down hard by Franklin on the other side.

"You're a murderer," Susan glared at him, "and I think we've proven that we don't put up with murderers here."

"You're kidding, right? I mean, c'mon guys. I *really* didn't do it! Swear to God! I didn't do it!"

Franklin looked across Malik's pounding chest at Darius, mouthed a word, and received a nod in reply.

"Cliff."

They lifted Malik and slammed him face down in the sand. Darius twisted the prisoner's arms behind him while Franklin held him steady.

"Matthew! Rope!"

Matthew obliged, once again blurring the line between good guy and bad. Yanking the cord from his belt, he whipped it around

Malik's arms, cranking it down tightly until it bit into his dark skin. Blood seeped out around the overly tight binding.

"No fuckin' way! No way!" Malik screamed into the sand, his voice muffled by the coarseness of it on his tongue, and in his throat.

The two big men lifted him up again and began to walk quickly up the beach, heading for the path to Gissler's cave, and more precisely, to thousands of miles of empty ocean air just beyond it.

They were nearly to the trail, the others trailing dutifully behind, when they heard a hoarse voice rising behind them.

"*Stop*! He didn't do it!"

Franklin and Darius spun to see Old Joe running up the beach, headlamp bobbing to and fro with each step.

"Sumbitch didn't do it!" he repeated as he came to a stop, slipped around behind Malik, and cut him free.

But the two big men did not let go.

"Explain, fast!" Darius breathed heavily, eyes reflecting the orange flame of the burning cabins, now mostly piles of rubble and blackened timber.

"I follered his tracks. Right to a fresh, steamin' wet mess. He's tellin' the truth. He was takin' a leak. Wadn't no tracks from there towards the cabins, neither."

Malik twisted free, pushing off his captors.

"Get the hell off me! See, I told you, I told *all* of you!"

Old Joe's machete was still in the "I will cut you" position. And he kept it out, rotating to face each Castaway in turn. Their faces glowed with hatred, even those of Kinnary and Danielle, women he once counted on to be level headed and kind.

No more would Old Joe make the mistake of trusting them to do the right thing. Any of them.

"Y'all were 'bout ta kill a man, judge and jury, with no ev'dence at'all! What the hell does that say 'bout ya? Bunch a sorry sacks a shit, 'fya ask me. God damn gold fever, that's what it is!"

"Don't you dare judge us, Joe!" Susan sneered, pointing to the flaming shacks. "We just saw three of us murdered in their sleep! And not only was this asshole not in his bed when that thing blew up, he lied and said he was!"

"That's because I knew you psychos would hang me if I said I was gone. And guess what?" he glared at them, his fear replaced by rage, "What did you do!"

147

"Shut up, Malik," Matthew spoke, "Nobody trusts you. Not now, not ever." A look of mob rage covered his face like no one would have believed he could muster.

"Ya know what?" Old Joe finished with disgust, "Murderers don't scare me all that much. But y'all? Y'all scare me! And I don't scare easily! Now good frickin' night! Anybody comes within twenty feet of my tree, ya get three or four o' these," he shook the arrows in his fist, "fer yer trouble!"

Old Joe stormed off to the jungle, while the others just stood frozen, gazing at each other, suddenly noticing the changes in the people around them. Changes that were permanent, and deep.

But a few minutes later, they dispersed back to their two camps, the once flaming cabins smoldering in ruins like charcoal briquets. Malik, stung bitterly by their betrayal, grabbed his bed and canteen and stormed off in the direction of Gissler's cave.

"The cave is mine!" he screamed as loud as he could so the whole beach could hear him, "You want to come get me? I hope you try. I really do!"

Averting their eyes, the Castaways pretended he didn't exist. Joe's findings aside, no one could be sure he hadn't really done it. Could he have peed and then hiked through the jungle to the cabins and blown them up, so as not to trek across the sand, open to the view of anyone awake?

He certainly could have.

Back in the relative serenity of their camp, Jason Oliver sat down on a stump between Randy and Susan, staring into the fire.

Moments later he grabbed a stick and began to draw on the beach, while the other two leaned in to watch. When he finished, they glanced silently at each other, sharing a wiry, mutual, knowing grin.

Written in the sand was, 13-3=10.

21

Day 10 ~ It Was a New Day, Yesterday

The next morning the blackened piles where the cabins once stood were cool enough to be searched. Virtually nothing could be salvaged. Food stores in the medical cabin had vaporized. The radio was now mere bits of silver glitter strewn about in the sand like deconstructed stars. The cabins themselves had burned to ashes. And there was no sign of their last remaining lifeline to the mainland, Taylor's satellite phone.

Strangely, there were no bodies either, though they did find bits of charred bone scattered here and there.

Matthew and Darius wondered allowed to each other as their hands filtered through the ruins in the growing light of dawn.

"You know what I think?" Matthew said. "I bet Taylor did this. I think he's still alive. Maybe he killed the other two, knowing we wouldn't be able to tell who, or even how many people died in there."

Darius nodded, "You're not the first one saying that that this morning. It's a pretty popular theory." He paused, kicking aside a big piece of bone, maybe a femur. "Me, I'm still partial to the Malik theory myself."

Matthew hung his head, his indecisive nature returning after last night's retreat. "I don't know what to think. The only thing I know now, is none of us are safe." He paused and looked around to be sure no one else was near.

"Me and Kinnary were talking this morning. We think we should bunch together at night, for safety. No way somebody tries to pull something with us all together."

Darius cocked a skeptical eyebrow and looked Matthew in the eye.

"You really think so? What about the dynamite? One stick, and we're all dead in one shot. You know," he pointed to the black chunks in his hand, "like this?" "Nope, we're better off splitting up."

Danielle slipped behind them and joined the conversation.

"You're both right. I mean what other choice is there but to stick together? But the first thing we have to do is get rid of that damn dynamite!"

Darius stood straight up, and took another look around the beach. His eyes focused squarely on one camp, where the dark side of the force was just beginning to rise from its slumber.

"Hundred percent. But we better do it before those guys try to change our minds. If there's anybody here gonna toss some TNT into a campsite, it's one of them."

"You do realized," Matthew mused, "the game isn't really over. Look at what we're talking about right now. Alliances. They've got theirs, that's plain to see. Black hats. We could have one too. White hats."

"Funny. But who else would be white hats?" Danielle asked with interest, increasingly desperate for any kind of security in the face of what felt to her like imminent destruction.

"Well," he expanded his thought, "as far as I can see, they've got three. Maybe we add Malik to that. And Joe doesn't seem to want to team with anybody. Can't say that I blame him.

"A floater," Danielle nodded.

"Precisely," agreed Matthew. "So, that leaves the two of you, me and Kinnary, and Frank. That's five. Versus three or four, and one floater."

Darius nodded, scanning the beach for Franklin. He was out in the water, desperately hunting for protein now that their food was merely particles blowing in some far off wind.

"I like those numbers. Let's talk about it when Frank's back. But first," he peered intensely at Matthew, "let's get that dynamite."

"Yes!" Danielle shrieked. "I'll keep the others distracted," she smiled before turning around and strolling quickly towards the beach.

Matthew waited near the burned out cabins while Darius quietly slipped into the jungle, re-emerging moments later next to the quonset hut. Danielle had made it to the dark camp, and was taking one for the team, chatting up the waking black hatters. Seizing the moment, he entered quickly and closed the door, and then, looking around to be sure no one was watching, Matthew followed.

Inside, Darius quickly grabbed the box of remaining dynamite, perhaps twenty sticks.

"Take a look outside," he prodded.

Matthew slipped the door open a couple of inches, but saw no one. Giving an all-clear nod, he took one side of the box from Darius, and together they stepped into the morning light.

Veering quickly into the jungle to avoid being seen, they slowly picked their way through it until they found the trail to Gissler's Cave. Unseen, they strolled casually along it without worry.

Matthew was relieved that at least one risk was about to leave the island. A big risk. There might be a million ways to kill someone on Cocos Island, but only a few ways to kill a lot of people at once. And the only one he knew of for sure, would soon be on the ocean floor.

At top of the hill they caught sight of Malik, and froze in their tracks. He was sitting outside the cave with his back to them, building a fire pit from the remains of the smoke bomb Joe had made just days before.

"Dumping it, are you? Seems a wise choice," he said without even turning around.

"Seems the best thing for everyone," Matthew replied with a quiver in his voice, unsettled that he somehow knew what they were doing without even looking.

Malik turned and sneered. "Speak for yourself, Sporty Spice. Some of us might like a little insurance."

Darius glared at the camera jockey, his eyes burning holes in the smaller man's skull. "Why don't you come and get one, little man."

Malik laughed like they'd never heard, lifted himself from the ground, and faced them. "Nah, that's ok. Had enough of you for a while, big boy. And besides, how do you know I didn't grab some last night?"

The self-satisfied grin fell from Darius' face. No, it was true, he had not considered that possibility.

"What the hell is wrong with you?" Matthew yelled, his straight man interior failing to comprehend the crazed visage before him. "Why can't you stop fucking with all of us? What's your deal?"

"My deal? My deal!" Malik, suddenly catlike, moved closer with a leap. Shocked at the strange move, Darius dropped his side of the box, spilling red sticks across the ground. Matthew quickly set his end down, gathered the wayward sticks and stuffed them back in the box. But Darius didn't take his eyes off of the strange, and somehow scary threat before him, and took a step back in case he had to unload on the wiry miscreant.

"How about the fact that I'm the only guy left who *ain't* a millionaire?" Malik continued. "Huh? Sound like a *deal* to you? How's that grab you, Boy?"

"Look man," Matthew argued, "we competed, and we won. Nobody got handed a damn thing. I'd think you'd be grateful to have been part of such a huge show! You got a check from it every year— the rest of us, just once."

Malik cackled, slapping his thigh. "Aww man, that's rich! You're quite the lawyer. Real sharp argument. Yeah, my little bitty checks and zero screen credit were right up there with your million dollar, fame-choked extravaganzas, you self centered jackass!"

His senses regained, Darius once again picked up his side of the box, and motioned for Matthew to do the same.

"Don't let him get to you, man. Guy's a loser."

"Says the dipshit from the projects who blew *his* million bucks! Least I wouldn't a done that!"

Dismissing them with a wave, Malik headed back to his rock next to the cave mouth. "Least I still got money in the bank. If I had kids, at least *I* could feed 'em!"

His senses once again lost, Darius dropped the box and started towards Malik.

"D!" Matthew yelled, again scraping up the fallen sticks, "C'mon man, like you said, guy's a loser! Don't let him goad you into something. He's probably got a knife."

Malik waved a bony finger at his would be attacker, "Yeah D! I probably got a knife! Or even better, a gun! No wait, better yet," he leapt closer again, "maybe some dyno-mite!"

He picked a stick up off the ground, tossed it at Darius, and screamed, "BOOM!", before cackling to the high heavens and returning to his rock.

Darius stood dumbstruck at the bizarre creature before him, a feeling growing inside him that the island was somehow *alive* inside Malik, twisting his soul and mind, and it suddenly occurred to him that it had done just that with the original killer. Surely, he now believed, Malik had indeed killed the rest of the crew.

Shaking the creepy feeling off, he returned once more to the box and the task at hand. Hoisting his side as Matthew did the same, they quickly tossed the contents over the cliff. Bright red sticks tumbled and twisted down the steep hillside into wet oblivion. Bouncing briefly on the same rocks where two days before Leticia had given her life for the team, soon, just like her, they were swallowed up forever by the emotionless maw of the Pacific Ocean.

On his way back to the trail, Darius couldn't resist one last poke at the crazy caveman.

"I'll see you pay when we get back. Personally."

Malik didn't even bother to look up. But when Darius turned away to ramble down the trail, his nemesis muttered just loudly enough to be sure he was heard, "Ain't nobody goin' back, boy. Nobody."

That night, everyone but the wild man on the hill, and Darius, who simply refused, feasted on rats, provided by Old Joe in the spirit of simply moving on from the ugliness that had gripped them the day before. Piles of them. The little buggers were everywhere, and all who attended were glad that someone was working hard to take the nasty little bastards out. That they could be converted into halfway decent protein was icing on the cake.

Together they dined at the big fire pit where Gissler Point met the waters of Wafer Bay, impossibly tall waves colliding with impossibly sharp rocks in a violent display right before them. It was the perfect backdrop for what was to have been the scene of the weekly Execution Ceremony, where one by one they would have been regularly ejected from Execution Island, albeit in the standard version of the game, still alive.

They barely spoke, and sat divided, "good guys" on one side, "bad guys" gazing warily back at them through the flames on the other. Old Joe sat at a small extension of the pit between the two groups, exactly where Taylor would have hosted the Executions, were he still alive.

It seemed there was still a game to be played, but no longer for a ten million dollar payday. The reward now was simply survival, with a small "s" instead of a grandiose capital one. Five "white hats" stared at three "black hats". And one guy who would wait to choose his hat until the day it became clear which color looked good one him sat in the middle. Trust among the Castaways was a distant memory, the lust for gold having taken its place.

Finally, Franklin broke the silence, his booming voice echoing across the flaming expanse.

"Who thinks Taylor might still be alive?"

Jason grinned, crossing his skinny legs.

"It has certainly entered my mind. You?"

Franklin nodded, crunching down on another bite of jungle rat, calcium-rich bones and all.

"It don't exactly make me feel secure knowing that his body might, or might not, have gone up in smoke," he added.

"Me neither," Susan nodded slowly. "Still," she smirked with narcissistic glee, "Taylor *was* stupid. Brazen. Foolish. Look at all the missteps he made with his ridiculous plan. Not to mention letting the show's ratings slide into oblivion in the first place."

Old Joe stared into the fire, ruminating. Moments later he spoke, once silence had again taken its hold.

"Anybody notice how all a sudden he found his softer side when he blowed up the money hole? Like he was preparin' us fer somethin'. Felt a bit like a show," he nodded, to himself more than anyone else, "like he was on display, preenin', dancin' fer us, sayin' hey y'all! Looky over there!"

The ever observant Randy had noticed the very same thing, but thought he was the only one.

"I hear you, Joe. The showman, a magician, pointing to the hole while he slipped a knife out from under a handkerchief. Hell yeah, I'd lay odds that son of a bitch is watching us right now."

Danielle, cracking like an egg inside her own skull, put her hands to it, ripped at her hair, and shrieked into the night sky.

"God! Make it stop!" Her pitiful wail trailed off into the pounding of the waves, and she fell, as she so often did, to the sand and sobbed.

Darius put his hand softly on her back to soothe her, halfheartedly.

"I can't take it anymore! I can't!" she gurgled into her palms, tears, snot, sand, and strands of hair merging into one.

"Look girl," Darius cooed, "you just got to make it five more days. Boat comes five days from tomorrow morning. Just hang on, now."

"Five days …" Old Joe's voice trailed off into the flames, a campfire storyteller winding up towards the big scare. "Five damn days. We got a maniac in the hand, Crazy Malik, who *might* be a killer, and two maniacs in the bush, Taylor and Ricardo, who if alive are *for sure* killers. Either way, y'all," he peered around at his fellow Castaways, "the name of this here game is still the same. Execution Island. Only now, it ain't fake."

Jason Oliver's inappropriately giddy voice rose suddenly above the crashing waves.

"Ahh, ahh, ahhh, ahh, Stayin' Aliiiiiiiive!"

"You're sick, Oliver," Kinnary spat with palpable disgust. "Fucking sick. You sound like a killer yourself, creep."

"As if!" Jason laughed a bit more happily than the maniac on the hill, "With these arms?" He raised his scrawny limbs up to the light. "Not bloody likely!"

The desperate mood briefly broken, they laughed as one, black and white hats sharing a brief moment of connection, for what would be the very last time.

22

Jason Oliver ~ 2000's

"Outta my way, douchebag ..."

The words spoken behind him were calm, emotionless, clear. Anyone on a sports team, any stoner, any tough chick, or ... well, *anyone,* knew that if Jason Oliver Walton was in your way, he'd get out of it if you simply commanded him to. There was no need to oversell it.

And indeed he did, slipping deftly aside as Brian Taylor, a defensive end on the football team, blew by him headed for his own locker.

Jason feigned coolness, whispering "Hey, Dude," with his trademark smirk, but there really was no point. At the very bottom of the high school social ladder, at the bottom of even the "nerd class", Jason Oliver was a ship without a port.

In fact, the only people who thought he was cool were his Mom, which only made his social alienation worse, and his teachers, which made it *way* worse. He ate lunch alone each day, or sometimes in the teacher's lounge, where they had long ago taken pity on him, mercifully breaking the "no students allowed" rule.

Mr. Payton, the AP Chemistry teacher, took special pity on him and allowed him to hang out in his classroom whenever he wanted. Before or after school, Payton even took the rare and dangerous step of giving the young boy a key to his classroom, so he could retreat to a safe space whenever he was picked on or pushed around. The teachers saw the way the poor kid was treated, and came together to offer him tiny islands of refuge in the stormy waters of high school.

Jason Oliver, skinny, frail, gangly and awkward, with oversized, curly brown hair that was years out of style, glanced around nervously to be sure no more threats were imminent, and then quickly stepped away from his locker and into the hall. School was out, and while other kids rushed to the bus, or to cars waiting in the parking lot, Jason simply tried to survive until most of them were gone, so he could make his way home in relative safety.

Once in the flow of the hallway's stream, he moved purposefully, head down, aiming for Mr. Payton's classroom to wait an hour or two before walking the mile and a half to his house. To try to do so immediately after school was just too risky. Potential threats were everywhere. In the halls, in the parking lot, on the streets. A master of self preservation, Jason Oliver had learned how to survive these afternoons so that perhaps he might make it to the next socially awkward day, in one piece.

Letting himself into Payton's classroom, he sat down at his desk. He set his backpack on the ground and pulled out the Dr. Pepper he'd begun to drink at lunch, gulped, and exhaled. This was his element. The very same things in this room that made other kids cringe and count the seconds on the clock, made him feel like he was at home. The classroom-standard Periodic Table of Elements on the wall. The tables filled with bunsen burners, beakers, and protective goggles. The emergency eyewash station. The dippy bird pecking away at a glass of water in the corner of Payton's desk. And the books, with esoteric titles like "Horizons in Organic Chemistry", "A Molecular Approach to Physical Chemistry", "The Birth of the Atom", and scads of others that most of the students had never bothered to notice.

But he had.

And as he spent much of his waking life in this very room, most often alone, he even read the ones on the highest shelves. These books weren't really meant for the general curriculum, but were there either for occasional background research, or for interesting anecdotes that Mr. Payton might use to actually pique the interest of the students from time to time. Fascinating tidbits like, "Do you know why the attempted murder of Rasputin with cyanide didn't work?", or the ever popular, "Did you know that Teflon was discovered totally by mistake?"

Unfortunately those little gems only served to wake the half-asleep texting machines, otherwise known as his classmates, for mere moments at a time before they went back to not giving a shit and trying to figure out where they were going to score beer or pot before Friday night.

But for Jason, these tomes were the stuff of life itself. And it was actually the little item about Rasputin that got him thinking one day. Rasputin was a powerful, mysterious mystic who scared the hell out of everyone in the Russian court, many of whom were hardened veterans of the military. He was a man who seemed untouchable. So then, how does one go about taking down someone who seems untouchable, if one has no power oneself?

Among the books on the top shelves, out of sight and laying on its side, was a dusty book he found one day after a particularly demeaning journey through the halls, moving rapidly on his way to the safety of his protective classroom. He'd escaped the interior hallways of the school, which then left him only to run the gauntlet of asphalt walkways that led to the "temporary" classroom buildings, set apart from the main building. Payton's Chemistry classroom was one of these, although in rural Northern California, "temporary" seemed to mean a really long time.

And here he ran into the two headed monster he feared most.

Football players. And cheerleaders.

It wasn't that each on their own were that bad. It's just that when you put them together, the twin toxins of popularity and testosterone combined to create a compound highly fatal to scrawny young men like himself. And this time, the explosion started from a less likely source. A cheerleader.

Tammy Wendover. She was high on both herself, and the pheromones drifting from David Yodner, the dipshittiest dipshit of the whole bunch.

"Hey, *Jerkoff* Oliver!" she began, not so innocently. He quickened his pace while nervously smirking at the two walking swarms of hormones like a beaten dog. "Cheer tryouts are today! You should join the squad!"

Laughter, giggles, and guffaws.   He kept moving.   But, unfortunately for him, he had to go through them.   Payton's classroom lay just beyond their classless cluster.

"Aww, shit," Yodner joined, his manhood rising at the possibility of making someone else feel like shit, so that he might look manly in front of his mentally undercooked girlfriend.   "You wouldn't even have to try out, Oliver! You got more pussy than any of these girls!"

Now the laughter reached a fever pitch.   Each of the walking magazine cutouts wretched and reeled with it, slapping Yodner on the back.   Two girls with more brain cells than the rest held back, repulsed, but not enough to make a scene and end up where poor Jason Oliver was.   Better to let the dog that was used to being beaten take this one too.

Jason smirked, but then made the mistake of continuing the conversation on a much more objective level than the Baywatch B-team could compute.

"Good one, Dave!   But, you know, there actually are male cheerleaders.   Just not here."

Yodner stopped cold, taking his arm from Tammy's shoulder. The dumbass grin dripped off his face, his mouth becoming a fine crease.   Slowly the others took his lead and stopped laughing as well.

"You wanna be a girl, *Jerkoff*?

Now Jason knew he was in big trouble, his geek senso-meter pegged at a full "OH SHIT!".

"Nah, man," he chuckled painfully.   "Just sayin'.   Hell no, me, a cheerleader?   Shit, man.   That's funny."

But the cat, or the pussy in this case, was out of the bag.

"Where you goin', Oliver?" his tormenter asked.   Rhetorically, of course, since there was no possible answer David Yodner would accept.

"Payton's," he mumbled, looking away.   "You guys take it easy."

"Oh yeah?   Cool.   Guess that means," he turned to survey the pavement behind him, "you gotta go through us, huh?   And since you wanna be a girl, I think you better show us your pussy if you want to pass.   What do you guys think?"

This time the response was definitely segregated, with most of the guys, and only one girl, Tammy, repeating Yodner's command.

"Yeah, show us your pussy!"

The smarter cheerleaders began to slip-slide away behind the larger group, clutching their bags as talismans against what could only be a very bad thing headed this way.

"Male cheerleaders? Lame, man. Totally. I'm cool." Jason was so scared that the words just dripped out of him without any sense of flow or meaning. There just weren't many verbal life rafts that would float in this river.

"Pussy. Now, Oliver. Or I'm gonna do it for you. Drop 'em."

The two girls of slightly higher moral fiber finally peeled away from the group and disappeared back the way they had come. But no one came to his aid. Jason began to walk backwards, realizing that retreat was his only option. Sensing this like a predator, Yodner leapt at Jason, who spun on his heels, tripped over his own feet, and ended up face down on the pavement.

Yodner was on him in seconds. Jason whimpered and squeaked as the group behind shouted and hollered for him to "show us your pussy!" David ripped at the scrawny kid's pants while Jason went limp, smart enough to realize that the coming humiliation, his stock in trade, was a far better choice than a severe beating, which would surely be handed him for refusing to let the moron have his way.

His face scraping the asphalt and beginning to bleed, Jason Oliver felt his pants and underwear ripped down to his ankles. Without a fight he was rolled onto his back and exposed to the world, while Yodner hopped off and accepted the congratulations of his peers.

High fives and back-slapping atta-boys all around.

The girls laughed and pointed. The guys jumped up and down in animalistic glee, chemicals coursing through their brains and causing the needles on their brute meters to go directly to full asshole.

Jason lay motionless, his manhood, or at this point in his life, his boyhood, exposed to the air and shriveling in the cool breeze. He stared hopelessly up at the clouds, simply waiting for this too to pass.

"Looks like a pussy to me! Good luck in cheer squad, *Jerkoff*!"

David Yodner stepped over him, quickly followed by his henchmen and woman. Their laughter poisoned the air until finally they turned the corner, and disappeared into the building.

Jason waited until they did, sighed, then slowly stood and pulled his pants up. His smirk twitched uncontrollably from left to right, and a few small tears trickled down his face and onto his curled lip.

160

On the outside, he was typical Jason Oliver. Meek in the face of absolute degradation, harmless.

But inside, he was on fire, plotting revenge as he headed for Payton's door, locked it behind him, and ripped the dust ridden book off the top shelf.

The next morning he made a side trip to a nearby trailer park that left him with an extra bit of pep in his step, but he carefully dialed it back once he stepped onto school grounds, so as not to alarm the natives. He made it through the day through sheer will and an amazing ability to become invisible. After school he rushed to Payton's room, going to work on a side project he'd come up with the afternoon before. Staying until nearly dark, he used the bunsen burners, beakers, and a beaten old refrigerator water filter his Dad had in the "throw away someday" box in the garage. Before he went home, he made one last detour, then left the school grounds practically levitating.

The next day, he grinned as he noticed funny looks on the faces of those who frequented the gym. They were pale, looked serious, and some even a little grim. A cheerleader vomited, right in algebra class! And even old David Yodner himself rushed by Jason Oliver with a horrid, twisted look on his face, right into the bathroom. His smirk in full glory, Jason couldn't help but follow, but once inside, the combination of sounds and smells emanating from Yodner's stall sent him right back into the hall, where he laughed his ass off, pounding his locker in joy with tiny fists.

The next day, two football players, two cheerleaders, and four basketball players went home sick in the middle of the day.

Jason flowed through the hall with renewed vigor. He even walked right out in the middle of the damn thing for the first time in his life, and no one batted an eye! He felt so emboldened that he even shoved past Brian Taylor to get to *his* locker after the bell rang at the end of the day! No one messed with him, blinked at him, touched him, all day long! Their slowly rebelling internal organs required all of their focus, and they simply had none left for him.

The next day was even better. Yodner and Taylor didn't even come to school. A cheerleader was in the hospital, supposedly suffering seizures after raging bouts of diarrhea left her totally dehydrated. When he later learned it was Tammy, he couldn't help but puff his chest out a little further as he boldly strolled straight home, right after school, for the first time in years.

The tigers had been tamed, the bullies had been castrated, and the smell of vomit and diarrhea filled the school's bathrooms to such a degree that when he had to pee, he went out behind Payton's portable classroom to do the deed.

But when he heard the next day that six more athletes had gone to the hospital, he knew the jig was up, and it was time to pull back.

After school he slipped back into the old Jason Oliver routine. He went to Payton's classroom, making sure that the book titled "Popular Poisons from a Historical Perspective" was tucked under several others, back-side up, and re-covered by hand with dust he brought in from outside. Waiting for dark again, he headed for the gym.

A screwdriver emerged from his backpack, and he quickly removed the bottom metal sheeting from the water fountain that sat between the entrances to the boys' and girls' locker rooms. This particular water fountain was so popular that there was often a line when activities were taking place either on the field, or inside the gym. Setting the sheeting aside, he quickly went to work removing the old water filter he had installed in the water line just days before, where there once had been a basic filter cartridge. Carefully he slid his homemade filter into a plastic bag and slipped it into his backpack. Replacing the old filter cartridge, he raced to put the whole shebang back together.

The intensely corrupting pulse of real power flowed through his body and mind for the first time in his life, and it was not one he planned on letting go anytime soon. Unlike anything he had ever felt, he realized with a smirk that *this* was what guys like Brian and David felt like every day! It wasn't fair that they came by it naturally, but he was just glad he had finally come by it at all, thanks to the glorious wonders of a big brain, and chemistry.

He'd nearly killed them all. Yet he hadn't. But he could have. And the power raging through him, the power to take their lives with impunity if he so pleased, or to simply punish them with a few days worth of vomiting, diarrhea, and the occasional seizure or minor kidney failure, was a power that was his and his alone. No one would ever know how it beat there within his bony chest. He'd turned it off, this time, but could just as easily turn it back on whenever he wanted.

The next morning he left home early so he could walk by the trailer park and sit on the little bench beside the bitterly scented flowers growing there. With a confident air and a lightness in his heart, he took a few happy moments to quietly admire the delicate, dangerous beauty of the oleanders planted against the fence, inhaling deeply the strongly scented fumes flowing into his nostrils from just a few feet away, smirking with newfound content.

23

Day 10 ~ Night Train

He didn't want to get up. He really, really didn't want to get up. To do so would mean leaving the safety of the fire, the security of the group. But boy oh boy, he really did have to pee.

Matthew twisted and turned for what felt like hours in his bed of palm leaves, his body crossed numerous times by various beetles and ants as they went about their nightly duties. But it wasn't *their* nightly duties that worried him, it was his own.

He tried to hold it. He pinched it off with his hand. He tried to cross his legs like Jason, but their bodies were completely different, and there was no way he could make it physically work.

He could put it off no longer. He had to go.

Sleeping next to him, Kinnary felt a tap on her shoulder.

"Hey. Hey, Kin? Sorry to bug you, but I need to take a leak."

Kinnary rolled over, eyes half open. "So go take a leak! What the hell does that have to do with me?"

He looked at her like she was speaking in a foreign tongue. "Remember where we are? Come on. I can't go alone."

She opened her eyes, and suddenly did remember exactly where they were.

"Shit. Ok," she wiped sand from the corner of her eyes, "you want me to go with you?"

"Please?" he whined, obviously in pain. "I'll do it for you when you have to go."

She laughed, patting him on the kneecap.

"I've got the bladder of a horse, Wonder Boy. Won't be necessary. But sure. Let's go."

They crept together through the soft, cool sand under the low light of the crescent moon, right up to the point where beach became jungle.

"Don't go in there," Kinnary warned, tugging at his shoulder for him to stop.

Spinning him around, she pulled him close and thrust her tongue into his mouth. His eyes grew wide as he felt her soft arms wrap around him and pull him towards her. His Mormon upbringing got the best of him and he hesitated, until something animal took over. He wrapped his own tongue around hers and put his hand in her shirt, feeling the soft fullness of her athletic breasts.

"Ohhh . . ." He moaned.

"We've waited for this for so long," she teased.

She pushed hard against his pelvis and he returned the motion, grinding up against her, feeling himself rising to a ready position.

"Oh my god, I know! But,"

Kinnary put her finger over his mouth, shaking her head. "No buts, Wonder Boy. It's time. For all we know, we could die tomorrow. Do you want to die without having this?"

She stepped back, and in one dramatic motion, ripped off her shirt. Nothing stirred on the sands behind them. And before them, the jungle lay quiet as well.

Her hands slid his shorts down over his knees and then went to his manhood, feeling its girth. This boy, this mildly religious boy, had rarely if ever been with a woman, and that thought made her even more excited than she already was.

"Of course I don't ..." he trailed off.

She slipped off her shorts with a flourish and threw them on the ground.

"Well then what are you waiting for!"

He could hardly believe what he was seeing, what he was feeling. She reached in and kissed him again, and, tugging him by his member, pulled him onto her, and they tumbled to the ground as one.

165

"Life is short, my love, take me now!" she whispered passionately into his ear as she softly slipped him inside of her.

His penis throbbed, and there was no longer any doubt in his mind that she was the one. Unable to resist the beautiful woman before him, he was nevertheless powerless to resist the pain just above his waist.

"Damn! Stay here!" He kissed her deeply. "I'll be right back!"

Leaping from the ground, he took three long steps towards the thick jungle behind him.

"Oh," Kinnary giggled in the moonlight, "right. Forgot."

Waiting a moment for his swollen penis to settle down long enough to do its day job, he then had to wait another moment, as it was even more swollen than he'd ever thought it could be. Finally, as tends to eventually happen, nature took its course.

He beamed, relishing the pleasant feeling of his over-inflated bladder slowly coming back into its original and naturally intended shape, and fantasized about the life changing moments still to come.

Kinnary rolled over and spread her shirt out on the ground and lied back on it, waiting for the pleasure she'd always known would arrive. She and Matthew, as it had always been meant to be.

Now soaked with urine, the Killer had also been waiting, waiting for hours for someone to leave the fireside, a baby wildebeest separated from the herd. Watching as the two lovers stirred, the Killer used the roaring waves as cover, side-slipping through the brush, crouching low, stalking them with precision to exactly the spot where the star crossed lovers' trajectory across the silvery sand would end. It was a lucky break that the good guys had made their camp at the Execution Grounds, where the waves were closer, and particularly loud.

And of course, the Killer grinned, it was a fitting spot for one of them to exit the island as well, just as originally intended.

That the Killer was forced to endure watching these two rutting animals awkwardly try to mate, and *then* be urinated on, only made the gruesome task that much easier to perform.

Matthew finished with a shake and a shiver, just as a sharpened two inch thick branch burst out of the jungle and into his abdomen, piercing his liver.

166

There was no scream. He just fell straight forward into the still steaming, piss-laden leaves of the jungle, as the Killer turned tail and bolted through the brush and away from the scene of the crime, the rapid, but decreasing sound of the culprit's exodus completely drowned out by the pounding surf.

Kinnary, still unaware, lay cooing on the sand, staring at the beautiful night sky, the silvery crescent moon, and the shimmering sands of Cocos, oblivious to the small, guttural sounds Matthew was now emitting into the ground. Having always had a crush on the Boy Wonder, her long sought romantic feelings peaked within her at the very same time that all feeling left her lost love, Matthew, for good.

"Come on, now, Matty boy," she toyed coyly, "Mama's waitin'!"

She sat up, expecting a still-exposed and no doubt stunning penis to greet her lusty gaze, but what she saw instead was Matthew's entrails hanging from a hole in his side, blood gurgling in a steady stream from his open mouth.

She screamed. Screamed, grabbed her clothes, and ran as fast as her sprinter's legs could carry her.

Old Joe sat up too, the scream rousing him from his light slumber. But instead of quickly sliding down the hillbilly elevator, he listened carefully as the screaming continued. Had to be Kinnary, he figured, as he knew Danielle's painful shriek all too well, and Susan was probably not even capable of screaming. Far off, he heard the waves too.

But then his old ears picked up on something else. It too was pretty far off, and might just be one of the plentiful (and extremely hard to catch) goats on the island. But something, something pretty fast and agile, was just now rushing through the brush near the end of his river valley, where it emptied into the sea in a towering waterfall. This thing wasn't running on the trail, but through the jungle itself— he could hear limbs tearing and breaking in its wake.

Grabbing his weapons he slid slowly down his rope, still trying to listen, while also staying silent.

But the sound was gone. Must have been an animal, he thought, because it covered ground so quickly, already well over the next hill.

"Dang Killer's scared off a meal!" he grumbled into the air. Shaking his head, he very slowly and stealthily moved towards the beach, emotionlessly expecting a massacre.

167

The Castaways were gathered at the far end of it, near the Execution Grounds. Moving slowly across the sand, he knew full well that this new Killer had proven there was no need to hurry. No one survived an attack on Execution Island.

Arriving, he sidled up to the crowd, observed the scene, and kindly draped an arm around Kinnary, who was already being consoled by Danielle. Of course Danielle needed consoling too, as always. He gave Kinnary a grandfatherly kiss on the forehead, patted Danielle on the hand, and then gratefully detached himself from the two sobbing women. Darius and Franklin lifted Matthew's limp, bloody body, and began to carry him up the beach, toward the makeshift graveyard.

Old Joe waved for them to stop, and quickly scanned the wound for clues. It was a very large through and through. The poor boy's intestines hung out his back, and his liver was severed, a tattered piece hanging from his abdomen.

"Killer carries a big stick," he mumbled into the air.

"Is that a fucking joke?" Franklin exhaled angrily, aghast, glaring at this man he once looked up to.

Nerves on the island were frayed to their limit, and people with frayed nerves were prone to misunderstanding.

"No sir. Truly not. Jus' a real stupid comment. Accidental."

He rose, and waved the two men back on their way without another word. Turning towards the graveyard, Franklin still glared back at him over his shoulder.

Susan tapped him on the back.

"What happened, Joe?"

Old Joe was not just some sweet old guy. But, he was no superman either, and his nerves were every bit as frayed as anyone else's. He too, like most men his age, had a crusty and crotchety side. And it was starting to show.

"Hell's bells, Susan! What in hell do *you* think happened?"

"Jesus, Joe!" she was taken aback, "What's gotten into you? It was just a simple question."

"A simple question? Is that what ya said? Lemme ask ya somethin' Susan. Ya really think there's any *simple* questions on this here island? Now do ya? 'Cause I'm here ta tell ya, I do not believe there are. No, ma'am, I do not! And frankly, I'm plum tired of the whole Hillbilly Detective Agency thing. It don't suit me."

"Fuckin' A!" Jason Oliver grinned like a murderous clown, "You're heading south too, aren't you Joe!"

"Gone south, son. Already gone."

"Well," he patted Joe on the back, "welcome to the dark side, my man. Welcome, welcome, welcome!"

Old Joe threw Oliver's hand off his back and strode to the spot where Matthew's body was found. He stared at the dark pool in the sand. He looked beyond at the urine soaked leaves in the trees. He started to move forward, to look for footprints as he had each time someone was killed in the past. But this time, at the jungle's edge, he stopped, waving his hand in dismissal at the dark mass in front of him.

"Aww, fuck it!" he yelled, totally out of character. It was the first time any of them had heard Old Joe cuss in anger, ever.

Turning and stomping away from the campers, he headed back to his treetop refuge.

"Aren't you going to track the Killer?" Kinnary lifted her tear-stained face, chilled to the bone at the prospect that Old Joe, their rock throughout the murders, the one thing they all had clung to for a sense of something solid, was leaving them.

"Y'all don't need me! Stay the hell alive! That's all ya gotta do!" he yelled over his shoulder.

Far behind him, Jason Oliver began to break into the Bee Gees again, but this time Kinnary leapt to her feet and punched him so hard in the face that he spun on his heels, collapsed face first into the sand, and went right to sleep.

"Joe!" Danielle pleaded, grasping for any thread of security, "Won't you stay with us? It's got to be dangerous, alone out there in the jungle! The Killer is out there!"

Joe chuckled knowingly, but kept moving straight ahead.

"Seems to me, lady, there's nowhere on Cocos that the Killer *ain't*!"

169

24

Day 11 ~ Scorned

"I'm taking him out," Kinnary said calmly.

No one was surprised to hear these words. Each had thought the same, at least once. Silence permeated the air around the fire pit, where they had gathered for their meager breakfast.

Old Joe took a deep breath, exhaled slowly, and stood. He always did his best thinking upright.

"I'm in," Franklin said.

"Hundred percent," Darius nodded.

Danielle was silent, while Susan, Randy, and Jason Oliver were smart enough to sit back and let everyone else fight their battles, until the day came when they were forced to fight their own. The trio simply munched their tiny breakfast of poached booby eggs and crab meat, and watched.

"Y'all," Old Joe began, then quickly stopped, realizing he was no longer the accepted voice of wisdom. "God damn…"

In truth, he hardly gave a rip anymore. This much blood, this much fear, this much paranoia… any one of them alone was enough to fry a good man's brains, and Joe, well, he *was* a good man. But he was no genius, and his simple brain was growing very tired of the constant drama. All he wanted to do now was sit quietly in his tree, and wait for the boat to arrive.

"I could tell y'all that we still can't be sure it ain't Taylor. Or that sumbitch Ricardo for that matter."

"Oh yeah?" Kinnary practically levitated with negative energy. "Is that what you think, Joe?"

Susan nudged Randy to take note at how another of the righteous had descended to their level, or below, after the events of the past week.

"Why, li'l girl, ya know somethin' I don't?" asked Joe.

"Sure as shit do."

She opened a bag that she brought to the fire ring earlier, and dumped its contents into the blaze. Three skulls rolled out, bounced on the hot coals, and rolled off in different directions.

"Oh my God," Danielle moaned, while the others just sat, stunned.

"It took me every hour since the sun came up," she explained. "But I found them! Oh, I found them."

"Wow," Randy started in, logic slapping him right in the face. "He *is* the fucking killer. I mean, that's it, right? Either it's one of us, or it's him. Three dead, three skulls. Taylor, Carl, and Ricardo."

"Well now that's whatcha might call a hasty assertion, buddy," Joe began. "Y'all don't think that mebbe somebody coulda dug them skulls up from the graveyard, and tossed 'em in there when he blowed it all sky high?"

Randy shook his head. "There were only two bodies in the graveyard when it blew. Matthew wasn't dead yet."

"Sure, but if Taylor's our Killer, he only needed one skull ta shine the light on ol' Malik. Even if it was Taylor *and* Ricardo, well, they already had ol' Carl's head now didn't they?"

The Killer was no dummy, figured Joe, and anything was possible at this point. But he was ignored, and the hive mind moved on.

Darius had been twitching nervously, but now spoke up.

"Look, when we were up there dumping the dynamite…"

"You did *what*?" Susan leapt to her feet in a rage. "Without asking the rest of us? Who do you think you are!"

"I think," he responded calmly, "I'm the guy who kept you from being blown up the last couple nights. That's who."

Susan was not to be trifled with. Alpha, from top to bottom.

"Look, Jackass, you do *not* make the rules here. You do *not* get to unilaterally decide what we do and do not throw out! Capiche?"

Randy was nodding along, and spoke calmly in defense of his raging sister.

"She's right. We shoulda voted. Mighta used it for something important. You never throw away a valuable tool that can do jobs nothing else can do."

"We just saw three guys…" Darius paused and pointed to the skulls in the fire, "look, we even have props! Three guys blown to smithereens! It was the responsible thing to do."

"Still," Randy stood up with angry eyes, a fever growing inside him just as it had in some of the others, "not your call. Don't pull that kinda shit again. Who knows what we coulda used it for? Blowing up palm trees to make a raft, on the possibility Taylor might have called off the boats permanently, or blowing up the sea bed for food… anything! Literally, a million and one uses!"

"Okay," Darius put his hands up in surrender, "Noted. It was a tense morning, maybe we didn't think it through. Now, as I was saying, when we were up there he was out of his gourd. I mean, like speaking in tongues type of crazy."

"He sounded," Darius went on, "like he was channeling the killer. Or," he paused, not wanting to sound like a nut, but then realizing it hardly mattered anymore he added "the island itself." He stared out to sea, playing the scene back in his head. "Last thing he said was that none of us would ever leave here."

"Well, ladies and gentlemen," Kinnary announced, "that is about enough for me!" Her mind's eye was filled with the painful image of Matthew, bleeding out on the sand.

Good, sweet, overly innocent Matthew, she thought. Her Matthew. Dead. By Malik's hand. Like her nemesis, Susan, Kinnary was a doer. She wouldn't, and in fact couldn't, sit around while garbage needed to be taken to the curb.

Picking up the bloody spear found near her almost-lover's body, she began a steady march towards Gissler's Cave. She didn't care if no one else came, she was on a mission and would happily do it alone if she had to.

Franklin and Darius glanced at each other, and then followed. Randy, always game to watch any kind of competition, joined in.

Jason Oliver and Susan hesitated briefly, but rose as well. Old Joe finally gave in too, while Danielle, predictably, stayed behind.

Malik sat in the very same spot where Franklin and Darius had seen him the day before. Sitting outside the cave, tending his fire, talking to the wind. Long, white tendrils of smoke blew all around him, swirling in the sunlight and never once touching his skin, rising in an unseen draft like a column above his head.

It was a strangely spiritual scene, and each member of the execution party stopped in their tracks, gaping in awe and fear, except Kinnary, who kept moving in defiance of the spectacle. Finally she sat on a boulder, directly across the fire from the maniac.

More than one shared the same thought. The island seemed to *like* him.

Kinnary glared intently at the crazy, erstwhile holy man.

"You see!" he screamed into the fire, "It's just as I said! They have come to kill me. They *have! It's my right!* And I won't fight, no I won't fight, the dying of the light, the warm, welcome, bright and right dying of the light!*"

"Holy shit," Randy whistled in wonder, "The son of a bitch is quoting Dylan Thomas? And poorly at that. You guys weren't kidding."

"Sure as hell wasn't," Darius shook his head in bewilderment, "but this is even weirder. *Mother fucker.*"

Old Joe backed off a few yards, closer to the trail and further from the edge of the cliff. He'd seen many rabid animals in his hunting days. A raccoon was dangerous even when it was healthy, but when rabid it was one of the most deadly prey in the world. It could rip a man apart, though outweighed by a hundred pounds. And this crazy being in front of him was the closest thing he'd ever seen to a rabid raccoon on two legs.

"Joe!" Malik turned his gaze to the old man, as if on cue, "you needn't worry. No, no my friend. You see I have watched this scene play out, and you don't need to be here. All of you can leave, in fact. This is only for Kinnary and I. As it should be." He turned his head back to the fire, before adding, "Your turns will come."

"Like hell we're leaving her alone with you!" Franklin, playing the chivalrous gentleman, ignored the fact that Kinnary was at least as dangerous as was he, maybe more.

"It's ok," Kinnary waved them off with a thin smile, "this one's mine. I got this."

"Yes, yes, she's quite right, you know. She does have this," the island's high priest spoke, staring back into her eyes. "I've seen it. It is Cocos' will."

"Are you fucking batshit, man?" Susan was dumbstruck. "Seriously, you've slipped a brain disc, buddy. The island, as has been made quite clear, doesn't give a rat's ass about any of us. Much less you, camera boy."

Malik turned his gaze to meet hers, an omniscient smile dawning on his soot-stained face.

"You blew a hole in her side! She's not at all happy about that, oh no! But it's not your turn, rich girl. Yours is coming, yes, I have seen that too and it's a hell of a good one, but it's not your turn today. Get back in line. It's my turn to die, *bitch*."

With an audible huff, Susan walked away, yelling as she did, "Gladly, dickweed!" Grumbling as she moved down the trail, she added, "Ain't nobody killing this girl. Nobody…"

One by one they peeled away until Kinnary found herself alone with a madman. Which was right where she wanted to be.

"How many did you kill, shitbag?" she asked, pulling the Killer's long, sharp spear from the ground and sticking its tip into the fire.

"None, actually," he smiled with a sudden sincerity, "It wasn't me. It was Cocos."

Kinnary grinned back, a devious, sarcastic smirk. "Yeah, right. Let's count them, shall we?"

"Please," he nodded, "yes, I'd like that."

"Taylor. One."

"Not me, though I'd truly love to take the credit. Shoulda done that one long ago, would have saved us all this trouble! But please, please go on."

"Ricardo. Two." She exhaled the words softly, with purpose, as if they were an incantation.

"No, but Goddamn I wish I'd had. Guy was bad news." He bent his head down, hands together in a prayer position. "Oh thank you, great and wise Island of Cocos."

"Carl. Three."

174

"Nope, I never would have killed Carl. Harmless, really. An asshole, but totally harmless."

She paused, pulled the spear from the fire, and blew on the tip of it, stoking the tiny flame that stuck to the end.

"And my Matthew. My poor, ignorant, marvelous Matthew. Man of my future. Did you kill my boy? Did you kill my Matthew?"

Malik stared into the fire.

"You know, I'm not really sure. I blacked out last night, in front of this very fire. I had visions, I do know that, visions of the past, visions of the future. I saw his death, in fact I know all of it, every death, every thrill, even what happens at the end. It's something, I can tell you that. Something none of you are even thinking about! *None* of you."

"Did you kill him, you fucking shit storm! Did you!"

"Well," Malik rose to grab another palm log, throwing it into the fire, "I might as well have, really. I woke up in the sand, down there," he pointed to the beach. "The visions, they took over. I don't know exactly what happened, for most of the night."

"Well then," Kinnary said, rising to face him across the fire, "let's just say you did. Five days from now the rest of us will leave Cocos and split the treasure eight ways, but you won't. And you're right, Malik. I'm here to fulfill the prophecy. I'm your deliverance. It's your turn."

Malik nodded his head very quickly, as a strange sound rose into the air.

"Oh yes! *Yes!* And it could be yours! Yours too! Isn't it wonderful? Just have a seat, and we'll stay here, together, *forever!*"

Kinnary heard it, plain as day. A snake! It was the sound of a hissing snake. She looked down and saw it, its tail twitching and twirling in the fire. Somehow it had fallen into the pit, though she had seen no snakes on the island. Its tail had caught fire, and it was going to die with him...

"Run!" screamed her brain, and her highly trained body leapt directly away from the fire, towards the trail that led back to the beach, and safety. But her foot caught one of the large boulders that made up the fire ring, and she fell face first into the dirt, just as the snake exploded.

The dynamite blew Malik straight back into his beloved cave, exactly as he had imagined and been instructed to make it so. His body was smashed to a bloody pulp against the wall inside, quickly buried in rocks and earth as the cave collapsed around him.

Gissler's Cave was no more. Nor, it seemed, was Malik. The two had become one, the Island of Cocos granting them eternity, together.

Far below on the beach, Jason Oliver gave a whistle at the thunderous sound.

"Day-um! Looks like the Wonder Twins have deactivated!"

Randy nodded, running his fingers through his medium length, dark hair. "Saw that one coming. Never face down a guy who has nothing to lose. And that guy... holy shit, if anybody I've ever seen had nothing to lose," he pointed demonstrably at the hill above, "*that was him.*"

Susan smiled. She looked at her boys, and then at the goody-goodies up the beach. She would split the treasure three ways, and quite happily at that. But seven? She thought not. However, she was not about to go crazy and start killing goody-goodies. No, she was fairly certain one of the others would do that for her, providing her all the cover she would need back in the World.

But as she turned to gloat about one more share being added back into the pot, Kinnary's bloody body, still very much alive, came stumbling slowly down the trail. The Goodies hurried to help her, while Susan and her crew just sat, mouths agape, staring at the Wonder Boy's wonder woman who had somehow made it through impossible odds, yet again.

"Shit," she moaned to her boys, "foiled again! Fucking Indian princess!"

For a moment she stared out to sea, tuning out the joyous celebration behind her as the white hats welcomed their conquering heroine back into the fold. Then, looking down at the sand, she dragged her big toe through it, drawing something familiar.

"I guess this is where we are now."

A large "8" stood out in the white grit below their feet.

Jason giggled liked he'd just been goosed.

"I like this better," he grinned, rubbing out half of her "8", making it a "3".

25

Days 12/13 ~ Alliances

Once again, it seemed the Castaways could breathe easy. Another murderer had been removed from the Island.

The original killer who began this bloody cycle— gone.

Malik, who almost surely was the new Killer— gone.

Yet relief was in short supply on the beach. A dark mood descended over the remaining players, mirroring the dark sky that poured ceaselessly upon them all night long. They remained divided into two camps, with a third consisting only of Old Joe. In fact, the black hats increased the divide that morning, moving their camp closer to the treasure hole, just to keep an eye on it.

With the boat's arrival in four days, a truce was called long enough so the eight of them could work together to extract the gold coins. Despite their division, they worked more as a unit than might have been expected. Though the rain refused to stop, they began and ended each day the same way, like wet rats, shoving heavy wheelbarrows through mud, bodies itching from fungus, knees and hands scarred from constant slips on the trail between the two camps.

Darius chose cave duty, and was lowered into the hole on a rope. All day long he filled buckets taken from the quonset hut— only halfway, of course, as the gold was very heavy. Franklin then hauled each bucket up by rope, emptying it into one of three wheelbarrows that, just like the buckets, had been used to haul and shape sand for

177

competitions. These were filled well below halfway due to the ever increasing mud on the trails, and Randy, Jason, and Old Joe took turns pushing them the mile or so to the quonset hut at Wafer Bay.

There, Danielle and Susan broke down sturdy, plastic crates that once held items for the show, filling them with just enough coins to make the weight close to correct. Then they re-stuffed the area around the coins with various discarded Execution Island bric-a-brac, and eventually, the rest of the material removed from the crates was simply thrown out to sea. The two women and a partially broken Kinnary, quietly resting her torn body on a blanket in the corner of the hut, were the only players to escape the rain, all too pleased to be indoors.

The temporarily unified tribe labored nearly all day after Malik blew Gissler's cave off of future maps of Cocos Island. There wasn't much else to do anyway, and each player rarely spoke to any of those on the other side of the divide.

Danielle gave the black hats an especially wide birth, certain that they were up to no good. Working next to Susan scared the hell out of her, but she knew very well that if she didn't, her coworker would almost certainly find a way to pocket more of the take. She glanced often at Kinnary, hoping the stronger woman would stir, but it was not to be, as the injured athlete spent most of the time fast asleep in her corner. Danielle had taken notice of the black hats' whispered conversations as well as their pointed remarks by the fire, and wouldn't put murder past any of them if it meant a greater share of the treasure.

And though she was on the right track, it wasn't murder they were chatting about.

"This three to five thing is not conducive to my plans for global domination," Jason Oliver joked that same night at their new camp just down the ridge from the hole. It was a well chosen spot, next to a creek that brought them fresh water, and the meat of thirsty rats.

"What's cooking in that brainpan, Dr. Evil? Spill." Randy bit into a hunk of charred rat flesh, his analytic eyes squarely on Jason.

"Well, I haven't been totally up front with you," he began. "Truth is, Frank and I have a pact. Well, had a pact, I guess, to go through to the end together. And though the game may be over, I'd still like to take him. He could be very valuable to our side."

"So what, we kill the other four?" Susan said calmly. "Danielle's easy," she nodded, "but Darius, he's above my pay grade. And Kinnary? That girl just won't die. Believe me, I'd try if I thought it was possible, but even dynamite couldn't kill the Indian princess! And who the hell gets Joe?"

Jason and Randy sat in shocked silence. Susan had moved well past strategy and straight to slaughter. Just like Malik, she was devolving right before their eyes.

"Jesus, Susan. Nobody is killing anybody. Simmer down, Dragon Lady," Jason teased lightly to avoid the she-devil's wrath. "No," he paused to shake it off, "but I'd like to grow our share. And I think we need Franklin's help."

"Because?" Randy perked up, enjoying his teammate's mastermind routine.

"I'll pull him aside. Make a pitch. You and I can do it, while Joe is off on a wheelbarrow run and we're waiting our turn. We just call him over and pitch it to him."

"And what exactly are we pitching?" Susan interjected. "That *he* kill the other four? 'Cause," she began to cackle, "there is no *fucking* way!"

"Holy shit, Susan," Jason exploded, leaping from his seat by the fire, "nobody is going to die!" "God, woman, get ahold of yourself!" The two men exchanged a flashing glance that instantly screamed "don't let this crazy bitch out of your sight!"

"I can see you two rolling your eyes!" she said, missing nothing. "But what I don't think you two dimwits understand, is that maybe one of *them* is the Killer."

Randy shook his head and fingered his hair. "Not on your life. The killers are gone, plain and simple. I mean, look who we're talking about."

"Yeah, Susan," Jason agreed, "Don't overthink this. Focus on the gold, and we're golden."

But her mind was on it's own, and she stared into the fire in a fugue state. "Darius. I think it's him. Guy's got three kids to feed. A man, a *real* man that is, and I have no doubt that he is one, will do anything to take care of his kids. *Anything...*" she repeated the word with a lustfulness never accounted for in Webster's.

Jason could take no more. Truth was, she was starting to scare him, and in just over an hour he'd be sleeping near her in the same camp. Rising from his seat, he walked over to her, and shook her by the shoulders.

"Earth to Susan! Come on now, wake up! We need you. Yer either with us," he faked a Western drawl, "or you're agin' us."

She snapped her head up at him, glaring with laser hot eyes. "That's what you think? That I'm against you?"

"Of course not!" Jason shook his head. "Bad humor, it's my thing, remember? But you clearly aren't *here* with us, right now. I need you to be here *now*."

The darkness dripped off her face, replaced instantly by a grin that could even be considered slightly above abnormal. "Yeah, ok. I'm here. Go on."

"OK," he sighed in relief, "now, just to reiterate, *nobody* dies! But, if the four of us are together on this thing, we can make sure there are extra boxes, crates, or even something more devious, where gold is stashed that only *we* know about."

"Then tell me, boy genius, why do we need Franklin," Randy probed. "I mean, what's so special about him that he has to be in on this? The three of us simply get in there at night and move shit around. We already know they can't hear us from their camp."

"Well, there is actually a specific reason. First, I like the guy. But that's not it. Would you agree that gold is heavy?"

Susan threw up her hands in irritation. "God, man! You're losing me with this ridiculous kindergarten routine! Speed it up, and skip the kiddie crap."

"Sheesh, tough crowd. I'm talking about the GPR unit. That thing is frickin' heavy. Everything else heavy, it seems, we're already using. But the GPR unit, nobody left alive even cares about it or really even notices it's there. Except, that is, for Franklin."

"Ok, now we're getting somewhere," the gambler nodded, sensing the makings of a plan.

"Franklin knows stuff. First of all, he'd notice if we paid any interest to the GPR unit when we get back to the World. Second, if *he* paid interest in it, nobody would bat an eye."

"Well now, I can't believe it, but I'm actually starting to like this stupid plan," Susan smiled, now fully awake.

"I know, right? Genius, if I do say so myself. Third, if we're going to be tearing hunks of metal out of the thing, we need Frank for that. He's the only one with the knowledge to do it, get the right parts out, and make it look legit at the end. Bingo, bango, bongo, I think we can get another five percent each out of the deal, just by doing that."

"Do it," Susan commanded, "Tomorrow. We're running out of time."

But Randy was not fully convinced. "What's your plan if he freaks out? What if he tells the others instead of joining the bad kids? You do realize there's a much higher chance of that happening than of him going along with us."

"Big whoop," Jason Oliver shrugged. "Then we're right back where we are now."

"And *then* we kill him," Susan added, quite seriously.

"I guess you're right," Randy ignored Susan's insanity while he sifted through his mental storehouse of probabilities, "I suppose that's true. But he still might get violent. And then, maybe he brings Darius along for fun."

"An off chance, I think, yes?" Jason offered, though he couldn't help peeking in Susan's direction. "Even so, we high-tail it to the other side of the island, and wait it out. Boat comes in three days. We can hide from any of them, except Joe."

"Who no longer gives even the smallest of shits, as he has said many, many times," Susan reminded them. Pointing a long, bony finger in Jason's direction, she commanded, "Get it on."

The next day as the rain poured on the labor force a the hole, he got his chance with Franklin. Darius was below, filling the next bucket when Jason sidled over to the man at the top.

"Look Frank," he began with as authentic a smile as he'd ever mustered before, "I've got an idea. You and I started out as friends. I want you to know in all candor, I'd still like us to end that way."

Franklin's lifted his eyes from the hole below, eyes that glowed with a distinct lack of trust.

"I am *not* killing anybody, Oliver! You're barking up the wrong tree."

"My God, man!" Jason stepped off in surprise, "Why the hell is everybody around here so trigger happy? Wow," he shook his head to clear his mind, "no, that's not what I had in mind at all!"

He quickly sketched his plan out, just as he had for the other two. With one minor change.

"And then there will be *another* compartment, that *only* you and I know about. And we end up just like we would have, had the game continued. Winning. Sitting together at the end, just like we talked about. A win-," he pointed his finger at Franklin, "win!" he finished gleefully, pointing back at himself.

Franklin shuffled his feet momentarily, looking at the ground and giving the idea at least a little thought. "You'd seriously screw your buddies over there out of that extra stash?"

"Damn right I would. It's my way of staying loyal to you. Pretty brilliant, if you ask me."

But, it then dawned on Franklin, that was the problem.

"Right," he nodded, sarcastically, "But by the same token, if you're willing to screw over two people you've been thick as thieves with, and I mean that literally, why would I trust you not to do the same to me?"

"Look, Frank, I'm being honest here. This is as sincere as I have ever been in this game." Jason Oliver did his very best to appear that way, but for him, it was simply an impossible task.

Franklin laughed quite suddenly, "Which is not at *all* sincere! You're the same guy who once told everyone in America you beat cancer so you could win a game! The answer is no! No way!"

But the big man wasn't done. He stepped forward, grabbed Jason Oliver by the collar, lifted him from the ground and spoke forcefully, his lips pushed up right next to the smaller man's face.

"And you better understand that I will inspect that GPR unit once we get to the dock. Closely. That ship has sailed, pal, and I don't want to hear any more of it! Equal shares, eight ways. The only way it ends up seven ways is if I toss you off that fucking cliff. Got it!"

Jason quickly realized the oddsmakers in his head were wrong on this one. Violence, it turned out, was more probable than he had concluded. Everyone, even Danielle, was on a razor's edge, and he should have realized that.

"OK, OK! I'm sorry, Frank! But really, my intention was to help you. Truly."

Franklin dropped him hard and quite suddenly from a foot off the ground. Jason Oliver's feet scraped for a hold in the slippery mud, but lost it, and he slid several feet down the ridge on his backside.

"The word 'truly' should never leave your lips. Now," Franklin gathered himself, "let me fill your wheelbarrow, and let's get back to work."

His tail now firmly between his legs, Jason Oliver did just that.

That night, hiding from the pounding rain under Leticia's old tarp, he relayed the humiliating tale to his crew. Minus the little buddy-money idea, of course.

"Looks like you might have miscalculated, just a bit!" Randy enjoyed a good laugh at the failure of Jason Oliver's gamble.

"My ass sure agrees."

Susan was all business. "He'll tell the others," she spoke into the fire, her mind drifting again. "Guaranteed."

Jason nodded sheepishly. "I bet he already has. No big deal. I'm sure they expected it anyway."

"Yeah," she said, "only now you gave him an idea! Sure he's gonna check the GPR over and over, because the son of a bitch is going to fill a chamber for himself! And maybe for all of them! God damnit, Jason! You fucked this one up royally!"

"Seriously, Susan," he leaned away from her just a bit, noting the darkness in her eyes, "you agreed with the plan, remember?"

But she didn't answer. Lost far back in her own mind, she was imagining that goddamn stupid football player, who was probably even richer than she was, grinning like Richie fucking Rich as he tore open the GPR unit in some empty warehouse in Costa Rica.

26

Susan ~ Eight Years Earlier

She sat at one end of the long conference table, the chairman at the other, the rest of the board gathered along the sides. Sipping from her water glass, she was quaking on the inside. But on the outside? Solid granite.

"Susan," the chairman droned on in monotone, "you've done well for yourself here, and we're all aware of it. You've shown grit through adversity, real heart, and a rather stunning ability to move through obstacles as if they weren't even there. Safe to say, we're impressed."

She smiled, ever more confident that she would indeed be made Chief Executive Officer of Sierra Western Holdings sometime in the next few hours.

"Thank you, sir. I appreciate your support, and," she nodded to her left and right, "the support of the board. I've given Sierra Western my very best, and I'm grateful you've noticed. Nothing would please me more than to lead our next leg of acquisitions. In fact, I've outlined a strategy for our move into Colorado over the next three years. I think you'll all be quite excited about it. I know I am."

Susan opened her briefcase, producing a leather binder. Removing a pile of documents printed on linen cardstock, she began to pass them around the table.

"As you'll see, I believe it would be wise for us to produce a secondary offering in the Spring. With these funds, we can easily begin that expansion and have substantial reserves left over, which will come in handy should we decide to push east from there. I'm hearing good things about Omaha," she chuckled, quickly joined by many around the table.

But at the opposite end, the Chairman wasn't laughing.

"Right," he he slid back his chair and cleared his throat, "and, I think we all agree that you have the bull by the horns when it comes to moving us into the next decade here at the firm. But Susan..."

She froze. But? Why the hell was there a but? How could there possibly be a but?

"...I must inform you that you are not our only candidate."

She gulped. They wouldn't fucking dare. "Really? But I thought..."

The chairman put his hand up and cut her off. "I'll be frank. There are some at this table, Susan, and I am not afraid to say I am among them, who believe that your methods can be..."

"Ruthless," rose a shrill voice from her left. It was Cindy Meadows, the current CFO. Susan glared in her direction. She thinks I'm ruthless, she thought, I'll show her ruthless.

"Yes," Chairman Handel continued, "ruthless is as good a word as any for it, I suppose. "There was that nasty business with Dave Cherkoff, just a few months ago."

"Cherkoff?" She was aghast they would bring that up. "Cherkoff the jerkoff? He grabbed my ass, Lloyd! Not just touched, but grabbed!"

"You cut his finger off!" Cindy shrieked. "How is that justified?"

Susan used her twitching hands to smooth over the few remaining wrinkles in her suit jacket, hoping to distract them from the desire to rip Cindy's throat out.

"In some cultures, Cindy, I would have been justified to cut off his penis, for god's sake. Lucky for him, I showed restraint."

Around the room, male board members shifted uneasily in their seats. Some coughed. Others grunted. Cindy sighed, maybe a little too derisively.

185

"Oh come off it, Cindy!" Susan's composure continued to slip towards the floor. "What would *you* have done! Blown him for god's sake!"

"I'd have notified my supervisor, and he'd have lost his job," Cindy replied, rather haughtily, disgusted that a colleague would use such language in the boardroom.

"Bullshit." Susan coughed, quickly regaining her calm. "They wouldn't have fired him. He'd have been sent in for "sensitivity training", and probably moved to a corner office when he finished. He would have continued to do to others what he did to me, with a wink and a nod from the boys above. And that, and now let *me* be frank, Lloyd, is part of the problem here, no offense to you nor to the other distinguished gentleman seated here. There is an old boy's culture at Sierra Western that must be addressed. How many complaints have been filed against this firm by women in the last five years? How many harassment suits have been settled in that time?"

No one answered. Susan had them by the balls, literally. Only Cindy was woman enough to answer her call.

"Deondre Theroux."

Susan was livid, picturing Cindy draped over the hood of her car with a bullet in her brain. "Are you really bringing up Deondre fucking Theroux, Cindy? Really? The woman was a total incompetent. She had to go."

"You shredded her family photos! You purposely broke the "world's best mom" mug that her kids, the ones *in* those photos, gave her for Mother's Day!"

Susan slammed her fist not he table. "She violated policy, Cindy! You know personal items aren't allowed on the floor. Period. So I put a stop to it."

Cindy sat back in her chair, nervously tapping her pencil on the embossed leather pad in front of her. Susan folded her arms and turned a withering glare in the chairman's direction.

"So Lloyd, just who then is this other candidate?"

"Well," he paused to clear his throat, "we've narrowed it down to Carter Hughes, from Pogram and Sons."

Susan was livid. "Carter Hughes? You're kidding me, Lloyd! Do you realize how many times I've bested Carter Hughes in negotiations? He's never beaten me. Not once! And this firm," she slammed her pointer finger into the table with each word, "has benefitted mightily from me kicking his sorry ass!"

"Now, now, Susan," Lloyd waved his hands in surrender, "no one here denies that. You are indeed the superior competitor in battle, can we all agree to that?"

Heads nodded, all around the table. All but one.

"But this is a different era," Cindy began, "it's not all about winning. One needs tact. One needs to be a team player. One needs to keep the troops happy, or they will go somewhere else."

"Oh really? Is that right, Cindy? They'll go somewhere else, even when their wallets grow fat on the acquisitions I'll make, at lightning speed? Acquisitions that will double company profits in ten years! They'll jump ship, what, to be paid less somewhere else?"

"They're mostly millennials now, Susan. They don't just care about their wallets. They care about quality of life, and quality of work environment."

Susan nodded violently. "You're right, they *are* mostly millennials. And you know what millennials do, just like any other generation, Cindy? They fall right the fuck in line behind people who can lead, people like me. And gentlemen, that is exactly what I intend to do *when* you elect me Chief Executive Officer tomorrow. Or, I'm sorry to say, I'll be the one who is leaving. Maybe Pogram and Sons needs a sharpshooter?"

"Now Susan! We don't want to lose you to the competition, we all agree on that. It would indeed be our loss. We've yet to interview Mr. Hughes, and you know you have our full confidence. Let it play out, and we'll discuss it immediately afterwards. No matter what the outcome, I will personally guarantee that you are heavily rewarded. Trust me. We know your strengths, and they are formidable. No one wants them in enemy hands."

"Goddamn right you don't." With that, and a plan already forming in her head, Susan stood, grabbed her briefcase, and moved quickly towards the exit.

"Until tomorrow, gentlemen."

Six hours later, Carter Hughes left work late, as usual. He was a devoted servant, and if not the brightest bulb in the box, he at least made up for it by working harder than anyone else. Tomorrow was a big day for him, a day that would bring him the CEO position he had dreamed of his entire working life. Cindy Meadows at Sierra Western had virtually guaranteed him the position was his to lose.

His silver Mercedes SL sat gleaming in the parking garage. He fired it up with his clicker, opened the door, and hopped inside. It hummed like the fine machine he knew it to be, and instantly began to warm the cold air inside to his liking. He tossed his briefcase in the seat next to him, and called his wife.

"I'll be home in about an hour, hon. Yeah, just gonna stop and have a pint of barley wine with the boys. Yes, just one. Don't worry," he laughed, "Tomorrow's a big day! I'm not gonna mess this up!"

After saying good bye, he eased his land yacht out of its reserved spot and into the exit lane, heading for the Bull's Blood tavern, a mere three Manhattan miles away.

Six spaces to his left, a thick shouldered teenage boy with dark sunglasses, equally dark gloves, and a large afro bursting out of his black hoodie sat in the driver's seat of the Escalade he had just hot-wired. The big engine purred as he too slipped out of his spot, following the silver Mercedes out of the garage and into the streets of New York City.

Staying just behind the sleek automobile as it twisted and turned its way through the heavily trafficked streets of Manhattan, he crossed the bridge into Brooklyn. The man in the Mercedes was in no hurry and paid no mind to the large, red SUV shadowing him all the way. The thickly muscled young man kept his eyes on the car, eyeing each turn with renewed interest. They followed the Belt Parkway along the Bay, before exiting at Shore Blvd in Manhattan Beach. Before long, the silver Mercedes turned into the parking lot of a tavern with a prime location along the Brooklyn waterfront, facing out towards JFK.

Carter Hughes parked in his usual spot, sideways so that no one could park next to him and spoil his paint job.

The muscly young black man's Escalade purred in the entrance to the parking lot. He looked behind, left, then right, as Carter Hughes rolled his hundred and fifty thousand dollar automobile to a stop right where the young man knew he would.

The teenager revved the engine, let go the brake, and the big SUV tore across the parking lot, closing the distance to Carter's driver's side door in just moments.

Unaware of the huge hulk speeding towards him, Carter opened that door very briefly, but seeing a sudden flash of red, he paused and instantly looked up. His mind was unable to process what it saw next, as the massive grill of the red SUV plowed into his door, throwing him across the car. The heavily outweighed Mercedes took to the air like a golf ball off a tee, flying sideways out of the parking lot and over Sheepshead Bay until, looking a bit like the re-entry capsule from Apollo 11, its silvery mass splashed down, bobbed for just a moment, and then began to sink beneath the frigid surface on an inevitable slip-slide to the bottom of the bay.

Carter Hughes wasn't aware of any of this. He was out cold.

Several witnesses later testified that a black teenager then bolted from the Escalade and ran across the parking lot, while four men dove into the Bay to save the battered and broken Carter Hughes. Luckily for him, the impact had shattered the driver's side window, and a volunteer firefighter who was drinking at the Bull's Blood that night managed to get a hand on his sport coat and pulled him back to life before his car plunged to the bottom for good.

These witnesses would later testify that the assailant had huge shoulders, a big afro, and was unmistakably a black teenager. He was fast, scary, and while more than one of the onlookers dialed 9-1-1, none dared to give chase. After all, this was New York!

The heavily muscled teenage boy raced through the alleyways near Oxford street, and back to a waiting car parked at Manhattan Beach Park. Jumping into this stolen red Toyota Tercel, he hit the gas.

The assailant drove back through the city the very same way he'd come, and in twenty minutes slipped back into the garage where the stolen Escalade had been parked, less than an hour before.

The teen leapt out of the car and ran through the parking garage to the next level above. Once there, he pulled out a key fob and punched the button to start up a waiting black Bentley sedan. Safely inside, he slammed the door shut, and gasped for breath.

Rushing to tear off the wig, the football pads, the dark glasses, and the hoodie as soon as she was safely inside the darkly tinted fine automobile, Susan shoved them all into a large, black trash bag. Shriek laden laughter filled the top-grain leather clad space all around her. When she finally regained control of herself, she eased the heavy luxury vehicle out of its spot and headed for her apartment on the Upper West Side.

There she very cautiously threw the the trash bag into the incinerator.

The next morning she went to work as normal, feigning shock at the unfortunate crippling and lengthy hospitalization of Mr. Carter Hughes. When Cindy Meadows dared glance her way, Susan narrowed her eyes like an angry cat and hissed loudly at the mousy woman, who, quite frightened and quite certain that her nemesis had added attempted murder to her list of career accomplishments, dove around a corner for safety.

And then, Susan went calmly into the women's bathroom, entered a toilet stall, bolted the door, and laughed her damn head off.

27

Day 14 ~ Play Ball!

The next morning Franklin's head was nowhere to be found.

Instead, the spot where it *normally* might be found was occupied by a long, silver machete, blade-down in the sand, where it had apparently completed the task of removing it from his shoulders. His headless body lay as though sleeping, on its back, undisturbed under a blanket of palm leaves, looking like he hadn't even awakened when his head was forcibly removed from his spine.

On cue, Danielle panicked yet again and ran down the beach, while Joe took a quick look, just for old time's sake.

"Musta been one helluva stroke," he spoke into the jasmine scented ocean breeze. "Guy had a thick neck. That's one sharp machete."

Plucking it from the sand, he inspected the edge.

"Sharpened all to heck. Mine sure don't look like that."

Darius, visibly angry and nervous at the same time, paced rapidly next to Old Joe.

"*Now* what the hell do we do? Throw all the damn machetes into the ocean too? Christ man, when does this all end?"

Joe dropped the machete to the sand and pretended to look at an invisible watch on his wrist.

"Looks like it all ends when that boat pulls up tomorrow afternoon. 'Til then, try ta keep yer head, son."

Truth was, it just slipped out, and he instantly regretted it.

"That is so sick, Joe," Darius eyed him warily. "Man, have you changed."

"Well ain't that the pot callin' the kettle black! And I didn't mean it that way. Just come out wrong. Figger a speech is all. Plum dumb luck."

Darius didn't completely buy it, but let it go for now. "Sure, Joe. I'll take your word for it. But there's no goddamn way I'm sitting here waiting for my own head to disappear." He looked back down the beach, and then towards trail. "I'm checking machetes. I see you have yours."

Joe nodded. "Never leaves ma side. 'Sure as hell ain't now."

"And as you see, I've got mine. Danielle!" he turned and yelled across the beach.

The sobstress was face down in the sand, trying very hard not to commit suicide to avoid being murdered, the second of which she figured might actually happen at any moment.

Raising her head ever so slightly, she looked over at them, her face a mass of tears, sand, and horrible, visible stress.

Darius held up his machete. "Where's your machete?"

She pointed halfheartedly at the fire pit, and Darius jogged over to confirm that yes, indeed, she had not killed Franklin. Not that it had really been a possibility, but he wanted to be thorough before he went about killing anybody himself.

"I'm going up to check shit camp," he huffed to Joe. "You comin'?"

Joe exhaled, very, very wearily. He'd truly rather just curl up right there on the sand in the pouring rain, bury his face in it like Danielle, and wait for the boat to come.

"Dear God, son, do I got a choice?" he moaned.

"Sure you do. But if they kill me because I'm alone, it just makes it tougher on you tomorrow."

"And so we're just gonna leave *that,*" Old Joe pointed to the sobbing pile of human goo on the beach, "all alone, just a sittin' there? Served up like Peking Duck?"

Darius peeked again at the woman alone on the sand, and shrugged. "What difference does it make? She'll probably head into those waves in the next ten minutes and try to walk home anyway."

Joe agreed, but somewhere inside, he had just barely an ounce of chivalry left.

"I gotcha, son, but I'm gonna go check on her. Hang on a sec."

Joe jogged over and touched her on the shoulder. She went suddenly taut, like electricity had bolted through her entire body.

"Hey girl," he purred into her ear, "hang in there now. Boat's a comin' tomorrow. Everthin's gonna be fine."

She turned her filthy, tear-stained face to look at him.

"Really? Really, Joe?" she sobbed, barely audible. Then she shook her head, just a little. "No, no it's not. You *know* it's not. It's true. Malik was right. None of us, not a single one of us, is ever going to leave here. Ever."

Being not altogether sure she was wrong, Joe simply stood, ready to move on with the task at hand.

"Ok, then. Me n' Darius are gonna go check machetes in the other camp. But I'm plum worried 'bout leavin' ya here by yerself. You gonna be all right?"

She stared longingly back out to sea, as though the boat might come a day early, slipping mercifully over the horizon to rescue her.

"I'll stay. Doesn't matter, really. If I go, they'll probably kill me. If I stay, they'll probably kill me. See? It doesn't really matter now. For you, either. There's no free will here, Joe. Everything is predetermined. Everything."

"Mebbe so, darlin'. Mebbe so. But we'll see ya in 'bout an hour or so."

She raised a limp hand to wave as he stood to go, then let it drop to the ground, like it wasn't even hers.

"Holy sheepshit!" Old Joe exclaimed to Darius as they moved towards the trail. "That one's 'bout as gone as ol' Malik was 'fore he gave up the ghost. I think yer right, she might jus' do herself in 'fore we get back."

Darius didn't care. He was focused purely on himself.

"I gotta make it, Joe. I gotta. Three kids, man."

Old Joe, like everyone else, was pretty sick of hearing about Darius' kids.

"I know, I know all 'bout yer three kids, son. Now hows 'bout somethin' new."

"Look, I know I'm a broken record," Darius admitted, "but I mean it. I can't lose this game. I blew it for my kids, and this is my chance to make it up to them. I won't let anyone take it from me."

"Game's over, son," Joe said calmly as they began to walk at, what was for Old Joe, a very fast pace.

"You know what I mean. I won't let them kill me. I'm not sleeping until that damn boat gets here. No way somebody takes me out. No way."

"Right there with ya, Pardner. Right there."

Things looked bleak, but when they reached the trail, they suddenly got much worse. They froze, shocked to their very cores, on a day when they were certain they already had been.

Smack in the middle of the trail, at the point where loose sand gave way to compacted soil, was Franklin's head. But it wasn't just lying there.

The severed head had been carefully teed up, football style. A palm leaf, folded into a makeshift tee, sat on the ground with Franklin's head perched on it like a ball waiting to be kicked. Scrawled in the sand to the side of the display was a single word.

PUNT!

"Aww, shit," Old Joe turned away, "If that don't beat all. It ain't enough ta kill a man, ya got to humiliate his corpse. Lord, I seen it all now."

Darius simply stared, seething, his chest rising and falling to its fullest extent with breaths of pure, hot rage. To see his friend first dismembered, and then disgraced, was twice more than he could bear. Wincing as he plucked the head softly from the tee, he slipped it carefully into the bag on his shoulder.

Then, without another word, he took off sprinting toward the black hat camp.

"Now hold on, son! Why in hell would they put it *here*, on the way ta their own camp!" Joe shouted after him, but Darius was too far ahead. The Old Man started to jog as quickly as his old legs would carry him, but it was a mismatch.

Fifteen minutes later he caught up to the big man, who stood brandishing his machete menacingly, hulking over the three dark siders. Cornered against the hill, all had their arms raised in standard "please don't kill me!" position.

"It was her!" Darius, seeing Old Joe arrive, yelled as he gestured towards the three with his machete. "Her machete is gone!"

"Joe," Randy pleaded, his wits still somewhat on display, "I've been trying to tell him! That doesn't prove a thing! Somebody could have taken her machete in the night. In fact, I'd lay odds somebody did just that!"

"He's right, son," Old Joe nodded his head, "Don't prove nothin'. Besides, why would she put the gol'durn head on the path ta her own camp? Don't make no sense, does it?"

"It's a trick!" he boiled as he paced up and down the line of thieves, his own sanity having momentarily left the building, "It's a trick, Joe, don't you see that? She knew you'd think that! She knew it." He paused, a scary sneer on his face, and waved his machete to and fro to drive the point home. "She's fuckin' smart, Joe, real smart! A snake. She knew you'd think one of them wouldn't do that! That's why she put it there!"

"What?" Susan said, dropping her arms, "somebody put it near here? On the way here? Are you serious?" she smirked right back at him, "Joe's right, man, why would I do that? If it was me, I'd have put it by *your* camp. Maybe in your bed!"

"Shut up!" Darius seethed, "Just shut the hell up! You are *not* getting out of this!"

"Not only that," Randy continued to work the problem calmly, "but is she even strong enough to cut through Franklin's huge neck? I doubt it. Guy was solid muscle, double X-L."

"Well now, truth be tol', this here machete *was* sharpened, like a razor," Joe answered sheepishly. "But, I guess that don't really help her case."

"Even so, what about you, Oliver?" Darius got right up in the deviant's face. "Frank told me you tried to get him to help you cheat us all. Maybe *you* did it, and made it look like *she* did!"

Susan turned to Jason Oliver, a dark, mischievous grin spreading across her face, sarcasm oozing into the air with every word. "*Yeah*, Oliver, what about that? Did you turn poor Franklin's head into a football?"

"Shut the fuck up, Susan!" Jason shrieked, spit flying from his mouth, his trademark, self-satisfied smirk nowhere to be seen. "This isn't funny! And I did *not* kill him! Hell, my arms are skinnier than hers!"

"Still," Susan turned calmly back to Darius as though she were in on the investigation, "I wouldn't trust this guy. He's got a track record. Plus, I'd bet my life that he had a grudge against football players." Her cackling laughter ripped a hole in the air, as she added, "Fucking nerds! Am I right! So predictable!"

"SHUT UP!" Jason screamed, flew towards her, and uncharacteristically shoved her to the ground. "That's enough! This is no joke, Susan! People are dying out here, and you get shits and giggles out of it! Maybe you *did* kill him. Maybe the others too!"

"Hmm," she put her finger to her chin and tilted her eyes up introspectively, "Maybe! But that's for me to know, and you to find out," she laughed wildly.

"Jesus, Count a' Monte Cristo!" Joe yelled as his last marble blew from his head, "is *everybody* plum crazy on this gol-durned rock?"

"Step aside, Jason," Darius ordered, "You too, Randy. For your own good. I don't want to miss and take one of you guys out. I've got all the proof I need."

"What?" Susan teased him fearlessly, "you gonna kill me in cold blood? Father of the year? Really? Hah!" she doubled over and slapped her knee for emphasis, "I doubt it! You don't have it in you. But here," she nodded vigorously, stepping towards her would be executioner, "let me help you, since you're such a fucking pussy."

Susan dropped to her knees on the muddy ground, and calmly set her head face down on one of the rocks that made up the fire ring.

"Here you go, big boy! Guillotine style. I'll play Marie Antoinette in your little stage play. Now you *can't* miss!"

Darius was torn. He wanted her dead, for everyone's safety, but somehow this little tableau jogged a nerve that made him realize he might *also* be going a little crazy.

"Don't do it, son," Old Joe set his hand softly on the thick arm brandishing the machete. "If we make it back ta the mainland, ain't no way you'll ever see them three kids agin. Son, they'll throw away the key."

"He's right, D," Randy nodded, no longer willing to let gold fever blind him to the true nature of his companion, "don't let her goad you into it. Don't do it man. She's fucking nuts. We'd all be best off just staying away from her until tomorrow."

"*Jesus* Christ!" Susan sat up, "What *is* this Island, a pussy forge? God damnit, Randy, grow a pair!"

"Susan, that's enough," Randy stepped into her space. "You shut your damn mouth, or I swear to God I'll knock every tooth out of it."

Meanwhile, Darius had cooled. Old Joe was right. Now, more than ever, he had to be sure he got back to his kids. One way or another he had to get home, and cold blooded murder would almost certainly keep that from happening.

Unless, he suddenly realized, unless he were the only one left to walk off this rock alive. To tell a tale entirely of his own making. But while the thought sparked briefly in his mind, it was just as quickly gone.

"Bitch," he pointed at her with his machete, "come for me. Do it. Because I *will* kill you, I'm just not dumb enough to do it on *your* terms."

Susan hopped to her feet with a grin. "And I so hoped you *were*! Thanks for the invitation, Daddy-o. Sounds like a hell of a party."

"Get the fuck outta here, Susan!" Jason gave her one more uncharacteristic shove towards the trail.

"Et tu, Oliver?" she huffed. "That's ok. I was planning to make my own way until tomorrow, anyway. I trust you goodie-goodies will keep my gold safe?"

No one answered.

"No matter," she waved them off, "I'll be sleeping with it, just in case. Now, boys!" she bowed to her former clan, "Nice knowing you. Hope you all, and I *almost* mean this sincerely, make it through the night."

"TEETH!" Randy shouted, moving towards her menacingly.

"I'm going!" she threw her hands up in the air. "God, man, don't bust a nut! But, I'm taking Leticia's tarp. I think she'd have wanted me to. One queen bitch to another."

She gathered the tarp and some of the food left from the night before, then paused on her way out of the camp to smile back at the group, a quizzical look plastered on her face.

"May I borrow a machete?" she smirked, "I seem to have *misplaced* mine."

Eight silent eyes looked back, blood shot, and glaring.

"Psyche!" she shouted with childlike glee, thumping her chest and laughing with wild abandon. "Had to ask!"

Her shrieking laughter sizzled in the air behind her as she hit the trail, heading in the direction of the treasure hole.

"Girl Power!" she yelled back at them, her middle finger raised in salute.

197

28

Day 14 ~ Night ~ The Tempest

The wind picked up just before dark, and then the sky *really* broke loose. Palm trees went horizontal under a mighty gale and the ocean pitched a fit, swells rising several feet, swamping the Execution Grounds under two feet of water.

Danielle, Darius and Kinnary moved quickly to the quonset hut, carrying everything they could with them. The hastily built structure creaked and groaned under the weight of wind and rain, and every time a coconut or a branch was ripped from a tree and slammed down onto the metal roof, Danielle shrieked, certain that the Killer was coming for her at that very moment.

Darius pitied the woman, but wished he could get out of there. Taking care of himself was one thing, but taking care of her at this point was like taking care of a baby, and doing so would leave him vulnerable as the Killer's next victim. He wondered where Susan was spending the night. Hopefully, he thought, not nearby.

But like any enterprising millionaire, Susan headed straight for the money at the treasure hole, and using the rope, lowered herself to the bottom. Still very wet inside thanks to the giant hole in the roof, Leticia's tarp kept most of the rain off, and she was at least out of the wind. Besides, sleeping next to a pile of gold was better than a plush king bed at the Four Seasons, as far as she was concerned.

Kinnary felt much better, but had missed most of the insanity of the past two days as she healed. When Darius told her about the scene with Susan, she knew she was the only person who could take her on. So with the storm intensifying, she went into action and separated herself from the pair in the hut. Wrapped in a blanket and an Execution Island windbreaker and hat, she hugged Darius, patted poor Danielle on the head, and headed for the first cave entrance they'd found such a long time ago. Darius told her that Susan was headed for the treasure, and there was no way she'd leave that bitch unattended. She'd stay close, until the moment to make a move finally came.

Battered by the elements, she inched her way through the jungle towards the cave. She passed the treasure hole as silently as possible, but with the wind howling so loudly, she could have stepped right over Susan's sleeping body and not been heard. Arriving at the original entrance, she slipped through the crack and made herself a bed on the first little shelf that led to the deeper chasm below. The walk had done her good, the strenuousness of it filling her body with vigor, and she felt ready for anything.

Jason and Randy were up a creek without a paddle. Susan had wisely taken the tarp under which they'd been surviving the formerly mild rain. But now they felt like they'd wandered into a biblical hurricane, with no ark to be found. Their first thought was the quonset hut, but on arrival they found Darius and Danielle had beat them to it. Darius was absolutely, and quite violently it turned out, opposed to the two joining them under its rattling tin roof.

But after some begging, he let them have one of the large banners left over from the Execution Island stash for cover, and they greedily took it before leaving. He immediately barred the door behind them, running the handle through with a thick bamboo rod, once destined for minor fame as an authentically rustic, tv show flagpole.

But where to go? The whole island felt like it was coming down upon them. A vinyl banner wouldn't be much help if it blew away in the gale, a distinct possibility, for the two men felt like they might be blown off the island as well. They could search for another cave, but it might take hours. Hours they didn't have. The sun would soon set, if there was even a sun out there behind the thick, dark clouds above.

Randy and Jason Oliver were about to spend the most miserable night in Execution Island history.

They poked through the cabin wreckage, thinking they might tie the banner to some downed timbers, but those timbers had nearly all burned to ash. Unable to hear each other speak, and battered by ocean spray that crossed hundreds of feet of beach to sting their faces with tiny needles, Randy simply waved for Jason to follow.

They hiked up to where Gissler's Cave once stood, praying there was enough of it left to shelter them. No one had seen the cave since Malik became part of it, and when they rounded the bend, the wind shoving them around like paper dolls on the exposed ridge, they were crestfallen to find there was no longer even a cave mouth left for cover. Boulders completely covered the entrance, and there was scarcely enough room for a piece of paper to slide between them, let alone a full sized man.

They gazed at each other in agony. It was quickly becoming dark, and they were soaked to the bone. Objects ripped from trees pelted them, and bits of flying sand slashed their skin like microscopic razor blades. Randy motioned to head back down the trail, and Jason had no choice but to put one foot in front of the other, and follow.

Halfway down the trail Randy noticed something unexpected. A gust of wind blew the huge, fan shaped leaves of a grove of banana palms apart, suddenly and momentarily exposing a hidden trail. They'd always gone straight to the cave when walking this unremarkable, densely green section of the main trail before, so no one else had noticed it either.

Randy bent into his companion and yelled with glee, "Trail! Has to go somewhere!"

Jason didn't see it and only caught the "somewhere" part of Randy's yell, but being out of options, he just nodded. But when his following feet suddenly stepped through the bushes onto a worn strip of compacted dirt, his jaw dropped. Their spirits picked up immediately, and their pace quickened to match.

Meandering up through a series of small hills, the trail left them exposed once again, and they bent low to keep their weakened bodies from taking to the air. Further they went, up and up into the raging maw of the storm, but soon the trail thankfully descended once more into the relative safety of the trees. It wasn't long until a strange and new coastline began to come into view behind the sheets of water dropping before their eyes. At first, it was just a bunch of water logged rocks and two points of land, but soon after, a beach, nearly as wide as the one at Wafer Bay came into view, and then...

"Fuuuuck me!" yelled Jason, the first to see clearly the device of their deliverance from the tempest. Barely able to control himself, he leapt onto Randy's back, hooting, hollering and gesturing towards the sandy beach below. Randy briefly entertained the thought that perhaps Jason Oliver actually *was* the Killer, a mere machete strike from taking down his former teammate.

But the look on Jason's face was unmistakable joy, and Randy turned his gaze to follow the bony arm gesturing vigorously towards the sea.

It was a cabin, just like the ones at Wafer Bay. Exactly the same, in fact.

They ran like stallions when just moments before they could barely walk. Bursting through the door when they arrived at the small structure, Randy slammed it closed once Jason was through.

"We must be dead, because this *has* to be heaven!" Jason squealed in delight, dropping the now useless banner and his small pack to the floor.

"Fuckin' A!" the usually calm Randy exhaled, "How the hell is there a cabin here that nobody knew about?"

Jason shook his head. "Not such a surprise. You know how these Execution Island things are," he said, poking around the room. "Walled gardens, man. Tourists on towels right around the corner if you know where to look. But they find ways to hide them."

"Like a hastily planted grove of banana palms," Randy nodded.

"Exactly. Shit to create a finite game space. Australia, Nicaragua, Fiji, all the same. Just a few miles away, people and food and houses. No surprise at all that this sucker is here."

"You're right," Randy nodded. "The surprise is that two brainiacs like you and me were too stupid to look for it. We knew the drill. But every time, Taylor pulls his hypnotist routine, and we fall for it."

"Well, I have it on good authority that won't ever happen again," Jason joked, pawing through the papers and books in the room. There was a desk, a couple of bookcases, and a pair of tables as well.

Randy busied himself by poring over the maps and photographs of the flora and fauna of the island, which covered nearly every inch of the cabin's bamboo walls.

"Rangers," he said as he put it all together. "Map says this is the only other cabin. Chatham Bay . . ."

He suddenly paused, hearing a thump. And there it was again. The unmistakable sound of something hitting the floor, from underneath.

Randy stepped softly towards his companion and tapped him on the shoulder, a finger to his lips.

Jason Oliver froze, and listened. And he heard it. One thud... then another. Not from above, where it might be blamed on the storm, but from below.

Randy grabbed his machete and crept towards the door. Opening it very slowly, he poked his head out just far enough...

Rats. The little monsters scurried in every direction, coming right from the crawlspace beneath his feet.

"Hah! It's just the rats! Little bastards need someplace to hide too, I guess."

Relieved, Jason smiled and went back to snooping through the cabin. Tearing through the desk drawers, his normally pale face suddenly glowed like the Sun.

"Well, God bless the Rangers! It looks like our boys in green have something in common with yours truly!"

His hand produced a bottle of rum, about three quarters full.

"Hallelujah!" Randy exclaimed with childlike eyes. Crossing the room, he sat down across the desk from Jason, who was already pulling a mightier swig from the bottle than would be thought possible for one his size.

"Oh Baby that is *so* very good!"

Randy took an even larger pull, rotating the bottle lovingly in his hands, gazing at it as if it were a tiny angel descended from on high.

"Nicaraguan, aged 12 years."

"Well, God bless Nicaragua, too!" Jason beamed.

He took another turn at the bottle, while Randy dug through the piles on the desk, an idea taking shape in his mind.

"Did you see a pen in there? Scissors maybe?" he asked.

Setting the bottle down, Jason opened the middle drawer.

"Why yes," he smiled, "there are indeed. What have you in mind, young sir?"

Randy, a much more regular drinker than Jason Oliver, pulled another swig. "See these folders? I'm gonna make us a deck of cards. Then, not only can we drink our way through Hurricane Susan…"

"Oooh, nice touch."

"… but we can have a bit of fun while we do."

"I'm tearing up with joy," Jason grinned, "you're killing me."

Randy snickered, the liquor taking hold in his empty stomach. "Better me than Susan!"

"Hah! You should get stuck in a storm more often! Brings out the joker in you!"

"Well then, God bless the Storm!" Randy mimicked his friend, before dumping more liquid Nicaraguan candy down his greedy gullet.

Quite unexpectedly, the two men had gone from sharing the worst night in Execution Island history, to sharing one of the happiest.

And while "Team Frat Party" was having a ball under the tempest, Old Joe was doing some unpleasantly necessary deliberating. At the base of his tree, he stared at his belongings, now spread all over the ground. His old home shifted wildly from side to side, now on his left, then on his right, bending nearly in half to become parallel with the dirt, before springing back again.

"Ok, Fella. I git what yer sayin'" Joe spoke earnestly to his former castle in the sky.

Picking up his goods, he wrapped them in a tarp he'd long ago removed from the quonset hut, and slung the whole thing over his back with his bow. Peering around the jungle, it was hard to get his bearings. Nothing was as it had been before the Storm. Nothing. His trails were gone, covered in multiple layers of palm fronds. Even the rats had disappeared, wisely retreating into underground dens, where they were no doubt at this very moment a hell of a lot warmer and drier than he was.

He looked up at the sky and noted the speed of the clouds, swirling and racing, emboldened by having crossed thousands of miles of Pacific Ocean with not a single thing to slow them until they hit Cocos Island. It was humbling, and he felt like dropping to his knees and praying to the sky.

"Sure don't have storms like this in West Virginia," he said, savoring each word leaving his mouth as an individually packaged totem against the tempest.

Old Joe lowered his head, beaten. In the gale, the only thing he could cling to that was as before— for the most part, anyway— was the river. He knew that if ever lost in the woods, all one needed to do was find a river, follow it downstream, and eventually you'd find civilization. It bewildered him how so many tourists got lost in the mountains, crossing one stream after another on the way to ignorant oblivion.

"Poor dumb bastards," he said, grasping again at his own voice for some sort of illusory security.

But there was no civilization here, anywhere, so instead of heading downstream, he headed up. He followed his little river, now not so little as it filled with runoff water, mud, and debris. Up and up, hoping against hope to find something, anything which might shelter him. A cave. A group of large boulders he might hide under (he came oh-so-close to that one, multiple times, but they weren't quite large enough). A stand of fallen trees where he might do the same. He walked and walked, up into the low hills in the center of the island. The canyon narrowed and he was faced with another waterfall, not quite as large as the one he'd camped above— the second largest on the island— but a wider one which blocked nearly the entire narrow canyon from side to side, leaving him scant room to climb around it.

"Shit," he said to no one at all.

Ever resourceful and currently quite desperate, Joe stepped onto the steep side of the slope that wound around the river, hoping his feet would grip the wet ground just long enough to get past the thundering falls. The slick ground steepened with every step, and when he lost a foot and tumbled to the water's edge before catching himself, he wasn't sure that he even cared if he made it or not.

"Death by waterfall sure beats death by machete," he exhaled against the groan of the falls.

But as he steadied himself with one arm and tried to keep ahold of his bow, arrows, and the tarp-bag on his back, a sudden gust blew hard against the liquid curtain, pushing it away from the slope for just a moment.

"Holy sheep shit!" he gasped, "I believe there's room at the Inn!"

Behind the waterfall he had briefly glimpsed what appeared from his vantage point to be a cave. A cave that was not by any means huge, but easily large enough to fit him and his gear for the night. If he was lucky and there was anything dry inside, there might even be room for a fire.

He dared not think of such luxuries, but immediately hoisted himself up with newfound energy. Steadying himself on his bow, he used his other hand to grab the dirt above for balance, and then put one foot in front of the other, toe to heel, step by step, until he stood beside the raging lip of the falls, right against the stone ledge that was the reason those falls existed in the first place.

Old Joe steadied himself with his right hand on a nub in the rock face, making sure his feet had good purchase on the soil below, and reached out as far as he could with his left hand for any kind of hold.

He found one. Holding tight, he swung his left leg over to do the same. Scraping and clawing at the wall with his shoe, he kicked a chunk of it loose in the attempt. A shoebox sized rock he'd hoped would be his next foothold tumbled end over end and plunged twenty feet, crashing loudly against sharp lava in the pool below.

Yet in kicking one toehold loose, he had created a better one, just about the right size for his boot. Joe slipped his foot into the gap, wedging it in tight. Lifting his right foot from the safety of the ground on the slope, he brought it directly under his right hand, which he then shifted onto a new handhold on the slab's face.

Old Joe now stood completely suspended above the pool below, the waterfall splashing his shoulders with icy green fluid, spraying his eyes with a mist that blocked his view of the next set of holds.

He was but one faith-fueled step from either the cave, or a wet ride down a one way slide. Pushing down hard on his right foot, he made sure it would be stable if he lifted his left one from its safer perch. Indeed, it appeared it would hold on the small rock nubbin on which it rested.

Old Joe, sixty-seven years young, swung his left leg up and onto the cave ledge, gripping it tightly with his knee. With a deep breath and the thrusting force of a much younger man, he rotated his body upwards to follow.

Collapsing with a gasp on the cave's hard stone floor, he kissed its wet, lichen-covered surface for a full thirty seconds.

When he finally stood, he discovered the cave would be darn near comfortable. There was no wind, and the far end of it, though dark, was relatively dry. Scooting back as far as he could from the misty front of the cave, he dropped his gear and pulled out the tarp, covering himself with it in a notch where someone had clearly slept before. Covered with withered palm fronds, it served as a nice, semi-soft bed.

Old Joe exhaled in relief and stared silently through his window of water at the front of the cave, wondering how the rest of the Castaways were making it through the night.

Then he rolled over, faced the wall, closed his eyes, and decided he really didn't give a shit.

29

Day 15 ~ Castaways

Morning dawned to more of the same. The storm raged on, though the wind blew wasn't quite as strong, and the rain lessened from liquid sheets, to mere marble-sized droplets.

Susan woke first, the smell of gold being her perfect alarm clock. Without so much as the thought of a cup of coffee, she took time to stash a small bundle of gold under a hunk of lava beneath the cave's pool. She did so simply because she *had* to win. If she were to leave the island with an equal amount of treasure, well, that would be the same as losing, to her. Even if chartering a boat to come back and get the coins in her little stash cost more than they were worth, the feeling of victory would be priceless.

A half hour after she began her cache creation she felt satisfied, and climbed the rope back up to the surface to search for something to eat. Now, her only remaining teammate on Execution Island was hunger.

Joe was the next to rise, a stone in his liquid-curtained bedroom jabbing into his backside. The roar of the falls had rocked him to sleep, keeping him in bucolic bliss all night long. Even though the biggest storm he'd ever seen raged just outside his door, it might as well have been on another planet. All he could hear on his rocky perch was the roar of the falls, and neither raindrop nor gust of wind disturbed the best sleep he'd had in weeks.

Rising from his palm leaf-laden bed, Old Joe rubbed his eyes. Yep, he thought, it was still there, that gorgeous liquid curtain shielding him from the world outside.

"Gol dang that's a beaut!" he chanted into the ether, this time out of sheer joy instead of the need for a protective incantation.

He stared at it a long while, letting it soothe and clean his mind as only a luxuriously translucent waterfall can. Few would ever be able to get the kind of view he was privy to, however, and boy did he know it.

"Shit, I might just come on back here n' live for the rest a my days. Man could get used ta that, right quick."

He quite happily let the sheer emerald green of the river soothe him into meditative bliss, until one word slipped into his brain, shook him awake, and had him on his feet in the next second.

Boat.

Today was the day the boat was to arrive, though he realized there was now a very good chance it wouldn't, thanks to the storm. But he had to see for himself, had to get to the beach and look out upon Wafer Bay to see if perhaps it had somehow made it through.

He also realized how important it was that he get there first, to be the very first one to tell the tale of bloodshed and insanity that consumed the final season of Execution Island, to get the real story out before some black hat, or some terrified ninny with the vapors, gave a version that was highly less accurate.

Of course, he still wasn't sure how to get around discussing the gold as one of the instigators of the Cocos Island massacre. He might be honest but he wasn't stupid, and did indeed want his portion of the treasure, so he'd have to be careful how he told the story, while making sure the others were as well. He was an old man, but this visit to the other-than-the-serial-murders magical Cocos Island, and especially his night in the waterfall, had filled in the blanks for him as to how he wanted to spend his remaining days.

Old Joe wanted a boat of his very own. His dreams in the tempest had filled him with delightful visions of a life at sea, a life spent in the South Pacific, cruising slowly from one island chain to the next, learning about their cultures, tasting of their wilderness, flora and fauna, swimming in their rivers and pools, and relaxing on their beaches while a Polynesian princess cared for his every material need.

It was as if the wind itself had blown the vision into his brain during the night, carrying on jasmine scented tufts an invitation from the various islands it had visited along its way to his cave.

Old Joe was very much ready to accept this ethereal invitation from beyond the sea.

When he returned home, he planned to sell all of his possessions, run to his bank account, and buy himself a sailing yacht with all the accoutrements he'd need to finish his life in the South Pacific. He would not only need money, he would need a *lot* of money, and he intended to get it, one way or another.

No matter what it took, or who got in his way.

But for now, he still needed to get off Execution Island, and not in a long box like most of the other contestants.

Peeking out at the edge of the falls to his left, he realized it would be a hell of a lot harder to get out of his little hotel than it had been to get in. When he arrived he hadn't cared whether he lived or died, but after his night's dreamscape, he wasn't only ready to live, but was actually passionate about doing so.

He peeked through the green curtain on the other side, hoping for a miracle.

"Aww shit, Joseph!" he teased himself when he saw it, "Always on the wrong side a the tracks!"

There, cut into the face of the fall, were actual steps, clearly made by a human being, perhaps Gissler himself, or Bloody Sword Bonito's crew on their way to stash gold in this very same cave. It was strictly a one toe at a time affair, but it got him out of the cave alive, in seconds.

Standing on the steep canyon wall next to the fall, he announced to it as though it were a living person, "I *will* be back," before heading down the trail under a dripping black sky.

Snoring like men much older than their years, the frat boys were not about to wake up. Truth was, they hadn't gone to sleep until nearly sunrise, and the cover of the waning storm provided enough darkness to keep them slumbering much of the day. When they eventually did awaken, a mutual hangover kept them moving very slowly. It took a while, but eventually it dawned on them too that this was to be the day of their escape.

Kinnary awoke with a start. Susan. Today was their day to meet, and for the last time.

She rose quickly, peeking out of the crack at the sky. Dark it was, but unmistakably day. She squeezed herself through the opening, and loped down the hill towards the coin cave.

In a minute she was there. Dropping prone, she slid cautiously to the edge, stuck her head just over the side, and . . .

Gone. Susan had flown the coop. Jumping quickly to her feet, lest she be stabbed in the back, Kinnary pivoted to see all around her. But there was only rain, wind, dirt, and in the distance, jungle.

"Damnit, Kinnary!" she yelled at herself. The weight of her injuries had led her to sleep too long, and had cost her the element of surprise. No matter, though. Susan didn't know she was coming, and wouldn't be ready when she did. The older woman might be brilliant, but Kinnary was brilliant *and* strong, one of the most well balanced players to ever set foot on an Execution Island challenge course. She would have her moment, and soon.

Hell, she thought, if I have to throw her off the rescue boat, so be it. No way that murdering scum was going to make it back to the mainland to twist the story of the final season of Execution Island in her favor.

No way.

She headed for the trail, keeping her head on a swivel.

Danielle hadn't slept a wink. Her eyes were pinned open all night, staring at the vibrating metal roof of the quonset hut, watching drips slide down the round walls from places where screw holes and seams let them in, listening to the continual pounding of coconuts and tree branches overhead that sounded to her like auditory murder.

Worse than all of those, however, was the door that Darius had barred. Through the night, the wind shook and rattled it, and every time it did, her mind's eye saw the Killer rushing through it with a machete, destined to be buried deep in her skull.

She was the very image of the last remaining patient left alone in an abandoned mental hospital, forced to fend for herself when her caregivers had long since forgotten the place, rocking to and fro with an absolute inability to care for her own needs. The mother of the tribe had become the child, and all it took were a dozen murders and accidental deaths to make it so.

And one very loud, very scary storm.

Darius had wisely moved as far from her as he could, to the very back of the hut, nestled behind sheets of plywood that had been intended to build ramps, docks, climbing walls and platforms for a game that almost certainly would never take place again.

Or would they, he wondered? People do slow down and gaze at a train wreck or a car crash, no matter how horrifying and bloody, don't they?

Yes, he realized as he stirred from sleep, the show probably *would* go on. Only now with a bigger viewing audience than ever, and stakes even higher than anyone in their right mind ever thought they could be.

Disgusted by this accidental realization of humanity's true nature, he rose and looked for Danielle.

And there she was, just as he had left her, staring at the door he'd barred the night before, on her haunches, arms wrapped tightly around her knees. Pale as a bleached white sheet.

"Aww, damn," he said under his breath.

Rising, he made sure to speak her name before daring to touch the wounded animal.

"Danielle! You ready for the boat?"

She turned her blackened eyes his way and sheepishly repeated, "Boat?"

"The boat! Our boat! We're getting the hell out of here today! Aren't you excited!"

He made his way to her through piles of lumber and materials. Reaching her, he put his hand on her shoulder and found it cold as ice.

"Hey girl, we gotta get you warmed up! How come you didn't grab something to sleep in?"

"Door," was all she could muster in reply.

"Well," he said, trying his best to be uplifting, "looks like it held. Seems like that was about the best night we could have had, under the circumstances."

She merely stared silently at him through dark eyes. Emotionless, pale.

Darius poked around, found a bundle of burlap cloth once set to be part of a challenge wall's surface, and wrapped it over her shoulders.

"Here, this'll warm you up."

She clung to a wad of it in front of her chest and tried to smile up at him, but it didn't take.

"I'm gonna peek outside, ok?"

Her eyes quickly grew from mere slits to half dollars.

"Don't open it! He's out there!"

Darius took a breath and put his palm to his forehead.

"There's nobody out there. If we want to get on the boat, we have to go out there. But I'll go first, ok?"

She didn't answer, her violent trembling shaking the table against which she leaned.

"Hey..." he gave her a hug, only to have her start sobbing on his shoulder. "Danielle, we're going to get on the boat and go home, ok?"

"Home..." she sobbed into his shirt, now wet with saliva and tears.

"Yes, home! See your family?"

"Family..."

Jesus, he thought, this is impossible. He felt terribly for her, and just wanted to scoop her up and take care of her. But always in the back of his mind was the fact that if he allowed himself to be exposed, he might be next.

"Yes, family. Boat. Home." He felt like he was talking to someone from a foreign country. "Now, I'm gonna go out there. You are safe. I promise."

She sobbed and whimpered, scooting back against the table as far as she could go, wadding herself into a ball. Darius removed the bamboo rod and reached to push open the door, when it was suddenly yanked open from outside.

A dark figure stood in the doorway, and Danielle screamed.

"Holy sheepshit, woman! Relax, it's just me!" Old Joe stepped through the doorway and into the hut.

"God damnit, Joe!" Darius yelled, "I just got her to chill out!"

Her screaming continued unabated, and she refused to look their way.

"Gol-dang, she been like this all night?"

"Pretty much," Darius shrugged. "Let's step outside. Maybe she'll stop."

The two men stepped out and closed the door behind them, but the screaming continued.

"That girl's done gone off the other side, son. Over the cuckoo's nest."

Darius sighed. "Believe me, I know. We gotta get her outta here. I'll need your help to get her on the boat."

Joe shuffled his feet, looking out to sea.

"Yeah, well, son, I hate to tell ya, but that's why I come ta see ya. Ain't no way that boat's a' comin'."

Darius froze, letting the screams from inside the hut fill his ears.

"C'mon," Old Joe put a hand on his shoulder, "I'll show ya."

Joe led him down the beach to a spot where they could see the open sea, and pointed.

"Take a look at them waves. Now, I'm jus' an amateur boatsman, but I kin tell ya there ain't no way that boat launched with these seas. And they'd a had ta launch yesterday, when it was even worse."

"Shit." Darius dropped his eyes from the raging sea and gazed at his feet.

"Does that mean it's not coming for another week? Because I don't know if we'll last a week unless you and me kill every one of the rest of 'em."

Old Joe shook his head, his gaze remaining on the ocean.

"I doubt that. Coupla things goin' on here. They ain't had no contact with the radio or Taylor's phone for close to a week now. That's got ta have 'em worried. Now, that same boat can't come, we know it's got other jobs ta do in between. But I bet the ol' network is workin' on gettin' somebody here as soon as this here storm clears up."

Darius shifted his feet.

"I can't stay with her, Joe. I can't. I just can't do it."

Old Joe grabbed him by the shoulders and shook him.

"Hell's Bells, son! Nobody said ya had to! This here is kill or be killed right now! One of them three is slaughterin' us like goddamn veal calves in a box! Now we got mebbe three, four days left if we're lucky. Ya gotta make it. You got kids ta feed, boy. That girl in there..." he pointed towards the shack, "son, I hate ta say it, really I do. But she ain't gonna make it. No way, no how. She's done fer."

Tears welled up in Darius' eyes, and he immediately wiped them away.

"Yeah. Yeah, I know. I just hate letting her down."

"Son, only people you can't let down is them three kids and yer wife. That's what God intended. He did not put you here ta care for some crazy lady who ain't got the intest'nal fortitude ta make it off a this here rock. Now we got three sons a bitches out there, one of 'em 'bout as pure evil as kin be right now. One of 'em is gonna try and kill us before that boat gets here. I aim to stop 'em from getting' me. I suggest ya do the same."

"They're killing the good guys, Joe," Darius pleaded, "We should join up. Watch each other's backs. Get Kinnary and maybe go looking for Susan, do something about her before she does something about us!"

"You so sure it's Susan? Are ya? Think about it. We got three possible killers', leaving' out the possibility of Taylor still being' on two legs, n' if that's it, well we might as well go carvin' pine boxes right now. But, that aside, I'm leavin' out the earlier murders, 'cause any of them other folks coulda done that, and odds are Malik or Taylor, or both, killed some of 'em. I'm jus' gonna focus on that last death."

"Franklin."

"Yep. Now ol' Evil Oliver, kid's scrawny as a calf who's mama's teats done run dry. Susan's a pencil pusher and ain't no muscle girl neither. Seems ta me only one a them three coulda had enough juice to cut right through Frank's neck like 'at."

"Randy? But nobody has even had a beef with him, or suspected him at all? He's barely even a black hat!"

Joe grinned. "Son, d'ya think real deal serial killers go 'round yellin' ta the world, 'look at me! I'm the murderer!'"

Darius nodded, not intending that he thought they actually did, but that he understood.

"No, siree. They hide in plain sight. So, 'fya ask this ol' boy, the Chicago kid's my number one suspect." Old Joe paused, then added, "Unless it was you."

"Me! Come on Joe!"

"Well, son, ya are in plain sight, ain't ya." Joe's eyes betrayed that he wasn't actually joking. Truth was, he was testing Darius, waiting for his answer. "After all, ya do make a big deal 'bout them three kids a lot. Man'll do anythin' for his kids."

Darius' eyes turned to slits, and he gave Joe a long look before answering, "You're more in plain sight than anybody, aren't you, Joe?"

"*Now* ya git what I'm sayin'! Ya cain't trust nobody! Not me," he jabbed his own chest with a finger, "and not you," he poked Darius.

"Right. So we're not joining up then." It was a statement, not a question.

"Not on yer life. Or mine. And not just for that reason. If it is Randy, or that crazy hellcat Susan, or even toothpick boy, it'd make us a helluva big target if we paired up. Only one I got some trust for is the Indian girl. She done risked her life ta take out nasty ol' Malik, and that there seems pretty virtuous. I don't know where the hell she's gone, but her I ain't worried about."

"Joe," Darius looked intently at the old man, "I didn't want it to end this way."

Joe scanned the horizon one last time, but saw nothing.

"Son, I think that 'bout goes fer all of us. 'Cept mebbe one or two."

"Or three."

"Hells bells, I don't even wanna thinka that," Joe replied. "If that's the case, we might be sunk. But, good luck to ya. May the good guys win."

The two men shook hands, preparing to split up until the moment they stepped onto the rescue boat, in who knew how many days.

"May the good guys win," Darius repeated, though he was no longer so sure just exactly who the good guys were.

Old Joe crossed the beach and disappeared into the jungle, while Darius stood and watched him go. The old guy had more weapons than anyone, which was smart. It was probably time he made some of his own, though he wouldn't be able to do it as well as Old Joe, of course. But he'd been studying that bow, and those arrows, and he figured he could make his own with a little effort.

Ok, he thought, maybe a *lot* of effort.

He crossed the beach and prepared to enter the quonset hut to get his things and scram, before Danielle could latch onto his arm and force him to drag her along.

Steeling himself before the door, he opened it very slowly, just in case she had armed herself against the Killer that seemed destined to take her life.

But when he opened the door wide, he discovered, with a strange mix of sheer terror and utter relief, that Danielle was gone.

26

Day 15 ~ Christmas Ornament

It was late in the afternoon when Randy and Jason Oliver finally came stumbling up the trail. They'd had a barn burner of a night, more fun than either thought possible on this godforsaken green rock in the middle of the Pacific Ocean. They drank. They told stories. They played poker into the night, and Randy even let Jason win a couple times. And they slept late.

When they finally awoke they had no idea what time it was. Randy poked his head out of the cabin door, but couldn't find the sun to tell him the hour. Still, they knew the boat wouldn't leave without them, so they very slowly gathered their things and began the trek to Wafer Bay.

They didn't speak. Not because they didn't want to, but because they simply couldn't. Their heads throbbing from the rum they'd poured down their throats, every step shot another jolt of pain up their spines and into their temples. It was the longest short hike either had ever taken.

Jason paused once on the trail to unpack the contents of his stomach, and emerged from the experience feeling slightly better. Randy wasn't so lucky. A veteran of frequent nights partying in Vegas, his stomach churned, and unlike his less experienced drinking companion, his system refused to give him any relief, until finally, only a few hundred yards before they reached the quonset hut, an unexpected opportunity to vomit proved impossible to refuse.

There, hanging from a stout limb on a length of official Execution Island braided rope, soaked through and swinging ever so slightly, was Danielle's very dead body.

"Fuck …" Jason exhaled, before falling to the ground with dry heaves. Randy's deliverance came immediately after, his beleaguered stomach splattering the trail with the source of it's pain.

Relieved for a moment, he rose and returned his gaze to the swinging corpse.

"Jesus. I saw that coming, but still…"

"Yeah. I know. Look…" Jason pointed at her shirt. On it were two very appropriate words, written in what appeared to be charcoal.

Dead Meat.

"Man," Jason continued, "you can say *that* again. Looks like a god damn human Christmas ornament."

Randy examined the rope tied around the tree's base.

"No way she did this herself," he shook his head, "Too high, and nothing near it she could have jumped off."

Jason pointed once more. "Blood. On her forehead."

"Yep," Randy nodded. "The Killer probably knocked her out, dragged her here, and strung her up. Too bad."

"Susan?"

"Maybe," he pondered, analyzing the possibility. "If she leveraged the rope just right. But I'm not sure she's strong enough to hoist her up. Or for that matter, to drag her here in the first place."

Jason Oliver agreed. "Hell, I'm not sure *I'm* strong enough to lift her up there!"

"God," Randy felt his stomach heaving again, "Let's get out of here. I can't take this right now."

"Please, lead on."

Minutes later they arrived at Wafer Bay. One glance instantly told them there was no boat. Disappointed dread dripped from their eyes, while rain dripped from their noses.

"Let's see if anybody's around," Jason said, looking for some kind of distraction from the heavy gloom.

"Sure thing," Randy nodded.

He knocked on the door of the quonset hut, and a very gruff voice answered.

"What do you want!"

"Hey, Darius. Any news of the boat?" Randy asked.

"Are you stupid?" the angry voice yelled back, "Did you see the ocean?"

The party victims gazed at each other, their unspoken fears now real. Leaning into Randy's ear, Jason whispered, "Ask him about Danielle. See how he reacts."

Randy nodded, and spoke again to the metal door. "Hey, Darius, is Danielle in there with you?"

The door burst open, and Darius stood before them with machete in hand, chest rising and falling rapidly with his heavy breath. He looked like a rabid animal, and a very large one at that.

Jason panicked and tripped over his own feet as he attempted to back away, tumbling into the heavy wet sand. "Hey, man!" he pleaded, "We didn't do it!" Randy stepped back too, but managed to keep both his footing, and his composure.

"Didn't do what!" Darius yelled, brandishing the machete menacingly, "Tell me now!"

He was a fearsome sight. Neither of them would be a match for him if he suddenly went full pit bull on them, and it looked like he might.

"Shit man, relax!" Randy's composure slipped, and his own anger at even having to be in this predicament took its place. "We were together when we found her, just now. We're really hung over man. Seriously, we came across her just a few minutes ago."

"Show me!" the rabid man commanded.

"Sure, c'mon." Randy turned to lead Darius back down the path, but the big man didn't follow. Instead, he waved his machete towards Jason.

"Get up, Oliver. No way I'm letting you get behind me. You two try anything and I will fucking cut you in half, no questions asked."

Jason stood and put his hands in the air. "We won't man. Seriously, it's been a rough morning. We're both pretty sick. Even if we wanted to, there's no way we could."

Gesturing again with the machete, Darius simply commanded, "Move!"

Jason quickly got in line behind Randy, his feet once again flailing pathetically in their attempt to follow his brain's instructions.

When they reached Danielle, the two black hats scooted as far from Darius as they could, while he took in the grisly spectacle for himself.

He circled around the swinging corpse, before inspecting the knot on the tree.

"Look, look man, we're telling the truth," Jason begged. "Vomit, right there. That's Randy's."

"Yeah, that was me," Randy affirmed, "I saw her, and that's all it took."

Darius glanced briefly at the still steaming pile of muck on the sand, before turning back to the twins. He was calmer now, realizing how ridiculous it would be for the Killer to vomit in the face of just another murder.

"So who did it, Big Brains? She couldn't have done this herself."

Suicide, of course, had been his first thought when he saw her swinging there.

"Well," Randy offered, "it wasn't us. And I'm guessing by your reaction, it wasn't you either."

"Susan…" Darius exhaled her name into the air.

"Or Joe," Randy continued, "I know he doesn't seem the type, but I'm not sure Susan could have lifted her. Or dragged her here in the first place. To be honest, you were my first suspect."

"And no offense," Jason added, feeling less likely now to be split by a machete, "but why the hell does no one ever suspect Kinnary? She could lift her. And when was the last time anyone saw her?"

Darius ignored Jason Oliver as if he weren't even there. He respected Randy, but the other guy? Not so much.

"The knot is basic," he replied to Randy, "nothing special. If it was Joe, and at this point I'm not putting it past him, but the knot would have been more sophisticated. That's just a friggin' granny knot," he pointed at the base of the tree.

Randy nodded, "Yeah, I noticed that too. Of course," he added with a tilt of his head, "But Joe would know we'd suspect a quality knot."

Darius nodded. "And, she might not have been dragged at all. She was a mess. Suicidal. She would have done this herself if she'd had the strength."

Randy and Jason exchanged surprised glances. While they were out partying on the other side of the island, the game had not only continued, but had apparently escalated.

"Shit, man. Rough night?" Jason smirked.

Darius shot him a deadly look, before turning and storming off.

The two friends stood in silence, stunned from the events of the past half hour, until Jason finally spoke.

"Man, what the fuck do we do now? Did you hear him? He wouldn't put it past *Joe*? Danielle would have killed herself? Shit. What the hell happened last night?"

"Strange," Randy agreed. "Not what I expected. And if those three are that bad..."

"Susan is ballistic. Yeah, I was thinking about that. Goodies turning on other goodies, Kinnary nowhere to be seen, Susan turning on us..."

Randy fell silent again, his calculating mind filled with thoughts he didn't think Jason was ready for. Violent thoughts. But when he'd sorted them out, he spoke the truth.

"Look, Jason. This is a *zero* trust situation now. We can't trust anyone."

"Except me, right?" Jason replied, only half jokingly.

Randy continued without responding. "We have to split up. Darius is in rough shape, mentally. He's dangerous, and if he thinks Joe is dangerous too? Nobody is safe. If you and I are together, we're an easy target. Better to get out on our own, easier to hide. Each man for himself."

Jason's face, usually dripping with sarcasm, now betrayed his own truth. Being alone, in an environment like Cocos, scared the hell out of him.

Visibly shaken, he finally mustered, "Wow, I... I guess you're right. Shit, not really excited about that. I'm fucking hungry as it is, man. Starved. And without you, or Joe? Man, I'm not exactly Daniel Boone."

"Well, buddy, we've all got something to learn out here. I'd work the fish angle. Find something to make a net from, get out in the water. Hell, the rats are easy to catch, they practically attack if you get close enough."

"Yeah, sure." But Jason Oliver wasn't buying it. Still, he thought, he could be pretty good at becoming invisible. But he needed an edge, and he knew just what would give him one.

"Can I have the Chatham shack?"

Randy knew the question was coming, and smiled. "If you want it, sure, buddy. I think it's too much of a target anyway, the Killer is bound to find it. But go ahead. It's yours if you want it."

Jason knew the ranger station might be a target, but had some ideas of his own to make it less so. Besides, he knew there were rats there, and he was starving.

"Thanks, man" he said, feeling a little better, "What about you?"

"Hike into the jungle, I s'pose. Maybe the unexplored area on the other side. I'm thinking we've got a few days at most before a boat comes, but probably at least 2. Guess I'll lay low, try not to get killed, make no sudden moves. Find some high ground. Keep my eye out for Kinnary and Joe. Darius I can avoid- he's too big to hide, and it's not his style. He's a face to face kind of guy. But those two? Wild cards. Keep your eyes open."

"I hear you," Jason nodded. "Sounds like as good a strategy as any."

"We'll see." But Randy didn't look so sure. "I hate to say it, but I don't think I know just what a good strategy looks like anymore."

"You and me both," Jason agreed, stopping next to the little grove of banana palms that hid the Chatham trail. He shuffled his feet, not wanting this moment to end, or really, for the next one to begin.

"Well," he croaked, "you're going that way, and I'm going this way. Guess this is it?"

Randy smiled, as big a smile as he had shown since leaving home. Jason Oliver was the closest thing to a friend he'd had on the island. After their night together, it felt wrong to be splitting up, each to his own devices, throwing caution to the wind. But, he knew the odds favored it, and Randy always took the path with the best odds. Always.

"I guess so, man. Had a great time hanging with you. When this is over, let's get together in Vegas and blow it out."

"Amen to that, man! I'm there." Jason Oliver offered his hand to the only player he sincerely hoped he'd see at the end. "Best of luck to you. May this be the first season with two Champion Castaways."

Randy grabbed the outstretched hand and pulled the skinny guy in for a hug. "You too, Jason. I hope you're right. Oh, and hey," he stopped in mid-step, "remember, if you see the boat first, have them shoot a flare. They probably will anyway, but I don't want to miss that thing."

"You and me both, buddy. Take care."

Randy stepped through the palms and was gone. Jason gulped, and turned to stroll back to Chatham Bay, where he planned to first find something to eat, and then to make some alterations to his cabin and surroundings that would hopefully allow him to stay alive until the boat arrived.

He hadn't gone far, though, when he heard the scream.

30

Day 15 ~ Soloists

Susan crept slowly past the three men on the beach at Wafer Bay. Randy, Jason, and Darius appeared to be in a heated argument. When Darius raised his machete, she knew there wasn't a single reason to get involved, and millions of reasons not to.

But if Darius took those two out, it would suit her just fine. She had no love for any of the Castaways, past or present, and would be altogether glad to split the remaining loot with Darius, Old Joe, and if she was forced to, Kinnary. But then again, she thought as she slipped off the trail and tiptoed through the jungle until she was beyond eyeshot, if Darius did take one or both of her former buddies out, that would give her the necessary cover to take him out as well. He would be a bona fide murderer, and killing him would be self defense.

Duly noted, she thought, now wondering what had become of Old Joe and Kinnary, the only two players missing from the little beach powwow.

She headed for Gissler's Cave to see if there was enough of it left for her to hide in until the boat came, either later that day, or maybe in the morning if it was delayed. It wouldn't be the best spot to camp since everyone knew its location and it was close to the beach, but she would booby trap it, and if she could get to the very back end of it, she could hide and launch a terrific assault on any intruder.

Truth was, she was no outdoors-woman, and probably wouldn't fare well by heading off into the jungle alone. She was starving, and at least she was familiar with this area, the only corner of the island she knew well, which offered a chance to hunt and capture rodents and birds where she had found them before. She might even dig up some crabs from the shallows out in the reef. She'd watched Old Joe and others bring in food, always with an eye towards taking care of herself in the end stages of the game. One thing was for sure, when the boys' little beach meeting was over, she would return and search the quonset hut for any kind of weapon, since she was now the only player without a machete.

Several minutes later she rounded the corner of the ridge, and was instantly depressed to see what remained of Gissler's Cave. It was literally just a pile of rocks, and there would be no refuge to be found inside.

She sighed and closed her eyes, instantly depressed. Now she'd have to come up with yet another plan, while so hungry that her brain was functioning poorly. Gazing around at scads of coconuts dropped by the raging tempest, she just could not bring herself to eat one more.

"God, I am *so* tired of freaking coconuts!" she yelled into the wind rising from the edge of the killing cliff.

She walked to the edge and sat on a boulder to collect her thoughts, the wild wind blowing her dark hair behind her like angel wings. Misty raindrops pelted her face. She wiped them on her shirt, realizing that her skin must need a serious deep cleaning about now. She'd get a facial and massage, a full spa day, once she got back to the mainland.

Her eyes scanned the endless Pacific for any sign of a craft, this being one of the best viewpoints on the island. But there was nothing. Only huge rolling swells and white capped waves, as far as the eye could see.

Kinnary scraped her way through the jungle, careful not to make too much noise. Things were . . . strange. Twisted. Since Franklin's head was found, paranoia had crept back to the island with renewed force, and none of them could escape its grasp. None, perhaps, but she.

She still knew who she was. She still knew she was not a killer, not going to flip flop and murder people whom she had laughed and joked with just days before. Old Joe had changed. Darius had changed. Danielle was practically gone. And the other three? Well, if they started out greedy and selfish, one could now add dangerous to the mix.

But Kinnary was still Kinnary. Dangerous in her own right, but not like them. She was cunning, she was smart, and she was strong. Those were the things that made her a threat, not a sudden lack of morality. She would kill if she must, but she wouldn't go looking for the opportunity unless it came to her.

And being cunning, she wouldn't set foot on the trail or beach if she could avoid it. Instead, she crept stealthily through the bush, just meters from the trail, so she could spot anyone there without them seeing her first. It was tough going, but not as tough as being dead.

She heard yelling, and paused. Unable to see anything, she crept closer to the sound, coming within six feet of the trail. And there, she dropped to her knees. Three men were arguing on the beach, and between her and them, creeping on all fours on the trail, was Susan.

"Bitch," she mouthed silently into the air.

Softening the focus of her eyes, she took it all in at once, and though detail was low, no motion escaped her view.   Susan was trying to get past the men without being seen, while they were engaged in some kind of argument that Darius looked certain to win. He was the aggressor, while the other two were on their heels. Jason Oliver slipped and fell, Randy momentarily looked like he might actually put up a fight before calming down, and then the three men finally took off up the trail.

Meanwhile, Susan had managed to get beyond their line of sight, jogging quickly towards Gissler's Cave.

"Only one place for her to go," she thought, pulling her gaze away from Susan. "But where are *they* going?"

She let them get a little further ahead, and then followed, but not too close. They would have to run into Susan, and she wanted no part of that battle. Two, maybe even three of them might be tossed off the cliff if they met, and there was no reason to get involved, no matter who that might be.   The rage she'd seen on Darius' face scared her, and she didn't scare easily. She'd give him a wide berth until the boat arrived.

"Where the hell are *you*, Joe?" she whispered to herself as she slid through the foliage.

Randy stopped suddenly, and so did she. And when she saw him move the palm leaves aside, a wily grin spread across her face.

"You sneaky bastards!" she whispered into the wind. "How long have you known about this?"

Her heart raced as the three men stepped onto a new path, and she followed. But shortly thereafter she stopped cold, her heart collapsing into her stomach.

"Oh my God!" she exhaled, a little too loudly.

But the men, too busy being shocked themselves, heard nothing. Her knees buckled, and she slid to the ground.

"Which one of you did this?" she wondered. Certainly the frail woman hadn't done it herself. She doubted Susan was strong enough. But she was smart— scary smart— and she could have figured out a way to pull it off. Jason held about the same odds, but the greater odds were that it was Darius, Randy, or Joe.

The wind was weaker back in the trees, and she was close enough now to hear them kicking around ideas. When they mentioned her name, she almost laughed.

Darius turned abruptly and left, and she followed him. Stepping back onto the main trail, he turned towards his refuge in the hut.

She suddenly realized that she was the only one who knew where Susan was at that very moment. And that being so, it seemed the time had come for their inevitable moment together.

Susan sighed yet again from her cliffside perch. There would be no boat today. Maybe tomorrow.

"Tomorrow, tomorrow, I love ya, tomorrow!" she sang into the wind with a wicked grin, before rising and turning to leave.

But as she did, she caught a momentary glance of something so frightening, so unexpected, that she went stone cold stiff, half-crouched, half-risen, half-turning.

"You gotta be fucking kidding me . . ." .

They were the last words Susan ever spoke. She was immediately slammed in the gut and flew backwards off the cliff, ejected into open air, mimicking almost exactly Leticia's plunge a week before.

But instead of going down boldly fighting as Leticia had, she went down screaming bloody murder. The realization that she was about to die like some common person was terrifying to this narcissist with an ego so large that she was certain she was immortal. Her endless drive to collect and secure money was her path to insure that immortality. Whether that meant a bionic heart or a robotic shell in which her brain could be implanted, the bottom line was that her life was to be endless.

The pain of being so unexpectedly average in death turned Susan's final moments into the most horrifying seconds of her suddenly shortened life. To her, those two seconds seemed to last forever. But by the third, she was just as irreversibly dead as any of the bodies buried in the ground on the beach at Wafer Bay.

Randy took off running when he heard the scream. There were two women left on Cocos, and that meant that either Susan or Kinnary was in trouble. But he wasn't running to help. Instead, he hoped to catch the Killer in a compromising position, perhaps ending this whole murder spree once and for all before he became part of it himself.

Arriving at the hidden trail junction, he dropped behind the banana palms, waiting quietly to see if the Killer would run by. The scream came from the ridge top, and that meant there was only one way out. This way.

He crouched low, only to be hit in the back moments later by Jason Oliver, who had been so focused on the scream he'd missed his friend hiding in the bushes.

"Shit!" Jason shrieked, but seeing Randy's finger go to his lips, crouched quietly behind him. "Sorry, man!" he whispered. "See anything?"

Randy shook his head no, and kept his eyes on the trail. Several minutes later, when no one had come by, he rose and stepped out of the bushes.

Unsheathing his machete, he crouched low again, moving towards Gissler's Cave. Jason hesitated, but quickly realized the two of them stood a much better chance of ambushing the Killer right now than they would alone over the next couple of days. With a deep, confidence building breath, he pulled his own machete from its sheath, and followed Randy up the trail.

They moved slowly, halting to listen for footfalls several times along the way. Drizzling rain formed crystalline beads on their blades, before sliding to the ground on a journey back to the Mother Pacific. The only sounds in the air were the Cocos constants— wind and rain, the sounds of millennia gone by, and millennia to come.

Randy moved on and Jason dutifully followed, his heart beating rapidly. He felt more awake than he'd been since he boarded the plane in St. Louis, bound for Costa Rica. While Randy moved like a panther, muscular, steady, and low, Jason Oliver looked more like a flamingo, standing too erect, skinny legs stretched, head bobbing back and forth on a stick-like neck. They were an unlikely pair of gladiators. But this was their lucky day, for there would be no fight.

They rounded the top of the ridge to see a wide open, empty scene before them. Only boulders, charred remains of Malik's explosion, Joe's smoke fire, puddled raindrops, and the cloudy sky beyond filled their eyes. Randy remained alert, spinning in slow circles to be certain he missed nothing, no one hiding behind a boulder, or at the top of the hill above the blown out cave.

He peeked behind the boulders, then peered up at the hilltop for a bit while Jason Oliver moved closer to the cliff's edge. When the oddsmaker in Randy's brain told him that the chance of ambush was low, he joined the stick figure peering over the abyss.

"Hey," he said to Jason Oliver, whose eyes were fixed on the rocks below, "we shouldn't look over the cliff at the same time. Too easy to give us the bum's rush. Tell me what you see, and then face this way so I can look. Keep your machete ready."

"What do you think I see, man!" Jason whined in fear, "Susan! She's dead. Splattered, man! She's not the goddamn Killer!"

"Shit. Lemme look," Randy commanded, his brain whirring, unhinged by what it had just heard. Once Jason was able to break his gaze free of the shocking scene below, he turned his tear laden eyes towards the hill, and Randy took his turn.

The ocean, still raging from the last gasp of the storm, was in low tide, and the reef below was fully exposed. There lay Susan's broken body, splashed by sea foam every few seconds, not yet dragged out to sea. That would take a couple more hours, he figured. When the tide rose back to nearly full, she would become part of it.

He spun quickly back around, fear now clouding his practical mind. "Shit. Shit! I guess that's that."

Jason, eyes closed, tried to slow his heartbeat, "Darius," he breathed out slowly, "I mean, who else? It looked like he was going for her when he took off. Had to be him."

"Yeah, true. But where is he? He didn't go back down the trail, and he sure didn't go off the cliff."

"Up there," Jason pointed above the cave. "I bet he went over the top, bushwhacking over the hill. And from there…"

"From there, he'd see Chatham Station."

Jason gulped. "Shit."

"Shit is right. You still heading there?"

"Yeah, but since he's probably not at Wafer Bay, I'll go back to the quonset first and grab some stuff. See if there are any rations left hidden in there. Then I'll hide and wait for him to pass. After that, I'll roll back to my beach and leave him to his."

Randy nodded. "Makes sense. I'll come too, split after we load up."

"Dude…" Jason returned briefly to his senses, "we're down to five. That's a decent split, if you ask me."

"Yeah," Randy nodded, "it would be. Only somebody thinks that's four too many."

31

Darius ~ Not Long Ago

"What do you mean, it's *gone*?"

Darius' hands shook uncontrollably, threatening to drop his brand new Iphone to the floor. He was in shock.

"Look, D, I mean the costs man. The frigging costs…"

Darius was stunned. Costs? Those weren't his problem! Those were Lance's purview, not his. His job was to drum up business, to hit up big box stores, distributors, and spokesmen for the new line of e-bikes they were putting together. Lance was the money end, he was the guy who won Execution Island, and opened doors to the world of commerce.

E-bikes were the future. When he bought in, Lance assured him this deal was a lock. Chinese manufacturing would ensure high margins. A rapidly growing market would ensure big sales. And their designs were much more radical than anything else on the market. Carbon fiber frames with diamond-shaped cutaways, top tubes shaped like lightning bolts, and quality suspension systems at a fair price would make sure they got noticed. And now Lance wanted to talk about costs?

"You better tell me what you mean, right now Lance. I mean *right* the fuck now."

"Look, D, it's not just you!" the voice on the phone pleaded, "I'm losing everything! Everything I have!"

Darius put his hand to his forehead and slumped in his chair. He tried not to look across the pool to where his wife lay in her swimsuit, smiling and applying sunscreen to their kids. A wife who was proud her husband had taken his Execution Island winnings and invested them in the future. A future now very much in doubt.

"One more time. Slow down, and tell me where the money went. It can't *all* be gone! All five hundred grand!"

There was silence on the other end of the line, and then the chinking of a bottle against a glass.

"Are you *drinking*, Lance? It's eleven in the morning for god's sake."

Lance chuckled. "You got a better idea?"

The familiar creep of rising rage moved up Darius' thickly muscled back, through his neck, and nested in the temples of his forehead. In the past, that feeling had meant somebody was about to get hurt.

"You've got five minutes Lance. Or I'm grabbing my nine and heading for your house. Five."

"Darius, the carbon is shit, man! The designs won't hold. They're delaminating under pressure. And without the designs, we have just a plain old e-bike like every other one out there, with a tenth of the funding of those companies. That," Lance paused to drink, "is it in a nutshell. Now, join me in a drink."

None of this made sense. Five hundred grand, vaporized? With no notice? It just wasn't possible.

"There's no god damn way you could just be learning this today. No way. Keep talking."

"It's not just your money, Darius. I'm in for three hundred myself! It's not like I just used your money to pay for the production run, I used all of mine, too. But we've still got close to a hundred in the bank for marketing and promotion. I mean, that's your end, of course, but you haven't spent it, right?" A pause, and then "*Tell* me you haven't spent it yet."

"God damnit!" Darius was about to jump through the phone. "Where did the rest go!"

"Where do you think it went! Don't yell at me, asshole, I was just doing my job! Count it off with me so I don't have to go through this again— and by the way, you approved all of these line items! Three hundred for production of the frames, tubing, molds, and so on, all paid for in advance. Gone! Two hundred for the rest of the parts to build the bikes. Gone! Seventy grand for the assembly of those bikes in Shenzhen. Gone! About eighty grand for packaging and shipping of the initial run, prepaid so we could get bikes to market by Christmas. Gone! Another fifty to grease Chinese officials and plant operators. Gone! Fifty for pre-production stress tests. Gone! It's all just gone, man. Vapor. Now have a goddamn drink with me!"

Darius smelled the stink in that list the moment he heard it.

"Hold up. Fifty grand for pre-production stress tests. We *passed* those tests, Lance! Passed them! I've seen the reports, was *there* that day when they put the press to the frames, and one by one all of them made it way past the point of no return."

Lance coughed. "I was there too."

"Right, so then how can you be telling me now that they aren't holding up? Who fucked up, and why, and when will that asshole have my money!"

Lance gulped. His voice began to slur.

"Well, man, that's where the problem is. The carbon. It wasn't the same."

Darius was bewildered. "The same as what?"

"The same as we went into production with. Look, D, the fact is we couldn't afford the good carbon. It would have doubled the price of the bikes, putting us out of business before we even started. So, I had to make an executive decision, and switched it out for a looser weave. But look man, it ain't my fault! The production guys assured me it would be fine! Their engineer signed off on it!"

Darius couldn't speak. He bit into his cheek and blood trickled into his mouth. His huge right hand threatened to crush his phone. The fingers on his left hand dug into his forehead, and blood began to flow there too.

"Darius. I'm sorry, man. It seemed like the best idea. Look, take the hundo in the marketing account. There's almost fifty left in the production account- I'll split that with you too. And remember, we can sell back some of the parts... not the carbon, but we should be able to get another fifty or so for what we can salvage. That's something man. And we still have a chance to get other investors on board. If we can come up with another five hundred, we can go back into production, but change… I don't know, something. The carbon, the manufacturer, the designs, we can still make it, man. Trust me."

But Darius was no longer there. Lance was speaking to the grass in Darius' back yard, where the he had dropped the phone before silently leaving his chair and walking to his garage. He reached under a blanket on the top shelf of his tool cabinet, a spot the kids couldn't reach, and pulled out his nine millimeter. Jumping in his car, he left the house without a word to his wife.

Twenty minutes later he stood in another garage. Lance's. And Lance, drunk or not, had wisely gotten the hell out of Dodge once he realized his large friend was no longer on the phone and quite probably headed to his house to put several bullets in his brain. His leased Range Rover was gone, and the two-car garage sat empty, except for a trio of prototype e-bikes, a kayak, and four sets of snow skis.

Darius stood shaking in the garage of Lance's nine hundred thousand dollar house, and began to cry. The gun dropped from his hand and clattered onto the concrete. And then he followed, crumpling to the ground in a sobbing ball. There he stayed, for about three minutes.

But then, suddenly, he bolted upright. He jogged back to his car and drove it around the block, parking at the 7-11 two streets over. He opened the glove box, pulled out a pair of tire changing gloves, put his gun inside, locked the car, and began to walk.

He'd wait for Lance, and then break his neck with his own two hands.

Moving carefully, he hopped the back wall of a neighbor's house and entered his partner's yard the same way so no one would see him go in the front of Lance's home. One by one he tried the patio door handles. When that didn't work, he tried the sliding windows, finally finding one at the master bathroom that slid open. Popping the screen out, he climbed inside.

He moved cautiously through the house on the off chance Lance had *also* hidden his car around the block and returned to take Darius on. But instead of finding his former friend, he found a note on the kitchen counter.

It read:

Darius, I really am sorry man. I know you are pissed, and I know that means I have to get the hell out of here. I've seen you go off, and I don't want to be the cause of you doing something you'll regret for the rest of your life. Maybe I deserve it. Maybe I don't. But I didn't intentionally screw you. This was my fuckup, and I own it, but I didn't do it on purpose.

I'm heading to China to see how much I can get back. I'll do my best, but in the meantime, take the hundred you have access to. I'll recover what I can, and we'll split it when I get back.

Still your friend,

Lance.

Darius crumpled the paper into a ball and threw it angrily into the kitchen. His hands flexed and squeezed together tightly, robbed of the chance to spread themselves across Lance's throat and crush his windpipe.

But he wasn't done. No, Darius had a temper that was famous for not cooling off until it had blown off. And it was time to blow.

His eyes scanned the kitchen and living room nervously. In the end, it was an easy choice.

Opening a valve on the gas stove, he grabbed a pot from the sink, filled it with water, and set it on top.

Then he walked to the gas fireplace in the front room, and simply switched it on before leaving the house the same way he came in.

He'd already pulled out of the 7-11 when he heard the explosion, and saw the column of smoke begin to fill the sky. When the authorities found what he had done, Lance would be forced to claim his own negligence in order to get an insurance settlement out of it. He'd simply left for a trip and forgot he left the stove and fireplace on. He was, of course, quite distressed due to the sudden failure of his new business and hadn't been thinking right.

But meanwhile, he lost everything else he treasured. Personal keepsakes, heirlooms, trophies, files both physical and digital, photos of his long since exited wife and kids.

Not to mention a hundred grand in cash hidden behind the desk that he had embezzled from the rapidly failing company they had founded just a year before.

Darius breathed hard, his chest filling with air. He felt better. His hands relaxed on the steering wheel. All within him, for the moment, was good.

But that moment ended when he got home, knowing he'd have to tell his wife that he'd foolishly lost most of that money she had been so proud of him for winning in the first place.

32

Day 15 ~ Fishing Lure

Darius was not about to give up his hut, or his beach.

As far as he was concerned, if there was still a killer out there, he or she knew where he was, and was welcome to try to boot him out. But this beach had become his home, and there was no doubt it was allowing him to eat better than anyone else besides Old Joe. He spent a large part of his days floating the reef, using a makeshift spear to catch fish, digging up clams, oysters, and crabs, and he knew that it was making a difference in his strength.

He'd gone searching for Susan at the treasure hole after leaving Danielle's hanging tree, but never found her. Hopefully, he thought as he'd strolled back to his hut, Old Joe had already taken her out. He didn't know that the boys had seen her dead body smashed on the reef, and so in his mind, she was still the biggest threat to his survival. But he believed with certainty that his beach, filled with seafood delights, would have him ready for her if she came.

Unlike Joe, he refused to eat rat. He was the only one who hadn't done it yet, and sure as hell did not plan to anytime soon. He'd made a bow and arrows like Joe's, but so far they hung unused by the door inside his hut. He just felt much happier with seafood in his teeth, instead of rat meat.

The afternoon after searching for Danielle was spent swimming in his sea, fishing on his reef, cooking on his fire pit at the Execution

Grounds, and sleeping safely and warmly in his quonset hut. His presence there also made him the keeper of the gold, he figured. Better him than any of the others, even Old Joe.

While he still believed the old man was mostly good, he couldn't trust him. The words spoken between them on the beach had sunk into his soul, and though he realized Joe only intended to wake him up, he'd seen something in the old man's eyes that day that he had never seen there before.

Desire.

Where it had come from, and why it burned there he did not know. But Darius knew well that sort of raging desire, the kind that could lead a man to do things he would otherwise never attempt. It was the same desire, he realized, that Joe probably saw in his own eyes when he looked at him.

That's what this game is all about, Darius thought as he floated peacefully above impossibly colorful corals, sea urchins, anemones, and tropical fish. Desire. It wasn't even greed- money was just one piece of a much larger pie. It was more complex than that, and the form it took depended on the player.

For some it was simply the desire to be the best. To show those people who'd once said you weren't good enough— parents, bosses, teachers, classmates, exes— that not only *were* you good enough, you were better than they were! Jason and Leticia were archetypes of this group.

For those like Darius it was the desire to secure the future for one's family, and one's self. He definitely fit into this box, as did Danielle, and maybe Tonya as well.

For still others, it was simply the all consuming need to win. To beat the competition at all costs. Perhaps to soothe the inner demon of ego, the narcissistic voice inside that said you *are* better than everybody else, and if you don't win, your entire, carefully constructed illusory self image will come crashing down. Susan, Randy, and Franklin were archetypes of this group.

For the last subset it was the desire for adventure. These were the happy ones. They were fan favorites, every time the game was played, because they played for fun, and the audience could *feel* it. They enjoyed the exotic locales even though they were hungry and tired, because they were on an *adventure*! Matthew, Kinnary, Amy, all of them made people smile and made others have fun, even if they didn't feel it themselves.

But that left Old Joe. Where did *he* fit? *Why* was he here? Why did he ever join the game in the first place all those years ago? He didn't fit any of these stereotypes, had never seen the show, yet succeeded in the game, and could even end up the last man standing on Cocos Island.

The realization that Old Joe was more than the classic floater, added to the unexpected raging inferno of desire he'd seen in his eyes the last time they spoke, led Darius to give the hillbilly a wide berth. He'd avoid all contact with the man, but if confronted by him, he'd either charge like a rabid buffalo, or back off and run like the wind.

Not that Joe would give him the chance, of course. If Old Joe really wanted to come for him, and who could say for sure that he didn't, chances were fairly good that Darius wouldn't know about it until he was already dying.

Yet, floating out in his very own ocean, thinking with a brain that was fueled by actual food, Darius decided there was no reason to hide. If Old Joe was the man he had once believed him to be, he was safe and there was no reason to go overboard with paranoia.

And if Old Joe was now someone else entirely, a demonic source of the inferno behind those eyes, then Darius was already a dead man and he may as well enjoy his last days on Earth to the hilt.

He saw no one and heard nothing but birds and waves as he floated above the happy world of the fishes. Happy, that was, until his spear pierced one's scaly side and ruined its day, destined as it was to be roasted over an open fire. He focused on his fishing, kept an eye out for the boat, did a little body surfing, and as a special treat, tried an idea he'd had for cooking crab inside a fresh coconut, until their juices combined to create a symphony of delights in his protein hardened stomach.

He enjoyed his swim, he enjoyed his cookout, and he enjoyed a good night's sleep. He even felt like the best fisherman in Execution Island history as he carried in a basketful of silvery beauties and colorful blue crabs that evening, thrilled to provide for himself in a way only one other person on the island could. He was proud, he was full, and he felt relaxed.

He returned to his quonset hut without a care, but before falling into a peaceful sleep, regained his sense of the greater world for just a moment. He thought about his family, and his eyes teared up. He made a silent prayer that he would live to see them once more, and more than that, that he would make them proud of him again. Having their respect meant everything to him, something he hadn't really understood until he'd lost it.

The next morning he awoke again, a mellowness in his mind and a song in his heart, and headed out for another day of bliss in the water.

He strode outside without a care, and had taken just a few steps when the first arrow slammed home between his shoulder blades, followed almost instantly by a second.

Darius spun to face his attacker, blood pulsing through his veins only to gush out of the holes in his back. But the last thing he saw froze the scream rising in his throat. The Killer, devouring his fear, stared him down with a grin, aimed again, and the third arrow thudded home in his chest. Darius fell backwards to the ground in agony, forcing the first two arrows deeper into his body. They splintered and broke as his body's full weight fell upon them.

Darius had a strong will, and it took several minutes for him to die. Like it had for Susan, it proved to be far too much time to ponder all that had gone wrong in his life.

Randy was at the same time shocked and yet not a bit surprised to find Darius with Old Joe's arrows sticking out of his back. Touching the man's neck and finding him warm, he dropped instantly to the ground next to the body and lay there frozen, terrified to move even an inch. Old Joe was a crack shot, and might have an arrow stretched and ready to fly across the beach at that very second. Randy knew he was being watched. He could feel it.

He lay still for several minutes, face burning on the hot sand, sweat pouring out of his scalp, feverishly searching for a solution.

Speed was the key, he figured. It was quickly growing dark, and speed combined with the oncoming darkness just might save his life.

He caught his breath, counted to five, and burst from the sand. Sprinting for the trail with legs pumping, he bobbed and weaved from side to side to make Old Joe's job as difficult as possible. Reaching the jungle he slowed a bit but kept running, as the tree cover was thick enough to keep any arrow from dropping him once he hit the bush.

Run he did. But his was not the only life to be saved, so he bee-lined it for Jason's cabin to tell him Old Joe was the Killer, and to stay the hell off the beach!

Kinnary, still hiding in the brush behind the quonset, was playing the smartest game of all, save perhaps Old Joe. No one had seen her since Susan's heart stopped beating. Keeping to the thick jungle, she dared move or make noise only when the subjects of her observations moved on.

No one saw her, but she saw everyone. Everyone, that is, except for Old Joe.

Glimpsing Darius dead on the beach from the safety of the trees, she waited for someone to pass. The arrows sticking out of the big man's chest told her all she needed to know.

Old Joe had gone rogue. For some reason he'd turned, taking out not only black hats, as might be expected, but white ones as well. Who lost his mind first, she wondered, Joe, or Darius? Had the big man gone rabid, forcing Joe to drop him from afar, or had Joe struck for no other reason than to sweeten his own pot of gold?

That didn't make any sense. It just couldn't be.

And yet, there lay Darius. Dead as a stone, with all evidence pointing sharply towards Joe, so to speak.

She waited, hoping Old Joe would come by again and confirm her suspicions. Her hips and back ached from lying in the same spot for so long, but she was too smart to move even a little bit. For all she knew, the woodsman could be right behind her.

Hours later though, it wasn't Old Joe who came by, but Randy. And his reaction made it very clear that he wasn't the Killer, at least not *this* Killer. His appearance also confirmed that he was alive, which meant that the four smartest players in the game had made it to the end.

That was not good news.

There was no way she was about to expose herself to help Randy. Though she was so hungry she could eat her own arm, her injuries screaming with every step, Kinnary decided the only way she could keep on living was to stay covered, stay quiet, and continue to play detective, watching Randy lying on the sand behind Darius' cold corpse.

He looked as scared as she was, but soon leapt to his feet and bolted towards the trail. Coming within twenty feet of her, he plunged unexpectedly into the jungle, heading towards the secret trail he had unwittingly uncovered for her.

Randy's fear smelled like panic, and he made no attempt to be quiet. Lifting her head up just a little, she craned her ears, straining with all of her senses to figure out where he was heading. When his thunderous footfalls began to sound inland, she knew.

And so, rather than follow him, she once again waited, silent, gathering intel.

If Old Joe *was* somewhere in these trees, and every bone in her body told her he was, he would soon drop and follow Randy, knowing the gambler would lead him straight to Jason Oliver and a two-for-one kill.

Yet thirty minutes later, nothing. Strange, she thought. Perhaps the old hunter had gone for Jason Oliver first, taking out the easy prey before concentrating on the big game—herself, and Randy.

So, very cautiously, she moved through the jungle towards the secret trail, pausing every few feet to listen for a follower. When she was sure there were none, she quickened her pace, ever so slightly.

33

Days 15/16 ~ Final Suspect

Jason Oliver rushed back to his home at Chatham Beach with new gear on his back to help secure it against an intruder. He and Randy had raided the hut while Darius was gone, waiting quietly until he returned. Surprisingly though, when he did it was from the direction of the treasure hole, not from Jason's secret lair. They'd assumed he'd gone over the hill after killing Susan and then found this new cabin on the other side of the island. They were puzzled, but had no time to chat, and quickly got out of his way before they were seen.

As far as Jason Oliver knew, everyone was dead now but three other men and one woman, and since he wasn't very good at killing, fighting, or even lifting heavy objects, his focus could only be one thing. Staying alive.

The song entered his brain once again, and he couldn't help but sing it as he skipped happily onto the beach at Chatham Bay. The sky was beginning to clear, and though he was now totally alone, he felt a real lightness in his heart.

Susan was dead, and to him, she had been the scariest bogeyman left in the game. Oh sure, Old Joe, Darius, or Kinnary could kill him if they wanted to, but he didn't really believe that they did. Darius had wanted Susan dead and probably made it so, and who could blame him? And now it appeared that none of them even knew about this shack on another beach. There was no reason for any of them to kill anybody else. That much gold split five ways was still a hell of a lot of gold, and he doubted any of them would split hairs, or his skull, to gain more.

His stomach screamed. Emptied of all its contents from the night's revelries, it reminded him that if he wanted to make it a couple more days, he would have to get some food, and pronto. Rats, fish, coconuts, anything… and soon.

Gratefully, the storm had dropped thousands of coconuts on Cocos island, and he picked up several and stashed them in his bag on the way down the trail. Greedily, he burst into his cabin and began chopping them up for both their calorie filled white meat, and more importantly, the precious water and electrolytes they held inside.

Nature had provided, and no one would starve on Cocos Island before the boat came to rescue them. They might be hungry as hell and would probably never eat another coconut again, but they would live. Or if not, at least it wouldn't be hunger or thirst that killed them.

After several minutes he'd had his fill of both coconut water and the white flesh that held it. He dropped the husks on the floor, then scooted them out of the garbage chute. With any luck that would attract more rats, and he'd have a meal tonight that wasn't vegetarian.

"Rat," he giggled at his cleverness, "the *other* other white meat!"

Satisfied for the moment, he looked over the items he'd brought from the quonset hut— a wicker basket and a long length of rope. These were to be the first leg of the safety net on his beach. The plan was that if someone came down his trail, he could either take them out completely, or at least knock them out and run like the true Castaway he was.

Leaving his hut, he strode across the sand, confident as ever. The idea had come to him when he'd seen Danielle swinging from that branch, and his devious mind thought, "hmm, I can do something with that."

Now he needed two more things that only nature could provide. A very large rock, such as might flatten someone's skull if dropped from above, and a tall tree, such as might hold the weight of said rock until someone like him were to release it and send it crashing down upon the hopefully unwitting, and absolutely deserving, Killer of Cocos Island.

He wanted it to be close to the junction of the beach and the trail, so he could easily mark the spot in his mind and pull the rope at just the right moment. Plus, he figured he could find a way to lead the Killer to that very spot, by running either towards, or away from it.

There were many arboreal candidates, as trees grew tall on the leeward side of the island, protected by hills and cliffs from the raging winds out of the west. Selecting one, he began the process of getting the rope up and over a high branch.

But that proved difficult, as one of the things that physically weakness limited was his ability to throw objects high in the air. His first attempt was pathetic and barely reached ten feet overhead. He tied a small rock to the end of the rope to give it momentum, and tried again. This time he got it up to maybe fifteen feet, but it wasn't enough. The Killer would see the basket hanging from the trail, and wouldn't be dumb enough to stand under it long enough to become a pancake.

He tried again, but it just wasn't working. So he found another rock, large enough to have more momentum, but not too large for him to throw. He took aim, mustered all of his strength, and threw!

This time the rock hit the intended branch, before clattering to the ground at his feet.

"Arms, you are not helping," he teased himself. "Guess those guys in school were right."

Taking a moment to think, he finally figured it out. This time he backed up first, and then sprinted towards the tree, letting go of the rock at the highest zenith of his arm's arc, like a wannabe high school shot-putter, destined to not make the team.

But it worked! He jumped up and down with glee, proud of himself for actually succeeding at something athletic for once in his life. His chest filled with confidence, and he knew he had the task at hand licked.

Now he needed a much bigger rock, and as there were none to be had on the beach, he hiked up the trail to find one. Minutes later he did, and instead of carrying it down the hill, he rolled it in front of him with his foot, all forty pounds of it.

When he got to the bottom of the trail he loaded it into the thick basket, tied the end of his tree-branch rope to the handle, wisely tying it around the rock as well for good measure. If the sky opened up again a wet basket could fail, and he didn't want the rock popping through the bottom of it unless he told it to.

Wrapping the rope around the tree's base, he sat on the ground with his feet up against the trunk, and began to pull. It was harder than he thought because the tree gave the rope resistance he hadn't factored in. Still, inch by inch it rose, until it hung high enough overhead that it started to really scare the crap out of him. Pulling just a little more until the basket was hidden behind a large palm leaf, he then tied the rope off to the tree.

Jason Oliver collapsed on the sand and closed his eyes, his chest rising and falling wildly from more physical labor than he'd done in most of his life. With a groan he realized that this was only the first of his boobytraps, and none of them would be easy to set.

"Ugh."

And that meant he better get more to eat before he continued. So he rose, gave himself a nice, self-congratulatory pat on the back for his good work, and headed back to the cabin to work on a fishing net.

But when he stepped on the porch, he instantly felt like he had been stung by a very large hornet, and his body, suddenly completely out of his control, slammed up against the cabin's wooden door.

But it was no insect.

"God, no!" he screamed as he looked down at the narrow gap between his chest and the partly opened door, now joined together by a hand-made arrow.

He touched it for just a moment, in shock and still not fully understanding the gravity of the situation, and was instantly hit by another. Helplessly he watched as it too burst through his bony chest and slammed into the door. Rolling his head back to look up at the sky, searching for some kind of meaning to all of this, he momentarily sensed a third arrow pierce his heart, and then, Jason Oliver, bad boy of Execution Island, simply died.

He hung silently overnight from the door on those three shafts of hand hewn wood, the breeze wafting around him as rats gathered below his feet to lap up the pooling blood. His eyes remained open, and when Randy came down the beach just after dark the next night to warn him that he'd found Darius on the beach with three arrows in his back, the first thing he thought was how strangely peaceful Jason Oliver looked.

But that flashing moment of peace was shattered when, looking down, he saw that his friend's feet were gone, devoured by hungry rats during the night.

34

Days 16/17 ~ Endgame

Randy vomited. His blood chilled at the sight of his friend hanging from the door of Chatham station, his back a carbon-copy of Darius', with the added horror that his feet were gnawed to bony stumps.

Both men were hit by precise arrow strikes, which, to Randy, could mean only one thing. The ugly confirmation of his theory made every small hair on his body stand on end. He suddenly found it very hard to breath— an anxiety attack, something he thought he'd left behind in childhood.

Old Joe was the Killer, his mind screamed at him. Old Joe, the guy everyone believed would win the game, the guy everybody trusted, the guy with the perfect bluff, the perfect poker face, the guy who really *did* hide in plain sight, was the Cocos Island Killer, and Randy was one of only two targets left for his homemade arrows.

He dropped immediately to the ground for the second time that day, his breath threatening to cease for good. Old Joe had killed in so many ways that murder could occur at any moment. He'd have to be nearly perfect to make it to the end with someone like that at his back. But hunger, cold, and the constant discovery of murdered companions had left his brain exhausted. He was no longer the guy who could sit across the poker table from seasoned veterans of the circuit and take them for all they had. He was, he realized painfully as he struggled to breathe beside his dead friend who had literally been hung out to dry, a possible victim.

He scraped his way into the cabin and sat on the ground with his back against the wall, straining to regain control. After a few minutes, he did so in the same way he'd always done when he was a kid— he started making plans for the future, and in doing so, took his mind off the present.

Realizing he'd fare better if he worked by night, he had very little time. Dawn was only hours away. Kinnary was not a threat, and was no doubt smart enough to be hiding back in the caves far from the aim of Joe's arrows, waiting out the boat that must surely come soon.

Shit, it occurred to him, they might even have a final two deal, where Old Joe did all the killing and her only job was to shut the hell up about it.

Randy absolutely had to take Old Joe out before he himself was taken out. He had no choice. This was Execution Island. Fortune favored the bold. And bold he would be.

Joe would expect him to hole up somewhere, just like Kinnary probably was. Cowed and afraid. But now, the hunter would become the hunted. Old Joe had always been the predator, not the prey, and there was no way he'd be expecting it.

Randy went immediately into military mode. Stepping back outside the cabin, he began chopping palm leaves with his machete, his back to the door, constantly scanning the jungle for signs of movement. He spent a good twenty minutes doing this, before hauling the cut pieces back inside. Safely under cover again, he whipped together a gilley suit, like those snipers wore to blend into their surroundings, by shredding the leaves into strips and then weaving them in and out of his clothing. He stuck a bunch of them under his hat and tied them to it as well, so they hung down over his back and shoulders.

It took just a half hour, leaving him a good deal of time. Unsheathing his machete, he slid out through the garbage chute to avoid being seen by anyone but a large group of very confused rats.

Kinnary stayed put, fifteen feet inside the jungle near the end of the trail to Chatham beach, where it hit the open sand, Jason Oliver's useless and forgotten booby trap swinging heavily above. She saw it. She saw everything.

Jason's body was bolted to the door by arrows, how many she couldn't see. Randy had slipped in and out of the cabin there, and she lay in the bushes, ants crossing her torso in a steady line but not sensing enough life in her to want to bite. And she waited.

What? Was that him? What the hell . . .

It looked like the Swamp Thing had just crawled out from under the cabin, and then raced up against the treeline to blend in.

Holy shit, she thought. Boy's gone bush blind. But at least he's thinking.

She watched him sidling along, and instantly knew he was heading towards some weird date with Old Joe, the kind where only one of them got to leave afterwards.

"Oh my God," she whispered into the jasmine scented breeze, "this is gonna be nuts."

She stuck to the vegetable phantom like glue, that was if glue could hang back about fifty feet and still stick.

"If I could only lay odds . . ." she thought with all intended irony.

Slipping off the open beach in the soft light of a quarter moon, Randy sidled up next to the edge of the jungle, where his suit allowed him to blend in perfectly. He walked steadily but slowly, soft on his feet, staying right against the bushes as he moved up the path towards Wafer Bay.

Reaching the hidden trail junction, he decided he'd better be thorough and check everywhere that Joe could possibly be holing up on this end of the island. Taking a right, he slipped through the night air, making it to Gissler's Cave in minutes. Once there he dropped to the ground, just another bush, and surveyed the scene.

Satisfied Joe was not there, he moved on, back to the trail, this time intent to scope out the entire Wafer Bay complex a little at a time, always from the cover of the dense jungle foliage.

Kinnary paused and waited for Randy to survey Gissler's Cave, knowing full well Joe wasn't stupid enough to be in the open.

"City boys," she teased quietly into the ocean air, "do you even realize that trails are only a suggestion?"

Quickly he seemed to figure out that the spot was a no-go, and she let him blow on by before resuming her cautious recon. He was moving slowly and deliberately, giving her plenty of time to insure that she made no noise.

Randy stopped at the quonset hut and lay prone again, waiting. After ten silent minutes he moved further down the trail to the edge of the jungle where the path turned towards the caves. Here he followed the foliage back towards the beach, staying against the tree line where Matthew had been murdered in cold blood. There was no one on the sand as far as he could tell, but he wouldn't know for sure until he laid eyes on the Execution Grounds.

Rounding the bend in the cliffs that blocked the site from the rest of the beach, he fell again to the ground, silent, as the glow of a burning fire filled the sky.

There walked Old Joe, milling around the fire pit, gathering wood, tinkering about. Just *exactly* what he was doing, Randy could not see. But he stayed flat on the ground, watching, surveying Joe's movements. Now that he'd found the old man, the actual moment of his real execution could wait until the perfect chance presented itself.

"Jesus," thought Kinnary, "this movie gets better and better."

Dropping to the ground in unison with Randy, she could just make out Old Joe by the fire at the Execution Grounds, her view slightly blocked by the many leaves and fronds between her body and the open sand.

She found herself asking yet again, "What are you *doing*, Joe?"

The old man seemed to have not a care in the world, shortly after killing some of the game's top players with two of the most competent still threatening. It made no sense. He couldn't possibly be this capricious, unless of course he hadn't turned as she'd thought, was actually waiting for the boat like a good boy, even sending out a freaking signal light to boot.

No, she realized. That wasn't it at all. A smile grew on her face, a big smile that lit up the night with its toothy joy.

"He's toying with you, dumbass. Oh my God," she whispered again into the night air, "this is going to be one for the ages."

251

Old Joe continued to tinker, before finally sitting down, facing the jungle instead of the ocean. Smart, thought Randy. The old geezer hadn't gotten this far by turning his back on his victims. Randy sharpened his focus through the misty ocean air and saw that Joe was making some kind of long, spear-like weapon out of one of the individual Castaway's flags, which in the original game would have been tossed in the fire each time a player was sent home, in essence burning the loser in effigy.

A spear, mused Randy? Was he tired of arrows? Maybe he wanted his last kill to be up close and personal, like a Native American warrior delivering the final coup-de-grace to his last victim.

Well, that he would get, thought Randy, only in reverse. It was a pity there was so much open ground between them right now, because it would have been fitting to win the game at the exact spot where it would have originally been won, around the fire pit at the Execution Grounds. But it was a small detail. Randy was a very patient man. He would lie in wait, like any good card shark, striking only when the odds favored him.

He stayed still until nearly a half hour later, when Old Joe finally rose from the Execution Grounds and began to move across the beach towards the trail. Once the old man stepped onto its hard packed surface, he quickly disappeared into the jungle on the lava cave trail.

Randy slowly rose from the ground, a smile spreading across his face. He had him now.

Machete in hand, he crept quietly along the edge of the jungle until he also reached the trail. Stopping for a moment, he listened for anything that might be amiss, but heard nothing. No footsteps, no rustling in the bushes. He crept on.

Moving smoothly and calmly, he strode the trail towards Mount Iglesias. His mind was in full tournament mode, the lightly moonlit world around him crystallizing into analytical data for him to process, coldly and objectively. Hearing a noise, he stopped instantly, without hesitation. When it was clear again, he moved fluidly, part of the environment itself.

As the minutes went on the sky began to brighten, and doubt too began to creep into Randy's normally doubtless brain. If the sun rose before he caught the old man, he would lose his edge, and might have to either risk a face to face confrontation, or give it up until the next night and find somewhere very, very secure to hide.

Joe was smart too, of course, and Randy was not in any hurry to face the old woodsman in mortal combat. Surely someone who had successfully vanquished all of his competition under such harsh environmental conditions as these would have tricks up his sleeve that Randy could not possibly predict.

No, he would have to finish the hillbilly tonight. He was smarter, he already had the edge of being behind his intended victim, and for a little while longer, he would have the cover of night.

Again he reminded himself of one very important fact— no one had hunted Joe before. Though the old man certainly knew he had just two competitors left, he wouldn't expect that one of them would be reckless enough to come after him now that the truth was out. He would no doubt imagine that Randy was hiding in the jungle to avoid being killed, perhaps snuggling alongside a shaking Kinnary, waiting for the boat to come. Old Joe's actions on the beach practically screamed that scenario. He was operating out in the open, whistling even, totally unafraid.

After all, if you *are the Killer*, what is there to be afraid of?

These things all added up quickly in Randy's mind, and he quickened his pace so he could indeed bring an end to the chaos on Cocos Island, tonight.

Thoughts of how he'd spend his winnings briefly entered his head, but he quickly swept them away. Focus came easily to Randy, and his intensity was stronger than it had ever been.

Suddenly he stopped dead in his tracks. There was movement— noise on the trail ahead. He knew he was close to Gissler Point, as the open sky over the ocean was now visible through the trees to his right. He cocked his ear and listened. More noise— footfalls, scraping. Yes, Joe was indeed up on Gissler Point. But what the hell was he doing there? Resting, perhaps from the climb? If so, it was another notch in Randy's favor. A tired victim would be a victim indeed.

He crouched and softly slid all the way to the ground. On his belly now, he crawled like a commando up the trail, staying close enough to the jungle on his left to seem a part of it. His gilley suit, made of fresh, green vegetation, was flexible and soft enough to stay relatively silent as it moved over the ground.

Reaching the top of Gissler Point, he grinned at the fortunate scene before him. Joe sat silently on a tree stump, facing the ocean with his back to the trail. Randy could hardly believe it, but Old Joe appeared to be waiting patiently to enjoy the sunrise.

Wilderness types, Randy thought, suckers for old-timey, romantic visions of Mother Nature's splendor. Well, this particular romantic moment would be Old Joe's last.

Randy crept slowly to his feet and tiptoed towards the Killer of Cocos. Eight very soft steps later, he was directly behind Old Joe. The old man was a sitting duck, served up on a platter in the rising light of the new day.

He sighted in on Joe's neck, pulled his machete-laden arm back, and swung with all his might.

And he hit a home run. Old Joe's head left its body and flew in the direction of the swing, the old man's torso slipping off the stump and slumping to the ground.

But instead of feeling elated at his victory, Randy's heart and lungs froze, as he instantly realized there was no blood spurting from the wound, and something had felt very wrong about how easily the head had separated from the man. He'd been ready for blood— had even steeled himself against the coming sight of it. A sudden, intense sense fear of having missed something crucially important stole the breath from his lungs at the very same moment a speeding arrow sliced through the back of his neck, slipped his spine, and plunged through the front of his throat.

The gambler had played his last hand, and lost. He fell to the ground clutching his throat as blood bubbles popped and spit the scattered remnants of his life into the misty air of Cocos Island.

That's what it looks like, the thought passed through his darkening mind as the red liquid dripped into his eyes, that's what blood looks like.

In the brush thirty yards to the Northwest, Kinnary buried her head in her hands to stifle a scream. She'd been prepared for a brutal scene, and for one she could not stop. But Randy had walked straight into what, to her, had been an obvious trap from about five hundred steps ago.

The ruthlessness displayed by Old Joe in propping up someone else's dead corpse (Susan? Matthew? Who?) to fool the hard charging Randy was beyond the pale. She hadn't expected that level of cunning, that level of willingness to sink to dishonor. Not from Joe.

And yet, here it was, right in her face. Randy gasped for air on the ground, blood gurgling from his mouth, some unknown head having been ejected from its body and sent into the weeds of Cocos. And worse.

She watched as Old Joe dropped from the trees, striding slowly and confidently towards Randy. Her heart nearly stopped, at the very same moment her mind came alive like wildfire.

Should she take him out now? Her hands tightened their grip on the jungle floor, and her toes straightened themselves like a sprinter's, ready to bolt into the fray and take on Joe where he would never expect it.

But . . . No. She would win this contest. Not only that, *she* would kill the Killer of Cocos island. But not this way. Her way, like in her victories before, would be a victory to be talked about, over water coolers, and on internet chat rooms and fan boards.

Kinnary would kill Old Joe. She had no choice but to do so, or she would certainly be killed herself. And she would do so in a way that would not simply add to her legend, but would strengthen it, as perhaps the greatest player of all time.

And she would do so by out hunting the hunter.

35

Days 17/18 ~ Memory Lane

Old Joe crept down from his perch in the big, old Ceiba tree, unsure whether Randy was really dead, or just playing. Inching his way across the twenty yards between them (helluva shot!), his bow was fully stretched and ready with an arrow in the breech, aimed at the back of Randy's head. But when he came within ten feet, he dropped his ready stance and strolled casually to his victim.

Randy was still breathing, but just barely. He lay on his side, just a few feet from poor Matthew's twice-dead body, now dressed in Joe's clothing. Blood gurgled from Randy's throat, forming crimson bubbles on the arrow's shaft. Joe rolled him over, snapping the arrow under the larger man's body. Randy gazed up at him, eyes searching for something to hold onto in his last moments. The arrow's point stuck straight out of his throat, a nearly perfect shot with a far less than perfect weapon.

"You?" Randy gurgled.

"Yep, sorry son, me. Guess ya didn't see it comin'."

Randy's hands clawed at the thing stuck in his throat.

"Son," Old Joe went on, "I like ya, quite a bit as a matter a' fact, but it just come down ta me or you. Love the leaves, by the way. Thought that was a real nice touch." He smiled sincerely down at his victim. "I guess this here's where they would put the ol' Castaway necklace on me. But since we ain't got a necklace, I'll take that there." Reaching down, Joe plucked a string of tightly tied leaves from Randy's head, and placed it on his own.

Randy managed to let one softly whispered word slip through the muck. It was mangled by a heavy combination of blood, mucous, and saliva, but was intelligible nonetheless.

"Kinnary . . ."

Joe shook his head. "I don't s'pose she'll be no trouble, son. Don't think she got it in her. I'll give her a good share though, don't you worry 'bout that. Fair's fair. Still, I done the work here, and I'll take the lion's share. This thing here really just come down ta you, and me. And so," he stood up and held his head high, "I hereby crown Ol' Joseph Stabler the winner of Execution Island, Cocos edition."

He took a step forward and turned around to face where he had stood, pretending he was now Taylor, barking in shrill glee the final mantra of the show to end all reality shows.

"Old Joe is the Strongest.
Old Joe is the Smartest.
Old Joe lasted the Longest.
Old Joe stands alone.
Old Joseph Stabler is the winner of the final season of Execution Island."

He rotated again to stand in the winner's spot, leaving the bitter taste of Taylor's persona behind, and bowed to the phantom host.

"There. That'll have ta do. That, and millions in gold coins."

Satisfied, but still not very happy about it, Old Joe turned his focus to his victim. Randy's suffering looked like it might continue for hours, and while he had no choice but to kill the man, he didn't like seeing anyone, or anything, suffer.

"Son, I just cain't take that yer in pain. It ain't right. Ya came in second, after all. Just wouldn't be right. So, I'm a gonna say my good byes, and let ya go. Good bye, now."

Old Joe planted his boot in Randy's side and rolled him straight off of Gissler's point, watched him fall three hundred feet before the killing blow came courtesy of a lava boulder. Randy's lifeless body twitched and bounced down the last hundred feet of slope, twisting and turning as his bones popped, until he came to a stop, next to the frothy ocean waves.

"Aww, damn," Joe muttered, "you're s'posed ta git something' for comin' in second. Here ya go."

Pulling a gold coin from Matthew's shirt pocket, he flipped it over the cliff. Seconds later it slapped down next to Randy's limp body, bounced high above him, and plunged into the sea.

"Close enough."

Old Joe dropped his bow to the ground and stood with his eyes closed facing the glorious Pacific Ocean, breathing deeply the scented air of the tropics, letting it fill his chest as Cocos Island had filled his soul. He stayed for a good while as the sun rose higher, and let the cleansing saltwater wind scour his conscience and steady his mind.

The killing was done. He hadn't liked it, but he'd also had no choice. It was kill or be killed, and once the game had devolved into some kind of "Lord of the Flies" campout, well, he wasn't about to let them take him. Not with the life he now planned to live, now sitting right there in his grasp.

Filled with the spirit of the Islands, Joe turned his back to the sea to face what was to come next. Hard work. He was not a big believer in the plan to stash the gold in crates and then hope it got through whatever chaotic mess was to greet them on the mainland, especially after all of the deaths. As the Ultimate Castaway and one of only two left alive from the show's final season, there was no way he'd be able to move around unnoticed and unbothered once he was back in the World.

No, there would be cameras, hangers on, interviews, lawyers, and god knew what else. But the forensics and bodies, and Kinnary if she had any sense at all, would back up his story, which went like this; Taylor's secret plan and lust for gold led him to call off the boats and begin killing his own contestants with the help of a conspirator already on the island. That led the players to go crazy and murder each other out of sheer terror and paranoia, until finally Joe had no other choice but to defend himself against the remaining murderer. Randy.

He headed for the quonset hut, tearing open the crates where the gold had been stashed by Danielle and Susan, one at a time. He poured them little by little into the wheelbarrow, and headed back up the trail. Only a couple of main criteria were required in his chosen stash spot. One, it had to be away from the bodies, which would certainly be dug up. And two, it had to be near the trail, or he'd never get that many pounds of gold to it in the first place.

And he thought it fitting, as he began to dig once more into the sandy flesh of Cocos, that it be buried in the former camp of the black hats. Each one had tried to kill him, just to get that gold.

Well, now they could have it. Temporarily, of course.

Old Joe would bury his gold there, and then clean the whole mess up to look somewhat normal. Luckily for him it was only half way to the original cave hole. By the time anyone was the wiser, the quick growing foliage of Cocos would cover all tracks and it would just be another patch of green ground off the trail.

But Old Joe was an outdoorsman. Taking a compass reading, he scratched it carefully into the leather of his bag, ready to use on the day he came back to Cocos with a boat of his own. He'd have to be careful, but he'd thought of that too. He'd simply get a week's diving permit, moor his boat off the southwest of the island, and under cover of night row ashore with a soundless dinghy. Equipped with night vision goggles, a shovel, and a heavy canvas backpack, he would simply haul as much back to his boat during that week that he could. He could simply return, yet again, if he had to.

There was still the matter of Kinnary, technically his runner up. With each passing hour that she refused to show herself, he reckoned that made her share of the pile smaller. After all, the least she could do is help with the physical labor. But the hours clicked by, with no sign of her.

And as those many hours ticked by, Old Joe begin to feel nervous. Paranoia, it seemed, was still a contestant in this game.

Lifting his head for a moment, he looked into the trees. "Girl, I know you're out there!" He paused, his chest heaving from the labor. "Seems like we're in this together? Mebbe ya'd like ta grab a shovel and help? I kin assure ya, I ain't got no ill will towards ya! I had ta take Ol' Randy out! Ya must know that! He was comin' fer me, plain'n simple!" He paused again, listening. "I mean, the man was wearin' half the jungle on his body! What do you think that meant?"

He paused again, his old ears straining to hear any sounds that might be out there. For a moment, he was sure he heard something in the trees, moving forward towards him at a good clip.

But a moment later, four giant rats emerged in a tangled mess, locked in their own violent, winner-take-all struggle over a hunk of dead bird carcass.

"Sonsabitches," Joe grumbled, before returning to his work.

He spent those next two days working very hard. Eating rats and coconuts three times a day for strength, he filled and wheeled the barrow, and dug like the rats themselves. He dragged Darius' arrow-filled body from the trail and buried him properly at the graveyard, as the good man deserved. A graveyard, he realized, filled only with white hats. The last two black hats were still where they had dropped, exposed to the rats and the elements, as he thought it should be. But he'd be damn sure the last white hat was buried, proper like.

He might have slept in the quonset hut now that everyone else was gone, but why? His waterfall cave had kept him alive, kept his enemies from finding him, and given him the inspiration that would make the rest of his life a pleasurable one.

So there he slept on his straw-covered stone bed, feeling each bump and scrape with pleasure, knowing he would soon be back in the land of the living, where things would not be so pleasant.

But first, there was Kinnary. He'd have to pull her aside to be sure she had her story straight. Make sure she was reasonably compensated so she'd keep it that way. Then he'd have to keep his wits about him and watch his own back 24 hours a day until that glorious day came, six months, a year, even two years from now when he could simply slip, forgotten by the fickle pages of history, onto a boat and motor out to Cocos to revisit his glorious achievement, and begin his life anew.

And now, he thought as he looked around the beach at an environment that had been burned, bored into, dug up, stabbed, scarred and charred, Old Joe truly did stand alone.

He fingered the crown of leaves still on his head, imagining it to be some gloriously complex totem, handed to him by Taylor in front of millions of people on live television.

A smile creased his lips. The boat would be along any day. One, maybe two. He'd spend those days huddled up, going over his plan and his alibi, drawing a map of every single death and event in the sand. Kinnary would eventually come out of hiding. She'd have to, and he'd work on a plan to make it so. They must talk before the boat got here, or things might spiral out of his control quickly. He even left about a fifth of the gold out in the open in the hut, just so he wouldn't have to lie about it. The closer his tale was to reality, the easier it would be to believe.

Shit, he thought. Matthew. He'd forgotten young Matthew. The kid wasn't one of the bad ones. In fact, he'd liked the guy. And he had served his purpose, allowing his body to be used in Joe's place, his head lopped off in a thoughtless desecration of the deceased, and yet Joe had forgotten all about him and left his body in two parts, up on Gissler's Point.

Rolling back down the trail to gather Matthew and give him his due, Old Joe thought it fitting to spend some time recollecting his fallen competitors, just as would have been done in a montage during the final episode of Execution Island, had there been one.

Tonya— she was a good egg. They could have gone far together. Of course she would still have had to settle for second.

Amy— he'd barely gotten to know her. She was nice to look at, but that was about all he could say about her. Still, seemed to be a nice girl.

The medical team, Sato and Jeremy— He'd barely said two words to either of them, and hadn't needed their services during his earlier season, so it was hard to even whip up a single observation about them. So, he simply moved on.

Leticia— holy shit! Damn near forgot about that one! That girl was a spitfire! Worst social game in the history of the show. Nasty, nasty woman. Just an awful human being. But she had dispatched the original killer, and in doing so, saved him a lot of work.

Taylor and his production team— By all rights, Taylor should have been the first to die. What a piece of shit. All of these deaths were his fault, as far as Joe was concerned. Wouldn't ever give him another thought, other than to cover his name in shit in the media once he got back home. Carl seemed ok. Malik too, but had just gone nuts under the strain, which was certainly understandable.

Matthew— lying right here before him. He was truly upset when Matthew was stabbed. Probably Malik's doing, as had been suspected. But this death in particular had changed the game for him.

261

Franklin— Arrogant. Too strong for his own good. Guys like that are always a target, in all walks of life. Had no chance from day one.

Danielle— he'd always thought she was nice, and might have helped her had the game gone as intended. But she had lost more than one step since her season, and was too nice, in fact, for Execution Island, losing all will to live under the strain.

Susan— Boy was he glad he hadn't been forced to take her out, though he had gotten up the gumption to at least think about doing so. She was dangerous, unstable, a loose cannon that somebody had to remove. He was glad someone did, and probably had Darius to thank.

Darius— God damnit he liked the guy! Really liked him. And that's why it had been so easy to put an arrow through Randy's throat. The bastards, one of them anyway, had killed a good man. He was just about to rescind the order that they split up when he'd found him dead. Pity he'd been too late.

Jason— Died the same way, probably by Darius as well. Fitting. Guy was ten pounds of shit in a one pound bag, as far as Joe was concerned. Hell, he'd have killed him the first time he faced him on the White Hats vs Black Hats season, if only it wasn't against the rules.

And Randy. Not that bad a guy, really. Had they met somewhere else, they might actually have gotten along. But Randy was the kind of guy who, although not bad himself, often rolled with a bad crowd, just for the juice. And this time, it had cost him everything.

Kinnary— Her story was yet to be written. And if Old Joe had his way, they'd write it together. As a team. He had nothing against her, even if she was a bit snotty. But if she'd play ball with him, he'd share his crown with her. And if not . . .

Old Joe rolled up to the Execution Island graveyard, dropped the barrow's handles, gazing at the many headstones there, mere coconuts jammed onto sticks. Franklin. Danielle. Darius. Amy. Tonya. And now Matthew would rejoin them.

He found himself fighting back a tear. Remembering what they had all gone through was a lot to process. He figured he'd spend the rest of his life sorting it all out, poring through memories and moments he'd suppressed just to stay alive. The friendships, the joys, and the many sorrows of his days on Cocos Island.

Matthew's grave was now dug up for the second time that week. Tossing the shovel behind him, he slipped the body softly back into the hole, and smiled. The twice buried lad finally rested peacefully, at least as peacefully as one could with no head. Old Joe was pleased, feeling a real sense of peace for the first time in weeks.

But it was short lived, for out of nowhere he felt a blast of pain hit his right shoulder. Looking down at the source, he was shocked.

A crudely made arrow, nowhere near as fine as those he had made, but still an arrow, stuck out of his arm and pointed into the jungle.

"Joe!" rose a high pitched scream from the trees, and he spun on his heels, dropped behind the wheel barrow, and gazed towards the sound. His wise old eyes scanned the foliage, but saw nothing.

"You're done!" Kinnary screamed. "This is *my* game. No way you're taking *me* out!"

Old Joe smiled slightly through his pain. "Well now, girl," he yelled as loud as he could, "the way I see it, we both won! I'll share my gold with ya, fair and square. There's plenty for us both."

He paused again waiting for his words to take effect.

"Why don't ya come on out," he probed, "so we kin talk? Ain't got nothin' 'gainst ya, I promise."

This time she was quick to reply.

"I don't talk to murderers, old man! You'll have to come and get me."

Joe was peeved. What the hell kind of game was she playing? "Aww, hell's bell's, girl! Randy had it comin'! He was comin' ta kill me, and you know it! I reckon ya seen the whole thing! He was wearin' a goldurned gilley suit! You don't put on one a them things 'less ya mean ta kill somebody! And he did *use* that machete, now didn't he?"

The jungle was silent. And then,

"What about the rest, Joe! Darius, Susan, Jason Oliver, hell, maybe all the way back to Taylor and his boys!"

"Girl," Joe shook his head in disbelief, suddenly realizing that this crazy situation was much worse than he thought, "have ya done gone off yer rocker? I ain't killed nobody but Randy. Plain and simple. I swear to it. Besides, it looked ta the rest of us like *you* killed ol' Susan! Not that anybody'd blame ya! So, that makes the count one to one. A black hat fer you, n' one fer me. Both of 'em cold blooded killers! Ain't nobody gonna hang for that."

"Arrows, Joe. They had arrows in their backs! Jason and Darius! Just like the ones you put into Randy. I just missed your heart by a mile, so it clearly wasn't me! And yeah, I went to confront Susan, but she was already dead!"

Old Joe thought for a moment as the voice trailed off. Some of that made sense. But how could those deaths be accounted for if it wasn't as he'd thought?

"Well then, maybe ol' Darius done killed Susan and Jason Oliver. Then Randy killed him in revenge. Signed, sealed, delivered!"

The jungle fell silent once more, as Kinnary now took her own turn to think. No, she decided, it was too neat, and there were too many others unaccounted for before those. She could place the names of killed and killer together, but the arrows still stuck, figuratively, in her mind.

"I'm not buying it. You've got two choices, Joe! You can sit there and get pin-cushioned, or you can try to come and get me!"

Once again, Joe was left without a real choice.

"Aww hell, girl," he moaned, realizing now that Kinnary had somehow gone to the dark side, "This here's your call, not mine."

And in the very next moment, Old Joe bolted for the trees, knowing that once inside, there was no way she could use the cute little toy bow and arrows she had apparently made.

36

Kinnary ~ The Year 2000

"I still don't understand why is this so important to you?" her mother chided. "Athletics is not a way to true success, Kinnary. If you just focused more on your studies, and less on these silly events . . ."

Kinnary turned and stormed off, leaving her mother alone in the stands at Hornet Stadium. Respect was certainly not something she expected from her. Or her father, for that matter. They didn't, and they wouldn't, ever understand her.

Achievement in sports meant nothing to them, only academic achievement. Her brother was well on his way to being an M.D. Her sister, a lawyer.

Never mind that neither of them *wanted* to be those things. What mattered, at least to her parents and their Indian expat friends, was that they brought wealth and status to the family, thereby improving the lot of the entire line. The caste system was well and alive in her parents, though they were several thousand miles removed from where it belonged.

Her father had done his part. He was a respected psychiatrist, the author of several books. Her mother, in the old tradition of the sub-continent, was just that, a mother. No one had expected *her* to do anything but be a matron, to produce children (preferably males) who would bring great honor and pride to their parents as high wage earners on the American continent.

But on this new continent, Kinnary was expected to be just like her father. Just like her sister. And just like her brother.

A source of familial pride. Not a silly jock. Never mind that all she had ever wanted to *be* was a jock.

So long ago she set her mind to achieving her *own* goals, despite their protests. Her dream was to succeed at the very highest level, the Olympics. And now here she was, preparing to qualify for the 2000 games in the 400 meter hurdles. She even held out the small hope that if she qualified, her family might actually become excited about it, and perhaps even change their minds about their youngest daughter.

The pressure of qualifying for the Olympic games was more than enough stress for any normal person. But for Kinnary, a second generation Indian-American female, that pressure was secondary to that which came from her parents.

Now here she was in Sacramento, in the qualifying trials that could win her a trip to the Sydney games. Though a mere three hour drive from home, her father hadn't made the trip, but said if she made the games, he would "try" to get to Australia for the real event. But he was a busy doctor, and couldn't make any promises.

Kinnary rolled her eyes thinking of his arrogance as she entered the locker room to prepare for her first race. She knew why people became psychiatrists. Because they were stark raving mad themselves.

Long ago she had stopped trying to please her parents. Like the song said, "You can't please everyone, so you got to please yourself". Since she was thirteen, that had been her mantra.

Kinnary gazed around the crowded locker room. The hundred meter dash had just finished its final race, and it was easy to tell those women apart from her fellow four hundred meter hurdlers. They were thickly muscled, while the women in her event were leaner, with tight, thin legs, necessary traits to make it the distance. She saw Marion Jones, who had just won her race. And Gail Devers, considered a lock to win the 100 meter hurdles as well, an event she had herself given up years ago, knowing she didn't have the muscle for it.

Kinnary was certainly no lock to make the team even in the 400, and she knew it. Her best time was only 55:54. Most of her times barely cracked 57 seconds. She'd have to step up big to make it here, or hope for someone else to stumble. She rarely hit hurdles, having very long legs that didn't need much help to clear them, but she had seen many of her competitors race, and thankfully some of them weren't as gifted.

She eyed each of them warily as she strolled the aisles, taking in the competition. Her nose filled with the familiar smell of the locker room, (is it different on the men's side?), her eyes filled her mind with the faces of her competitors, ferreting out who was nervous, and who had the eye of the tiger.

She'd be in heat two, and that was a fortunate thing. The real talent was in heat one, and the times those women put up regularly would beat her best on a good day. But Kinnary knew that the rarefied air of the Olympics made people bring out the best of their best, and she wouldn't be here at all if she didn't believe she could rise above.

Tossing her bag in a locker, she pulled out her cleats, and slipped them over her long feet with care. Her ankles were already wrapped in tape to help transfer every motion to the ground, keeping her stable as she exploded out of the blocks. Closing her eyes she pictured her parents, their judgmental gazes sliding off of their faces as she strapped on a medal— any medal—at the podium after the finals. Breathing deeply the pungent aroma of the locker room, she let it her fill her heart, and then opened her eyes once more.

Arrayed around her on metal benches were her opponents from heat two, having taken the places of the women from heat one who were now out on the track, stretching and getting into their blocks. She had keen powers of observation, a true competitor who took note of all of her opponents' weaknesses, and today was no exception. She wore her own UCLA jersey with pride, and knew a couple of the other girls by theirs. Dominique Calloway- she ran for Ohio State and was fast, probably the favorite of the group. Yvonne Harrison she only knew by reputation, because she was a sponsored athlete and not a student, but that reputation was fearsome. Sandra Farmer Patrick too was sponsored, by Nike no less. Again, she had never run against her, and didn't really know what to expect. And Nicole Thompson, from her own Pac 10 conference ran for Arizona.

Kinnary smiled, knowing she would beat that one for sure, as she always did. The girl was slow, at least slower than she was. Her gaze rested upon her, waiting for their eyes to meet. When they finally did, she smiled, knowing well that the meaning of that smile was understood. "I own you," she said with that grin, and when Nicole quickly looked away, she knew she agreed.

Only two of the five women sitting here would make the semi-finals tomorrow. The other three came here for nothing, and Kinnary didn't plan to be one of them.

Breathing deeply she stood up, hearing the gun fire for heat one. The other girls stood too, preparing to head outside with some more stretching, when Kinnary suddenly noticed something that made her heart pound faster in her chest.

Dominique's left shoe had a problem. A problem that gave Kinnary an edge against one of the women who just might beat her. The glue was "delamming", coming apart where the sole met the upper shoe. It was just a small tear, maybe an inch, but it would be just enough to slow her opponent down for the few hundredths of a second or so it would take to beat her.

Kinnary knew Dominique's usual times, and that little bit was all it would take.

Her chest rising and falling rapidly, Kinnary hesitated for just a moment, but then fell in line with the other girls and headed into the tunnel that led to the track. Out in the bright sunlight, she squinted to see the results of heat one. Joann Hayes, a newcomer, and Nikki Buoyer, another runner from Arizona, had made the cut. The rest of the girls filed into the tunnel, their heads hung low, their chests pumping furiously to gain oxygen.

Kinnary looked away. No sense getting that stink on her.

She headed for lane two and looked down at her blocks. She knelt into them, testing her cleats, and bolted. After a few steps, she felt secure, and turned back around. They had a few minutes yet to go, so she stretched, and focused.

Dominique had drawn lane one, right next to her. God, she thought, I hope she doesn't fall into my lane! It was a selfish thought, she knew, but this was war.

Keeping her gaze from falling onto Dominique, she instead knelt in the blocks and looked down the track, focusing on the first hurdle.

One at a time, her well trained mind repeated. One . . . At . . . A . . . Time.

Suddenly a high pitched voice pierced her mind's peaceful quiet. "Good luck, UCLA!"

She turned and saw Dominique, smiling at her. Unlike the grin she had aimed at Nicole, this one was harmless. One might even call it sweet.

She nodded. "Good luck to you, Buckeye."

Dominique nodded in return, before dropping her own gaze to the ground, kneeling, and stretching.

Kinnary saw the shoe again, the delam growing slightly worse. It would almost certainly cost her opponent the race.

But suddenly, for some damn reason she didn't feel so good about it. Would this moment haunt her if she made the semis? Would she think about it well after that, perhaps even into the Games themselves? Would it gnaw at her gut, and leave her with a bitter taste for years to come?

How would she react when Dominique dropped her head after the race and sauntered into the locker room, lost from the annals of Olympic history by an unfair circumstance she herself could have prevented?

"Damnit!" Kinnary muttered under her breath, before stepping out of the blocks, and raising her hand.

The whistle blew, and the other runners looked up, confused. Sighing, Kinnary turned to the girl from Ohio State.

"Hey, Buckeye. Your shoe. It's coming apart."

Dominique first looked puzzled, and then looked down.

"The left one," Kinnary pointed.

"Holy hell! Wow, Omigod! Thank you!" Dominique ran to the judge with the starter pistol, and pointed at her foot. A moment later she was jogging into the tunnel, while the other racers stood and stretched again.

"What the hell's going on?" Kinnary heard one of the girls say.

She knelt and did more lunges, but didn't look up. No weakness.

"Her shoe. It was delamming."

Giggles in reply. "And you told her?" Another voice rang out. "You here to win or make friends?"

Kinnary ignored them, looked ahead, and focused. Now not only was luck on her side, but, she hoped, karma too.

Dominique quickly re-entered with a new pair of cleats on her feet, softly patted Kinnary on the back with another sweet thank you, and the whole thing began anew.

When the gun fired, Kinnary left the blocks first. Her heart leapt. She focused on the hurdles, one… at … a … time, her lean brown legs clearing them with ease. She heard someone hit one, and then the sound of it clattering to the ground.

She assumed it was Nicole, but thought no more of it, focusing on the next hurdle. That left just three racers to beat.

Over another, then another, then another, her legs pumped furiously towards the last one. Sandra Patrick was next to her in lane three, and Kinnary glowed as she began to put the woman behind her. She could see Yvonne Harrison, the Fila sponsored runner, well out ahead of the pack in lane 5, so all she had to do was hang on and she was in!

Dominique was neck and neck with her, right on her pace. Kinnary pushed and pumped with all her might, knowing Karma was on her side, and that doing the right thing would certainly be just the edge she needed. She leaned forward, straining hard, and crossed the line!

At the same time as Dominique. The two of them turned in unison towards the board, each knowing her fate was in the hands of the timers.

The board was blank for just a moment, and then the times popped up.

LANE 1- 56.83
LANE 2- 56.85

Dominique squealed in glee while Kinnary fell to the ground, her head in her hands, tears melting into the red clay of Hornet Stadium.

A few hundredths of a second. That was all she had needed, that was all it would have taken. And she'd known exactly that, all along.

Karma, it turned out, really is a bitch.

37

Day 18 ~ Some Girls

Kinnary raced through the treetops, moving away from Old Joe on the very same path that had led her to him. She stayed above the ground, her lithe legs and lean body carrying her effortlessly from branch to branch, while Old Joe, quite distracted by the arrow in his body, followed much more slowly on the ground.

Stopping to catch his breath, he gazed at the young woman slip sliding through the trees. Something about it didn't quite sit right with him. She seemed to know exactly where she was going, like she was on a predetermined route. Kneeling on the ground, Joe stuck a piece of vine in his mouth, bit down on it, and ripped the arrow out of his shoulder, losing a piece of flesh in the process. It hurt like hell, and he screamed against the crushed vine in his mouth before gathering himself and spitting it out, and then slowly rose to get his bearings.

Kinnary had slowed her pace, but remained visible against the green of the jungle. To Joe, she seemed to be purposely keeping him just barely in her view, looking without looking from the corner of her eye.

He smiled through the pain in his shoulder. A tracker knew when he was being tracked. There was no damn way she could beat him out here, in his element. His head on a swivel, he scanned the jungle for a route other than the one she was clearly leading him down. He was certain there was a trap out there, somewhere on that path. A trap she was praying he wouldn't see. So he took a bead on her position, and the angle of her path, then quickly triangulated them both.

He bolted. Moving much more quickly with the arrow gone, he knew that she, no matter how fleet of foot, would eventually be forced to move more slowly through the thick trees than he could on the ground.

Old Joe began to gain ground, and Kinnary picked up her pace to match. She made no attempt to cover her tracks, escape, or be quiet. Indeed, to Joe the whole jungle seemed to be filled with the sound of breaking branches, crunching leaves and palm fronds, both in front of him, and even behind. Tuning out the noise, he focused instead on both the angle of his approach, and where his feet were falling. A twisted ankle at this point could mean his life.

Kinnary wasn't the least bit surprised that Old Joe had quickly caught on to her cat and mouse game, in fact, her plan depended on it. But she was surprised that he was gaining on her. In a few moments, she realized as she swung between two branches on a vine she'd placed there for just that purpose, she'd be forced to hit the forest floor and go the rest of the way on foot.

Which, she grinned as she ran the length of one last, massive Ceiba limb before leaping into the air, was just fine with her.

Old Joe was within thirty yards when Kinnary leapt from the branch. He watched as she hit the ground hard, dropped briefly to one knee to absorb the blow, then quickly took off again.

The older man groaned as his tired body strained to keep up. He had nearly forty years on her, not to mention a bleeding hole in his topside, and he began to lose ground again. Making matters worse, his role in this fight was much tougher than hers. He had to both track her *and* stay off of her direct path, somewhere along which certainly lay his intended doom.

"God," he puffed under his breath, "damn girl's half antelope!"

Kinnary's brown legs moved like a dancer's. Smooth and light were her steps. She softly swept branches behind her as she flew, every so often peeking over her shoulder to see where he was. She couldn't have known which side he would take, yet his tack was almost exactly how she'd imagined it would be. She'd known that beating a true woodsman would require not only distraction and confusion— the arrow — but she must also allow him to bring his own knowledge of nature to bear, and use it against him.

This, as Old Joe too wisely understood, was no spontaneous chase.

Minutes later, he discovered that what he had worried might happen, was indeed happening. She was clearly leading him into a box. Forced to side-step towards her track, the dirt under his feet began to fall away into a sharp canyon. Knowing what was coming, he allowed himself to be pushed halfway back to her primrose path by the rapidly angling ravine, and then, realizing the odds were no longer on his side, Old Joe stopped running altogether.

Kinnary peeked over her shoulder again and saw him slowing to a Sunday stroll, so she did the same.

"Well now," he panted with his hands on his knees, "Girlie, let's just see whatcha got planned fer Old Joe Stabler, shall we?"

Kinnary, breathing easily, placed her hands on her hips and glared at her competitor.

"Having some trouble there, Joe?" she teased.

He lifted his head, smiling confidently at her. "Ain't nothin' a coupla minutes won't fix."

His absolute confidence hit Kinnary hard in the stomach. Doubt, just a teensy bit of it, began to creep in.

"Well, please forgive me if I don't wait for you."

Turning on her heels, she calmly began to walk away.

"Where ya goin'? Seems like we got a bit a talkin' ta do yet."

Kinnary stopped once more, speaking with her back to him.

"Look, Joe. There's no way you can catch me out here. No way. I'll never even let you get close."

"No?" he perked up, his lungs beginning catch up. "What's all this here, then? Seems ta me like you got me on some sorta approach. Like this here's *all* parta yer plan. Don't kid me, girl. I know how these things go. This here's *my* world."

Kinnary laughed, though a bit less forcefully than she'd hoped she would.

"Well then, why are you following me? If you're so sure?"

Now Joe laughed. "Because. Like I told ya. I know how these things go."

273

Kinnary began to walk again, creeping doubt nipping at her heels. Joe matched her pace, and the two moved, as if joined by an invisible tether, in unison through the jungle of Cocos Island.

"Look now, ain't no reason for this, Girl," Joe returned to diplomacy. "Ya cain't beat me out here. You got ta know that. No matter what little booby trap you got waitin' fer Old Joe, he's seen it before. That, I kin promise ya."

Kinnary froze for just a second, and Joe noticed.

"Yeah, that's right. See, it don't really matter *what* ya got. Pit covered with leaves? Seen it. Spring loaded branches? Seen it. Vine loaded with something' heavy, just a hangin' way up high? Seen it."

Kinnary quietly cleared her throat. "Well then," she began, relieved that her voice didn't crack, "what do you propose we do, Joe?"

Joe stepped lightly, his gaze switching rapidly from every jungle branch, to every rock, to every patch of dirt on three sides. Scanning. Analyzing. A redneck robot.

"Well," he continued in a voice that, unlike Kinnary's, overflowed with confidence, "seems like ya got two choices. Number one is, ya die."

He paused to let the blunt moment take effect, and noticed by her wavering steps, that it did.

"Now, I got ta say, I don't like that option fer ya. Seems like yer a fairly nice sorta gal. But if ya don't go for option two, I don't see how there's a choice other 'n that. Ain't no way I kin sleep out here, knowing all the time that yer ready ta stick something sharp inta me while I do."

"Option two?" Kinnary paused her steps as she spoke.

Joe waited, seeing her pause, dropping low to his haunches to be sure he didn't miss anything that might be swinging towards him at that very moment. When nothing came, he returned to his pitch.

"We talk. And we come up with a plan. Together. But see here, you got ta come ta Jesus and git yer story straight. The story is gonna be that all these other poor dumb bastards killed each other. Now, like I say, I'll take the heat for Ol' Randy. I done that one, plain and simple. Had no choice. But the others? We got ta wind that tale up real tight, and stick with it. No ifs, ands, or buts."

Kinnary pretended to consider his plan as she crept ever closer to the end of the trail. Before her, about fifty steps ahead, stood a rock wall. That rock wall sat between two chasms, and there was no way, short of a rope, to get around it.

One way or another, that rock would be the end of the line.

"Seems like there's a third option," she said, confidence taking a step forward in the struggle for control taking place in her mind.

"What's 'at?" Joe was intrigued. Doubtful, but intrigued.

"You go back," she replied, "sit on the beach, leave me be, and wait for the boat. I promise I'll stay here in the jungle, and won't come out until that whistle blows. Then, we let the authorities sort it all out."

She'd moved ten more steps as she spoke, but wished she'd gone twenty.

"Well now," Old Joe shook his head in dramatic style, "that jus' don't work fer me. See, you're gonna tell one story, I'm gonna tell another, and they're probably gonna listen to yours. Seems like a lotta these fellas out here got arrows in their sides. That jus' don't look good for me, even if I didn't put 'em there. Ain't none a them dead bodies got yer mark on 'em. Not a one. Even if I could get 'em ta believe me 'bout Susan, they're gonna hang me fer the rest. No," he paused, noticing that she was letting him get closer, tightening her steps, "like I told ya. Two options."

"Well then," she said, turning to face him, "I guess you'll just have to come and get me."

Kinnary crept slowly backwards, now only fifteen steps from the rock wall. Joe had closed on her as they spoke, and was perhaps only twenty steps away.

And unbeknownst to her, he saw it.

He didn't let her know that he did, but Old Joe had just moments before noticed a branch that seemed out of place as she passed it, a branch that was bent in a way God had never intended. And now that she'd passed it, he knew what would come next.

Like he'd told her before, he'd seen it.

"Ok then, Girlie. Suit yourself."

Joe stepped ever closer, until Kinnary came within 5 feet of the rock wall behind her. His hunter's eyes caught every muscle twitch, every dilation of her eyes, every hesitation in her step. And when he finally saw them all add up to one conclusion, he was ready.

Kinnary kicked her left leg out and caught a long, thick branch that was precariously leaned up against a tree trunk, sweeping it away in one rapid motion.

The trap released and Joe dove. A heavy branch that was cocked like a spring flew from behind the tree with a whoosh!, slicing through the air with eight sharp stakes leading the way, plunging mercilessly into the very space where Old Joe Stabler had been just a fraction of a second before.

Boom!, it exploded under its own weight, its deadly spikes finding nothing but dead air as it flew the rest of the way through its arc, before crashing to the ground in shards.

Joe peeked up from the ground, where he had managed to ride out the murderous moment in relative safety, save for a chunk of the mess that fell on his back, adding a few harmless scratches to the bloody hole on Kinnary's scorecard.

Kinnary stood, shaking, her back against the rock wall. Her eyelids quivering, a tear rolled silently down from her right eye as she watched Joe rising from the ground.

He stood, brushed himself off, and leered at her. Reaching into the rear of his grubby waist band, he pulled out a four inch piece of sharp metal, a relic from the Execution Island hut that he'd been using to sharpen his arrows. Holding it now for a much more gruesome purpose, he moved towards her.

"See now, it's like I says," he chided her, "I seen it."

Kinnary's legs shook violently. There was nowhere to run. This, truly, was the end of the trail.

"Please, please Joe! Just leave me be! Go back to the beach! I won't say a thing!"

Old Joe shook his head. "Ya don't know how badly I wish I could, Deary. But in your heart, ya know ya done made that choice fer me, 'bout a half mile back."

"Please!" she screamed in agony, her fate now sealed, "God, Joe, stop! Please, please stop!"

Her legs gave way and she crumbled to the ground, helpless, begging for her life.

Joe watched her collapse, helpless in his own way as well, and not at all pleased about what he must do next.

But as Kinnary dropped, her knees came down with the full force of her body's weight (perhaps more, Joe would soon wonder), striking a tightly wrapped bundle of sticks she had tied together and buried there the day before. That bundle of sticks was connected to a pair of curved branches with a small cup at the end of them— a cup made from a coconut as a matter of fact— and in that cup was a long, thick, very sharp stick, much like a spear, that rose nonchalantly up the wall behind Kinnary, a stick which had previously been obscured from Old Joe's view by Kinnary's own quivering body, but which now became terribly visible to him as it slammed into his chest with tremendous force.

An atlatl. A levered spear, much like the one she had modeled it on that killed her friend Amy on the beach, in what seemed to her like years ago.

Joe was instantly blown backward by the force of spear breaking bone, the makeshift knife flying out of his hand and clattering down the canyon to his right. He lay there, looking up, barely thinking for a moment. His mind had simply not yet caught up with the events at hand, but it soon did. And when it did, he gasped wildly for air, unable, *unwilling* to believe that he'd somehow been beaten, by a *girl* no less, on his own battlefield! How could it be?

The shock rolled over him like a Sherman tank, crushing his will to live, ripping his dream of a new life right from his heart.

Old Joe was truly humbled as Kinnary leaned over him, and they caught each other's gaze. With a determined look on her face, she softly repeated the very words he had spoken to Randy that morning, only with a few minor changes.

"Kinnary is the Strongest.
Kinnary is the Smartest.
Kinnary lasted the Longest.
Kinnary stands alone.
Kinnary is the winner of the final season of Execution Island."

"Holy sheepshit . . ." the words gurgled out of Joe's mouth as truth took hold in the rapidly intensifying darkness of his mind.

But all of a sudden that mind jerked awake with a start, as he saw Kinnary staring down at him. He had to tell her. She had to know!

"I . . ." He struggled mightily to get the words out, but life was leaving him, "Kin . . . Randy . . ."

Kinnary leaned in closer, but not close enough for him to reach her.

"What? Last words, Joe? Tell me."

Joe's face, a writhing mass of pain, pushing, straining to get the words out.

"Randy . . . Just him! I swear! I didn't kill . . ."

And that was it. Old Joe Stabler, the odds on favorite to win the whole thing, was dead.

Kinnary stood up, stunned, in disbelief that he would use his last breath to lie. How could it be? Jason Oliver, Darius, they both had arrows, well placed arrows, in their corpses at this very moment. Susan . . . who did that if he didn't? Darius? And what about poor Danielle! Who lifted her up that tree? Couldn't have been Susan.

Her mind whirled out of control, her stomach spinning right along with it. She fell again, vomiting what little she had in her gut onto the ground, right next to Joe's motionless body.

Chunks dangling from her mouth and cold sweat dripping into her eyes, Kinnary felt very sick. She rose, steadying herself with hands on her knees, and gazed down at the man who would have been her teammate at this very moment, had she believed the very story he had chosen to make his epitaph.

Why the hell would he lie now? Was this just some kind of final jab? A stick in the gut, meant to haunt her for the rest of her life?

She straightened herself and ran her hands over her eyes, scraping off the sweat. She shook her head. It couldn't be. No, it wasn't possible.

And even if it was, she couldn't allow it to be.

"No way," she scolded his lifeless body, "No way, Joe! If I didn't kill them, and you didn't kill them, tell me who did!"

Preoccupied with their intense final conversation, Kinnary hadn't noticed any other sound since Old Joe hit the ground. But now, suddenly and unexpectedly, she heard the very last words she would ever hear, just before a crude stone axe struck her in the back of the head, opening its contents to the sky.

"I did, Bitch!"

38

Eight Years Later ~ Cast . . . Away

The Killer sat in a beach chair sipping cold Rum punch, watching the children laugh and play as waves splashed softly on a beach of pink coral sand. Huge fruit bats flew through the daylit sky like pterodactyls of old. Crisp white Fijian wedding flowers bloomed beside towering coconut palms. The air temperature was ideal, the breeze scented with spice.

It was a lovely spot to confess to mass murder.

The Killer believed there must be a record. The families of the deceased deserved to know what happened to their loved ones. But more than that, the Killer believed credit was due for a brilliant strategy, for truly being the *final* Castaway. Many lifetimes worth of gold was fine. But recognition of true greatness, even after death, was worth far more.

The pen moved across the paper ...

After I killed Kinnary, I dug up the treasure, which luckily Old Joe had moved closer to my boat. I spent the next two days loading it, and then, under cover of darkness, left Cocos Island for good. The island that had chosen me to exact its revenge had let me go, the ransom for my escape paid in the blood of those who would have done the same, if only they'd had the chance.

I headed out to sea, eventually landing on a small island near Ecuador. There, I filled my belly with bananas and crab, filled my tanks from a stream, and like the other Cocos pirates before me, buried the treasure yet again.   I took note of the location on the boat's GPS and then headed due east, eventually landing on the coast of Ecuador, at Atacames.

Most of the rest you already know. I went back and forth to my little island of buried treasure over the next few years, bringing the gold back a little at a time, learning a little more about seafaring every time I went. The two of you were born soon after. Once you were, the three of us later moved here to Fiji, far from prying eyes, far from suspicion.

My children, this island where we come to play, which I named Little Cocos, is where you will find the remaining treasure after I die. I have taken from it only to buy the things we needed for this new life. A new boat. The island itself. Our home near Suva. But I have not lived extravagantly, as that has never been my way. This money, this gold, it is yours. When I die, you will read this note, come to Little Cocos, find my prize, and do with it what you will.

But don't feel guilty about where it came from.   I don't. Remember, the people who died to make all of this happen would have killed me. In fact, they tried! If they'd succeeded, the two of you, my greatest joys in life, would never have been born.

I love you both. You are the only things in this life I have ever loved. And more than that, *you are the only things in this life that ever loved me back.*

One last thing.   You know me as your mother, Emilia De Castrugo. But that is not my real name, my children. And not yours, either.

My real name is Leticia Robles, and I am the real winner of the final season of Execution Island.

She closed the notebook.   Her eyes lovingly followed her children as she stood and walked across the center of her private island, to the large boulder in the middle. There she bent and scraped through the sand until she found a handle made of coconut husk, and lifted it.

Her gold coins shone back at her as brightly as the day she buried them.

Reaching in, she grabbed a few and placed them in her satchel. Then she carefully covered the hatch, placed a large rock over the handle just in case the sea decided to go wild again and tear away the sand, and made her way back to her children.

"It's time to go, my Loves!"

A deeply satisfied smile dawned on her sunny face as she looked across the reef at their home, perched on a hill on the main island of Vitu Levi. From the windows there she often looked back upon her Little Cocos, watching her very own Treasure Island with the eye of a mother eagle, protecting her nest, protecting her children's future.

"Head for the boat. Roast goat for dinner!"

The children hemmed and hawed, arguing briefly and dispassionately about leaving their little paradise, but eventually they crawled into her little motorboat, and the three of them set out across the short expanse of aquamarine waters towards their beautiful home overlooking the South Pacific, and Little Cocos Island.

As the sun began to slip over the horizon, she couldn't help but silently mouth these words once more, as she often did on the way back from her island. They were her mantra, words that had gotten her through the occasional feelings of guilt and doubt since that fateful day she fell from the cliff and awoke in the sea, somehow, alive.

Leticia Robles is the strongest.
Leticia Robles is the smartest.
Leticia Robles lasted the longest.
Leticia Robles stands alone.

Leticia Robles is *the* Executioner, of Execution Island.

Epilogue:

A Killer's Confession

My first lucky break came when I discovered the killer's boat floating in a huge cavern, open to the sea! I didn't know anything about the treasure yet, but when Taylor discovered it, that secret boat cave meant I was the only one who could leave the island alone, *with* the treasure! When that jerk told us he'd found gold, I almost had a heart attack I was so excited!

But when those idiots knocked me off the cliff and left me to die, it seemed my good luck was yet another brutal joke played on me by God. Battling the killer to save us all was the first time in my life I'd ever done anything selfless! And, I was determined it would be the last.

It happened so fast, but I must have landed on the killer's broken body, saved from certain death by the island itself. I awoke underwater, gashed by his knife and bleeding, but alive! Focusing on the bright light above, I swam, pulling hard at the water with battered hands, kicking furiously with my bloody legs, and finally popped out on the surface.

I didn't remember what happened at first and washed up on a strange beach. I thought it was another island, but when I saw a cabin and went inside, maps on the wall told me I was still on Cocos, at Chatham Bay. I found food, bandages, and even rum to clean my wounds. I ate like an animal from tins of meat and slept for two days. The island cared for me. It cradled me. We spoke to each other a lot, during those days. It told me that I was the only one worthy of it's gold, and I was determined to have it.

And then, days later, I heard it. Dynamite.

The island was angry that they dared put holes in her skin, and so was I. These nitwits brought dynamite to the island and risked all of our lives, so it was fitting to me to end theirs that way. That night I snuck into the quonset hut and found a whole box of it. I took two sticks, poked around for matches, and carefully stepped outside.

Slipping into the crew's cabin, I stole a machete to replace my own, slung it on my back and made my exit.

When my victims fell asleep, I made my move. Creeping quietly from the bushes, I scurried again to the crew cabin with a stick of dynamite in my hand. Lighting the fuse, I stepped inside and threw it.

When Carl raised his head, I winked at him, and was gone.

Running as fast as I could with my leg wounds, I dove into the jungle and tore through it until the quonset hut was between me and the cabin, and it blew.

It was so glorious! Flames filled the sky, and a dark cloud covered the moon. The screams of the survivors on the beach filled my empty heart with joy!

But the next day I was nearly caught. I'd gone up to Gissler's Cave while they looked through the wreckage. My plan was to lure people to the cliff and trip them with a buried rope I'd stolen from the hut, sending them over the edge to their doom, just like they had done to me.

But when I rounded the corner and saw Franklin and Darius dump the dynamite into the ocean (damn them!), I avoided Malik and snuck up the hill above the cave. I stayed silent in the dirt, and heard every word they said.

Malik was wild! I was a bit jealous, as it seemed that he too had connected with my island. But, the others thought *he* had blown up the cabin, and I could use that.

The next night I crept near their camp after dark and saw them split into two groups (teams! that's not allowed!) and then watched as they went to bed.

Matthew was my perfect first face-to-face victim— not too bright. I followed his march across the beach, and dropped at the edge of the jungle. For a moment I thought I'd have to kill him *and* Kinnary. But when she stopped him from going into the jungle, I breathed a sigh of relief.

Watching them try pathetically to have sex was bad enough, but when that bastard pissed in my face, it made me very happy to put my spear through his gut. I ran like the wind to the only place I knew on the far end of the island, just as Kinnary screamed.

That night I slept tucked inside the original cave entrance. Sharp lava scraping my skin, bats flying in and out above my head, and heavy thoughts of the work I still had to do kept me awake most of the night.

Before dawn I carefully hiked the miles back to my secret cabin at Chatham Bay, and slept. Hours later, another explosion woke me up! I closed my eyes again with a smile, happy that someone was probably just blown to bits.

But the next afternoon I watched angrily as they hauled gold from the cave back to the stupid quonset hut and further from my boat! Enraged, I grabbed my machete and headed towards their camp.

Sneaking onto the open beach after dark, adrenaline pulsed through me from my reptile brain (which always said fight, never flight). I found them sleeping near the water's edge, where waves would muffle any murder sounds, but if anyone woke up I would be a sitting duck. My heart beat furiously as I searched for the right target.

And, there he was. Franklin slept alone, far enough away from the rest to make him my only real choice. A rich white man with a privileged life, fawned over by millions. Bullshit American royalty.

There was no love lost.

Unsheathing my machete I stood over him, peering into that granite face. I'd planned a simple, artless killing, but looking down at his big pointed head, it was just so obvious! I took a practice swing, aimed, and…

WHANG! My blade slashed through his neck with the full force of my body weight, and I leaned in *hard*. His eyes and mouth flashed open as his head rolled away, my blade forced deep into the sand by a rage against privilege that had flowed in me my entire life.

His warm blood sprayed my face, and I left the machete where it was and dove to the ground, worried someone had heard my angry blade's thump.

But no one had. So, I rolled across the sand to Franklin's severed head, closed his eyes for good, and stuffed it in my bag.

284

Then came my second great idea of the night.

I already missed my machete, and then it dawned on me that my spree would be so much more fun if I pointed blame at a player after each killing! So, I headed for where the wild ones slept, in their new camp.

Susan was my first— no one would have a hard time believing she was a killer. So, I stole her machete and crept into the night, stopping briefly to hastily construct an American style football tee, then set it up for kickoff.

But the next morning I had a terrible thought. What if the boat came before I was done? I didn't even know what day it was! From then on I lived in fear of a boat's whistle, or a flare gun's shot. But the worst was to come.

That day a storm threatened to blow the roof right off of my little cabin, and I stayed inside through the gale. But just as night overcame the windy world outside, I heard voices, coming across *my* beach!

I was frantic! In a few more seconds they would catch me, and it would be the end. I quickly stuffed food and water my bag, grabbed the machete, and dove through the garbage chute just as the cabin door creaked open!

I hit the ground in an upside down wad, my feet hanging over my head. Rolling over, I slid silently beneath the cabin's floor.

I heard their stupid voices as they rooted through my home, drank my rum, and learned of the island's true layout. I stayed under there all night, safe from the rain but still exposed, wet, and freezing. Rats attacked me and I fought back, smacking the floor several times as I swung violently at the little demons, almost giving myself away. Eventually, we reached a truce—they huddled at one end of the muck and I huddled at the other, cold, wet, and hungry.

When morning came the wind subsided, but rain continued to pour. Crawling on cold-stiffened legs, I left my beloved cabin behind, resolved to end this nonsense as soon as I could, but too cold to do so right away.

Fate, as it so often does, intervened. The only place I might warm up was the quonset hut. But surely, I thought, others must be inside, taking shelter from the storm. Still, it was a chance I had to take.

I crept once more behind the hut, and lay still. I waited for an hour and was just going inside, when I heard voices. Darius. And a moment later, someone else. A whimpering voice I couldn't place. Yet I knew for sure that the owner of that voice was weak. Very weak.

Finally Darius left, heading for the beach. When he was out of sight, I gripped my machete, took a deep breath, and softly opened the door.

She barely noticed me. Her expression didn't change at all when she should have been shocked to see me, and I froze, staring at her. I truly felt sorry for her.

"You," was all she could say.

Filled with confidence, I reminded myself how awful she had been to me, and moved past her to grab a rope and a thick, canvas tarp from the back of the hut.

When I touched her arm, it was even colder than mine.

"Come on, Danielle. The boat's here. We're going home!"

"Boat?"

I helped her up and looped the gear over her shoulders. Leading her out the door like my very own pack mule, I bent to pick up a hunk of charred wood from the wreckage of the cabin before turning toward's Gissler's Cave. When we reached the secret trail, I pushed my mule through the bushes and followed.

We walked so very peacefully together on her death march. I held her hand and craned my neck upwards, until I finally found exactly what I was looking for.

"Stop here, honey. Let's rest. Just stand right there."

Her dead eyes stared straight ahead as I removed my tools from her neck.

"I'll write your name on your shirt, so the rescuers will know who you are!"

Kneeling in front of her, exposed but unafraid, I scribbled something to strike fear into my future victims. Then I stood, smiled with sincere kindness, and said,

"Now, go to sleep. I'll wake you when they come."

When I slammed the machete handle down on her head, the winner of Execution Island 14 fell to the ground like dead meat.

I tossed the end of the rope over a large branch above and tied it around her neck. Wrapping it once around the tree's trunk, I braced

286

my feet against it for leverage, and slowly hauled Danielle to her final resting place.

Still very cold and wet, I now had a blanket and a tarp, but nowhere to go. Darius had the hut, and Jason Oliver and Randy had stolen my cabin.

Desperately needing to get warm, I hiked up to the remains of Gissler's Cave and found a spot behind a boulder, where I wrapped myself up like a burrito in my new tarp, closed my eyes, and happily dozed off.

When I woke it was still daylight, and I felt much better. Blood coursed through my half-warmed body, healing myriad aches and pains known only to hard working mass-murderers like myself. Stretching my arms to the sky, I rubbed my eyes, then quickly rubbed them again, for I simply could not believe what the island had handed me as a gift.

Ever so quietly I moved towards the woman on the cliff. When I was just about to strike, Susan yelled into the wind and turned to me! All the better, for watching absolute terror rush through her disgustingly arrogant, rich woman's eyes was the icing on my murder cake.

I struck like a cat, the full force of my thick body blasting the fragile woman into the air. I even risked being seen just to revel in every twist and turn of this horrible woman's body as it hurtled through the air, smacking down with a heavy thwack! on the reef below.

Unlike me, she did not survive. Take that, all you skinny bitches!

Hearing voices, I gathered my tarp and scurried up the hill behind the cave. Randy and Jason rounded the corner, and my hair stood on end when they pointed towards my perch with their machetes. Luckily they didn't follow their own directions. But I did hear them blame Darius for Susan's ugly end, giving me a well deserved smile for the day.

Grateful to the island once more, I found my next scapegoat the next morning, still huddled in the hut! So predictable! Walls won't protect you, I teased him silently, from the Killer of Cocos Island.

When he left the hut to catch his supper, I stepped inside to find something I could use to blame him for my next kill, but found something very confusing! On the wall was a bow, and several

287

arrows! It was either Joe's, or Darius had made his own, and not very well. Either way, this made Old Joe my next scapegoat, not Darius.

Yanking the weapons from the wall, I raced back to find *my* cabin empty. Setting up a target at the far end of the beach, I practiced until I could hit the center of it from twenty yards. My plan was to go after Darius the next morning on his way out to fish, when he would be in the open in deep sand, and unable to escape.

It was a good plan, but the Island, I had learned by then, always had its own. When Jason Oliver strolled uninvited onto my beach, I dropped to the ground to avoid being seen! Then that chicken faced monster danced his way to my cabin, as though it were his!

When he went inside, I grabbed my new weapons and sprinted to the palm leaf targets I'd set up on the beach, tore them down, then ran back to the jungle and crept along it to where I could see the door of my cabin.

It wasn't long before Jason Oliver stepped into the light with a long rope and a basket, heading towards the trail. Intrigued, I gave up the easy shot and waited, fascinated to see Doctor Evil's brilliant plan.

When he tossed the rope at a limb above the trail, many, many times it turned out, I was so disappointed! He was supposed to be a genius? But all he could do was copy me? Jesus, I thought, they don't give out Execution Island titles for *that* kind of thinking!

The trap took a long time to set thanks to his limp little body, and when he finished he actually patted himself on the back! I mean for real! I giggled as he danced again, moving cluelessly towards my cabin.

Then, I dropped the smile from my face, set my jaw, held my breath, and aimed. My first arrow slammed him against the door. I hit him with another, and then a third, before stepping calmly out of the jungle to taunt him.

But damnit, he was already dead! I wanted so badly to taunt the "super villain"! But it wasn't to be. So I just shoved him aside, went in, and got some much needed sleep. When I left to kill Darius the next morning, he was still nailed to the door.

Repeating that killing, when Darius left the quonset hut, I quickly unloaded two arrows into his back. When he spun around I put a third one in his chest, and he fell.

Once I was sure no one was near, I walked over and straddled his big body. He was still alive, but his face was a bulging, red mass of rage and confusion.

I smiled down at him. "Oh my, I'm so sorry for your kids! I really *like* kids, much more than assholes like you in fact. Might even have some. So," I beamed proudly, "tell you what. I'll send them each a shiny gold coin to remember you by! And one for mama, too, to pay some of those bills you racked up!"

Rage became fear, until all emotion dripped off his face, and vaporized into thin air.

Three more. If I had pointed my fingers well, Randy would be gunning for Old Joe any minute, certain that he shot down Jason Oliver. And who knew, or even cared really, where Kinnary was. I was *so* over her.

And of course, I *had* played my cards right, and I got to watch the show while Randy and Joe played their little cat and mouse game. And, wonder of wonders! Kinnary was also watching! The brown skinned wench fancied herself a master of the game! Though it pained me to let her think she was Queen Bitch, I breathed through it and then watched in glee as Joe moved the treasure closer to my boat, floating near the western edge of Cocos Island.

But wait, behold again! Kinnary! Wow! She actually *might* have been the Queen of Cocos! She would have had I not survived my fall! It was beautiful watching her those last two days, as she set traps, stared into puddles like they were mirrors and talked confidence into herself, I mean, really. It was not only amusing, but I was quite proud of her. If circumstances had been different, and she hadn't been the goody-goody from hell . . .

But, sadly, she was. Quite brilliantly she led Old Joe to his death by playing upon his stupid masculinity (is there any other kind?), and he fell on his sword like a tin soldier with a red painted neck.

I actually hated to kill her! She was the only one worthy of sharing my crown. But as I followed them on their little death jog, I heard her refuse time and again Joe's pleas for a good story to tell the World. I just could not let such a person live. It would have cost me everything.

And so, I didn't.

I survived when no one else could. Against all odds, against the other contestants, against a psychotic host, against the elements, against certain death at the hands of a greedy killer, against fucking *rats*, against all of these I triumphed!

And I, *Leticia Robles*, am *the* Executioner!

Acknowledgments

The author would like to gratefully acknowledge the following persons for their assistance in honing the first draft of Execution Island into the work before you.

Maya Gardner

Paul S. Ross

Isaac Shepard

Linda A Gardner

Tim and Lori Wutzke

Scott and April Sullivan

Greg and Sharon Small